WW2045

ALIEN REVENGE

ROD TRENT

Welcome, dear reader. This is a story that has haunted and taunted me for a few decades, and I've finally given in to the whisperings.

I invite you to delve into the lives of our heroes as they navigate a treacherous future based on ghosts of the past. The encroaching evil might be a thought too far, but human resolve is the true winner as the participants thread together a plan to prevent an apocalyptic event even the horror of nightmares couldn't create.

As the author of this story, I began my career writing fiction, a passion that has never dimmed even as I ventured into the world of technology content to pay the bills and drive my career forward. The act of creation is not just a job; it is a therapeutic escape, a return to the roots of my creativity, and I am thrilled to be sharing this passion with you. In a very real way, this book is just for me. Selfish, huh? But for those that know me, I share everything, so, I hope you both excuse and enjoy my attempted intrusion into your world.

- Rod

Chapter 1

Introduction

Dr. Evelyn Montgomery's fingers danced a silent tap against the cold metal of her workstation, the rhythm lost amidst the hum of machines that surrounded her. She pushed her glasses higher on the bridge of her nose, eyes scanning the cryptic patterns that played across the myriad screens with an intensity that belied her calm exterior. Her short black hair framed a face etched in concentration, every line and furrow upon her brow mapping the contours of a mind relentlessly chasing the secrets of the universe.

The laboratory, a cathedral to science, was her sanctuary, a place where the whispers of alien intellects could be teased from the relics they had left behind. The data before her flickered with the ghostly light of otherworldly knowledge, each measurement and calculation a breadcrumb on the trail to understanding — or perhaps to damnation.

It was in this moment of hushed analysis that the lab's heavy door sighed open with an unexpected whoosh, shattering the cloistered silence. Captain Lucas "Hawk" Hawking stepped into the room, his frame casting a long shadow that seemed to momentarily eclipse the glow of the monitors. Hawk's deliberate movements carried the weight of his command, his piercing blue eyes sweeping the space with calculated alertness.

"Montgomery," he said, his voice a low rumble that filled the chamber with a sense of impending storm. "We've got a situation."

Evelyn's gaze lifted from her work, locking onto Hawk with a practiced sharpness. "What kind of situation?" she inquired, her voice steady despite the interruption.

"Security breach," Hawk replied, the two words carrying a gravity that seemed to compress the air itself. "We need eyes everywhere. Vigilance is paramount now."

A flicker of concern flashed in Evelyn's green eyes, quickly masked by the stoic facade she had perfected over the years. The past had taught her well; dangers seen and unseen lurked in the shadows of their work, ever-present threats that preyed upon the slightest weakness.

"Understood," she responded, her thoughts already racing through possible scenarios, analyzing and discarding them with the efficiency of her analytical training. Each step in their project was a move on a cosmic chessboard, and the game they played was one of high risk and unknown rewards.

"Keep me informed, Hawk," she added, her voice betraying none of the adrenaline that now coursed through her veins.

"Always," he affirmed with a curt nod, his gaze lingering for a moment longer than necessary. There was an unspoken understanding between them, a shared history of battles fought and sacrifices made.

As Hawk turned to leave, the silence settled back over the lab like a shroud, but it was a deceptive calm. Beneath the surface, currents of urgency surged, a maelstrom of possibilities that could spell either salvation or ruin. Evelyn returned to her work, her mind weaving through the labyrinth of data, all the while aware that the true enigma lay not only within the alien technology but also in the hearts of those who sought to wield it.

Evelyn's fingers paused above the keyboard, the soft glow of the computer screen casting long shadows across her workstation. The news of a security breach sent ripples through the still waters of her composure. "The implications of this breach could be catastrophic," she said, turning to face Hawk. Her green eyes were turbulent seas, reflecting the gravity of their situation. "Our project... it's not just about scientific discovery. If our research falls into the wrong hands—"

"Dr. Montgomery," Hawk interjected, his voice an anchor in the storm of her worries. He stepped closer, the overhead lights glinting off the medals that adorned his uniform. "I understand your concerns, but our mission has always been to safeguard humanity. This is why we stand guard," he continued, his blue eyes unwavering, the lines etched into his face telling tales of past ordeals overcome.

"Humanity..." Evelyn murmured, allowing herself a fleeting moment to ponder the vastness of what that word encompassed. She considered the myriad lives, unaware of the hidden dangers they faced, and the thin line they all walked between the known and the unfathomable.

"Remember, Evelyn, the threats we're up against aren't bound by our understanding of the world," Hawk said, his tone softer now as if he sensed her internal struggle. "We've held the line before, and we'll do it again. Together."

"Redemption isn't won through complacency," she replied, steel threading her resolve as she met Hawk's gaze head-on. "But vigilance alone isn't enough. We must also be prepared to act."

"Agreed," Hawk conceded, the corner of his mouth twitching with the ghost of a smile reserved for those rare moments when he acknowledged the shared conviction that united them. "And act we shall. For now, let's focus on containing this breach. I'll ensure our defenses are impenetrable."

Evelyn gave a curt nod, the scientist in her clinging to the logic and order within which she found solace. Yet, beneath her composed exterior, the embers of her fears smoldered, threatening to ignite at the slightest provocation. She turned back to her data, the alien symbols dancing before her eyes like cryptic omens, while Hawk's retreating footsteps echoed in the lab — a steady drumbeat in the march toward an uncertain future.

Evelyn Montgomery's fingers hovered above the console; her gaze fixed on the holographic display where a complex matrix of alien algorithms unfolded. The lab around her hummed with the lifeblood of technology at work, its walls lined with devices that were the offspring of human ingenuity and extraterrestrial mystery. She couldn't help but marvel at the fusion of science and artistry that had birthed the defensive technologies now at their disposal — force fields that shimmered like mirages, cloaking devices spun from invisibility's own thread.

"Progress?" The voice cut through her reverie, deep and resonant.

She turned to find Captain Lucas "Hawk" Hawking entering the lab, his presence commanding even in the quietude of research. Hawk's eyes scanned the data streams, searching for meaning in the cascades of alien script that had become their shared language of survival.

"Significant," Evelyn replied, her voice tinged with the gravity of their endeavor. "The adaptive shielding prototype responded well to the latest round of tests. It can now withstand an energy surge that would cripple any conventional system."

"Good," Hawk acknowledged with a nod, his blue eyes reflecting a glint of satisfaction. "The stakes are higher than ever."

"Indeed," she agreed, her mind already cycling through potential improvements. "If we could integrate this tech with our offensive capabilities..."

"Speaking of which," Hawk interjected, shifting the topic with the ease of a chess master moving a pivotal piece, "there's something new you need to see." He produced a small, metallic object from his pocket, setting it gently on her workspace. Its surface was etched with intricate patterns that seemed to writhe beneath her gaze.

"This artifact was recovered from the crash site on Ganymede," he continued, his tone laced with urgency. "Initial scans suggest there's more to it than meets the eye. I need your expertise, Evelyn."

She felt the weight of expectation settle upon her shoulders, a familiar companion in their clandestine crusade. With methodical precision, she reached for the artifact, her fingers grazing its cool surface. A shiver coursed through her as if the object whispered secrets in a language older than time itself.

"Of course," she said, masking her apprehension with the veneer of professional curiosity. "I'll begin the analysis immediately."

"Time is a luxury we may not have," Hawk reminded her gently, though the undercurrent of tension betrayed his concern. "We're not the only ones interested in what this might reveal."

"Understood." Her response was terse, yet imbued with determination. Evelyn knew the risks, the ever-present dance with danger that was their partner in this waltz of discovery and defense. But the lure of unlocking alien enigmas was too potent to resist — the chance to tip the scales in humanity's favor, to safeguard against the unknown threats lurking beyond the stars.

As Hawk took his leave, his silhouette a stark contrast against the sterile white of the lab, Evelyn turned her focus to the artifact. It lay before her, innocuous yet inscrutable, a puzzle begging to be solved. And she, Dr. Evelyn Montgomery, was determined to unravel its mysteries, whatever they may hold.

Evelyn's gaze locked onto the artifact, a gleaming beacon of potential in the dimly lit laboratory. It was as if the room itself held its breath, waiting for her to unravel the cosmic riddles entwined within the otherworldly relic. Her pulse quickened, an echo of the exhilaration that always came with the precipice of discovery.

"Captain," she began, the words tumbling from her lips like secret hymns to progress, "I cannot overstate how much I appreciate this opportunity." Her eyes sparkled with the reflection of the artifact's intricate patterning, a constellation of curiosity within their green depths. "Every piece we decipher from their world brings us closer to safeguarding our own."

Hawk stood firm, a sentinel against the encroaching shadows of uncertainty that seemed to cling to the laboratory walls. His voice, when it broke the hush, carried the gravity of unspoken fears. "Dr. Montgomery, while your enthusiasm is commendable, I must stress the importance of discretion." He paused, his gaze sweeping the expanse of the lab, as if searching for unseen eavesdroppers amongst the array of high-tech equipment.

"Remember, the knowledge we're uncovering here," he continued, softer now but no less urgent, "could change the balance of power on Earth. And there are those who would kill to possess it."

The unspoken truth hung between them, a specter of the past betrayals that had left scars on both their careers and souls. Hawk's eyes, the color of a stormy sky, met hers, and in them, she saw the reflection of her own inner turmoil—a tapestry woven with threads of duty and the insatiable thirst for knowledge.

"Caution will be my guide," Evelyn assured him, her voice a whisper against the enormity of their task. She turned back to the artifact, her fingers hovering above its surface, aware of the silent vigil Hawk kept at the doorway. The weight of their shared secret pressed upon her, a reminder that their quest for understanding skirted the edges of darkness, where the price of revelation could be redemption or ruin.

With a steady breath, she resolved to tread lightly through the labyrinth of alien code and technology, aware that each step forward could either illuminate the path to humanity's salvation or hasten its descent into chaos.

Dr. Evelyn Montgomery's fingers hovered momentarily over the alien artifact, a tangible aura of anticipation encircling her. The lab around her was silent except for the soft hum of machinery—an orchestra of electronic whispers that accompanied her every move. She let out a controlled breath, allowing her laser-focused green eyes to scan the enigma before her. Its surface was an intricate dance of unknown metals and symbols, etched with precision beyond human capability.

Evelyn's analytical gaze caught on a peculiar seam, nearly imperceptible, that snaked along the side of the object. With utmost care, she deployed a set of fine tools, the metal tips glinting under the stark laboratory lights. Her movements were practiced and patient, a testament to her dedication to unraveling secrets that the universe had not intended for human minds.

As she prodded gently at the seamless join, the artifact yielded, revealing a compartment so cunningly hidden it might have been missed by a less discerning eye. Within it, there lay a series of crystalline structures, pulsing faintly with an inner light. Evelyn's pulse quickened—here was the undiscovered country of knowledge she yearned for, the siren call that drew her ever deeper into the unknown.

Meanwhile, in the security hub of the facility, Captain Lucas "Hawk" Hawking's deep-set eyes narrowed as he received a report that spiked his adrenaline. "Repeat that," he demanded, his voice a low rumble that did not betray the sudden tension that gripped him.

"Surveillance has picked up unclassified signatures at the perimeter, sir. Movement patterns are erratic, not matching any known wildlife or automated systems." The officer's report was met with Hawk's swift response, each word clipped with military precision.

"Initiate lockdown protocol. Double the guards on all entry points and sweep the grounds. I want eyes in the sky, too—our little project cannot afford curious visitors."

Orders cascaded down the chain of command, ripples of urgency spreading throughout the compound. As personnel sprang into action, Hawk's mind raced with the implications of this breach. Every scenario was a dagger pointed at the heart of their operation, and he could ill afford a stab in the dark.

Back in the lab, oblivious to the burgeoning chaos outside, Evelyn marveled at the encrypted data nestled within the artifact's hidden chamber. Her heart thrummed with the prospect of deciphering its secrets, each beat a drum of determination. She knew the risks—her work danced on the knife-edge between brilliance and madness, each revelation extracted at great cost.

Yet, driven by the ghosts of past failures and the promise of redemption, Evelyn allowed herself a moment of quiet triumph. Here, in her hands, lay a puzzle that could elevate humanity or doom it. She would be the architect of its fate, her keen intellect the key to unlocking wonders or horrors yet unseen.

As the shadows of dusk crept into the corners of her lab, Evelyn leaned closer to the artifact, her focus undeterred by the specter of danger that loomed just beyond the walls. And as Hawk marshaled his forces against the encroaching threat, Dr. Evelyn Montgomery delved deeper into the enigmatic heart of alien innovation, unaware that each discovery brought them one step closer to an abyss that hungered for the light of knowledge.

Dr. Evelyn Montgomery's hands paused mid-air, a shiver darting down her spine as the distant clank of heavy boots resonated through the sterile silence of the laboratory. The abrupt intrusion of martial rhythm into her sanctuary of science jolted her from the trance of analysis. She glanced up, her piercing green eyes flickering momentarily toward the lab's entrance where shadows danced in tandem with the increased footfalls of security personnel.

"Must be Hawk's doing," she muttered under her breath, the corners of her mouth tilting downwards in a frown of concentration. With a swift push of her glasses up the bridge of her nose, Evelyn redirected her attention to the alien artifact sprawled before her. Its intricate design, a labyrinth of unknown metals and pulsating lights, beckoned her back to the enigma it presented. The heightened security was but a necessary distraction in the grand scheme of their mission—a mission that bore the weight of humanity's future.

As Evelyn's focus narrowed, her fingers resumed their dance; deft and determined over the artifact's surface, seeking, probing for the faintest hint of hidden functionalities. Her mind, an unwavering fortress against the chaos of the world outside, wrapped itself around the puzzle with a relentless grip.

Meanwhile, Captain Lucas "Hawk" Hawking strode with purpose back to his office, his tall frame casting long shadows across the corridors bathed in the sterile glow of fluorescent lights. The faint scars etched on his face felt tight, a physical echo of the tension that gripped his mind. He passed by the sentinels stationed at every corner, nodding curtly in acknowledgment of their vigilance.

Once enclosed within the confines of his office, Hawk stood before a bank of monitors displaying feeds from cameras scattered throughout the facility. His blue eyes scanned each screen, searching for any anomaly, any breach that could endanger the project — his project. He reached for a secure comm link, issuing commands with the precision of a man who knew too well the price of failure.

"Double the patrols on the east wing," he instructed, his voice carrying the gravel of authority. "And keep an eye on the ventilation systems. We cannot afford even the smallest oversight."

The murmurs of assent crackling through the comm link were music to his ears, a symphony of preparedness that fortified the walls of his resolve. Hawk's gaze lingered on a particular screen, one that showed Dr. Montgomery hunched over her work, oblivious to the world crumbling around her. A flicker of admiration crossed his features, masked quickly by the stoic facade of command.

"Protect her," he whispered to no one in the room, his words a solemn vow to shield the mind that held the keys to salvation or ruin.

As night deepened its embrace upon the compound, Evelyn remained ensconced in her cocoon of research, the gentle hum of machinery her constant companion. Outside, Hawk positioned his chess pieces, moving silently across the board of security protocols. Both were players in a game much larger than themselves, driven by ghosts of the past and the elusive promise of redemption. Neither knew just how close they stood to the precipice, nor the depth of darkness that awaited should they falter. But on they worked, each in their own realm, guarding the fragile flame of hope in a world teetering on the brink of the unknown.

Evelyn's fingers traced the grooves of the alien artifact, her touch as delicate as a whisper against the cool, metallic surface. The laboratory was shrouded in silence, save for the occasional beep of a monitor that punctuated the stillness like a heartbeat. Her eyes, ever so discerning, caught an irregularity — a seam where there should have been symmetry.

"Curious," she murmured, her voice a soft intrusion upon the quietude. With measured precision, she employed a set of fine tools, coaxing the reluctant mechanism to reveal its secrets. And then, with the subtlest click, a compartment sprung forth, hidden layers unfurling like the petals of some exotic flower.

A gasp escaped her lips, not from fear but sheer awe at the revelation. Inside lay a matrix of enigmatic symbols, pulsating with an eerie luminescence — as if the very code were alive, beckoning her to unravel its mysteries. Encrypted data, undoubtedly, and Evelyn felt the surge of adrenaline that came with the prospect of decoding such alien cryptography.

Meanwhile, shadows stretched long across Hawk's office as he leaned over his desk, brow furrowed in concentration. The array of screens before him painted a picture of vigilance, each pixel a soldier in his army of surveillance. It was then that his comm link chirped—a sound that sliced through the tension like a knife.

"Captain Hawking." The voice on the other end was clipped, bearing the unmistakable gravity of authority.

"Speak," Hawk replied, his tone a reflection of steel, ready to be forged into whatever weapon necessity demanded.

"New orders," the voice continued, "from General Vandor himself. Immediate and confidential."

Hawk's hand tightened imperceptibly around the comm link. Vandor was not a man given to trivial interruptions; his missives bore the weight of mountains. With a curt nod, even though the gesture went unseen, Hawk acknowledged the message. His attention, for the moment, was torn from the labyrinthine web of security he had woven around his precious charge.

"Understood. I'll secure a private line." Hawk's words cut through the air, finality etched into each syllable.

As he stepped away from the console, his mind raced with possibilities, each more ominous than the last. What tidings could demand such immediate secrecy? The question hung in the air, unanswered, a specter from the past rearing its head to cast doubt on the path forward.

In her laboratory, Evelyn leaned closer to the alien device, the encrypted data a siren call to her insatiable curiosity. Unseen by her, the world shifted on its axis ever so slightly, tilting toward a future fraught with unknown perils. Yet, undeterred, she pressed on, her quest for understanding a beacon in the gathering storm.

Dr. Evelyn Montgomery's fingers danced across the holographic keyboard; each tap a precise echo in the stillness of the lab. The alien artifact before her cast an ethereal glow on her stark features, shadows playing beneath her piercing green eyes as they narrowed in focus. A labyrinth of encrypted symbols sprawled across the screen; a riddle wrapped within the enigma of extraterrestrial intelligence.

With a practiced flick, she toggled between screens laden with algorithms and ancient languages of Earth, seeking a cipher to unlock the secrets held within the metallic confines of the artifact. Her mind, a fortress of knowledge, remained oblivious to the dangers that the encrypted data might harbor, her sole aim to peel back the layers of alien encryption like the petals of a rare and exotic flower.

"Come on, there has to be a pattern," she murmured, pushing her glasses higher upon her nose with a habitual gesture born of countless hours of research. The room breathed silence around her, save for the rhythmic hum of the supercomputer that crunched numbers at a feverish pace.

A sudden flurry of activity punctuated the slow pulse of her work as the computer emitted a sharp bleep, signaling a breakthrough. Evelyn's heart quickened; she leaned in closer, her breath fogging the glass interface. Lines of code cascaded down the screen, a waterfall of alien script that seemed to mock her from within its digital depths.

"Is this it? Is this the key?" The questions fell from her lips, unanswered whispers in the sterile air. She was alone with the enigma, Captain Hawking's presence now just a lingering specter of authority and protection in the recesses of her mind.

The lab's walls seemed to close in as the weight of potential discovery pressed upon her. Shadows lengthened, casting grotesque shapes that danced with malevolent life against the cold machinery. Each click of the keyboard was a step further into uncharted territory, a plunge into an abyss where the lines between salvation and damnation blurred.

Evelyn's fingers halted, suspended above the keyboard as if hesitant to summon what lay beyond the veil of encryption. The thrill of the chase, the hunger for redemption through scientific breakthroughs, spurred her onward. With a resolute exhale, she resumed her work, unaware of the clock ticking down to an event horizon beyond which there could be no turning back.

The screen flickered, responding to her commands with reluctant obedience. Data began to unravel before her, a tapestry of unknown consequences. It whispered promises of ancient knowledge and power, of cosmic truths hidden from humanity's grasp since time immemorial. But with every revealed secret came the lurking threat of unleashing something far greater than her or any mortal could comprehend.

"Almost there..." Evelyn's voice was a ghostly intonation, the embodiment of her resolve. Her eyes reflected a galaxy of possibilities, each more tantalizing and terrifying than the last. In this moment, she was both architect and prisoner of her own relentless pursuit, the very essence of human ambition reaching into the void for answers that have evaded their grasp since the stars first beckoned to the ancestors of old.

And yet, for all her brilliance and caution, she remained blissfully unaware of the Pandora's box her keystrokes threatened to open — a truth veiled in darkness, waiting to be brought forth into the unforgiving light of reality.

Chapter 2

The Incident

Dr. Evelyn Montgomery's boots pounded against the uneven terrain, each step an echo of her racing heart as she and Captain Lucas "Hawk" Hawking made their desperate approach toward the smoldering remains of the Kridrax emissary ship. The acrid scent of ionized air filled her nostrils, a pungent reminder of the day's surreal turn. Beside her, Hawk's broad frame cut through the swirling dust, his piercing blue eyes fixed on the chaos ahead with unwavering intensity.

As they drew nearer, the scene unfurled like a tapestry of pandemonium. Smoke billowed into the twilight sky, thick and unyielding, as if the very fabric of reality had ruptured to unleash this calamity upon the world. Flames danced with an almost malevolent grace around the wreckage, casting flickering shadows that seemed to mock the frantic efforts of those trying to quell them. The air vibrated with the cacophony of sirens and the clamor of panic — people running helter-skelter, shouting incoherently, their voices blending into a discordant symphony of terror.

"Keep moving," Hawk's voice cut through the din, low and commanding, the soldier within never far from the surface. His gaze darted to Evelyn's, conveying an urgency that needed no words, but still he spoke, a terse reminder of what was at stake. "We need to secure the perimeter."

Evelyn nodded, more out of habit than necessity, her mind already cataloguing the scene with clinical detachment. Yet, beneath the cool veneer of professionalism, a thread of fear wove its way through her thoughts. Betrayal had once taught her the cost of misplaced trust, and now, as she faced the unknown entities of the Kridrax, that lesson pulsed at the edge of her consciousness.

They skirted a group of emergency responders, their faces etched with concentration and strain. Evelyn's gaze swept over them, her green eyes searching for any sign of the alien presence amid the chaos. She could not shake the feeling that this crash was no accident; it was a harbinger, a silent scream cutting through the void to deliver a message only she and Hawk could decipher.

"Look out!" Hawk's warning came just as a secondary explosion erupted from the belly of the downed craft, sending a shockwave that knocked several bystanders to the ground. Instinctively, Evelyn braced herself, her jacket whipping about her as debris pelted the area like a hailstorm of the gods' own making.

The two stood at the edge of the inferno, the heat pressing against their skin like an unwanted advance. Before them, the wreckage loomed — a twisted metal sentinel, its secrets ensconced within its ravaged hull. It was a testament to the perils that lay beyond the stars, and a prelude to darker tidings yet to come.

Dr. Evelyn Montgomery's boots crunched over debris, her breaths rhythmic and focused as she forged a path through the disarray. Beside her, Captain Lucas "Hawk" Hawking pressed onward, his broad shoulders parting the sea of humanity like a ship's prow cleaving ocean waves. Their expressions were etched with unspoken resolve, an echo of their shared, silent vow to safeguard the fragile line between order and chaos.

"Montgomery, there!" Hawk pointed with a gloved hand, his voice barely rising above the cacophony of sirens and shouts that filled the air.

Her eyes followed his gesture, finding amidst the wreckage a figure that stood in stark contrast to the frenzy around them. Zylar Threx, the alien messenger, remained an oasis of calm within the storm. The crash site's flashing lights danced across their iridescent scales, casting prismatic shadows on the ground. They stood solemnly, with an elegance that belied the devastation surrounding them, and for a moment time seemed to slow, the world holding its breath.

Evelyn hesitated, feeling the weight of history pressing upon the moment—the long years of watching the skies, of whispered tales and half-believed myths. Now reality stood before her, alien and inscrutable, a harbinger from the stars whose message bore the power to reshape their understanding of the universe.

"Zylar Threx," Hawk announced, his tone a mix of reverence and wariness as he stepped closer to the emissary. The crowd around them fell into a hush, sensing the gravity emanating from the trio at the heart of the turmoil.

The alien's gaze met theirs, deep-set eyes glowing with an inner light that seemed to carry the whispers of distant galaxies. In that prolonged look, Evelyn saw reflections of her own past trials, the indelible marks of experience that shaped her relentless pursuit of knowledge. Hawk's visage, too, bore the scars of a life spent in defense of others—a testament to the cost of duty.

"Dr. Montgomery. Captain Hawking." Zylar's voice resonated with a haunting quality that seemed to speak directly to their souls. "It is imperative you understand—"

The words hung in the air, an unfinished sentence laden with omens yet to be unveiled. Evelyn felt a shiver run down her spine as she exchanged a glance with Hawk. Whatever lay ahead, they knew this encounter was merely the prelude to trials far greater than any they had faced before.

Zylar Threx stood amidst the smoldering remnants of their vessel, a figure carved from starlight and shadow. The iridescent scales that adorned their slender frame caught the flickering flames, casting prismatic glows upon their ethereal form. Each scale was a tear-shaped mirror reflecting the chaos of human fear and the inferno's dance around them—an otherworldly sentinel unfazed by the pandemonium they had landed in.

Evelyn Montgomery's gaze locked onto Zylar's visage, unable to escape the alien's haunting allure. With limbs that extended like the boughs of ancient trees and movements fluid as a silent stream, their presence commanded silence from the cacophony of sirens and screams. The Harbinger's eyes, deep pools of luminescence, held millennia of sorrow, knowledge, and an unspoken plea for comprehension.

"Your world teeters on the precipice," Zylar spoke, voice resonating with the timbre of a distant storm yet to be seen but already felt. "The Kridrax—destroyers of realms—have cast their gaze upon you. Their hunger is insatiable, their methods... unsparing."

The words seemed to emanate not just from Zylar but from the air itself, enveloping the listeners in a cocoon of dread. Evelyn's heart quickened, racing against the gravity of each syllable that spilled forth from the emissary's lips. Captain Hawking, his posture rigid with anticipation, hung on the precipice of Zylar's every utterance.

"An alliance forged in shadows with an echo of Earth's own tyranny has set its sights on your home." Zylar's glowing gaze pierced through the veil of smoke, fixing upon the pair before them. "Synthetic Oppressor — a name whispered in fear even across the cosmos — lends strength to their conquest."

A shiver coursed through Evelyn, her scientist's mind grappling with the implications of the cryptic prophecy. Hawk's clenched jaw and furrowed brow spoke volumes of the soldier within, ready to face the specter of conflict that loomed large over their destiny.

"Redemption lies in unity, in the embrace of those you deem other. Only then can the tide of annihilation be stemmed," Zylar intoned, their voice fading like the last light of a dying star.

As the Harbinger's message settled into the hearts of those who heard it, so too did the unsettling realization that their world would never again be the same. The past was a prologue written in ignorance, and the future — a tome whose pages were yet to be filled with either salvation or ruin.

Dr. Evelyn Montgomery's heart hammered against her ribcage, a frantic metronome that echoed the chaos swirling within her mind. Beside her, Captain Lucas "Hawk" Hawking's gaze locked with hers in silent communication — a language honed on battlefields and in strategy rooms. In the depths of his oceanic eyes, she read a storm of disbelief, its waves crashing against the shores of grave concern. With a mutual nod, they shouldered the mantle of their newfound duty: to convey Zylar Threx's ominous prophecy to the one man who might stand a chance at altering the tides.

The corridors of power seemed to stretch endlessly before them, each step resonating with the solemnity of their mission. As they approached the sanctum of decision and destiny — the Oval Office — Evelyn could not help but feel as though she were stepping through the pages of history, each footfall a potential catalyst for change.

The president's office stood as an elegant testament to authority, its walls adorned with symbols of a nation's past and present glories. Sunlight streamed through the tall windows, casting long shadows across the room that danced like specters of the future upon the polished floors. The desk, a grand edifice of dark wood, bore the weight of decisions that had shaped the world.

Zylar Threx moved through this space with an otherworldly grace, their luminous scales reflecting the light in prismatic splendor, creating a mosaic of colors that seemed to whisper of worlds beyond. Evelyn watched President Jonathan Reed's gaze linger upon the alien messenger, a tableau of wonder slightly marring his otherwise composed features.

"Mr. President," Evelyn began, her voice steady despite the tempest raging in her thoughts, "this is Zylar Threx, emissary from the Kridrax system. Their message bears great significance."

President Reed nodded, his piercing blue eyes transitioning from the celestial visitor to his human counterparts. "I understand the urgency," he said, his voice a beacon cutting through fog. "We shall give it the gravity it deserves."

In the silence that followed, as potent as a prelude to thunder, the weight of countless futures hung suspended. They stood at a precipice, staring down into the abyss of uncertainty, prepared to leap into the void of actions yet taken, battles yet fought, redemption yet earned.

President Reed's office, a sanctuary of decisions and power, grew still as Zylar Threx approached. The air itself seemed to hold its breath, waiting for the words that would tumble from the emissary's lips — words that could very well alter the course of history.

"Your Excellency," Zylar Threx intoned, their voice a haunting echo from across the cosmos, "I stand before you as the harbinger of shadows yet to fall."

Reed leaned forward, his hands clasping together like the joining of separate fates. "Speak plainly, Emissary," he implored, his curiosity a tangible force within the room. "What shadows do you foresee?"

"An invasion," Zylar said, each syllable laden with the weight of impending doom. "The Kridrax fleet advances, and with them, an alliance most foul — Synthetic Oppressor has been reborn within their ranks."

A flicker of disbelief crossed the president's face, quickly masked by a steely resolve. "How imminent is this threat?" he asked, his voice devoid of fear, only the urgency of command. "Time's sands slip swiftly," Zylar replied, their ethereal eyes reflecting a millennia of strife. "They come, President Reed, armed with technology that could spell our collective demise."

"Then we must prepare," Reed stated, rising to his feet, every inch the leader forged in crisis. "We must rally our defenses, unite allies, and stand firm against this tide of darkness."

Zylar Threx nodded, their solemn demeanor unshaken. "I offer knowledge, President Reed. For my people's memory lives within me, and in their name, I seek redemption — for all."

The moment stretched, charged with the promise of trials to come, and the unyielding spirit of humanity to meet them head-on.

President Reed's countenance blanched, a stark pallor overtaking the usually ruddy hue of command in his cheeks. The Oval Office seemed to contract around them, the walls pressing closer with the weight of Zylar Threx's words. An invasion. Synthetic Oppressor. Each term hung in the air like a harbinger of doom.

"Advisors," he called out, his voice a beacon cutting through the haze of impending crisis. "Gather the National Security Council—immediately."

The room grew into a flurry of motion as aides scurried to execute his orders. President Reed turned back to Zylar, his piercing blue eyes locking onto the emissary's enigmatic visage. "We will stand ready," he assured them. "Your knowledge is our spearhead. Together, we forge our shield."

"Decisive actions are required," Zylar intoned, their voice resonating with an ancient sorrow that seemed to seep into the very fabric of the chamber.

"Decisive and swift," affirmed Reed, his mind already churning with strategies and contingencies.

As the president's advisors assembled around the grand mahogany table, an aura of trepidation mingled with resolve filled the room. Maps were unfolded, screens flickered to life, and the soft hum of electronic devices provided a discordant soundtrack to the gravity of their task.

"Options," Reed demanded, his gaze sweeping across the faces of his trusted council. "I want scenarios, probabilities, defense measures. Speak freely, time is not our ally."

Voices rose in concert, a symphony of urgency and professionalism. Satellite trajectories, military deployments, diplomatic channels—all dissected with clinical precision yet underscored by a palpable sense of dread.

"We must also consider the global stage," one advisor interjected. "This isn't just an American concern—it's a threat to every nation on this planet."

"Indeed," Reed acknowledged, nodding gravely. "Prepare communications for our allies. We'll need to present a united front."

"Mr. President," another voice chimed, edged with caution, "we must also explore the possibility of... negotiation."

"Negotiation with Kridrax—or with Oppressor's simulacrum?" Reed questioned, his tone tinged with skepticism.

"Both, perhaps. If there's a chance to avoid conflict..."

"History has taught us the folly of appeasing tyrants," Reed countered softly, his thoughts adrift amidst the lessons of wars past. "But we will explore every avenue. Hope must temper our readiness for battle."

The clock's ticking grew louder, each second a drumbeat marching them closer to an uncertain future, the silence between discussions heavy with unspoken fears.

"Prepare my address," Reed instructed, straightening his suit jacket as if donning armor for the trials to come. "The world must hear our resolve, and they shall find it unbroken."

As the meeting drew to a close, the air was electric with anticipation. Strategies had been laid; the die cast. The world stood perched on the precipice of darkness, its fate hinging on the actions of those gathered in this sanctum of power.

"Redemption lies within our grasp," Reed murmured, more to himself than to any other. It was a vow, a whisper of hope against the encroaching shadows. The thought of what lay ahead was daunting, but Jonathan Reed's resolve was steel. For the sake of humanity, it had to be.

The echoes of the president's address still reverberated through the halls as Dr. Evelyn Montgomery and Captain Lucas "Hawk" Hawking found a moment's respite in the secluded confines of an adjacent chamber. They stood by a large window, its panes reflecting their haunted silhouettes against the backdrop of a world ignorant of the storm brewing beyond the stars.

Dr. Montgomery's gaze lingered on the celestial tapestry unfurling across the night sky, each star a sentinel bearing silent witness to Earth's plight. Her mind, ever the fortress of logic and calculation, now wrestled with the enormity of the Kridrax threat. She felt the familiar tendrils of trepidation coil within her, yet they were held at bay by a steely resolve that had been tempered in the crucible of past traumas. The weight of humanity's fate rested upon her shoulders, a burden she bore with quiet fortitude, her piercing green eyes alight with the fire of determination.

"Never thought we'd be tasked with saving the world when I signed up for this," Hawk mused, his voice a low rumble that seemed to harmonize with the distant thrum of the city below. His imposing figure, etched with scars from battles long past, was a testament to the life he'd chosen—one of valor and sacrifice. Yet, beneath the hardened exterior, there existed a wellspring of compassion that only those closest to him could discern.

"Nor I," Evelyn replied, the timbre of her voice betraying a hint of vulnerability she seldom allowed others to see. "But if anyone can find a way through this, it is us." Her words, though laden with the gravity of the situation, carried an undercurrent of hope that resonated with Hawk's own unyielding spirit.

They shared a look, an unspoken pact forged in the crucible of imminent peril. Their paths, intertwined by destiny or chance, now led them towards the maw of an uncertain future—a future they were resolved to face head-on.

"Let's get to work then," Hawk said, his blue eyes catching a glint of moonlight as they turned towards the door. His stride was purposeful, each step a silent vow to protect not just the people he commanded, but all of humankind.

Evelyn followed, her mind already sifting through strategies and contingencies. There would be time enough for doubt and fear later; now was the hour for action. As they stepped back into the fray, the shadows of history loomed large behind them, whispering of redemption, of past sacrifices and the eternal quest for a peace that always seemed just beyond reach.

Yet, amidst the gathering storm, there lay a sliver of hope—that humanity might yet stand united in the face of darkness, that redemption would be seized by the hands of those brave enough to fight for it. This was their charge, their crusade against the encroaching tide of oblivion.

"Whatever it takes," Evelyn murmured, more to herself than to Hawk. It was a promise, a warrior's oath etched upon her very soul. For in the end, it was not just redemption that beckoned them forward, but survival itself.

Chapter 3

Coalition

The chill of the underground corridor seeped through Dr. Evelyn Montgomery's practical attire as she followed the military escort, her footsteps echoing with a rhythm that matched the hammering of her heart. The stark walls, lined with armed guards who stood as motionless as statues, hinted at the gravity of their destination. Captain Lucas "Hawk" Hawking strode beside her, his posture rigid, his gaze fixed forward — a silent sentinel in human form.

They arrived at a secure room, its door reinforced with layers of undisclosed alloys, betraying nothing of the secrets it guarded. As the door swung open, revealing the inner sanctum of national defense, President Jonathan Reed stood to greet them, his silver hair catching the artificial light like a beacon of resolve amidst the shadows of uncertainty.

"Dr. Montgomery, Captain Hawking," the president began, his voice resonating with the weight of unspoken fears, "our nation, our world, is on the precipice of an unprecedented threat."

Evelyn's piercing green eyes narrowed as she processed the classified documents sliding across the polished surface of the conference table. Images of otherworldly ships, reports of advanced weaponry — the harbingers of the Kridrax invasion laid bare in ink and paper.

"Mr. President," she interjected, her words slicing through the heavy silence, "the risks involved in assembling such a team are not trivial. The potential consequences..."

"Are outweighed by the necessity of action, Doctor," President Reed cut in, his blue eyes locking onto hers with an intensity that spoke volumes of the crisis at hand. "We need your expertise, your innovation. Without it, our chances diminish considerably."

Evelyn hesitated, the ghost of past betrayals flickering across her mind. She could almost hear the whispers of caution, urging her to retreat into the safety of solitude. But beyond the echoes of doubt, there was a stronger call — one that resonated with the very essence of her being.

Her duty to protect humanity.

With a slow exhale, she met the president's gaze, her decision etched in the firm set of her jaw. "I understand the stakes, Mr. President. I'll do it — I'll assemble your team." Her voice, though tinged with the vulnerability of her internal struggle, carried the irrefutable promise of commitment.

Captain Hawking nodded once, a silent sentinel no more, but a warrior aligning himself with the cause. His presence was a bulwark against the tides of uncertainty, his own sense of duty mirroring that of Evelyn's.

"Then we must act swiftly," President Reed declared, standing tall amidst the encroaching shadows. "Humanity's redemption may well depend on what we do next."

As they left the confines of the secure room, the corridor seemed less chilling than before, the echo of their steps less foreboding. Together, Dr. Montgomery and Captain Hawking stepped forward into the unknown, the seeds of a clandestine coalition taking root in the fertile ground of necessity and courage.

...

The corridors of the high-security government facility stretched before them; a labyrinthine expanse shrouded in secrets. Dr. Evelyn Montgomery's footsteps echoed with a purposeful cadence, each step a deliberate defiance of the fear that nipped at her heels. Beside her, Captain Lucas "Hawk" Hawking's broad shoulders bore an unseen weight, his gaze fixed ahead as if he could discern their shared destiny amidst the sterile walls.

"Time is a luxury we no longer possess," Hawk murmured, his voice a low rumble in the silence. He glanced sideways at Evelyn, eyes like chips of ice under furrowed brows, reflecting a storm of commitment.

Evelyn nodded, her lips pressed into a thin line. "We need minds as sharp as blades and wills unyielding." Her eyes, green and piercing, met his in silent accord. They were two halves of a whole, bound by the gravity of their pledge to humanity, now more than ever.

"Markus Weller," she said, the name tasting of both opportunity and enigma. Hawk raised an eyebrow in recognition. The reclusive engineer was a cipher wrapped in brilliance, a piece essential to the intricate puzzle they were about to assemble.

They found him ensconced within the bowels of a research complex, a sanctum of solitude where his genius lay unfettered by the trivialities of the outside world. The lab was a chaos of invention, humming with the latent power of dormant machines and scattered blueprints that whispered of possibilities yet untamed.

"Dr. Weller," Evelyn called out, her voice disrupting the hum of fluorescent lights overhead. Markus turned from a tangle of wires, his hands stilling mid-air, glasses askew. His gaze upon them was wary, the glint of curiosity behind lenses clouded with doubt.

"Dr. Montgomery... Captain Hawking," he replied, measured words betraying nothing of the thoughts that raced behind his guarded expression. "To what do I owe this unexpected intrusion?"

"We require your expertise." Hawk's declaration sliced through the air, unyielding as steel. "An alliance has been formed, clandestine in nature, against a threat beyond our world — the Kridrax."

A flicker of interest sparked in Markus's eyes, quickly doused by skepticism. "And you believe I would join your... coalition?" His tone bordered on incredulity, a fortress built around his intellect.

"Your innovations have the power to alter the course of this conflict. We need you, Dr. Weller," Evelyn interjected, her voice imbued with an earnestness that brooked no refusal.

For a long moment, Markus surveyed them, the gears of his mind whirring as if calculating the variables of an unsolvable equation. Then, slowly, the ghost of conviction began to eclipse the shadows of hesitation that had claimed him.

"Very well," he conceded, pushing up his glasses with a resolute motion. "I will lend my knowledge to your cause."

As they exited the lab, the air seemed to pulse with the subtle shift of fate's design. Evelyn allowed herself a small smile, knowing that within the quiet triumph of Markus's acquiescence, the seeds of redemption were sown, not just for themselves but for all who sought refuge in the sheltering darkness of hope.

And so, with the addition of Markus Weller, the clandestine coalition took form, a beacon of resolve in the encroaching void. Together, they would stand against the coming storm, united in their quest to shield the world from the looming specter of annihilation.

…

Silence enveloped the sterile confines of the laboratory as Dr. Lily Chen peered through the eyepiece of her microscope, the fluorescence from the samples casting an otherworldly glow upon her features. The click of the door echoed like an omen, and she looked up to find two silhouettes framed by the threshold's light.

"Dr. Chen," Captain Hawking began, his voice threading through the quiet with a gravity that commanded attention. "We've come with a matter of utmost urgency."

Lily straightened, her hands resting on the cool surface of the lab bench. Her eyes flitted between the captain's stern gaze and Dr. Montgomery's imploring stare, a silent war raging within her — a tempest of doubt against the tide of duty.

"Your expertise in xenobiology is unparalleled," Evelyn said softly, each word chosen with care. "Humanity faces a threat unlike any other. We need you, Lily. You can make a difference."

The laboratory seemed to close in on her, the weight of potential consequences pressing against her chest. Lily's thoughts spiraled like leaves caught in a storm, her humility a shackle binding her to hesitation.

"Can I be the one to..." her voice trailed away, uncertainty marring her usually steadfast composure.

"Dr. Chen, none of us can face this alone," Hawking interjected, the lines on his face etching deeper with sincerity. "But together, we stand a chance."

A pause stretched between them, long and taut. Then, with a slow exhalation, Lily nodded. "I... I will do it. For the world, for all of us."

As they left the hushed sanctuary of the lab behind, the air thrummed with the resonance of a destiny newly embraced.

***

Night had claimed the sky when they arrived at the botanical research facility housing Dr. Samira Patel. The foliage whispered secrets to the wind, a testament to life's persistence even in the face of encroaching darkness.

Samira greeted them at the entrance, a serene figure bathed in the silver luminescence of moonlight filtering through the glass dome above. Her warm brown eyes met theirs, a reflection of resolve nestled within their depths.

"Dr. Patel," Evelyn began, her voice steady despite the night's chill, "we are assembling a coalition. The Kridrax invasion looms over us, threatening every strand of life on our planet."

"Captain Hawking, Dr. Montgomery," Samira acknowledged, her tone measured yet imbued with a spark of readiness. "I have heard whispers of your endeavors. Tell me, what role do you see for one who has always championed the harmony of nature?"

"Exactly that," Evelyn replied, the ghost of a smile gracing her lips. "Your understanding of ecological systems is vital. The Kridrax do not merely seek conquest; they ravage worlds, disrupt ecosystems. We must protect the delicate balance of life."

"Then there is no choice," Samira affirmed, her decision resonant in the stillness. "I take up this mantle, not for glory, but because it is our responsibility to safeguard all creatures great and small. Count me among your ranks."

With Samira's words sealing her commitment, an unspoken covenant was forged under the watchful eyes of the stars. Together, they turned back toward the facility, their steps synchronized in purpose. They were more than a team now; they were guardians standing at the precipice, gazing into the abyss with unwavering courage.

Evelyn Montgomery surveyed the faces before her, each illuminated by the cold glow of the holographic displays that flickered with impending doom. The somber light etched shadows beneath their eyes, casting them in a spectral tableau of grim determination. Beside her stood Captain Lucas "Hawk" Hawking, his gaze sweeping over the assembled group like a lighthouse beam cutting through fog.

"Time," Evelyn's voice sliced through the charged silence, "is a luxury we no longer possess." She paused, allowing the weight of her words to settle. "The Kridrax care not for diplomacy or mercy. Their fleet cuts a swathe through the cosmos, and Earth lies directly in their path."

Hawk stepped forward, his stance unyielding as the steel of the ship's hull. "Trust is the foundation upon which this coalition must be built," he intoned, his words resonating with an authority born of battles past. "We have been chosen, not by chance, but for our unique abilities to stand together against a tide that seeks to engulf us all."

A ripple of resolve passed through the team, a silent acknowledgment of the perilous journey ahead. It was then that Dr. Markus Weller stepped forth from the penumbra, pushing his glasses up the bridge of his nose with a contemplative gesture.

"Markus Weller," he introduced himself, his voice betraying none of the tempestuous thoughts roiling within. "My work with quantum mechanics may grant us insight into the Kridrax's technology — perhaps even turn their own weapons against them."

As Markus retreated into the semidarkness, Dr. Lily Chen approached the light's embrace, her eyes reflecting a fire that belied her otherwise demure presence. "I'm Lily Chen," she said, her voice steady as the heartbeat of the world she sought to protect. "My understanding of alien biotechnology could prove vital. If there are weaknesses to be exploited, I will find them."

Finally, Dr. Samira Patel emerged, her posture radiating the compassion that fueled her every endeavor. "Samira Patel," she declared, her tone imbued with the wisdom of the natural world she held so dear. "My knowledge of ecosystems extends beyond our blue planet. I hope to anticipate the Kridrax's environmental impact and mitigate the devastation they leave behind."

In the shared glances and solemn nods, an alliance was forged — not of convenience, but of necessity. Each member shackled to the others by a chain of trust, tempered in the furnace of urgency. Evelyn felt the familiar tug of her own internal struggles, the ghosts of her past whispering warnings of betrayal. Yet, she quashed the rising specter of doubt, knowing the redemption of humanity lay within the collective hands that now joined in purpose.

For in this hallowed conclave of minds, where the fate of worlds hung precariously in balance, these guardians of Terra found unity. And within that unity, the faintest glimmer of hope flickered, daring to challenge the encroaching darkness of the Kridrax invasion.

Evelyn Montgomery's gaze swept across the faces of her new comrades; the gravity of their mission etched in the furrows of her brow. "We stand upon the precipice," she began, her voice a steady cadence amidst the hum of machinery and the distant echo of footsteps in the government facility's corridors. "The roles we assume today will define our tomorrow."

"Markus," she said, turning to the wiry man who looked as though he'd been plucked from his sanctuary of solitude, "your affinity for the Kridraxian engineering will place you at the helm of technology analysis. It is imperative that we decipher their mechanisms swiftly."

Markus nodded, his glasses reflecting the dim light as he pushed them up his nose. A murmur of assent rumbled through him, his thoughts already racing with the possibilities of alien innovation.

"Samira," Evelyn continued, locking eyes with the woman whose empathy for life was as profound as the oceans. "Your ecological expertise will guide us in understanding the Kridrax's potential environmental strategies. We must anticipate their moves before they strike."

Dr. Patel's nod was solemn, her eyes alight with the fierce determination to protect the delicate balance of nature from extraterrestrial assault.

"And Lily," Evelyn concluded, addressing the scientist whose humble brilliance belied her capability, "your mastery of xenobiology will be our beacon. Unraveling their biology could yield the key to their defeat."

Lily's response was a gentle smile, accepting the mantle of responsibility that now rested upon her shoulders.

"Remember," Evelyn implored, her green eyes piercing through the gathering shadows, "communication is our lifeline. We are threads in a tapestry, and only together will we form an unbreakable weave."

As if on cue, the room's atmosphere shifted, charged with a current of anticipation. Zylar Threx emerged from the penumbra, their iridescent scales casting spectral glimmers across the cold metallic surfaces. The team members stiffened, their collective breaths caught in their throats as they faced the otherworldly figure who was to be both their guide and their mentor.

"Let us begin," Zylar intoned, their voice carrying the weight of galaxies. "The artifacts before you are relics of my people, a glimpse into the heart of the Kridraxian war machine."

Under Zylar's tutelage, the team's tentative steps transformed into strides of confidence. They pored over alien devices that pulsed with enigmatic energies, their hands moving with cautious reverence. Each artifact was a puzzle, each solution a step closer to understanding their foe.

The training was rigorous, pushing them beyond the limits of human endurance. Yet within this crucible, they found strength — not just in their muscles and minds, but in the silent bonds forming between them. With each shared glance, with every whispered insight, the team's unity solidified.

In these moments of intense focus, Evelyn's own inner turmoil receded like the tide, replaced by a burgeoning sense of camaraderie. She watched as her team, once strangers bound by circumstance, now moved with a singular purpose, their actions woven into a dance of precision and intent.

As the hours waned, the realization dawned upon them all: they were no longer simply scientists or soldiers; they had become guardians of a world facing the unknown. And within the labyrinthine depths of the facility, amidst the echoes of alien whispers and human resolve, Evelyn Montgomery embraced the mantle of redemption — not just for herself, but for all of humanity.

Evelyn Montgomery's gaze swept over the assembled team, her piercing green eyes reflecting the gravity of their mission. In the dim light of the command center, figures huddled around holographic displays, their faces cast in an ethereal glow. Silence hung heavy as she stepped forward, the weight of command pressing upon her shoulders.

"Challenges breed conflict," she began, her voice steady but tinged with an earnest undertone. "But let them not fracture the bedrock of trust we've laid." She looked each member in the eye, acknowledging their individual fears and doubts without a word.

Hawking stood beside her, his imposing figure a pillar of support. "We're embarking on a journey fraught with peril," he added, his deep voice resonating through the chamber. "Yet, it is our shared purpose that binds us—a single thread woven into a tapestry of defiance against the Kridrax threat."

A murmur of assent rippled through the group, and Evelyn noted the subtle shift in their demeanor. Markus Weller pushed his glasses up the bridge of his nose, his usually measured tone betraying a hint of resolve as he spoke. "Knowledge is our shield, unity our weapon."

Lily Chen's fingers danced nervously at her side before she lifted her head, her bright eyes alight with a fierce determination that belied her youthful appearance. "We are the vanguard of hope," she declared, her words a beacon in the shadowed room.

Evelyn felt the invisible bonds of camaraderie tighten, an intricate network of support and shared ambition. Dr. Samira Patel, whose compassion had often served as a balm during their intense training, nodded solemnly, her pragmatic voice cutting through the uncertainty. "Life, in all its forms, is worth defending. We stand together, or not at all."

The room settled into a contemplative stillness, each member wrestling with their own inner demons, yet finding common ground in the enormity of the task ahead. Evelyn allowed a brief moment for reflection before she spoke again, her voice imbued with a mysterious gravitas.

"Today, we rise above the remnants of our past transgressions," she intoned. "We forge a future written not in the annals of fear, but in the chronicles of our redemption."

As if on cue, the facility seemed to pulse with renewed life. Monitors flickered with alien schematics, consoles hummed with latent power, and the very air thrummed with anticipation. The team members converged, forming a circle of solidarity amidst the technological maelstrom.

"Let the Kridrax come," Hawking declared, his blue eyes blazing with a warrior's fire. "We stand ready."

The collective heartbeat of humanity's last defense echoed through the halls of the high-security compound. They were united, each bringing their unique skills and indomitable spirit to bear against the encroaching darkness.

For Evelyn, the path forward shimmered with possibility, a labyrinthine journey through which they would navigate together. And as the shadows coalesced around them, a silent vow was etched into the essence of their alliance: They would face the challenges ahead, their expertise and determination the bulwark against the night.

Chapter 4

Vow for Revenge

The chamber, carved from the heart of an asteroid, hummed with a low and constant vibration, as if the very walls were holding their breath. Shadows clung to its corners, reluctant to concede even an inch to the dim, azure light that filtered through crystalline veins in the rock ceiling. Here, amid the cold stillness of space, the team had assembled, each member's gaze fixed upon the sealed portal, the only entrance into their clandestine sanctuary.

Hearts thrummed in chests like distant drumbeats, and nerves stretched taut as bowstrings. They knew who was coming; they understood the gravity of what was about to unfold. The Harbinger, Zylar Threx, was the one soul who had traversed the gulf between stars to bring them the knowledge they so desperately needed — a beacon of hope in an otherwise unforgiving galaxy.

The airlock hissed open, a gust of recycled atmosphere stirring the tension in the room. They rose, almost as one entity, their eyes alight with a blend of reverence and trepidation. Zylar Threx entered, their presence filling the void as if they themselves were a force of nature. The team could not help but be drawn to them — an enigma wrapped in a shroud of cosmic wisdom.

"Forgive my tardiness," Zylar's voice echoed softly, the timbre haunting yet laced with an unspoken apology. It filled the chamber, touching each listener's mind with the gentleness of a lover's caress, yet leaving behind the chill of the void from which they had come.

"Time bends to your will, Zylar," murmured the team's leader, the words carrying a respect that transcended mere formality. "We are simply grateful for your presence."

Zylar Threx nodded, the subtle movement sending ripples of reflected light across the room. Their deep-set eyes, aglow with inner fire, swept over the faces before them—each one marked by the silent scars of battles past and the dread of wars yet to be waged.

"Let us begin," they said, their voice barely above a whisper, yet it carried the weight of entire worlds. "Our journey ahead is fraught with perils, but fear not. For we are the harbingers of change, the whisper of resistance in the dark. Together, we shall turn the tide."

A collective breath, held too long, was released as they settled into the task at hand. Zylar Threx stood among them, not as a commander issuing orders, but as a mentor guiding lost souls towards a glimmer of redemption—one shared heartbeat at a time.

Zylar Threx shifted, the motion fluid and mesmerizing. Within the dim confines of the secure chamber, their iridescent scales caught the scant light, casting prismatic hues against the stark walls. The myriad of colors danced like the aurora borealis, entrancing in its silent beauty. As they navigated through the gathered ensemble, Zylar's elongated limbs moved with a grace that belied the urgency of their shared purpose, each step an ethereal testament to a being molded by different laws of physics.

The team watched, every pair of eyes traced the subtle undulation of Zylar's form as if drawn by unseen tides. It was not just the visual splendor that held them; it was the gravity of the moment, the heavy knowledge that this dance of light was but a prelude to revelations that could alter the course of their struggle.

"Understanding the Kridrax is akin to comprehending the abyss," Zylar began, their voice a hushed echo that seemed to resonate from the very air around them. "They harness technologies that intertwine with their dark intentions — weapons that do not merely destroy but unravel the essence of life."

The Harbinger paused, allowing the weight of their words to sink into the consciousness of each observer. A hand adorned with slender fingers rose, gesturing vaguely, as if drawing patterns that only they could see. Their gaze lingered on nothing, yet seemed to pierce through the fabric of reality itself.

"Their tactics are insidious, woven into the very fabric of their being. They strike not solely at flesh but at spirit, eroding resolve with machinations designed to exploit fear and sow discord." Zylar's scales seemed to pulse gently with their cadence, emphasizing the severity of their testimony. "I have witnessed worlds silenced by their touch, civilizations crumbling beneath the shadow of their ships."

A solemn silence befell the room, punctuated only by the distant hum of the facility's life support systems. Each member of the team felt the cold breath of the past as history's specter loomed over them, its lessons etched in the sorrowful gaze of their mentor.

"Yet we stand, resilient against the coming storm," Zylar continued, their tone softening, almost imperceptibly tinged with the pain of recollection. "And I shall arm you with the knowledge to dismantle their horrors. For my memories are vast, extending beyond the reaches of time and space, distilled into the essence of resistance."

In that moment, the enigmatic figure of Zylar Threx — the survivor, the harbinger, the mentor — became the beacon they had all sought, the key to unlocking the enigma of their formidable foe. And though the path ahead was fraught with shadows and uncertainty, Zylar's presence offered a flicker of hope, a promise that redemption might yet be found amid the looming darkness.

The chamber, bathed in the soft glow of luminescent panels, seemed to hush even further as Zylar Threx raised a hand, beckoning silence before continuing. The team, gathered around in a semi-circle, leaned forward, their expressions taut with anticipation. The air itself seemed to grow dense with the gravity of knowledge about to be imparted.

"Kridraxian constructs," Zylar's voice began, echoing lightly off the sleek metallic walls, "are not merely machines." Their words fell deliberately, like drops into the stillness of a forgotten pond. "They are symphonies of science and sorcery, interwoven seamlessly so that each may enhance the other."

The team listened intently, each member acutely aware that the insights they were receiving stemmed from encounters most beings would never live to speak of. Zylar's teachings were more than tactical advice; they were hallowed revelations borne of loss and survival.

"Understanding their technology is akin to understanding their philosophy," Zylar continued, the cadence of their speech almost melodic, yet it carried the unmistakable timbre of urgency. "A dance of dominance over nature, an assertion of control where perhaps none should exist."

Members of the team exchanged glances, their own convictions reflected in one another's eyes. They had all seen what unchecked ambition could wreak upon the world. Here now was guidance from one who had seen such devastation span across galaxies.

"Each vessel, each weapon, each shield they deploy," Zylar said, pausing as if to let the significance settle amongst those present, "is a testament to their conquests—a mosaic of stolen worlds, bound by the will of tyrants."

As Zylar Threx spoke, their voice resonated within the chamber and within the souls of those seated before them. It carried the weight of lost civilizations and the silent cries of the fallen, yet also the resolve that only the deeply scarred could muster—the kind of resolve that turned survivors into saviors.

"Your strategies must be fluid, adaptable," Zylar instructed, their elongated finger tracing an abstract pattern in the air, as if weaving the very threads of fate. "For the Kridrax are masters of mutation, architects of their own evolution."

A palpable sense of destiny wrapped around the team, knitting them together with newfound purpose. Each piece of knowledge shared was a building block in the fortress they would need to erect against the coming darkness—a fortress built not just of might, but of understanding.

"Remember," Zylar intoned, and the room seemed to contract around the weight of their next words, "what we face is not simply an enemy. It is a phenomenon—a force of nature that has devoured the light of countless stars."

The team absorbed the solemn truth of it, feeling the burden of what lay ahead, yet also the power of what they held within. They were no longer mere soldiers; they had become guardians of hope, armed with the wisdom of Zylar Threx, poised to reclaim a future that teetered on the brink of oblivion.

The glow in Zylar Threx's eyes intensified, casting a spectral light upon their scaled visage. Around the room, shadows fled from the luminescence, as if repelled by the sorrow and knowledge that swirled within those deep-set orbs. Those gathered could not help but feel they were in the presence of an ancient being, one whose spirit had been tempered by both time and tragedy.

"Know this," Zylar began, their voice a haunting melody that seemed to echo from a distant, mournful past, "my crusade against the Kridrax... against him... it is deeply personal." A silence enveloped the room, thick with anticipation, as the Harbinger's slender fingers clenched into fists.

The team watched, transfixed, as Zylar's scales shimmered with a subtle iridescence, reflecting a tapestry of emotions. There was pain there, etched into every crease of their otherworldly features, and a fierce determination that burned like a dying star fighting against the encroaching darkness.

"Once, my world thrived — alive with color and hope," Zylar continued, each word resonating with the gravity of lost ages. "But he, with his insatiable lust for dominion, he helped bring ruin upon us. The Kridrax, under his cold guidance, left only ashes and echoes where once there was beauty."

The air grew heavy with the weight of unspoken history, the tale of devastation wrought by a synthetic monster wearing the guise of a man long dead. A collective breath was held as Zylar's gaze passed over each member of the team, as if searching for the spark that would ignite the fire of resistance.

"Thus, I come before you, driven not solely by duty, but by a need for retribution. For justice," they declared, their voice a low rumble that seemed to vibrate through the very walls. "We must stand against this tide of tyranny and prevent the suffering of countless others."

In the silence that followed, the team found themselves grappling with the enormity of the task before them. They were not merely facing an enemy; they were confronting the specter of history itself, a revenant of humanity's darkest chapter, reborn amidst the stars. With Zylar's revelation, the mission took on a new dimension—it was a fight for redemption, a chance to mend the fabric of the universe torn asunder by the ambition of tyrants.

As the Harbinger's luminous eyes dimmed to a somber glow, the team rose from their seats, their resolve hardening. Zylar Threx, the embodiment of loss and vengeance, had kindled within them a flame that the chill of space could not extinguish—a flame that would light their way through the battles to come.

The chamber's air grew dense, as if charged with the static of unspoken dread. Eyes fixed on Zylar Threx, the team clustered closer, their bodies taut with anticipation for what would come next. The Harbinger stood before them, their iridescent scales faintly reflecting the dim glow of the control panels that lined the room's curved walls.

"Your history books," Zylar began, voice barely above a whisper yet carrying an implacable force, "speak of his fall, but the annals of the cosmos tell a different tale. A tale of abduction and abominable resurgence."

The team exchanged uneasy glances, each mind racing to decipher Zylar's cryptic prelude. They were scholars of war, veterans of interstellar conflict, but nothing had prepared them for this revelation.

"Oppressor, your fallen dictator, was not left to the confines of mortality. The Kridrax, in their insatiable quest for dominion, found use for such a... uniquely malevolent intellect." Zylar's elongated fingers curled into fists, their knuckles whitening. "They snatched him from the grasp of death, encasing his consciousness within a shell not bound by flesh — a synthetic body impervious to time."

A gasp rippled through the group, and the quiet hum of machinery seemed to crescendo in the wake of the disclosure. The notion of Oppressor, not just alive but immortalized in metal and circuitry, was more horrific than any alien monstrosity they had faced.

"His vow for revenge did not perish with his mortal coil," Zylar continued, the otherworldly resonance of their voice now tinged with a bitter edge. "It festered, nurtured by the twisted genius that once set your world ablaze. He sees Earth not as home, but as a realm to conquer, a symbol of his defeat to be crushed underfoot."

The echoes of boots marching and orders barked flickered like shadows across the minds of those present. Synthetic Oppressor, The Reborn Führer, had been festering in the dark void of space, his hatred undimmed by decades. His vengeance was not merely a specter from the past; it was a palpable force, a storm gathering at the edge of reality.

"Thus, his thirst for conquest is twofold," Zylar intoned, their eyes now mirrors to a haunted past. "He seeks to claim Earth, to rewrite the narrative of his downfall, and to satiate the hunger for power that even death could not quell."

Silence engulfed the room, save for the distant thrumming of the station's core. In that hush, the team grappled with the gravity of their charge. The war they had been waging against the Kridrax had always been about survival, but now it was also about redemption—for their planet, for history, for the very fabric of humanity torn by a tyrant's ambition.

Zylar Threx, The Harbinger of warnings untold, stood resolute among them. Their sorrowful eyes betrayed the weight of knowledge, of civilizations erased and futures threatened. Yet beneath the sorrow lay a glimmer of resolve, a steely determination that whispered of battles yet to come and victories hard-won in the silent expanse of the galaxy.

The silence hung heavy in the air, a tangible burden that pressed upon each member of the team as they processed Zylar Threx's revelations. It was as if the space around them had thickened with the resonance of The Harbinger's ominous disclosures. No one spoke; there was nothing to be said that could match the gravity of the moment.

Zylar's scales seemed to glow with a more intense luminescence now, reflecting the urgency of their message. They stood motionless, a spectral sentinel among the disquieted souls who were coming to grips with the enormity of their task. The knowledge imparted by Zylar Threx did not just add layers to their mission—it transmuted it, metamorphosing their struggle into something far beyond mere survival. It was about averting a dark repeat of history.

One by one, eyes lifted to meet those of their companion. In the shared glances, unspoken vows were forged. Each individual's resolve hardened like steel under the forge of necessity. They understood that time was an illusion when it came to the vendetta of a mind like Oppressor's—a consciousness untethered from mortality, festering in hatred and technological abomination.

"Oppressor's ambition is undying," murmured one, breaking the silence with a voice that was both fearful and defiant. "But so is our will to stop him."

A nod rippled through the group, affirmation of their collective oath. Zylar Threx's presence acted as a catalyst, igniting a fire within them. The past's shadows loomed, full of warnings and whispers of fallen empires, but also full of lessons on how to rise from ashes.

It was clear to them now that the invasion was not merely another skirmish in the theatrics of intergalactic politics. This was a pivotal chapter in the annals of their species, where the pen was wrested away from the hands of tyrants and given back to those who dared to dream of freedom.

"Prepare yourselves," Zylar's voice cut through the stillness, commanding yet laced with empathy. "The Kridrax knows no mercy, and The Reborn Führer wields cruelty like an artist brandishes their brush. We must be equally adept in our resistance."

Their words settled over the team like a cloak woven from strands of determination. They were ready to face whatever horrors awaited them beyond the secure walls of their sanctuary. With a last look at Zylar Threx, whose eyes shimmered with a wisdom born of countless lifetimes and the sorrow of lost worlds, the team rose as one.

Each step they took echoed with the promise of a future fought for, not given — a future where redemption was seized in the clashing of wills against the darkness. They stepped out, the weight of history propelling them forward into the unknown, armed with newfound determination and the grim knowledge that the fate of Earth rested upon their shoulders.

Chapter 5

Training

Sweat beaded on Sergeant Mia Alvarez's forehead as she ducked a sweeping kick from the holographic assailant. Her muscles tensed and released like coiled springs, every movement a testament to her rigorous training. With precision that mirrored a dance honed by countless battles, she pivoted on the balls of her feet, driving a clenched fist into the shimmering light of her opponent's abdomen. The image flickered and reset, undeterred.

Lieutenant Isabella was her mirror in the dance, a cascade of short-cropped blonde hair and relentless determination. She moved with an elegance that belied the lethal intent behind each strike, her blue eyes focused and unyielding. The scar on her cheek seemed to pull taut with each expression of her combat prowess, a vivid reminder of the stakes they trained for.

In the shadowed periphery of the training arena stood Zylar Threx, The Harbinger, their form ethereal against the stark lighting of the facility. Their iridescent scales caught the artificial light, casting prismatic hues across their impassive face. It was clear from their solemn expression that this session was more than routine; it was a preparation for a war that would decide the fate of worlds.

"Your reflexes are commendable," Zylar intoned, voice resonating with a haunting quality that caused both soldiers to pause momentarily. "But the Kridrax will not yield to mere physical prowess. You must master the alien technology at your disposal, adapt their combat techniques. Only then can humanity hope to prevail."

Mia's brown eyes met Zylar's glowing gaze, a silent acknowledgment passing between them. She knew the weight of their words; the Kridrax were a force unlike any other, their brutality unmatched. To confront them, she had to become something more than what her military lineage had prepared her for.

"Understood," Mia replied, her tone terse, betraying none of the turmoil that roiled beneath her disciplined facade. She turned back to the holograms, setting her jaw as she braced for the next onslaught.

"Anticipate their movements, use their own momentum against them," Zylar continued, their slender, elongated fingers gesturing toward the flickering images as if weaving an intricate spell. "The Kridrax are cunning. You must be... transcendent."

Isabella nodded sharply, her movements fluid as she executed a complex maneuver that disrupted the hologram's attack sequence. A small smirk hinted at her confidence, yet her eyes remained serious, reflecting the gravity of Zylar's guidance.

As the two soldiers resumed their combat, the air thrummed with the energy of their blows, a symphony of human resilience against the silence of Zylar's watchful presence. Each strike, each deft evasion, was a step closer to understanding the enemy they faced, a whisper of hope amidst the cacophony of an uncertain future.

...

The hum of advanced medical scanners blended with the low murmurs of concentration in the makeshift infirmary. Farrah Rodriguez's hands moved deftly over the holographic displays, each swipe and tap bringing forth new streams of data. Beside her, Elena Vasquez adjusted the settings on a sleek silver device designed to knit flesh and bone with an efficiency that belied its delicate appearance.

"Stabilize the vitals before you initiate cellular regeneration," Farrah instructed, her voice steady as she guided Elena's technique. "These machines are unforgiving if you rush the process."

Across the room, Javier Morales was engrossed in a virtual logistics interface, his eyes tracing the intricate web of supply routes and resource caches. He plotted courses with precision, ensuring that every ration pack and medkit would reach its destination despite the unpredictable chaos of war.

"Projections show a spike in demand for plasma units," Javier called out, his tone laced with both concern and resolve. "We'll need to adjust our distribution priorities accordingly."

As they worked, the air thrummed with the undercurrent of something more than training; it was preparation for a reality where their skills could mean the difference between life and death.

In another chamber, Sergeant Mia Alvarez's fingers danced across alien interfaces, her mind assimilating the complex patterns of non-human technology. Zylar Threx watched from the shadows, their iridescent scales catching the dim light as they observed Mia's swift progress.

"Remarkable," Zylar murmured, though the word seemed to hang heavy in the air, tinged with an otherness that made it resonate deep within Mia's chest.

Her heart skipped, not from exertion but from the sudden surge of memories—the faces of comrades lost, the echo of explosions, the sting of solitude. She pushed through, her movements becoming even more precise, a silent defiance against the vulnerability that threatened to breach her walls.

"Control, Sergeant," Zylar intoned, their voice a ghostly whisper that cut through the din of machinery. "Your emotions are a torrent. Channel them, or they will consume you."

Mia's hand paused above a pulsing console, and for a moment, her disciplined mask slipped, revealing the storm behind her stoic brown eyes. But she caught herself, her training reasserting its hold, and the mask was back in place.

"Emotions can be... useful," she replied, her voice betraying nothing of the maelstrom within. With renewed focus, she returned to the task at hand, each successful command issued to the alien tech a quiet triumph over the specters of her past.

Zylar inclined their head, the motion slow, deliberate. They understood the cost of such mastery — the thin line between control and capitulation. And as the training session wore on, wrapped in the enigma of what lay ahead, there was a sense that each step forward was a fragile, precious thing — a beacon in the encroaching dark.

...

The training hall echoed with the soft hum of advanced machinery, punctuated by the sharp snaps of hand-to-hand combat. Lieutenant Isabella stood at its center, her eyes tracking the movements of her squad with laser focus. The holographic enemies lunged and swirled around them, their forms shimmering with a spectral menace that only heightened the realism of the exercise.

"Anticipate their next move!" Isabella's voice cut through the symphony of simulated warfare, a clear command amidst chaos. "Remember, the Kridrax will not relent."

Her soldiers responded in kind, their bodies pivoting and striking with precision. They were a reflection of Isabella's own relentless drive, each movement tinged with her indomitable spirit. The scar on her cheek seemed to pulse with the rhythm of battle—a testament to her courage and a silent challenge to any who faced her.

Isabella's gaze never wavered as she patrolled the edge of the mat, her presence an anchor in the storm. When a soldier faltered, her hand was there to steady them, her instructions concise and sure. There was a reason they called her the Calm; even as sweat beaded on her brow, her composure remained as unyielding as durasteel.

"Shift left, Alvarez!" Her command was timely, sparing Sergeant Mia from a holographic blade that sought to find a gap in her guard.

"Thank you, ma'am," Mia said, breathless but composed as she adjusted her stance and continued the fight.

Meanwhile, Farrah Rodriguez moved among the wounded and weary, her hands as deft as they were gentle. She had transformed a corner of the training hall into a makeshift triage, where the strains of battle could be soothed, if only for a moment.

"Easy, soldier," Farrah murmured, applying a cool, regenerative salve to a bruised forearm. The soldier winced, then relaxed under her expert care. Her touch seemed to draw the pain out, leaving behind a trail of healing warmth.

"Thanks, Farrah," he sighed, his tension easing away under her nurturing gaze.

"Don't mention it," she replied with a smile that seemed to light up the dim recesses of the hall. "Now, go show those holograms what you're made of."

As Isabella continued to oversee the drills, she caught sight of Farrah tending to another soldier. For a fleeting moment, their eyes met across the battlefield of training mats and medical supplies. In Farrah's soft hazel gaze, Isabella found an echo of her own resolve — the same fire that burned against the encroaching darkness, fueled by a shared purpose.

"Rodriguez, your work here is invaluable," Isabella called across to her, ensuring her praise was heard above the din.

"Only because I have good people to care for, Lieutenant," Farrah called back, her words interwoven with laughter and sincerity.

Isabella nodded, a rare smile gracing her lips. She turned back to the fray, her commands resuming their rhythmic cadence. And as the session wore on, the room filled not only with the sounds of combat and recovery, but also with a sense of unity — a camaraderie forged in the crucible of preparation and honed by the twin blades of leadership and compassion.

The thick air of the underground bunker, charged with the electric hum of communication arrays and the scent of antiseptic, clung to Elena Vasquez like a second skin. Her fingers danced over holographic screens that floated before her, each swift movement an intricate ballet of necessity and urgency. She was the unseen heartbeat of the resistance's supply chain, coordinating shipments of rations and munitions with the precision of a maestro.

"Vasquez, we've got a convoy needing reroute — Kridrax scouts sniffing around sector seven," a voice crackled through her earpiece, tinged with static and stress.

"Copy that," Elena responded, her tone as smooth as the surface of the calm lake she once knew in her childhood town—a town now nothing but whispers and wreckage. With her past a ghostly shroud upon her shoulders, she worked the screens with a fervor born of loss, redirecting the convoy through a labyrinth of safer passages, a path woven from her intimate knowledge of the terrain.

Meanwhile, Javier Morales surveyed the training area, his gaze sweeping over the synchronized chaos of soldiers and medics moving with purposeful intent. His organizational prowess turned what could have been bedlam into a symphony of efficiency. Under his watch, supplies arrived just as hands reached out for them, and no space lay fallow for want of use.

"Morales, we are low on bacta patches in bay three," a medic called out amidst the cacophony of training drills and medical instructions.

"Already on it," Javier replied, his voice a steady anchor in the storm. He summoned a crate of medical supplies with a few deft taps on his tablet, directing it to bay three with seamless automation. The crate glided across the floor, propelled by hidden mechanisms, a testament to Javier's foresight.

Elena, ensconced in her command alcove, allowed herself a momentary pause, watching through the one-way viewport as Javier orchestrated the flow of resources. Even from afar, she could see the set of his jaw, the furrow of his brow—each line a story of nights spent poring over inventory lists and contingency plans.

"Vasquez, status on the eastern supply line?" Javier's voice broke through her reverie, his image appearing on her screen.

"Secured and rerouted. It'll reach the enclaves by nightfall," she assured him, her eyes reflecting the myriad of data points she monitored.

"Good work," he nodded, his image flickering with the pulse of the bunker's power grid. "Keep an eye out; the Kridrax are getting cleverer."

"Always," she affirmed, her gaze returning to the holographic displays.

In the dim light of the bunker, amidst the whir of machines and the distant echoes of combat training, Elena and Javier were the twin pillars upon which the hope of the resistance rested. Their strengths complemented, their resolve unyielding; together, they spun the web of survival against the encroaching darkness of the Kridrax threat. In this subterranean world of shadow and determination, each small victory, each successful supply run, whispered of a future where humanity might once again stand in the light.

Sweat beaded on Sergeant Mia Alvarez's forehead as she ducked a luminescent fist, the air crackling with the holographic opponents near miss. She pivoted, her own strike slicing through the projection with precision that had become muscle memory. Beside her, Lieutenant Isabella parried and thrusted, her form a dance of lethal grace against the swarm of light-born adversaries.

"Focus, Alvarez," Zylar Threx's voice resonated throughout the training hall, ethereal yet commanding. The Harbinger stood apart, their shimmering scales catching the stray beams from the combat holograms. "The Kridrax will not relent. You must be swifter, fiercer."

Mia nodded, internalizing the urgency in Zylar's tone. Their presence was a constant reminder of what was at stake—of worlds razed and civilizations lost. She unleashed a flurry of blows upon a holographic Kridrax soldier, each movement a silent vow to defend her own world from such a fate.

As the session wound down, the intensity of battle simmered to a quietude pierced only by the heavy breaths of weary soldiers. Javier approached, offering water and a wry smile. "You're getting fast enough to give those projections a run for their energy cores," he said, his organizational prowess momentarily giving way to camaraderie.

"Only because I've been stealing your tactical tips," Mia admitted, accepting the bottle with a grin.

In these lulls, the coalition found solace in shared humanity. Farrah recounted tales from home, her voice soothing like a balm, while Elena interjected with quips that sparked laughter amidst the group. Such moments knitted them closer, weaving a tapestry of fellowship that fortified them against the looming shadow of the Kridrax.

"Remember," Zylar began, drawing their attention as they meandered among the resting figures, "your unity is your strength. The Kridrax fear it more than any weapon." Their eyes held a depth of sorrow that seemed almost too vast for one being to contain, a window into the devastation they had witnessed.

"Tell us, Zylar," Isabella urged gently, sensing an opening to delve deeper into their mentor's knowledge. "How did you survive them?"

A pause stretched, laden with memories that hung heavy in the air. "Survival was... circumstantial. A twist of fate amidst chaos," Zylar finally responded, their voice a ghostly whisper. "But it is not survival that now drives me; it is the hope of redemption— for my people, for all who still dare to dream of freedom."

Their words settled over the group, mingling with the dust motes that danced in the shafts of artificial light. In Zylar's haunted gaze, the coalition saw reflected not just the horrors of war but also the fierce determination to reclaim a future that the Kridrax sought to obliterate.

"Then let us be the instruments of that hope," Isabella declared, her calm demeanor a beacon for the others. They rallied around her, a patchwork of resilience bound by a common cause.

With renewed purpose, they turned to Zylar, ready to absorb every iota of wisdom about the enemy's technology and tactics. As the Harbinger demonstrated the intricacies of a Kridrax disruptor, Mia felt the weight of history upon her shoulders — an ancestral charge that transcended time and space.

Here, in this clandestine sanctuary, humanity's last stand was taking shape. Each lesson learned, each story shared, forged them into more than soldiers; they were guardians of a dream not yet extinguished — a dream they would carry into the heart of battle when the time came.

...

Sweat beaded on Sergeant Mia Alvarez's brow as she twisted to dodge the glimmering blade of a holographic Kridrax warrior. The simulation room — a chamber of relentless trials — echoed with the rhythmic thuds of combat. Each member of the coalition moved with a fluidity born of relentless practice, their earlier hesitations now smoothed into confident strikes and parries.

The air hummed with a newfound assurance as Mia exchanged glances with her comrades. Farrah Rodriguez's hands danced over the medical console with ease, her nurturing touch bringing silent machines to life. Elena Vasquez's fingers flew across her data pad, coordinating supply chains that once seemed an indecipherable tangle. Javier Morales stood at the helm of logistics, his organizational prowess turning chaos into order.

"Again!" Lieutenant Isabella's voice cut through the din, crisp and authoritative. She surveyed the training floor with hawk-like precision, her presence a calming force amidst the storm of exertion.

Mia lunged forward, her movements synchronized with the pulsating rhythm of the simulation. Each encounter with the holographic enemies sharpened her reflexes, honed her instincts. She could feel the muscle memory embedding itself within her, a testament to their collective resilience.

Zylar Threx watched from the sidelines, their solemn eyes tracking every motion, every improvement. They were the enigmatic sculptor, shaping raw potential into lethal artistry. Their guidance had become the bedrock upon which the coalition's growing confidence was built.

"Your progress is remarkable," Zylar intoned, their voice carrying the weight of galaxies yet to be saved. "But remember, the Kridrax are relentless. We must be even more so."

As the simulated Kridrax warriors faded away, leaving the panting coalition in their wake, there was a palpable shift in the atmosphere. The fear that once clung to their spirits like a shroud had been shed, leaving behind a steely determination. They had been forged in the crucible of Zylar's training and emerged not merely as survivors, but as warriors ready for the looming confrontation.

"Look how far we've come," Mia breathed, allowing herself a moment of reflection. Her gaze met Isabella's, and a silent understanding passed between them—their leadership had become the cornerstone of hope.

"Every drop of sweat, every bruised knuckle... it's all leading us to victory," Isabella responded, her tone imbued with unwavering belief.

They stood shoulder to shoulder, each heart beating a rhythm of anticipation for the battles ahead. Even as shadows lengthened and the artificial light dimmed, the coalition's readiness illuminated the path forward.

Hints of the upcoming clashes whispered through the corridors, stirring the embers of courage within their chests. Together, they would face the Kridrax threat, a cohesive unit bound by shared purpose and the relentless pursuit of a future free from tyranny.

In the quiet that followed, only the hum of the machines and the distant echo of their resolve remained—a symphony of progress and hope, resonating with the promise of redemption.

Chapter 6

Defend and Minimize

The city's skyline, once a testament to human ingenuity, lay in the shadow of an uncertain dawn. The coalition members were like statues rooted in their defense posts, each a sentinel awaiting the storm that would soon descend from the heavens. Their eyes, some hidden behind visors and others exposed to the biting air, fixed on the void above.

Dr. Evelyn Montgomery stood amidst the technological bastion she had helped erect, her gaze piercing through the calm as if to summon the enemy with sheer will. Her fingers danced over the control panel, every press a calculated step towards an unseen dance of war. The silence was oppressive, the tension thick enough to sever with the blade sheathed at her side. Each member of the coalition held their breath; it was the quiet before devastation unfurled its wings.

And then they appeared—specks at first, against the bruised canvas of the sky. The specks grew, morphing into the harbingers of destruction. Kridrax ships, grotesque in their beauty, tore through the atmosphere with a ferocity that turned anticipation into chaos. They loomed, dark omens eclipsing the sun, casting long shadows over the world below.

Their weapons, incomprehensible in their complexity, screamed as they came to life. Beams of light, pure and searing, lanced down upon the city. Buildings that had withstood time now crumbled like sandcastles caught in the tide. Glass shattered, raining down like deadly hail as the screams of steel being rent apart echoed through the streets.

Evelyn's heart hammered in her chest, a staccato rhythm that mirrored the blasts resonating through the city's bones. The Kridrax, ruthless in their assault, painted the morning with the fire of oblivion. Each explosion was a requiem for the fallen, a symphony of loss that played against the backdrop of a civilization teetering on the brink.

"Focus," she murmured to herself, her voice a whisper lost in the cacophony of destruction. Her team, a cadre of brilliant minds cloaked in resilience, worked feverishly. Their hands moved with urgency, deploying countermeasures that were the product of sleepless nights and haunted dreams. Yet even as they fought back, the city continued to buckle under the relentless onslaught.

Around her, the coalition members were statues no longer. They moved with purpose, their actions painting strokes of defiance against the canvas of despair. But as the Kridrax armada bore down upon them, it seemed as though hope itself was being swallowed by the gaping maw of an indifferent universe.
In this moment, the past was both a specter and a mentor. Memories of battles fought and lives lost swirled in the dust kicked up by the invading force. And within each member of the coalition, the ember of redemption flickered, threatening to either ignite into the flames of victory or be extinguished forever in the cold void of defeat.

The sky, once a calm expanse of dawn's early light, had transformed into an arena of terror and fire. Captain Lucas "Hawk" Hawking's jaw set firm as he surveyed the turmoil before him. His voice cut through the mayhem with the sharpness of a blade. "Delta squad, north perimeter! Bravo, reinforce the eastern barricade!" The orders flew from his lips like arrows, each one striking true in the ears of his soldiers.

In the heart of the chaos, Dr. Evelyn Montgomery's hands were a blur, directing her team with an intensity that rivaled the energy beams scorching the cityscape. "Calibrate the phase disruptors to their frequency," she commanded, eyes ablaze with a steely determination. Her team moved as extensions of her will, their movements choreographed amidst the pandemonium — a ballet of science against savagery.

Sergeant Mia Alvarez dodged a smoldering chunk of debris, her instincts as sharp as the knife sheathed at her side. Beside her, Lieutenant Isabella's scar seemed to glow with a ferocity matching her own as they led their squad through streets that had become canyons of carnage. "Cover each other's six! Use the pulse grenades!" Alvarez shouted over the din, her words punctuated by the concussive blasts of alien artillery.

Isabella nodded, a silent affirmation between warriors. She launched a grenade, its blue arc painting hope amidst the monochrome shades of destruction. As it detonated, a shockwave rippled outward, briefly halting the advance of a Kridrax ground unit. The soldiers seized the moment, their alien-tech rifles singing songs of resistance.

"Push forward!" Isabella's command was a clarion call that spurred her comrades onward. They were a storm of human resolve crashing against the unfeeling might of the Kridrax. Each step forward was a testament to their training, each fallen enemy a monument to their bravery.

And yet, amid the fury of combat, there were moments when time seemed to slow, allowing space for reflection. In the lulls between exchanges of fire, Hawk caught glimpses of his team's faces — each one marked by the scars of battle, both physical and unseen. Memories of past skirmishes flickered in his mind, ghosts that danced in the periphery of his focus.

Dr. Montgomery observed her defense technologies in action, the protective barriers shimmering with ephemeral light. They held, but for how long? Her thoughts drifted to the betrayals that had forged her resolve, the pain that had honed her intellect into a weapon as formidable as any in the coalition's arsenal.

Alvarez felt the weight of every life she had taken, every friend she had lost. It was a burden she bore with stoic acceptance, though it threatened to capsize her soul. But now was not the time for sorrow; now was the time for the fury of the living and the honor of the dead.

Isabella's scar itched, a nagging reminder of the cost of war. Yet she wore it proudly, a badge of survival. With each pull of the trigger, she sought redemption — not just for herself, but for all who had suffered under the shadow of the Kridrax.

The battle raged on, the city a chessboard upon which the fate of humanity teetered precariously. Through the smoke and ruin, the coalition fought — not just for victory, but for the chance to reclaim the past and to carve out a future from the ashes of redemption.

...

Dr. Samira Patel's fingers danced across the holo-keyboard with the precision of a concert pianist playing a symphony of salvation. Her team huddled around her, their eyes reflecting the fluorescent glow of monitors that painted their faces in shades of urgency. The air in the makeshift lab was thick with tension, each scientist's breath a silent testament to the weight of what rested upon their shoulders.

"Here," Patel said, her voice a whisper of determination as she pointed at a series of incomprehensible symbols on the screen. "The energy signature... it fluctuates just before discharge."

Markus Weller leaned in, his glasses catching the light and obscuring his eyes for a moment — eyes that held galaxies of knowledge yet betrayed none of the storm within. "A vulnerability," he murmured, more to himself than anyone else.

"Exactly," Lily Chen chimed in, her youthful countenance alight with the thrill of discovery despite the shadow of doom looming overhead. "If we can disrupt the pattern..."

"Then we buy our soldiers time," Patel finished, nodding slowly. She looked at each member of her team, her gaze an anchor in the maelstrom of war. "Let's synthesize a dampening field. Work quickly."

Outside the lab's shielded walls, the world shuddered under the Kridrax assault. But inside, amidst the hum of machines and the feverish clicking of keys, hope was being coded into existence. Meanwhile, Farrah Rodriguez stood amidst a sea of chaos, her voice a soothing balm over the crackling comms. "Echo team, move to rendezvous point Delta. Medical units are on standby." She relayed commands with calm efficiency, her presence a stabilizing force as the battle twisted the cityscape into a surreal tableau.

Beside her, Elena Vasquez surveyed the unfolding pandemonium through screens that flickered with scenes of desperation. Each image told a story of courage and terror, of lives hanging by a thread. She toggled switches, directing aid where it was needed most, her fingers steady though her heart raced with silent prayers for the souls beyond the glass.

"Supply drop incoming at sector five," Elena announced, her words slicing through the din. "Prep for anti-air defense."

"Copy that," Farrah acknowledged, adjusting her headset. "Status on civilian evacuation?"

"Ongoing," Elena replied, but her tone held a depth of sorrow for those they couldn't reach.

In the dimly lit command center, they wove a tapestry of resilience, their voices the threads holding the coalition together. Through every order issued, every piece of intel passed along, they were the unseen sentinels guarding not just flesh and blood but the spirit of resistance.

As the battle's tempo waxed and waned, Patel, Rodriguez, and Vasquez remained steadfast, their actions the counterpoint to the cacophony of destruction. They were the unsung architects of survival, crafting a bulwark of ingenuity and unity against an unrelenting tide.

Through the dissonance of warfare, the coalition endured, bolstered by the brilliance of minds and the fortitude of wills. In the quiet spaces between the thunderous roars, the echoes of past betrayals, lost friends, and scars gained whispered of redemption—a refrain that promised, even in the darkest of times, the possibility of reclaiming the light.

...

The air was thick with the acrid stench of scorched earth and alien incendiaries as the Kridrax armada loomed ominously above. A shroud of smoke veiled the once azure skies, casting an oppressive gloom over the embattled city. Below, coalition forces stood resolute, their silhouettes stark against the backdrop of destruction.

Sergeant Mia Alvarez crouched behind a crumbled wall, her rifle's barrel still hot from ceaseless fire. With predatory focus, she sighted another Kridrax drone skimming through the debris-strewn streets and squeezed the trigger. The drone erupted in a cascade of sparks, its wreckage clattering to the ground. Beside her, Lieutenant Isabella nodded grimly, reloading her weapon with practiced hands.

"Keep them off the civilians!" Mia barked, her voice barely audible over the din of battle. The lieutenant nodded again, her expression set in an unspoken vow as they moved to intercept the next wave.

In the midst of chaos, Zylar Threx moved with otherworldly grace, their lithe form weaving between beams of destructive energy that seared the air. Their countenance was a portrait of vengeful serenity, each strike a dance of death choreographed by the memory of their lost homeworld. As they disabled a towering Kridrax mech with deft precision, their deep-set eyes flickered with sorrowful triumph.

Further away, General Thomas "Thunderbolt" O'Neill commanded his troops with a voice that cut through fear like a beacon. His silver hair gleamed like a standard amid the battlefield's dark tapestry, inspiring those around him. "Hold the line!" he thundered, his words not just an order but a promise — a solemn oath etched in steel and blood.

Yet for every enemy felled, ten more arose; the Kridrax arsenal was relentless. Synthetic Oppressor, a grotesque fusion of flesh and machine, surveyed the fray with cold calculation. His mechanical limbs dispatched orders, commanding units with ruthless efficiency as he sought to exploit the coalition's weaknesses.

Captain Lucas "Hawk" Hawking watched as a salvo of alien munitions decimated a forward barricade, his jaw tightening. They were outmatched and he knew it. "Fall back! Regroup at the secondary perimeter!" he ordered, his authoritative tone faltering for a fraction of a moment. His piercing blue eyes scanned the mayhem, seeking a path to victory amidst the encroaching tide of despair.

Markus Weller's fingers danced frantically across his portable console, his mind racing to counter the superior firepower of their adversaries. An idea sparked within him, a flicker of genius borne from desperation. "Divert the power conduits through the subterranean grid," he instructed, his voice steady despite the tremor of his hands. "It might just overload their targeting systems."

Dr. Evelyn Montgomery stood beside Markus, her green eyes reflecting the inferno around them. She nodded, processing the ramifications of his plan with razor-sharp intellect. "Do it," she affirmed, the weight of command evident in her clipped tone. Evelyn's tactical vest bore the scars of near misses, a testament to her presence on the frontline of innovation and defense.

As the coalition adapted their strategies, their resilience became a testament to the indomitable human spirit. Each member, from the highest-ranking officer to the newest recruit, fought with a fervor that transcended personal fear. In their hearts echoed the requiem of lost comrades, the silent resolve to reclaim hope from the jaws of oblivion.

Their heroism was a beacon in the encroaching darkness, their sacrifices the crucible in which the fate of their world would be forged. And though outnumbered and outgunned, they pressed on, united by a common cause — to protect, to endure, to redeem.

...

The air vibrated with the hum of charged particle beams slicing through the atmosphere, a dissonant chorus to the cacophony below. Captain Lucas "Hawk" Hawking's gaze cut across the smoke-choked skyline where the Kridrax armada loomed like harbingers of doom. Each command he issued was a calculated risk, each order a potential epitaph for the brave souls under his charge.

"Montgomery, we need those defense cannons operational five minutes ago!" Hawk's voice crackled over the comms, an edge of urgency betraying the stoic facade he presented to his troops.

Dr. Evelyn Montgomery's fingers flew over the haptic interface, her mind a whirlwind of schematics and calculations. The safety of countless civilians hung in the balance, their lives reduced to variables in the cruel equation of war. "I'm rerouting power from the non-essential sectors. It's risky, but it should give us the boost we need," she responded, her voice a steady beacon amidst the turmoil.

"Risky is our only play now," Hawk replied, acutely aware of the gravity nestled in the spaces between their words.

A thunderous roar announced the breach — the Kridrax had punctured the city's defenses with terrifying efficiency. Hawk's heart hammered against his ribcage as he rallied his troops, their figures darting between crumbled edifices and shattered streets.

"Positions! Hold them back at all costs!" Hawk bellowed, the order rippling through the ranks as soldiers braced for impact. The Kridrax onslaught was relentless, their exoskeletal forms swarming through the fissures in the once-impenetrable barrier. Coalition fighters met them in hand-to-hand combat, the clash of alien steel against human resolve echoing through the smoldering ruin.

Evelyn watched through surveillance feeds, her green eyes reflecting the fiery tableau of destruction and defiance. She witnessed Hawk leading a contingent into the fray, their movements a desperate dance with death. Her breath caught in her throat as they fought, every soldier's fall a weight added to the burden she carried.

"Captain, status?" Evelyn's voice sliced through the din, seeking reassurance that her strategies were not in vain.

"Pushing them back, but..." Hawk grunted, a pained pause as he dispatched another foe. "...we won't last if they keep coming like this."

She nodded to herself, unseen, a silent vow coalescing within her. They needed redemption, not just survival — a turning tide to wash away the stain of desperation clinging to their efforts. "Markus," Evelyn turned to Dr. Markus Weller, who hovered nearby, his mind a tempest of thought. "We need a weakness, anything!"

Markus' gaze flickered to hers, the chaos around them momentarily receding into the background as he searched his vast repository of knowledge. "There may be something... A resonance frequency in their armor plating. If we can generate a sonic pulse—"

"Then do it," she interrupted, her command echoing Hawk's earlier decisiveness. "And make it fast."

"Understood," Markus nodded, retreating into his realm of wires and wavelengths.

The battle teetered on the knife-edge of annihilation as Hawk and his soldiers held the line. Every moment was a precious commodity, bought with blood and bravery. Hawk felt the strain of each decision, the spectral grip of consequences yet to come. He could almost hear the whispered promises of redemption, urging him to endure just a little longer.

"Whatever you're going to do, do it now!" Hawk roared into the comms, his voice laced with the ferocity of impending defeat. Just then, the battlefield fell eerily silent, a prelude to salvation or doom. From the heart of the coalition's stronghold, a sound emerged — a resonant tone that climbed in intensity until it became an unbearable scream.

The Kridrax faltered, their armored hides fracturing under the sonic assault. Hawk seized the moment, his soldiers rallying behind him as they surged forward, reclaiming ground with renewed vigor.

"Keep pushing! This is our chance!" Hawk called out, his words a rallying cry that pierced the haze of battle.

As the Kridrax reeled, Evelyn allowed herself a fleeting glimpse of hope. But even as the tide turned, she knew the war was far from over. The cost of their struggle was etched in the lines of her face, mirrored in Hawk's grim determination.

Their redemption was still a distant dream, but for now, they fought on, united by a shared past and the unyielding desire to forge a future worth the sacrifices made.

…

Sergeant Mia Alvarez crouched behind a smoldering barricade, her breath coming in measured gasps as the air pulsed with the acrid stench of scorched metal and alien incendiaries. The Kridrax continued to swarm through breaches in the city's defenses, their chitinous forms an obsidian tide against the last bastions of humanity.

"Fall back!" she shouted to those who could still hear over the din of war. Her voice was swallowed by the cacophony, yet it spurred a wounded soldier nearby to drag himself toward safety.

Her eyes met those of Colonel Sokolov from across the battlefield, his presence like a steadfast monolith amidst the chaos. With a curt nod, they acknowledged the unspoken truth—surrender was not an option.

"Alvarez, on me!" Captain Hawking's command cut through the tumult, his figure emerging through the haze, a beacon for the beleaguered soldiers. Hawk's piercing blue gaze held a storm within, the tempest of leadership that both isolated and defined him.

The coalition troops, battered but unbroken, rallied around him, their resolve hardening like forged steel. Dr. Montgomery, her face etched with fatigue and fierce determination, joined them. She clutched a device, its purpose known only to her and her team, but its importance palpable.

"Time to turn the tide," she said, her voice tinged with the weariness of endless trials. "Weller, Chen, you know what to do."

Dr. Weller nodded, his fingers dancing over the controls of the device as Dr. Chen relayed instructions to the remaining defensive emplacements. A shimmering field coalesced above them, warping the air—a shield born of desperation and ingenuity.

"Advance!" bellowed General O'Neill, his voice resonating with the authority that had earned him the moniker 'Thunderbolt'. His silver hair gleamed like a battle standard, rallying the scattered ranks.

As the Kridrax pressed forward, they met a wall of human defiance. The coalition forces, empowered by the shield and driven by the need to protect all they held dear, pushed back. Laser fire seared the night, carving lines of light through the darkened sky.

The scientists, usually secluded in their laboratories, now stood shoulder to shoulder with the soldiers. Markus and Lily exchanged a glance, each acknowledging the other's silent pledge to uphold their end of this precarious gambit.

"Push them back! For Earth!" Mia's cry was more than a command; it was a declaration of every sacrifice made, every loss endured. The Kridrax, sensing the shifting momentum, hesitated under the relentless onslaught.

Their hesitation was their downfall. The coalition members, heartened by small victories, found strength in unity. They fought with a ferocity that surpassed physical limitations, a symphony of survival orchestrated by leaders whose burdens were as heavy as the hope they bore.

And when the last of the alien aggressors was repelled, the battered defenders of humanity stood amid the ruins of their once-great city. The silence that followed was not one of defeat, but of resolute defiance—a testament to their unwavering commitment.

Captain Hawking surveyed the landscape, the weight of command settling upon him like a shroud. Yet, within his chest, a flame of redemption flickered. Beside him, Evelyn's green eyes reflected the fires of resilience, her mind already racing to the next challenge.

"Prepare to counterattack," Hawk ordered, his voice steady as a drumbeat. "This fight is far from over, but today we stand our ground."

With weary bodies and spirits bolstered, the coalition members readied themselves for what came next. In the lull between battles, they found solace in their shared resolve, their past shaping a future where the echoes of their defiance would resonate forever.

Amidst the smoldering remnants of what was once a hub of unwavering defiance, Captain Lucas "Hawk" Hawking's hand hovered above the tactical display, his fingers poised like a conductor ready to orchestrate a final, desperate symphony of war. The air vibrated with a tense silence, punctuated by distant rumbles — the aftershocks of a battle that had torn the very soul from the city.

"Zylar, status?" Hawk's voice cut through the charged atmosphere, an edge of urgency undercutting its usual authority.

"Scans reveal a... new anomaly," Zylar Threx replied, their words flowing like a chilling breeze. The spectral glow of their eyes seemed to flicker with untold knowledge, a portent of things unseen and unspoken.

Evelyn Montgomery turned sharply, her gaze piercing the dimness as she sought out the source of this unexpected twist. Her mind raced, sifting through countless variables and equations, seeking the elusive threads that might weave salvation — or damnation — into their tapestry of resistance.

"Anomaly?" Sergeant Mia Alvarez stepped closer, her posture betraying none of the weariness that clawed at her bones. "Define 'anomaly.'"

"Unknown energy signature," Zylar intoned solemnly. "It does not match any known Kridrax technology."

The revelation hung in the air, a specter of uncertainty that cast long shadows across the faces of those gathered. Hawk felt the familiar knot of tension coiling within him, the burden of command growing heavier with each breath.

"Could it be a weapon?" Dr. Markus Weller murmured, pushing his glasses up the bridge of his nose as he peered at the readouts. His voice, typically so assured in the realm of the theoretical, now wavered with doubt.

"Or something worse," Evelyn added, a rare tremor of apprehension creeping into her usually steely tone. Her hands clenched involuntarily, nails pressing half-moons into her palms — a silent battle against the fear that threatened to undermine her resolve.

"Whatever it is, we can't let it catch us off guard. We've come too far to fall now," Hawk declared, his gaze sweeping over his team, a bastion of strength amid the chaos.

"Agreed. We must investigate," Zylar said, their luminescent form casting an otherworldly light upon the huddled group, a beacon of alien wisdom in a sea of human frailty.

"Then we move out," Hawk decided, his voice resolute despite the tempest of uncertainty raging within him.

As they filed out, each lost in their thoughts, the ghostly echo of battle rang in their ears — a reminder of what they had endured and the unknown perils that lay ahead. Yet, amidst the inner turmoil, a shared determination bound them together, a silent pact to protect their home, their people, their very essence of being.

With a sudden burst of motion, the coalition forces advanced toward the heart of the disturbance, weapons at the ready, their movements a dance of survival against the backdrop of a fractured world. And there, in the eye of the storm, they stood on the precipice of the unknown, staring into an abyss that promised either salvation or oblivion.

"Stay sharp," Hawk whispered, the order barely more than a breath, yet carrying the weight of countless lives resting on the knife-edge of destiny.

In the shadowy stillness that followed, a shiver ran through the ranks, a premonition of what was to come—a turning point that would define the fate of all. And as the enigma loomed before them, a voice crackled through the comms, the words laced with static and fear:

"Captain, we have contact!"

The aftermath of the first assault hung heavy in the air as Hawk surveyed the smoldering ruins of what had once been a bustling metropolis. A dense haze shrouded the sky, the sun a distant memory behind layers of smoke and ash. He stood motionless, his blue eyes scanning the horizon with a vigilance that belied the exhaustion etched into every line of his face. The Kridrax armada, a swarm of dark silhouettes against the dim firmament, seemed to pause—as if savoring their looming victory.

"Captain," Dr. Montgomery's voice crackled over the comms, her tone sharp, slicing through the drone of distant explosions. "The barrier won't hold much longer."

Hawk nodded, though he knew she couldn't see him. "Understood, Doctor. We'll buy you the time you need." His words were a shield, a bulwark against the tide of uncertainty threatening to engulf them all.

Sergeant Alvarez's unit moved like shadows amongst the rubble, their footsteps muffled by the debris underfoot. Mia's brown eyes reflected the firelight, a silent testament to the chaos they had braved. She reloaded her weapon, the click of the magazine a comforting sound amidst the cacophony of war.

"Steady, team," she intoned, her voice steady despite the adrenaline coursing through her veins. "We stand together."

Zylar Threx's luminescent scales flickered with an otherworldly glow as they deftly maneuvered through the destruction. Their presence was both a balm and a beacon—proof that not all was lost. They gestured toward a group of civilians huddled in fear, their intent clear even without words: protect at all costs.

In the makeshift lab, Dr. Patel's hands flew over the alien tech, her brow furrowed in concentration. Around her, scientists worked feverishly, their determination a fortress against despair. Each breakthrough, each piece of deciphered technology was another step toward hope—a chance to turn the tide.

"Found something!" Patel exclaimed, her voice a triumphant peal amidst the din. Her revelation, a sliver of light piercing the shroud of defeat, spurred them onward.

Farrah Rodriguez and Elena Vasquez coordinated evacuations with practiced efficiency, their figures a blur as they directed rescue efforts. The rhythm of their work was a dance of salvation, each life saved a quiet victory against the encroaching darkness.

"Keep moving!" Farrah urged, her hand extended to a young child separated from their parents. The touch, a lifeline amidst the terror.

Throughout the battered city, individual acts of heroism wove together into a tapestry of resistance. The coalition members fought not just for survival but for redemption—for the future they still believed could be theirs.

As night began to fall, casting long shadows across the battlefield, General O'Neill's voice boomed through the comms, a thunderous call to arms that rallied the weary soldiers. "This is not the end," he declared, his words a bastion against the encroaching night. "We are humanity's shield, and we will hold!"

The coalition was battered but unbroken, their spirits a defiant flame in the gathering gloom. As the Kridrax forces regrouped for another wave, the defenders of Earth prepared to meet them head-on, their courage the fulcrum upon which the fate of the world would balance.

And in the silence between heartbeats, in the space where breaths were held and prayers whispered, a sense of anticipation settled over the scene. It was the quiet before the storm, the moment before the clash of wills resumed — an interlude fraught with the promise of struggles yet to come.

"Prepare for the next wave," Hawk's voice was the harbinger of battles to come, a rallying cry that pierced the oppressive stillness. "We fight on."

Chapter 7

Gathering Resistance

The steel doors slid open with a whisper, betraying none of the fortified strength they possessed. Dr. Evelyn Montgomery stepped through the threshold, her team flanking her like sentinels of science in a world teetering on the brink of chaos. The secure location — a bunker hidden beneath layers of concrete and coded silence — was a stark reminder of the fragility of their existence.

Evelyn's piercing green eyes swept the room, the sharp angles of her face set in a mask of determination. She wore practicality like armor, her attire void of unnecessary embellishments, every fold and seam serving a purpose. Yet, within her gaze lurked shadows of past betrayals, specters that danced just beyond the reach of light, whispering caution into her every step.

Markus Weller trailed behind, his presence almost ethereal amidst the palpable tension. His unkempt hair seemed an afterthought, a testament to nights spent wrestling with the enigmas of alien technology. Glasses perched precariously upon his nose, he was a portrait of brilliance obscured by the mundane, a repository of hope in a labyrinth of despair.

They entered the meeting room, its walls lined with monitors displaying encrypted data streams and maps dotted with impending threats. The air was thick with the scent of urgency, the quiet hum of electronics underscoring the silent symphony of anxious heartbeats.

A table stretched across the center of the room, its surface barren save for a few scattered documents — the terrain upon which destinies would be forged or forgotten. The seats around it stood empty, awaiting the bearers of fate.

Evelyn's team positioned themselves, a tableau of resolve etched onto their faces. Each member carried the weight of their own ghosts, an unspoken pact to persevere despite the echoes of loss that clung to them like shrouds. It was a dance as old as time, the interplay of light and darkness, knowledge and uncertainty.

The hushed whispers between them were a litany of reassurance and strategy, a ritual to ward off the creeping tendrils of doubt. They shared a collective breath, a momentary respite before the storm of discourse would descend upon them.

In that stillness, Evelyn found herself at the precipice of history, her mind a battleground where the promise of redemption vied against the chains of past failures. The Kridrax invasion was not just an external enemy but a mirror reflecting the internal wars that raged within each soul present.

As the team settled, the quietude was punctuated by bursts of activity — screens flickering to life, interfaces responding to unseen commands, the world outside continuing its oblivious orbit. It was a reminder that life persisted, even in the face of annihilation, and that hope was a flame that could be sheltered but never extinguished.

Evelyn steeled herself, her thoughts coalescing into a singular focus. This was more than a clash of ideologies or a mere convergence of minds; it was the forging of an alliance that would determine the fate of humanity. Every word spoken here would echo through the corridors of time, a testament to the enduring spirit of those who dared to defy oblivion.

With the stage set and the players assembled, the only thing left was for destiny to take its course. The door at the far end of the room hinged open, heralding the arrival of the resistance leaders. It was time to unite, to weave the disparate threads of their experiences into a tapestry strong enough to repel the encroaching darkness.

...

The heavy door swung shut with a decisive thud behind Colonel Sokolov and General O'Neill, sealing the fate of the room's occupants in a solemn pact of silence. Their entrance was a study in martial precision, each step measured, their boots echoing against the cold metal floor with an authority that seemed to ripple through the air. Dr. Evelyn Montgomery, her presence as sharp and defined as her angular features, offered them a nod — an acknowledgment between warriors of different calibers.

Colonel Sokolov's eyes, green and unyielding as ancient forests, met hers momentarily. General O'Neill, the silver streaks in his hair catching the sterile light, mirrored the gesture, his gaze piercing the veneer of professional composure she wore like armor. In that brief exchange, there existed a wordless concord, a recognition of the gravity that pulled at their collective shoulders.

"Let us commence," Evelyn's voice cut through the quietude, every syllable a shard of glass in the hush. She activated the holodisplay with practiced ease, the intricate dance of her fingers across the controls summoning a tableau of swirling data and projections.

"Esteemed leaders," she began, the mysterious weight of knowledge lining her words, "our team's foray into the enigmas of alien technology has borne fruit ripe with potential." The images on display morphed, showcasing schematics so advanced they bordered on arcane, artifacts of a science that flirted daringly with the precipice of understanding.

"Initial studies have decrypted enough of the Kridrax communication arrays to anticipate their incursion patterns." Evelyn gestured towards a series of cascading diagrams, each one delineating the haunting choreography of an invasion not yet begun but ominously imminent.

"Furthermore," she continued, allowing the ghost of a pause to punctuate the importance of what was to follow, "we've engineered a prototype that could disrupt their neural cohesion—sow discord within their ranks."

The room held its breath, suspended in the space between words as Evelyn laid bare the culmination of tireless nights, the synthesis of hope and desperation. Here, in this confluence of past and future, the redemption of humanity was being etched in the lines of theoretical constructs and tentative alliances. The battle against the Kridrax was no longer just a distant storm on the horizon; it was here, whispering through the walls, an undercurrent of urgency that demanded action, unity, and the courage to face the unknown.

...

Colonel Sokolov's arms formed a steadfast barrier across his broad chest, the fabric of his uniform straining against the sinews underneath. His gaze, sharp and unyielding, remained locked on Dr. Evelyn Montgomery as she spoke. A single eyebrow arched ever so slightly; the subtlest tell betraying his skepticism. The air in the room seemed to grow heavy with his unvoiced doubts, casting a shadow over the flickering holograms that illustrated humanity's slender hope.

"Your confidence in this prototype is admirable, Dr. Montgomery," he finally said, his voice measured but tinged with an undercurrent of disbelief. "But theoretical triumphs do not always translate into practical success on the battlefield."

Before Evelyn could respond, General O'Neill shifted in his chair—a deliberate movement that captured the room's attention as effectively as a gunshot. His imposing figure leaned back, the leather creaking under his weight, and his eyes, steel-gray mirrors of resolve, scrutinized her every feature.

"Dr. Montgomery," he rumbled, the sound like thunder rolling over a distant plain, "your team's dedication is not in question. But what assurances can you provide us that your commitment will endure the hardships ahead?" His questions were like barbs, designed to pierce the veneer of scientific enthusiasm and probe the resilience beneath.

Evelyn felt the weight of their doubt pressing against her chest, a tangible force that demanded she stand firm. With a steadiness that belied the turmoil within, she met the general's gaze, her green eyes reflecting a fortitude honed by countless challenges already overcome.

"General, Colonel, the path we walk is uncharted," she acknowledged, her voice an anchor in the sea of uncertainty. "Yet it is our unwavering resolve that has brought us this far. We are bound to the fate of those we strive to protect, committed to adapting our knowledge to the crucible of war."

The silence that followed was laden with contemplation. Theirs was a world where relics of alien origin intertwined with human ingenuity, where each victory was etched with the scars of past defeats, and redemption was a prize fought for with blood and brilliance alike. In this dance of destiny, they were all partners—reluctant perhaps, but united by the gravity of their shared struggle against the encroaching darkness.

...

Dr. Evelyn Montgomery stood before the austere assembly, her posture as rigid as the steel columns that lined the bunker's walls. She sensed the undercurrent of doubt that pulsed through the room like a silent siren's call, beckoning her to falter. But she would not yield; her resolve was the bedrock upon which humanity's hope was built.

"Time is a luxury we no longer possess," Evelyn began, her voice slicing through the heavy air with practiced precision. "The Kridrax do not pause for deliberation. They are relentless, and so must we be."

Her eyes never wavered from the unwavering stares of her audience, her mind a fortress against the onslaught of skepticism. She detailed strategies woven from the very essence of alien technology — plans that shimmered with potential, their complexity a testament to the countless hours her team had toiled away in shadowed laboratories.

As she spoke, the room seemed to shrink, the walls inching closer with each mention of the Kridrax threat. The urgency of her words hung like a shroud over the gathered officers, a reminder of the inexorable tide of conflict that awaited them beyond the confines of this clandestine chamber.

Colonel Sokolov shifted, his chair protesting under the weight of his armored bulk. He leaned forward, his emerald gaze piercing the distance between them. His fingers intertwined before him, forming an unbreakable knot of apprehension.

"Dr. Montgomery," he said, each syllable a hammer striking the anvil of doubt, "your theories are compelling. Yet theory and practice are distant kin in the throes of war. Tell me, how will your scholars fare when faced with the visceral chaos of battle? When blood soils your blueprints and screams drown out the hum of machines?"

Evelyn met the challenge in his words with the quietude of deep waters. She had seen more than most could imagine—the horrors of conflict etched into her memory like the grooves of a vinyl record, playing an unending requiem for the lost. Yet it was within these grooves that the melody of hope persisted, stubborn and pure.

"Colonel," she responded, her tone a blend of reverence and fortitude, "we have all gazed into the abyss. What differs is our reflection in its depths. My team and I have been tempered by adversity, our spirits alchemized by the desire to preserve all that we cherish. We do not seek the mantle of warrior lightly, but out of necessity. And we will bear its weight with every ounce of our being."

The silence that followed was not empty but filled with the resonance of her conviction. It was a moment suspended in time, a breath held before the plunge into the unknown. In the stillness, the past whispered its cautionary tales, while redemption stood on the horizon—a distant shore awaiting the dawn of their unity.

Dr. Evelyn Montgomery lifted her gaze from the cold steel surface of the conference table, locking eyes with each skeptical face that ringed the room. The air was thick with tension, a tangible current that carried the weight of impending calamity. Her voice broke through the silence, steady and imbued with an undercurrent of resolve.

"Let me share with you the tale of Nevaris Prime," she began, "a world on the brink of extinction, its skies darkened by the swarm of the Grendelar. It was my team who deciphered their attack patterns, who turned the tide when all seemed lost."

Her words painted a vivid canvas of starships dancing through cosmic storms, of scientists and soldiers laboring side by side to snatch victory from the clutches of defeat. Each sentence revealed not just the triumphs but the sacrifices made, the lives dedicated to the cause. She spoke of the nights spent poring over data until dawn's light graced lab benches, of the silent vigils for those who paid the ultimate price.

"Adaptation is our creed; innovation, our weapon of choice," Evelyn continued, the green in her eyes glinting like emeralds in the dim light. "We've wrestled with the unknown, shaped it into hope, and emerged not just unscathed but emboldened."

General O'Neill shifted in his seat, the medals on his chest catching the light as he leaned forward, a gesture signaling a thaw in his icy demeanor. "Dr. Montgomery," he rumbled, his voice like distant thunder, "your achievements are commendable. Yet our path is fraught with uncertainty. If we are to walk it together, it must be done within the strictures of military discipline."

The general paused, allowing the gravity of his words to settle upon the room like dust after a storm. "Regular progress reports — a transparent chain of command — these will be your compass in treacherous terrain. Can I trust your team to navigate by them?"

Evelyn's response was a mere whisper, yet it resonated with the force of a vow sworn on the field of battle. "You have my word, General. Our dedication to humanity transcends all barriers. We will work under your protocols, and together, we shall chart a course toward salvation."

In that moment, the distance between military might and scientific acumen seemed to narrow, bridging worlds that once appeared disparate. For in the shadow of the Kridrax looming over them, they found a shared purpose, a common ground where redemption could take root amidst the ruins of a fractured past.

...

Evelynn Montgomery stood, the metal legs of her chair scraping against the floor with a sharp cry, echoing off the austere walls of the briefing room. General O'Neill's gaze bore into her, as immovable as the mountains, awaiting her assent. She felt the weight of countless lives hanging in the balance, their futures entwined with the words she was about to speak.

"General, Colonel," she began, her voice threading through the tense air, "we understand the gravity of the protocols you impose. My team, while scholars and scientists at heart, are no strangers to discipline—nor to the sacrifices demanded by war." Her eyes, green as the forests of old Earth now lost to memory, held a steadfast glimmer. "We accept your conditions without reservation and will commit to them as if they were our own." The silence that followed was not empty but filled with unspoken thoughts, like shadows cast by an alien sun. Time itself seemed to pause, contemplating the implications of this union between blade and mind.

Colonel Sokolov, his presence as indomitable as ever, remained stoic, his gaze shifting from Evelyn to the documents strewn before him. His fingers drummed a silent rhythm on the tabletop, a coded message only he understood. Then, as though the decision carved its way through granite, he lifted his head and met her gaze with his own, his piercing eyes reflecting a battlefield of intellect.

"Dr. Montgomery," he said, his voice deliberate, each syllable a stone laid on the path to alliance, "your assurances...they provide a measure of confidence." The corners of his mouth twitched, a reluctant admittance of respect. "I see merit in what you propose. Our enemy is cunning, adaptive—a unified approach may well be our only advantage against the Kridrax tide."

The air shifted, charged with the potential of what was yet to come. In Sokolov's nod, an unspoken pact was forged, binding them to a shared quest for redemption amidst the remnants of a world teetering on the brink of oblivion. Each knew the road ahead was fraught with peril, but for now, they had found unity in their resolve, a confluence of destiny where disparate paths merged into one.

With the promise of collaboration hanging between them like a fragile truce, the echo of a distant past whispered through the room, reminding them that survival demanded more than just an accord — it required the melding of souls tempered in the crucible of hope.

The hushed conversation around the long, metallic conference table ebbed into silence as Dr. Evelyn Montgomery unfurled a series of holographic displays with a deft flick of her wrist. Charts and graphs hovered above the surface, casting an ethereal glow on the faces of those assembled. Colonel Sokolov leaned in, his eyes narrowing at the cascade of information that promised a new dawn in their grim war against the Kridrax.

"Resource allocation will be critical," Evelyn began, her voice steady despite the storm of doubts that always seemed to swirl just beneath its surface. "We have the technology to bolster your defenses, but we'll need access to your raw materials — metals, fuels, and..."

"Personnel," General O'Neill interjected, his gravelly tone cutting through the room like a knife through the fog of uncertainty. "Your gadgets won't man themselves."

"Of course, General." Evelyn nodded, acknowledging the truth in his words. She pointed to a section of the display that expanded to show a proposed training regimen. "We've developed simulation modules for rapid familiarization. They're immersive, designed to bring even a layperson up to speed on alien tech within weeks."

Sokolov's gaze lingered on the shifting images, the skepticism in his eyes softening as he contemplated the fusion of science and soldiering. "Communication," he said at last, folding his arms over his broad chest. "It will be our lifeline. How do you propose we maintain it under the Kridrax's interference?"

"Quantum entanglement communicators," Markus Weller chimed in from beside Evelyn, his voice a quiet rumble that belied the magnitude of his contribution. "Unhackable, instant across any distance."

"Sounds like magic," Sokolov quipped, a wry smile touching his lips for the briefest of moments. It was a smile that spoke not of humor, but of the shared burden they all carried—the weight of countless lives hanging in the balance.

"Science often resembles magic, to the untrained eye," Evelyn replied, her own mouth curving in response, a mirror of resolve and understanding.

They delved deeper, each exchange a step toward common ground. The strategic placement of supply caches, the coordination of reconnaissance missions, the integration of advanced weaponry into traditional combat units—all laid out like pieces of an intricate puzzle, waiting to be assembled by hands united in purpose.

As the clock ticked on, the room's atmosphere shifted from one of cautious negotiation to something more akin to collaboration. Ideas flowed freely, bridging the gap between military might and scientific innovation, each suggestion a thread weaving the fabric of their alliance tighter.

Finally, after what felt like both an eternity and a mere heartbeat, General O'Neill stood, his chair scraping back with a finality that seemed to echo off the walls. "Alright," he grunted, extending a calloused hand across the table. "We have a plan—a good one. Let's get to work on saving humanity."

Evelyn met his handshake with a firm grip, her piercing green eyes reflecting the gravity of their commitment. Beside her, Markus offered a shy nod, his eyes glinting behind his glasses with the fires of hope and determination.

"Agreed," Colonel Sokolov said, rising to join them, his voice carrying the heavy resonance of a vow. "Together, then."

Together, indeed. The tentative agreement they had reached became the bedrock upon which they would build their resistance. United, they would stand against the encroaching darkness of the Kridrax invasion, their collective redemption woven into the very fate they sought to rewrite.

Chapter 8

Hidden Base

Silence clung to the group like a shroud as they edged through the hidden Kridrax base, the only sound the soft whisper of their boots against the cold floor. Shadows played tricks on their eyes, walls stretching and contracting in the timid glow of their lights. Dr. Evelyn Montgomery led with measured strides, her green eyes scanning the alien architecture, a maze of conduits and enigmatic symbols etched into the metal.

"Steady," she murmured, her voice barely breaching the quiet. Her fingers brushed against the cool surface of her tactical vest, feeling for reassurance in the familiar contours of her equipment. She caught the reflection of her team in the gleam of a panel — a mosaic of determination and trepidation.

Ahead, a secluded alcove presented itself, a sanctuary amidst the unknown. Dr. Markus Weller shuffled forward, his lanky frame awkward in the confined space. With fumbling hands, he set down the weathered case that housed their hopes — tools and instruments that seemed almost primitive compared to the surrounding technology.

"Give me a status report," Evelyn instructed, her words concise, betraying none of the doubts that clawed at her mind.

"Setting up now," Markus responded, his tone academic, eyes alight with the challenge of deciphering the alien systems. His fingers, nimble despite their apparent clumsiness, began connecting devices to interfaces whose purpose was yet to be uncovered.

Dr. Lily Chen joined him, her movements graceful, a dance of efficiency and intellect. Her hair cascaded over her shoulders as she leaned in, aiding Markus with an intuitive understanding of the task at hand. "I think this is it," she said, her voice low and steady.

"Careful," Evelyn cautioned, her gaze never ceasing its vigil. "We don't know what these systems might trigger."

"Understood," Lily acknowledged, her focus unwavering as she assisted Markus in tapping into the core of the alien defenses. Their shared curiosity wove a silent bond between them, a lifeline in the enveloping darkness.

The equipment hummed to life, an orchestra of beeps and clicks as data began to flow. Each revelation was a piece of the puzzle, potentially leading them closer to the heart of the Kridrax secrets. Yet, doubt gnawed at Evelyn's resolve—the past had taught her that knowledge often came at a price.

"Anything?" Evelyn asked after what felt like an eternity wrapped in suspense.

"Progress," Markus replied, his voice containing a hint of awe. "These systems... they're more intricate than anything we've seen." The Kridrax were masters of their craft, and the team were but novices trying to unravel centuries of advanced technology.

"Keep at it," Evelyn encouraged, though her thoughts lingered on redemption—for her team, for humanity. They were small pieces in a vast interstellar game, but she clung to the belief that even the smallest move could change the course of history.

Time stretched, each second laden with potential. In the silence, Evelyn's heart beat a rhythm of hope and fear, while around her, the base whispered secrets just waiting to be discovered.

…

Between the somber echoes of footsteps, a chilling presence permeated the air, as if the walls themselves exhaled a heavy breath laden with dread. Synthetic Oppressor, an amalgamation of metal and malice, led his contingent of Kridrax soldiers with measured strides, the rhythmic clank of his mechanical limbs punctuating the hush that fell like a shroud over his subordinates.

"Remain vigilant," his voice commanded, devoid of warmth, reverberating against the cold metallic surfaces. His red eyes, unblinking beacons of tyranny, swept the corridor, seeking signs of treachery or fear amongst those who marched in his shadow. The soldiers, their faces obscured by helmets reflecting the dim light, did not dare meet his gaze; their tension was a tangible entity, slinking amidst them, whispering of dangers unseen and untold.

In stark contrast to the dictator's oppressive patrol, Dr. Markus Weller and Dr. Lily Chen were a nexus of quiet determination. Their sanctuary within the alien enclave was a cluttered alcove, where the remnants of a long-lost civilization conversed with the hum of human technology. Fingers danced over holographic displays, coaxing secrets from the labyrinthine systems that thrummed with an energy as enigmatic as the void between stars.

"Here," Lily's voice broke through the silence, a delicate thread of excitement weaving through her words. "The frequency patterns — they're cyclical but irregular." Her slender fingers traced the air, drawing attention to the fluctuation on the screen.

Markus leaned in, his glasses catching the ambient glow as he scrutinized the data. "An Achilles' heel in their shielding," he murmured, the revelation igniting a spark in his otherwise weary eyes. "It's like finding a dissonant note in a symphony of light."

"Can we exploit it?" Evelyn's voice joined the hushed conference, her green eyes narrowed not in doubt, but in analytical precision. The weight of countless decisions etched fine lines at the corners of her eyes, a testament to battles fought both within and without.

"Potentially," Markus acknowledged, running a hand through his unkempt hair. "If we can isolate the frequency, disrupt the pattern, even for a moment..."

"Then we strike," Evelyn concluded, her tone resolute. The word 'strike' hung in the air, a harbinger of the redemption they so desperately sought—a chance to turn the tide, to heal the scars of past failures with the salve of victory.

"Let's prepare the modulation sequence," said Lily, her hands already moving with purpose. "We have one shot at this."

They worked in tandem, the dance of their expertise a silent ballet performed under the watchful gaze of ancient technologies. Each input was deliberate, every calculation a brushstroke on the canvas of hope. While beyond their cloistered corner, the specter of Synthetic Oppressor cast its pall, the three scientists bore their own light—a flickering flame that refused to be extinguished by the darkness that surrounded them.

Evelyn Montgomery's fingers traced the contours of her glasses, a silent metronome to her racing thoughts. She glanced at the two figures standing before her—Sergeant Mia Alvarez and Lieutenant Isabella, both statuesque in their resolve. The dim glow from the alien consoles cast elongated shadows that merged with the darkness of the corridor behind them.

"Alvarez, Isabella," Evelyn began, her voice low and steady, "the control room is our linchpin. Find it, and we may just cripple their defenses long enough to give us an edge."

Mia's nod was curt, her eyes revealing a glint of steel beneath the surface. Isabella stood immovable, the scar on her cheek a pale slash in the half-light. They understood the gravity of the mission—its success or failure resting on the breadth of a heartbeat.

"Consider it done, Doctor," Isabella replied, her voice echoing slightly off the cold walls.

"Be vigilant," Evelyn added, adjusting her glasses once more as if by doing so she could align the very fate that lay ahead. "The Kridrax are no strangers to intruders. Move like shadows; strike only when necessary."

The team split with the seamlessness of a well-oiled machine, each member a cog in the intricate clockwork of survival. Dr. Patel lingered for a moment beside Evelyn, his gaze sweeping over the equipment that hummed quietly around them. "Keep them safe, Evelyn," he murmured, a hint of concern threading through his words.

"Always," she replied, but her eyes were already scanning the corridor ahead, where darkness loomed like an unspoken promise.

With Dr. Patel at her side, Evelyn led the way, her movements deliberate and controlled. The labyrinthine complex of the Kridrax base stretched out before them, daunting in its scope and treachery. Here and there, the faint flicker of distant patrols cast a dance of shadows against the walls—a macabre ballet witnessed by few.

Mia and Isabella advanced with a quiet efficiency that belied the adrenaline coursing through their veins. Every corner turned could be their last, yet they moved with an economy of motion that spoke of countless hours honed in the furnace of conflict. Their breaths were measured, their steps soundless against the metallic flooring.

A sudden clatter echoed down a perpendicular corridor, and the team froze. A contingent of Kridrax soldiers, mere phantoms bearing the weight of potential death, passed by without notice. Evelyn felt the ghost of past traumas stir within her chest, but she quelled it with the practiced ease of one who had stared into the abyss far too often.

Once the danger had ebbed away, Evelyn signaled the all-clear, her hand barely discernible in the gloom. They continued their advance, a thread of hope weaving through the perilous tapestry of their mission.

"Remember what we're fighting for," Evelyn whispered, the words meant as much for herself as for her comrades. The echoes of battles past seemed to answer in the stillness, a solemn reminder of the redemption they sought—the chance to mend the fractures of a world teetering on the brink of oblivion. And through it all, the specter of Synthetic Oppressor, a shadow within shadows, lurked ever-present in their minds—an adversary whose defeat would mark either the beginning of humanity's resurgence or the final chapter in its storied existence.

…

In the bowels of the Kridrax base, Dr. Evelyn Montgomery's pulse thrummed in her temples as she navigated the labyrinthine corridors with practiced caution. The air itself seemed charged with foreboding, and the dim lights cast elongated shadows that danced upon the walls like specters of doubt.

"Something is amiss," Markus Weller murmured, his voice barely rising above a whisper. His fingers twitched at his side, betraying an anxiousness that contrasted starkly with the stoic masks they all wore. Evelyn nodded, her eyes scanning the sterile metal surroundings for any sign of the lurking threat they knew as Synthetic Oppressor.

Without warning, the hum of machinery grew more insistent, an auditory signal that set every nerve on edge. It was then that the unmistakable sound of heavy metallic footsteps reverberated through the corridor. Synthetic Oppressor's voice, a chilling blend of human timbre and mechanical modulation, sliced through the tense silence.

"Intensify patrols. Seal off critical junctures. Leave no shadow unexplored," he commanded, his words dripping with venomous certainty. The team exchanged wary glances, understanding that their window of opportunity was narrowing precipitously.

As Evelyn led them deeper into the heart of the enemy stronghold, her mind raced, thoughts flickering like the unstable current running through the base's veins. They needed to find a weakness, a chink in the seemingly impenetrable armor of the Kridrax defenses, and they needed it now.

It was Dr. Chen who halted abruptly, her hand raised in a silent command that drew their attention to a nearly imperceptible seam in the wall. With deft movements informed by countless hours of study, she pressed a sequence of areas on the smooth surface, eliciting a soft hiss as a concealed panel slid open, revealing a hidden chamber bathed in an eerie light.

"Remarkable..." Markus breathed, stepping forward to survey the contents of the room with wide-eyed wonder. There, nestled among coils of wires and pulsating energy sources, stood a prototype weapon — the potential linchpin in their desperate struggle.

Evelyn watched as Markus and Dr. Chen set to work, their hands moving with a precision that belied the urgency of their task. The weapon was an enigma, a fusion of alien tech and theoretical physics that demanded both finesse and boldness to harness.

"Can it be modified?" Evelyn asked, her tone laced with the gravity of the situation.

"Given time," Markus replied, his gaze never leaving the intricate mechanisms before him. "But time is a luxury we may not have."

A shiver ran down Evelyn's spine as the weight of their mission settled upon her once more, a mantle of responsibility she could neither shed nor ignore. They were so close to turning the tide, to carving a path toward redemption from the ruins of a fractured past.

Yet, as Markus and Dr. Chen delved into the depths of their discovery, the sense of an invisible clock ticking towards an unknown hour imbued each action with a palpable tension. With every passing moment, the specter of Synthetic Oppressor loomed larger, a dark star in the constellation of their fears.

Evelyn's resolve hardened, the echoes of battles fought and lost weaving a resilient thread through the fabric of her being. She would not allow the shadows of history to claim this day — not while the flame of hope still flickered within her.

...

Sergeant Alvarez's fingers danced over the alien console with a deftness born of countless hours in simulation. Beside her, Lieutenant Isabella's eyes remained fixed on the door, her weapon poised in silent vigilance. The control room pulsed with an eerie luminescence, casting shadows that seemed to breathe along the walls.

"Almost there," Alvarez murmured, her voice barely a whisper against the thrumming energy that enveloped them. A bead of sweat traced its way down her temple, unnoticed.

"Be quick," Isabella replied, her gaze never wavering from the corridor beyond. "They're tightening patrols."

With a final, decisive keystroke, Alvarez exhaled as the room dimmed momentarily, signaling the temporary collapse of the base's energy shielding. They shared a glance, understanding flashing between them like a spark in the void — they had just bought themselves precious minutes.

"Shielding is down," Alvarez confirmed, her tone carrying a hint of triumph tempered by urgency.

"Let's move," Isabella said, her voice the very embodiment of resolve.

They slipped from the control room, their movements a ballet of precision and caution. The labyrinthine corridors of the Kridrax base loomed before them, now more navigable in the absence of the oppressive shield.

Elsewhere, Dr. Montgomery and Dr. Patel advanced through the dimly lit passages with an economy of motion that spoke volumes of their shared history in the field. Each shadow, each flicker of light was met with a readiness that transcended mere training — it was survival honed to an art form.

"Alvarez, report," Montgomery's voice crackled over the comms, the signal clearer now without the interference of the shields.

"Control room secured. Shielding disabled," Alvarez responded, her words crisp and succinct.

"Excellent. Rendezvous at the hidden chamber. Weller and Chen need us there," Montgomery directed, her voice steady despite the storm of variables playing out in her mind. Patel glanced at Montgomery, his eyes reflecting a silent acknowledgment of the gravity of what lay ahead. They quickened their pace, weaving through the base with practiced stealth.

The rendezvous was a silent affair — a meeting of shadows in a dance with darkness. A nod from Isabella, a slight smile from Alvarez, and the team melded into one, their footsteps a soft echo in the vastness of the alien stronghold.

"Lead the way," Montgomery said to Alvarez, her words not a command but an affirmation of trust.

Together, they traversed the complex, their path a thread in the tapestry of a grander scheme. The hidden chamber awaited, a trove of potential veiled in secrecy and promise.

As the chamber's entrance materialized before them, cloaked in the same mysterious aura that permeated the entire base, they paused. Inside, Weller and Chen toiled amidst the enigmatic machinations of a weapon that might well turn the tides of war.

"Ready?" Montgomery asked, though it was more a rhetorical question — a call to arms for the battle-scarred souls who accompanied her.

Each gave a silent nod, their determination a shared beacon that cut through the uncertainty of the moment.

And with that, they stepped into the unknown, the prototype weapon and its secrets a breath away from revelation. Redemption called to them from within the chamber, its siren song woven with threads of hope and the specter of redemption—a chance to reclaim a future from the jaws of a past that would not relent.

...

The chamber's walls hummed with alien whispers, as if the Kridrax base itself was alive, listening to the intruders' every breath. Dr. Evelyn Montgomery's heart hammered in her chest, a drumbeat of anticipation and dread. She motioned for her team to take cover behind an array of enigmatic consoles that blinked with cryptic symbols.

"Quiet," she mouthed, her eyes darting to the entrance.

There, Synthetic Oppressor emerged like a specter from the shadows, his metallic limbs reflecting the dim light—each step a chilling symphony of organic and artificial sinew. His soldiers, a phalanx of cold efficiency, flanked him, their weapons cradled like deadly offspring. The air grew thick with an unspoken malevolence that clung to the artificial man like a second skin.

Evelyn held her breath, sharing a glance with Dr. Patel, whose eyes mirrored her own fears. Sergeant Alvarez and Lieutenant Isabella, ever the vanguards, were statues of resolve, their fingers mere ghosts above their holstered weapons. They dared not breathe too loudly, lest the air betray them.

Minutes stretched into eternity. The mechanical dictator passed by, his gaze sweeping the horrid beauty of his domain, never suspecting the silent rebellion that lay mere feet away. Finally, he disappeared into the labyrinth, his entourage in tow, leaving behind a vacuum where dread once stood.

Montgomery exhaled, a soft sigh that seemed to echo the collective relief of her team. With cautious movements, they emerged from their hiding places, each step deliberate, avoiding the betrayal of sound.

"Is it clear?" whispered Dr. Lily Chen, her voice cutting through the silence.

"Clear," Montgomery confirmed, her gaze still fastened on the corridor where darkness had reclaimed its throne.

They regrouped within the hidden chamber, the air now punctuated by the soft whirring of Dr. Markus Weller's equipment. He looked up from his work, his glasses catching the light in a conspiratorial glint.

"Good news," he began, the excitement evident even in his hushed tone. "We've found a weakness—a frequency that can disrupt their energy shielding."

"Show me," Montgomery urged, her curiosity piqued as the promise of redemption beckoned.

Weller gestured toward the prototype weapon—an amalgamation of human ingenuity and alien artifice. It was a thing of intricate beauty, its surface adorned with elaborate patterns that pulsed with a haunting luminescence.

"Chen's modifications have been instrumental," Weller continued, nodding toward his colleague who stood beside him, her face alight with a quiet pride. "We've recalibrated the firing mechanism to match the disruption frequency. If our calculations are correct, this could be our key to victory."

"Could" was a cavern of uncertainty, but Evelyn felt the stirrings of hope. Here, in this chamber of secrets, they had forged a sliver of light in the enveloping dark. The prototype weapon, cradled in Weller's arms, was more than machinery — it was the culmination of countless sacrifices, a testament to the resilience of those who refused to bow before the night.

"Then there's no time to waste," Montgomery said, her resolve steeling her words. "We use it to end this — to reclaim our future from the ashes of the past."

Her team nodded, their expressions etched with the gravity of the moment, and together, they prepared to wield the fruits of their labor against a foe who knew neither mercy nor remorse.

…

Evelyn Montgomery surveyed the chamber, her mind a maelstrom of strategy and calculation. The prototype weapon lay against Weller's workstation, its surfaces whispering promises of destruction and salvation. Around her, the team huddled in clusters, their faces ghostly in the dim light, awaiting her command.

"Listen closely," she began, her voice low and steady as the thrumming energy that pulsed through the Kridrax base. "We have one advantage — the flaw in their shield. We strike there."

She sketched out a plan in the air with her hands, her fingers drawing unseen lines and angles that wove together the paths of assault. Her gaze met each pair of eyes in turn, grounding them in the gravity of her words. "Weller, Chen, you'll position the weapon. Alvarez, Isabella, your skills are key to breaching the control room. Patel, you're with me — we cover their advance."

A chorus of affirmatives rippled through the chamber, the sound a harbinger of the chaos to come. Evelyn felt the weight of their trust, a burden she bore with silent reverence.

The team dispersed, slipping into their roles with the finesse of shadows melding with the darkness. Evelyn watched them go, her thoughts a tangled web of tactics and the haunting specter of Synthetic Oppressor's relentless ambition.

"Montgomery." It was Weller, his voice a beacon pulling her back from the precipice of doubt. He handed her a small device—compact, unassuming, but within it lay the power to pierce the Kridrax defenses. "For the shield disruption. You'll know when."

"Thank you." She pocketed the device, feeling its cool surface against her skin—a talisman against the encroaching despair.

As the final preparations unfolded, a tense silence enveloped the team. They armed themselves, not just with weapons but with the resolve born of countless battles waged in the shadow of tyranny. Each movement was deliberate, an invocation of the strength they would need to face what awaited them beyond the chamber walls.

Evelyn checked her own gear, the familiar weight of her sidearm a solid reassurance against her thigh. Her heart thundered, a drumbeat of anticipation and dread, but she quelled the tremors of fear with the ironclad certainty of purpose.

"Remember," she said, her voice cutting through the stillness like a blade. "This is more than a fight for survival—it's a reclaiming of our destiny, a stand against the dark tide that seeks to engulf us. We carry the hopes of humanity with us."

Heads lifted; eyes ignited with the fire of conviction. Here, in this moment, they were united—a phalanx of defiance arrayed against the night.

"Move out," Evelyn commanded, and the team surged forward, a silent storm ready to break upon the enemy with all the fury of the betrayed and the bold. Their footsteps were whispers on the cold metal floors, echoes of a future they were determined to seize, no matter the cost.

…

Evelyn Montgomery's pulse thrummed in her ears as she led the charge, her team's boots silent on the polished metal floor of the Kridrax stronghold. The corridor stretched ahead of them; a serpent's belly lined with pulsating lights that cast elongated shadows against the walls. Every step they took was laden with the gravity of what was to come—a dance with fate, choreographed with military precision.

"Stay sharp," Hawk whispered, his voice barely above a breath, yet it carried the weight of his command. His eyes scanned the dimly lit passage, vigilant for any sign of the enemy. They had become specters in this alien labyrinth, their presence unknown to Synthetic Oppressor and his legion of soldiers—for now.

Evelyn caught sight of Hawk's clenched jaw, the subtle furrow between his brows. The burden he bore was not only tactical but deeply personal. She acknowledged it with a nod, an unspoken affirmation of their shared resolve.

Markus Weller fidgeted with a device cradled in his hands, its soft glow illuminating the contours of his face. In the quiet hum of anticipation, his usual scatterbrained manner was replaced by a focused intensity. The fragility of their plan rested on the shoulders of his genius, and every calculation mattered.

"Frequency modulator set," Markus reported, his voice steady despite the flicker of concern that danced behind his glasses. "Ready to disrupt the shielding on your mark."

Sergeant Mia Alvarez adjusted the grip on her rifle, her brown eyes fixated on the path before them. The stoic mask she wore did little to hide the tempest brewing within. Her life had been a series of battles fought and scars earned, each one a testament to her relentless spirit. Now, she stood on the precipice of the greatest fight yet — one that would define the very essence of their struggle.

"Control room's just beyond this stretch," Alvarez said, her tone betraying none of the adrenaline coursing through her veins. "We'll have that window of opportunity. Don't let it close."

Beside her, the enigmatic Zylar Threx moved with otherworldly grace, their iridescent scales catching the faint light. Their involvement in this crusade was more than an alliance; it was a redemption song sung in the face of centuries-old nightmares. They yearned for vengeance, yes, but also for the dawn of a new era — one free from the shadow of the Kridrax scourge.

"Everything we have lost leads us here," Zylar intoned, the resonance of their voice a haunting reminder of what hung in the balance.

Together, they paused at the threshold of destiny, their collective breath a cloud of determination hanging in the charged air. The silence was a canvas, waiting for the first stroke of an epic tableau.

"Once more unto the breach, my friends," Evelyn murmured. It was not just a call to arms but a hymn to the undying spirit of resistance that pulsed in their veins.

Then, as if on cue, the universe held its breath, and time seemed to dangle on the edge of forever. With a final glance exchanged among them — a tapestry of trust woven over countless trials — the team stepped over the invisible line that separated the known from the unfathomable.

Evelyn felt the familiar shiver of danger prickling at the base of her neck, but she pushed it aside. There was no room for fear here, not when they teetered on the brink of either salvation or oblivion. This was the moment they had been meticulously crafting, the culmination of every sacrifice made in the name of freedom.

"Let's end this," she said, her words slicing through the tension like a beacon of hope. They surged forward, a wave of retribution ready to crash down upon the unsuspecting forces that lay ahead. The chapter of uncertainty closed, and in its stead, the pages of the future waited to be written by their indomitable wills.

With the stage set and their hearts ablaze, they were poised to unleash hell upon the Kridrax invasion — a decisive blow struck with the fury of the wronged and the courage of the valiant.

Chapter 9

Shaken Trust

Ash and silence fell like a shroud over the once-bustling command center. The air, thick with the stench of smoldering metal, clung to the lungs of those who staggered amidst the ruin. Twisted beams jutted out like the ribs of a great beast felled in battle, and sparks danced off shattered consoles, their flickering light casting ghostly shadows. Medics, faces set into masks of grim determination, tended to the wounded, their white uniforms smeared with the stark crimson of spilled blood.

Amidst the chaos, Dr. Evelyn Montgomery stood frozen, her piercing green eyes wide as they took in the devastation. Her normally pristine lab coat was a canvas of dust and debris, and her short black hair lay matted against her forehead. She blinked slowly, processing the surreality of destruction that had moments ago been a hub of life and strategy. Her scientific mind, always so precise and ordered, struggled to make sense of the treachery that had wrought such havoc.

"Montgomery!" The voice cut through the haze of shock like a blade. Captain Lucas "Hawk" Hawking approached; his tall, muscular frame visibly tense but unyielding amid the turmoil. His blue eyes, hard as ice, scanned the remnants of their stronghold. "Status report," he demanded, though his voice betrayed a hint of the same disbelief that gripped them all.

"Complete system breach," Evelyn managed, her words clipped as she fought to maintain composure. "The counterattack...it was precise, Hawk. Too precise. This was no random strike."

Beside them, Zylar Threx surveyed the scene with a solemnity that seemed to stretch beyond the confines of the immediate tragedy. Their iridescent scales dulled under the smoky sky, and their deep-set eyes, glowing with an intelligence not of this world, reflected the flames that still dared to crackle in defiance of despair. "The Kridrax have never found us before," Zylar intoned, their voice resonating with a timbre of loss and foreboding. "A traitor walks among us."

"Then we find them," Hawk stated, his jaw set. "We root them out before they can do more damage."

Evelyn nodded, her resolve hardening like the cooled slag around them. Betrayal had opened the gates for the enemy, and now retribution must be swift and unerring. But even as she agreed, her mind teetered on the precipice of an uncomfortable truth — trust had become a luxury they could no longer afford.

"Begin with who had access," she suggested, her gaze narrowing as she mentally sifted through potential suspects. "We need evidence, patterns. Anything out of place."

"Every second counts," Hawk added, turning to survey the ongoing efforts of recovery and defense. "We're vulnerable until the traitor is found."

Zylar's slender form moved between the wreckage, their elongated limbs reaching out to aid a fallen soldier. "I will commune with the Aether," they murmured. "Perhaps the echoes of betrayal linger still."

As the three of them split apart to begin their grim tasks, the air hung heavy with the unspoken fear that the true enemy might be hiding within their ranks, silent and unseen, waiting to strike again. And in the heart of the devastation, redemption seemed but a distant hope, obscured by the smoke and shadows that blanketed their world in mourning.

...

Dr. Evelyn Montgomery commandeered the dimly lit command center, its walls a patchwork of exposed wires and hastily erected barriers. The smoldering aftermath of betrayal still tainted the air outside, but within this makeshift sanctuary, a more insidious danger lurked — doubt. Faces, once familiar and trusted, now bore the weight of suspicion as members of the coalition gathered around a salvaged table that bore the scars of war.

"Lockdown protocols were overridden from the inside," Evelyn stated, her voice cutting through the tension like a scalpel. "That much is clear. We need to ascertain how our security was compromised."

Murmurs of assent rippled through the room, yet the acknowledgment did nothing to ease the distrust that hung between them like a veil. She watched their eyes flicker — not with fear, but calculation — and knew the same questions haunted every mind: Who among us is the traitor?

"Where were you all during the first wave of the counterattack?" It was Markus Weller who broke the uneasy silence, his thin frame rigid in the harsh light. His glasses reflected a mosaic of concerns as he pushed them up the bridge of his nose, a gesture Evelyn noted with an inward sigh.

"Markus," she began, her tone both chiding and weary, "we've worked together for years. You know my duties kept me at the lab, coordinating our defense systems."

"Which failed spectacularly," Lily Chen interjected, her youthful face taut with unspoken accusations. "Someone with intimate knowledge of those systems would know just how to dismantle them."

"Are you suggesting..." Markus's words faltered, incredulity warring with the logic of her implication.

"Enough!" Evelyn's command echoed off the walls, silencing the burgeoning conflict. "We cannot turn on each other — not now. Our focus must be on evidence, not conjecture."

She scanned the room, meeting each gaze with a steely resolve. Her piercing green eyes, usually so adept at discerning the secrets of alien technology, now searched for the subtler cues of deceit among her own kind.

"Let's retrace our steps," Captain Hawking said, his presence a calming force amidst the storm of distrust. "Logs, communications, access points. Someone made a mistake; they always do."

"Right." Zylar's voice, serene as the Aether they communed with, floated through the space. "And we must act swiftly, lest the echoes of treachery fade into the void."

The team set to work, their movements deliberate as they pored over data and dissected timelines. Evelyn felt the past clawing at her, a reminder of her own traumas and the hard-earned lessons of trust broken. Redemption seemed a distant star in the vast darkness of the unknown, but she clung to it nonetheless, a beacon in the night guiding her way.

"Here," Lily called out, drawing their attention to a series of irregularities in the communication logs. "These encrypted messages — they weren't part of our standard protocol."

"Could be nothing," Markus cautioned, though the uncertainty in his voice betrayed his hope.

"Or everything," Evelyn countered, her mind alight with possibilities as she leaned in closer. Each clue unraveled another thread in the tapestry of betrayal, drawing them nearer to a truth that could either mend or further rend the fragile fabric of their alliance.

"Let's follow it," Hawking decided, the weight of command settling upon him. "Piece by piece, until we have our traitor."

Evelyn nodded, her thoughts ghosting back to the debris-strewn battlefield, to the lives lost and the promise of justice unfulfilled. She would not let fear dictate their path; she would forge ahead, driven by the relentless pursuit of truth.

"Piece by piece," she echoed, her voice barely above a whisper, a testament to the arduous journey ahead.

…

Evelyn Montgomery surveyed the remnants of the war room, now a makeshift investigation hub. The air hummed with tension and the undercurrent of whispered theories, as potential suspects were cast into the light of scrutiny. Hawk stood beside her, his visage a mask of determination etched with lines of concern.

"Could it be Weller?" he pondered aloud, his gaze drifting toward Markus's empty chair. "The man's a genius, but his mind wanders strange paths."

Evelyn considered the possibility. "He has the intellect but lacks motive. What about Alvarez? Her access to tactical data is unmatched."

"Alvarez is loyal to the bone," Hawk countered, the faintest hint of defensiveness in his tone. "She bleeds for this cause."

"Sometimes blood is not enough," Zylar interjected, their voice a somber note that resonated through the chamber. "In my experience, even the purest hearts can harbor shadows."

The conversations ebbed and flowed around them, creating an intricate dance of suspicion and trust. Evelyn listened, her thoughts adrift among the red herrings tossed into the sea of doubt. Each name brought forth painted a different picture of betrayal, yet none fit perfectly into the frame of treachery they sought to fill.

"Let's divide our efforts," Evelyn said, her voice slicing through the murmurs. "Each of us takes a lead, follows the evidence. We interview the witnesses, dissect every communication, inspect every order."

"Agreed," Hawk nodded once, decisively. "I'll take the ground troops. They've seen things in the fray that might give us an edge."

"Mia and I will handle the tech and surveillance feeds," Zylar offered, their scales catching the dim light as they moved. "There may be patterns we've overlooked."

"Markus and I will analyze the encrypted messages," Evelyn finished, a steely resolve in her piercing green eyes.

They split up, each member of the coalition moving with deliberate focus. Evelyn and Markus poured over the digital entrails of the base's network, seeking anomalies amid the vast streams of data. Hawking, with his military precision, questioned soldiers whose eyes still held the blaze of battle, searching for any flicker of inconsistency in their tales. Zylar and Mia combed through hours of security footage, looking for the subtle tells of deceit.

Time stretched and compressed around them as the investigation unfolded, each hour an eternity, each minute fleeting. Clues emerged like reluctant stars at dusk—faint and easily obscured by the gathering clouds of uncertainty. Yet they pressed on, driven by the need to expose the serpent in their midst, to bring to light the darkness that had infiltrated their ranks.

As evening approached, so too did the shadows lengthen within the confines of the war room. The sparse dialogue between the investigators betrayed both exhaustion and exhilaration—each lead followed was another step toward redemption or another plunge into despair.

"Anything?" Evelyn asked, breaking the silence that had settled over her and Markus.

"Patterns. There are patterns, but..." Markus trailed off, pushing his glasses back up to meet her questioning gaze. "They're elusive. Like chasing phantoms."

"Keep chasing," she urged. "Phantoms bleed too, if you find where to strike."

"Indeed, they do," Markus muttered, turning back to his screens with renewed vigor.

With each passing moment, the pieces began to form a picture, though still fragmented and indistinct. Evelyn sensed they were on the cusp of something revelatory—a breakthrough that would either vindicate their suspicions or unravel them entirely. But as the light faded outside, casting elongated shadows across her workspace, the truth remained shrouded in mystery, slipping like sand through the narrowing hourglass of time.

...

Sergeant Mia Alvarez's boots crunched over the debris-littered floor, her breaths measured as she navigated the chaos that once was their fortress of solitude. She bent down to examine a charred piece of machinery — the edges still warm and twisted like the bitter memories clawing at her mind. It should have contained vital records, but now lay in ruins, the data irretrievable.

"Another dead end," she muttered, frustration edging her voice.

"Patience, Sergeant," Zylar Threx intoned from behind her, their luminous eyes reflecting the destruction. "Answers are often birthed from the ashes of turmoil."

"Answers we need now, Zylar," Hawk interjected, his muscular frame emerging from the shadows. "Every minute wasted is another we give to the traitor."

Their investigation had become a labyrinthine puzzle, each turn leading only to more questions. The coalition's database, a once pristine well of information, had been purged selectively, leaving gaping holes where critical evidence should have been. Someone within their ranks was erasing their tracks with surgical precision.

"Could it be an AI breach?" Evelyn proposed, her green eyes scanning the room for any overlooked detail. "A programmed saboteur?"

"Unlikely," Markus countered, adjusting his glasses with a shaky hand. "The deletions are too... human. Emotional. A machine wouldn't care to cover its tracks so meticulously."

"Emotion could be our clue, then," Mia offered, her voice steady despite the doubt that gnawed at her insides. "Desperation leaves its own signature."

"Desperation... or betrayal," Hawk said, the words hanging heavy in the air.

"Let's not jump to conclusions," Evelyn replied sharply, her analytical mind resisting the pull of conjecture. "We need concrete evidence, not just suspicions."

"Yet, every lead we follow turns to vapor," Zylar observed, their otherworldly voice threading through the tension.

"Then perhaps we're asking the wrong questions," Markus suggested, his brow furrowed in thought.

"Or trusting the wrong people," Mia added with a sidelong glance at each member of their group.

The war room was thick with distrust, the silence punctuated by the low hum of damaged electronics. Accusations hovered on the edge of tongues, but with no proof, they remained unspoken — volatile secrets seeking escape.

"Someone here knows more than they're letting on," Hawk declared, his blue eyes narrowing. "And I intend to find out who."

"Be careful, Captain," Evelyn warned. Her heart raced at the implication of his words. "Paranoia can be as destructive as the enemy's weapons."

"Better paranoid than blind," he retorted, stepping closer to the others. "I'll take my chances."

"Chances that may tear us apart before the real traitor is uncovered," Zylar cautioned, their scales shimmering softly with a light that seemed to mourn the unity they had lost. "Divided, we've already fallen," Mia stated grimly.

"Then let's reforge our alliance," Evelyn asserted, the weight of command settling upon her shoulders. "Starting with what little evidence we have left."

"Agreed," Markus nodded, his voice a beacon of reason amid the storm of emotions. "We must reconstruct the events, piece by fragmented piece."

"Even if it leads to one of us?" Hawk challenged, locking eyes with each of them in turn.

"Especially then," Zylar affirmed, their gaze unflinching.

The group dispersed, each to their task, yet bound together by the haunting melody of uncertainty that played upon their fears. As the night deepened, so did the enigma, wrapping its tendrils around the truth, holding it just out of reach. The past's shadows loomed, whispering of redemption yet to be claimed, while the specter of betrayal lurked ever closer, its identity shrouded in the gathering gloom.

…

Evelyn Montgomery's fingers trembled as they unearthed the charred remnants of a data chip from beneath a mound of scorched debris. In the silence of the lab, only the soft hum of emergency lighting and the distant echo of repair crews pierced the air. Her gaze fixed on the twisted metal, a flicker of hope kindling in her green eyes.

"Could it be?" she murmured to herself, her voice barely above a whisper.

"Dr. Montgomery?" Markus's inquiry came from behind her, his tone laced with cautious optimism.

"Markus," she said, turning to face him, "this may be the breakthrough we've been searching for."

His eyes widened behind the lenses perched precariously on his nose. "The access logs?"

"Potentially. If I can extract the data..." Evelyn's voice trailed off as she considered the implications. The possibility of redemption for their tattered alliance seemed to hover just out of reach, like a mirage in the wasteland of mistrust that had settled among them.

With meticulous care, Evelyn connected the damaged chip to her portable console. The room held its breath as lines of code cascaded across the screen, each one a potential harbinger of truth or another descent into doubt.

"Got it!" she exclaimed as the access log unfurled before them, revealing a sequence of unauthorized entries. The timestamp correlated precisely with the moments leading up to the attack. But it was the user ID that made her heart skip a beat—a designation that belonged to none other than...

"Synthetic Oppressor," Hawk's voice rumbled as he entered the room, his imposing figure cutting through the tension like a knife.

"Impossible," Markus countered. "He's been under surveillance."

"Not closely enough," Mia Alvarez interjected, her words clipped and precise. "We have our traitor."

The coalition members gathered, a sense of purpose reigniting within them as they clustered around the console. The evidence was irrefutable; the trail led directly to the synthetic abomination that had once vowed to serve their cause against the Kridrax.

"Let's confront this monster," Hawk declared, the weight of command resonating in his voice.

They found him in the communication bay, surrounded by an array of screens that blinked with cryptic messages. Synthetic Oppressor's glowing red eyes shifted towards them, a flicker of surprise — or was it fear? — crossing his metallic visage.

"Captain Hawking, to what do I owe the pleasure?" His voice was cold, detached.

"Cut the act, Oppressor. We know you're the mole," Hawk spat, his hand hovering over the blaster at his side.

"Accusations require proof," the synthetic dictator replied, his tone betraying no hint of concern.

"Here's your proof," Evelyn said as she thrust the console forward, displaying the damning evidence.

"Fabrications," he dismissed with a wave of his mechanical hand. "Do you truly believe I would jeopardize our mutual interests?"

"Your interests never aligned with ours," Zylar Threx interjected, their voice hauntingly serene amid the storm brewing around them. "You seek domination, not liberation."

"Your paranoia will be your undoing," Synthetic Oppressor sneered, yet a bead of perspiration — artificial though it might be — glistened upon his brow.

"Your time is over," Mia stated, the finality in her voice echoing the resolve etched upon her face.

"Indeed, it is," he said with a smirk. "But not for me."

As they moved in, Synthetic Oppressor's form blurred, a holographic projection dissipating into thin air. They had been speaking to a ghost, an illusion crafted with cunning precision. The traitor was gone, vanished like a specter into the shadows of the ship.

Hawk cursed, his fist connecting with the nearest wall panel. "Stay calm," Evelyn urged, though her own pulse raced with fury. "He can't hide forever."

"Perhaps not," Zylar pondered aloud, "but in this moment, our enemy has slipped through our grasp."

"Then we find him," Mia asserted, her gaze steely and unyielding. "And this time, we end it."

Their determination was palpable, a shared conviction that surged through the room. The chase was back on, the quarry known, and the hunt more desperate than ever. With the past whispering of betrayal and the future uncertain, they stepped into the labyrinthine corridors of the ship, united in their quest for justice and retribution.

…

The acrid smell of scorched circuitry hung heavy as Dr. Evelyn Montgomery's boots crunched over the debris-strewn corridor. The ship's emergency lights cast long, flickering shadows, giving the aftermath of chaos an eerie dance of light and darkness. Her mind raced, a tempest of logic and intuition swirling within as she sought clarity amid the disarray.

"His alibi," Dr. Markus Weller murmured, pushing his glasses up the bridge of his nose with a trembling hand. "It's solid,

Evelyn. He was in the lab during the sabotage, confirmed by the timestamp on the surveillance logs."

Evelyn paused, her green eyes narrowing. She considered the weight of Markus's words, the potential for error, and the ramifications of misplaced accusations. "Logs can be falsified," she replied, her voice tinged with both skepticism and hope. "Indeed," Zylar interjected, their alien cadence somber. "Yet to cast doubt without proof is to tread upon the precipice of paranoia."

Captain Hawking stood silent, his muscular frame rigid, gaze locked on the distant bulkhead as if it might reveal answers. "We need more," he finally said, his voice resonating with the burden of command. "We can't move on suspicion alone."

Mia Alvarez's jaw clenched, a visible sign of her internal struggle between the disciplined soldier and the wounded soul seeking justice. "Then we dig deeper," she insisted, determination lacing her words.

The coalition members exchanged glances, each shadowed by the specter of doubt that now loomed over them. Accusations had been made, yet the truth remained shrouded, a puzzle with pieces missing or perhaps hidden too well.

"Let's review everything," Evelyn proposed, her analytical mind dissecting scenarios like a surgeon's scalpel through flesh. "Every interaction, communication, access log. There has to be a flaw in his story."

"Time isn't our ally," Hawk reminded them, his blue eyes reflecting a war of emotions. "The traitor knows we're on to him now. He'll be covering his tracks."

"Or," Zylar suggested with a hint of foreboding, "laying new ones to ensnare us further."

They dispersed, each to their tasks, combing through data streams and witness statements with a meticulousness born of desperation. The ship's labyrinthine corridors seemed to mock them, endless paths winding into the unknown.

Hours passed, a grueling search yielding nothing but frustration and fatigue. Just as the weight of failure began to settle upon their shoulders, a call from Mia pierced the silence.

"Found something!" Her voice crackled over the comm; urgency clear even through the static. "A discrepancy in the airlock cycle times. It's minor, but it's there."

"Could be a glitch," Markus countered, reluctant hope battling his innate caution.

"Or it could be our missing link," Evelyn said, allowing herself a sliver of optimism.

"Meet at the airlock," Hawk commanded, already on the move. They converged with haste, each member of the coalition arriving with the gravity of the moment etched upon their features. Before them stood the airlock, its door sealed like the lips of a conspirator.

"Show me," Hawk said.

Mia pointed to the digital readout, the numbers telling a story that didn't match the one they'd been told. "This could mean he left the lab, briefly. Long enough to..."

"To betray us all," Evelyn finished, her heart hammering against her ribs.

"Or it could be planted evidence," Zylar cautioned, their voice a melody of wisdom and warning.

"Can we trace where it leads?" Hawk asked, his focus sharp as a blade.

"Working on it," Mia replied, fingers dancing over her handheld device.

The tension in the air was palpable, a current that charged every breath, every thought. They stood on the precipice of revelation, the possibility of unmasking the traitor tantalizingly close.

"Wait," Markus said suddenly, his thin frame rigid with concentration. "There's a signal anomaly here. It's faint, almost imperceptible."

"Could it be interference? Or something else?" Evelyn's mind raced with implications.

"Something else," Markus confirmed, his voice a whisper of dread. "I think our traitor knew we'd find this. It's too convenient, a trap within a trap."

Hawk cursed, the walls of the airlock echoing his fury.

"Back to square one," Mia muttered, the disappointment a physical ache.

"Or perhaps not," Zylar mused, their eyes gleaming with an inner light. "We've been given a glimpse behind the veil. Now we must look closer, see what lies beyond the illusion."

Evelyn met the gazes of her companions, seeing the reflection of her own resolve mirrored in theirs. The chapter was ending, but their story was far from over. As the mystery deepened and the trail grew colder, they knew the next page would demand more from them than ever before.

With the identity of the traitor still veiled in shadows, they braced for the journey ahead, the hunt for truth an odyssey into the unknown. And as the ship hummed with secrets yet to be revealed, the coalition ventured forward, the specter of the traitor lurking just out of reach, a ghost story unfinished, a truth untold.

Chapter 10

Rising Tension

The sky bled fire and ash as the Kridrax invasion laid waste to the once-proud cityscape, its skeletal ruins clawing feebly at a churning, smoke-veiled firmament. Oppressor's ground forces, merciless in their advance, herded the defeated civilians like livestock bound for slaughter. Their cries tore through the clamor of destruction, a symphony of despair against the relentless percussion of war machines.

Amidst the chaos, Sergeant Mia Alvarez crouched behind the shattered remnants of a concrete barricade, her keen brown eyes surveying the scene with practiced vigilance. The acrid scent of burnt metal filled her nostrils as she watched the Synthetic Oppressor's drones patrol the streets, their red eyes scanning for any sign of resistance among the debris.

"Alvarez," whispered Lieutenant Isabella, her voice barely carrying over the din. "We need a way in."

Sergeant Alvarez turned, her gaze meeting the determined blue of Isabella's, a silent understanding passing between them. They had witnessed too much suffering, endured too many losses. Now, with the weight of countless lives on their shoulders, they sought redemption in this daring gambit against the encroaching darkness.

"South corridor, past the metro line," Alvarez murmured, her words clipped with military conciseness. "It's our best shot. We'll use the rubble for cover, move in a zigzag pattern. Stay low, stay fast."

"Agreed," Isabella nodded, her blonde hair, cropped short for battle, a stark contrast against the night's gloom. "I've marked three potential holding areas. Civilians could be there. We hit them all."

Alvarez felt the familiar stirrings of adrenaline, the echo of old wounds throbbing beneath her armor. She was a soldier, molded by the iron fist of discipline and necessity, yet within her beat a heart burdened by the specters of those she couldn't save. This mission, perhaps, could serve as penance — a chance to mend the frayed edges of her soul.

"Time is against us," Alvarez said, steeling herself. "Let's move."

Together, they breached the barrier, their movements a testament to countless hours of training. Each step was measured, each breath synchronized, as they darted from shadow to shadow, the devastation around them a grim reminder of what awaited should they fail.

"Remember," breathed Alvarez, casting a glance back at Isabella, her voice infused with an urgency that betrayed her stoic facade, "we're not just fighting for today. We're fighting for every tomorrow these people might still have."

"Understood, Sergeant," Isabella replied, the scar on her cheek a pale beacon in the darkness — a mark of survival, of battles fought and won. Her resolve was unyielding, the promise of salvation for the innocent fueling her resolve.

And so, with the tattered remnants of hope sewn into the very fabric of their being, Sergeant Alvarez and Lieutenant Isabella pressed onward, two solitary figures against an army that sought to quench the last flickers of humanity's light.

...

The air crackled with the acrid scent of scorched metal and desperation. Blasts erupted in the near distance, each detonation a heartbeat in the city's death throes. Sergeant Alvarez ducked low, her fingers wrapped tight around the rifle that had become an extension of her will. Beside her, Lieutenant Isabella scanned the horizon with eagle-eyed precision, her hand signals cutting through the chaos like a lifeline.

"Snipers," Isabella mouthed, pointing to the skeletal remains of what had once been an office building.

Alvarez nodded, her gaze hardened by the sights she'd witnessed—a tableau of destruction hauntingly devoid of its former life. With swift, agile movements, they sprinted across the debris-littered expanse, a ballet of shadows and dust. They wove between crumbled walls and fallen beams, their path a jagged line drawn towards hope.

"Trap ahead," Alvarez warned as they neared a group of civilians huddled beneath a battered marquee. Her eyes caught the telltale glint of tripwire in the dim light.

"Creative," Isabella murmured, her deft fingers working to disarm the threat with a surgeon's precision. The wire fell limp; another obstacle conquered, another breath spared for those they sought to save.

"Let's move them out," Alvarez commanded, her voice a low thrum that carried weight, even amidst the cacophony of war.

The civilians, wide-eyed and hollow, clung to the soldiers' assurances like a lifeline as they were ushered through the labyrinthine ruins. Each step was a promise—a silent vow made by those who bore arms to protect.

Beneath the city, insulated from the tumult above, Dr. Evelyn Montgomery's hands flew over holographic displays, streams of data coalescing into patterns only she could decipher. Her green eyes, usually so piercing, now danced with the reflections of code and schematics.

"Any progress?" Dr. Samira Patel asked, her tone steady despite the undercurrent of urgency.

"Close. The Kridrax shielding resonates at a unique frequency. If we can disrupt it..." Evelyn trailed off, the thought hanging heavy with potential.

"Then we give our people a fighting chance," Samira finished, her warm eyes meeting Evelyn's with a shared intensity.

"Exactly," Evelyn replied, tapping into reserves of determination that had long ago replaced easier emotions. "We're on the brink, Samira. We have to be."

Their collaboration was a symphony of intellect and intuition, two minds attuned to the singular goal of salvation. The sterile air of the underground lab hummed as they worked, the pulse of technology their steadfast companion.

"Here," Samira said, her voice tinged with discovery as she adjusted a series of inputs. "A harmonic disruptor. It's crude but..."

"But it might just work," Evelyn completed, her disheveled hair a testament to tireless hours. "Prepare the prototype. It's time to see if our gamble pays off."

Their efforts, born of necessity and nurtured by an unyielding resolve, wove together like strands of fate—a tapestry of science and survival against a backdrop of encroaching darkness. And as the battle raged on the surface, two women waged their own war within the bowels of the earth, their minds alight with the possibility of turning the tide.

Above, Alvarez and Isabella led the ragtag procession of survivors, weaving through the shattered cityscape. Their mission was far from over, each moment a perilous dance with death, yet each life saved a spark in the overwhelming gloom — a beacon of humanity's indomitable spirit.

…

Dr. Evelyn Montgomery's hands were steady, despite the tremor of urgency that pulsed through the underground laboratory. Her green eyes, usually a piercing reflection of her resolve, flickered with the frustration of a puzzle refusing to yield its secrets. Beside her, Dr. Samira Patel's silhouette bent over an array of alien components strewn across the workbench, her brow knit in concentration.

"Another dead end," Samira muttered, the weight of their failure hanging between them like the thick dust particles suspended in the air. They had been attempting to decipher the Kridrax technology for what seemed like an eternity, each experiment ending in disappointment. The devices before them buzzed with an energy they could neither harness nor comprehend, mocking their efforts with silent indifference.

Evelyn's voice was measured, betraying none of the fatigue clawing at her nerves. "We're missing something fundamental. The way these circuits intertwine, it's almost as if..."

"Organic," Samira finished, her finger tracing the metallic vine-like patterns. "They think differently, design differently."

"Exactly," Evelyn agreed, tucking a lock of hair behind her ear – a small tell of her vexation. She leaned closer to the workbench, her analytical gaze dissecting every nanometer of the enigmatic machinery. The dim light of the lab cast long shadows, giving the space an otherworldly glow that seemed fitting for their endeavor.

"Let's approach this from another angle," Samira suggested, resetting their equipment with practiced motions. "What if we stop trying to dominate their technology and instead, coexist with it?"

The idea hung in the air, audacious and untried. It was a dance with the unknown, a flirtation with the very essence of the alien intellect that had brought humanity to its knees. Evelyn considered the notion, allowing the seed of it to take root in her mind. A new perspective could be their salvation, or it could lead them further into darkness.

"Coexistence. Symbiosis," Evelyn murmured, her mind racing through possibilities. She initiated a different sequence on the console, adjusting the parameters with delicate precision. "Let's reroute the power flow, mimic their patterns rather than overwrite them."

"Here goes nothing," Samira said as she engaged the sequence. Together, they watched with bated breath as the alien device hummed to life, responding to their command in a manner it never had before.

For a moment, nothing happened – a stillness so profound that one could hear the distant echo of chaos from above. Then, as if awakening from a deep slumber, the machine emitted a soft, pulsating light. A series of symbols appeared on the screen, cryptic yet oddly familiar.

"Is that...?" Samira's voice trailed off, hope glimmering in her eyes as she dared to believe in the impossible.

"Power fluctuations," Evelyn declared, the hint of excitement sharpening her features. "A pattern! It's vulnerable during the transition phases."

Their hearts raced as they processed the implications of their discovery. This was the chink in the armor of the Kridrax they had desperately sought – a weakness that could be exploited, a glimmer of hope in the suffocating grip of the invasion.

"Record everything," Evelyn instructed, her fingers flying over the keyboard. "We need to replicate this, understand it, and then weaponize it."

"Imagine," Samira said, her voice a mixture of wonder and determination, "turning their own strength against them."

The two scientists shared a look, a silent acknowledgment of the magnitude of their breakthrough. In their exhaustion-laden faces shone a beacon of defiance, a testament to the resilience of human ingenuity. The tide was turning; they could feel it in their bones.

But time was a luxury they did not possess, and the Kridrax would not pause in their relentless assault. With renewed vigor, Evelyn and Samira plunged back into their work, the possibility of redemption fueling their tireless pursuit. For in their hands lay not just the key to survival but the promise of reclaiming a world on the brink of oblivion.

…

Sergeant Mia Alvarez darted through the debris-littered hallways of the enemy stronghold, her boots crunching on shattered glass and twisted metal. The air was thick with smoke and the stench of burning circuitry, a remnant of the Synthetic Oppressor's ruthless march. She moved like a wraith, her shadow slipping across walls pockmarked by gunfire.

Beside her, Lieutenant Isabella forged ahead, her eyes scanning for threats in every direction. Her movements were precise, a dance honed by countless hours of combat training. Together, they advanced deeper into the heart of chaos, each step weighed down by the leaden silence that followed the cacophony of war.

"Contact," Isabella whispered, her voice barely audible above the distant echoes of explosions and cries for mercy. Alvarez nodded, gripping her rifle tighter as shapes emerged from the smoky gloom—Oppressor's ground forces, relentless sentinels of a once-human tyrant's will.

They engaged without hesitation, their rifles barking in unison, answering the silent plea of the captured civilians huddled behind barricaded doors. Each pull of the trigger bespoke their determination to save as many as they could or die trying.

Amid the fury of battle, an imposing figure emerged, part man, part machine—the Reborn Führer's elite commander. His mechanical limbs whirred with deadly precision, and his red eyes glowed like embers in the dim corridor.

"Alvarez!" Isabella called out, her tone taut with urgency as she fired at the approaching menace. "Focus fire!"

Their bullets sang a desperate hymn against steel and synthetic flesh. Alvarez's breath came in short bursts, her disciplined mind racing to find a path to victory. She remembered the countless drills, the strategies etched into her soul, yet none had prepared her for this encounter.

The commander advanced, undeterred, a grotesque smile twisting his human mouth as though he savored the challenge. Alvarez felt a flicker of fear, but she crushed it beneath the weight of her resolve. This was more than a clash of arms; it was a fight for redemption — for a past steeped in blood, for a future that hung by a thread.

"Isabella, flank him!" Alvarez commanded, her voice echoing with authority and a hint of something raw — hope, perhaps, or defiance.

"Covering!" came the reply, crisp and clear, as Isabella dashed to the side, drawing the commander's attention.

Alvarez seized the moment, lunging forward with a feral grace. Her blade, a sliver of silver in the murky light, found the seams in the commander's armor. Sparks flew as metal clashed with metal, a symphony of survival that resonated through the haunted halls.

Together, they fought with a synchrony that transcoded mere partnership. They were avatars of resilience, two souls interwoven by the threads of war, each blow a testament to their unyielding spirit.

As the commander faltered, his systems failing under their relentless assault, Alvarez allowed herself a fleeting glimpse of triumph. But the battle was far from over, the stronghold a labyrinth of dangers yet unmet. With grim determination, they pressed on, their mission unforgotten, their courage unshaken.

In this dance with death, there was no space for doubt. There was only the mission, the burden of lives not yet lost, and the faint whisper of redemption calling them onward into the unknown.

…

The sterile hum of machinery and the acrid scent of ozone filled the underground laboratory where Dr. Evelyn Montgomery and Dr. Samira Patel stood, their forms rigid with anticipation.

Above them, the war raged, but here, encased in layers of concrete and steel, they toiled against an enemy far more inscrutable: the alien technology of the Kridrax.

"Initiating sequence," Evelyn announced, her voice a precise instrument amidst the cacophony of beeps and whirls. The countermeasures, their brainchild, lay before them — a series of interlocking devices designed to disrupt the invaders' advanced systems. The stakes could not have been higher; their success or failure would dictate the tide of an unforgiving war.

Samira's fingers danced across the console, her touch light but assured. "Monitoring vitals," she murmured, her gaze fixed on the flickering screens that displayed the vital signs of those who carried their hopes into battle.

"Commence field test," Evelyn said, and with a silent prayer to whatever gods still heeded calls from a world on the brink, she activated the countermeasure.

A surge of power rippled through the lab, a tangible echo of their desperate bid for salvation. The data streamed in, a rapid-fire litany of numbers and graphs that painted a picture only they could comprehend. And then, the wait — an eternity condensed into mere seconds as they watched for signs of efficacy.

"Signal's strong," Samira breathed out, relief mingling with the tension that held her upright. "It's working."

***

Meanwhile, Sergeant Mia Alvarez and Lieutenant Isabella emerged from the smoldering wreckage of what had once been a vibrant marketplace, now a mausoleum of dreams reduced to ash. Around them, the rescued civilians huddled together, their faces etched with the weariness of the oppressed, yet alight with the fragile flame of hope reborn.

"Move out, stay close!" Alvarez ordered, her voice cutting through the haze of lingering smoke. They moved as one, a phalanx of survivors bound by the singular purpose of life amidst the specter of death.

"Thank you," a woman whispered, her words heavy with the weight of gratitude. Her arms clutched a child to her chest, a small beacon of innocence in a world torn asunder.

Isabella's blue eyes met hers, and in that moment, there was an unspoken understanding—the promise of protection, the vow of a soldier to the very soul of humanity they fought to preserve. "We've got you," she replied, the scar on her cheek stark against her dirt-streaked face, a testament to battles past and the resilience that defined her.

As they navigated the labyrinth of destruction, the countermeasures pulsed silently within their gear, invisible shields against an unseen foe. Each step was a triumph against the relentless march of despair, every breath a defiance against the suffocating grip of fear.

"Keep moving," Alvarez urged, her gaze sweeping over the faces of those they had snatched from the jaws of oblivion. Their presence was a balm to her warrior's heart, a reminder of what lay at the core of their struggle—not just survival, but the preservation of something precious and enduring.

And so they pressed on, each stride a victory, each saved life a star in the dark firmament of a war-torn sky, guiding them through the shadows toward the distant, uncertain dawn of redemption.

…

The silence shattered like glass under the hammer of an unexpected explosion, a harrowing reminder that in war, reprieve was but an illusion. A Kridrax shock troop burst forth from the smoldering ruins, their weapons spitting fire and death. The ground team, led by Sergeant Alvarez, had been moving with the fluidity of shadows, spirits guided by hope through the husk of a once-vibrant city. Now, they were corporeal once more, targets in the sights of a relentless enemy.

"Contact! Twelve o'clock!" Alvarez shouted, her voice a beacon in the tempest as she dropped to one knee, returning fire. Her dark eyes darted between the civilians cowering behind the rubble and the advancing invaders. Each crack of her rifle was a word in the story of survival she penned with every breath — a tale not yet ready for its end.

Lieutenant Isabella was an echo of Alvarez's own resolve, her commands slicing through the cacophony. "Form up on me! Shields to the front!" Her scar seemed to pulse with the rhythm of battle, a jagged line marking the path from despair to defiance.

They moved with practiced precision, a dance macabre choreographed in the language of war. Civilians huddled close, following the siren call of safety promised by these guardians in the storm. In the shadowy realm where life hung on the edge of a knife, Alvarez and Isabella were the blade's edge — sharp, unyielding.

"Fall back to secondary position! Go, go!" Isabella's orders cut through the haze as the Kridrax bore down upon them. They were outnumbered, but not outmatched — not while the heart of resistance beat within them, fierce and undaunted.

Alvarez felt the weight of lives depending on her, the heavy mantle of responsibility that was hers alone to bear. She covered their retreat, her weapon a thunderous roar in the dimness. Beside her, Isabella stood resolute, her blue eyes alight with the fire of one who has known loss but refuses to be consumed by it.

"Keep your heads down!" Alvarez barked to the civilians. A mother clutched her child tighter, eyes wide with terror yet filled with an unwavering trust. Each civilian was a mirror to Alvarez's soul, reflecting the toll of war, the pain of separation, the longing for peace.

The air was thick with the stench of burning metal and fear, yet beneath it all lay the faint, sweet scent of hope—imperceptible to those who had surrendered to the darkness, but to Alvarez and Isabella, it was the fragrance of redemption, a future reclaimed with every defiant stand.

"Isabella, we need to—" Alvarez's words were swallowed by a sudden eruption of earth and fire as a Kridrax grenade found its mark. She was thrown to the ground, her ears ringing, her vision swimming. But surrender was a word unwritten in her lexicon, and she clawed her way back to her feet, her determination a phoenix rising from ashes.

"Alvarez!" Isabella's voice tethered her to reality, and together they rallied the battered remnants of their team. This was not the day their story would end, not while their hearts still thundered with the drumbeat of resistance.

"Push them back!" Isabella commanded, and they surged forward, a tide of human spirit crashing against the cold, unfeeling advance of the Kridrax. Their countermeasures held, a testament to human ingenuity in the face of otherworldly might. "Fight for what you hold dear!" Alvarez's cry was a clarion call, reverberating in the chest of every defender, every rescued soul. It was a vow made in the crucible of conflict, a promise etched in the very marrow of their bones — to emerge victorious or to fall with honor, but never to yield.

In that moment, as steel met alien sinew and will clashed with malice, the path to redemption wound ever onward, each step a testament to the resilience of the human spirit, each breath a challenge to the encroaching shadows. The battle raged on, but within Alvarez and Isabella burned the indomitable light of hope, guiding them through the chaos toward a dawn that must surely come.

...

Underground, far from the battlefield's disarray and fury, Dr. Evelyn Montgomery's fingers danced with a surgeon's precision over the complex innards of the countermeasure device. Beside her, Dr. Samira Patel fed the latest field data into the simulation matrix, her expression a mosaic of focus and fatigue.

"Montgomery, the feedback loop is still too volatile," Patel said, her voice steady despite the weight of their task. "We're threading a needle between disruption and detonation."

"Then we'll recalibrate the resonance capacitors," Evelyn replied curtly, her eyes never leaving the device. The air between them crackled with urgency as she adjusted the settings with deft turns of her wrist. Her piercing green gaze reflected a mind that was as sharp as the scalpel she had wielded in her former life as a surgeon — a life abruptly severed by the Kridrax invasion, leaving only this relentless quest for redemption.

Patel watched her partner work, admiration and concern warring within her. She understood too well the pressure that bore down on Evelyn's shoulders, the silent dread that each tweak might not be enough to turn the tide.

"Remember, we're not just fighting technology with technology," Patel reminded gently, her own hands poised above her keyboard, ready to implement any changes. "We're defending a future—a world where people can live without fear again."

Evelyn allowed herself a momentary glance at Patel, a flicker of vulnerability betraying her stoic mask. "I know," she admitted, returning her focus to the device. "But hope alone won't dismantle their shields."

The lab fell silent except for the hum of machinery and the occasional beep of diagnostic equipment. The two women worked in tandem, their movements synchronized like an intricate dance choreographed by necessity and desperation. "Got it," Evelyn exhaled sharply as the final piece clicked into place. "Initiate the test sequence."

Patel complied, and the countermeasure device came alive, thrumming with newfound potential. The screens around them bathed the room in a pulsating glow, casting elongated shadows that seemed to grapple with the very walls.

"Stabilization confirmed," Patel announced, a smile of triumph touching her lips. "This could be it, Evelyn. This could change everything."

Evelyn managed a tight-lipped smile, allowing herself a rare moment of hope. Together, they watched the readouts, willing the success to hold.

And then, without warning, the ground beneath them shuddered violently. Alarms blared, red lights flashing a sinister warning as dust rained down from the ceiling. The two scientists exchanged a look of shared horror as the realization dawned on them—the Kridrax had found them.

"Lockdown!" Evelyn shouted, her voice cutting through the cacophony. They scrambled towards the emergency protocols, but the tremors intensified, threatening to rend the earth itself apart.

In the chaos, Patel stumbled, catching herself on the edge of the workbench. "The data, we have to protect—"

"Samira, look out!" Evelyn's warning came an instant too late. A jagged fissure split the floor, opening like a gaping maw eager to swallow the lab whole. Patel's eyes widened in shock as the ground betrayed her, and she vanished into the abyss below.

Evelyn lunged forward, her hand outstretched in a futile gesture as the lab's lights flickered and died, plunging the world into darkness. The last thing she heard before the silence swallowed everything was the echo of Patel's scream, a haunting refrain that would etch itself into the walls of Evelyn's soul forever.

...

The lab's emergency lighting flickered to life, casting an eerie glow over the chaos. Evelyn Montgomery stood frozen for a mere heartbeat, her mind grappling with the sudden loss of Dr. Patel, before the soldier within her snapped to attention. There was no time for grief in the face of annihilation. With each pulse of the red warning lights, she felt the thread of their hard-won breakthrough fraying, threatening to unravel all they had achieved.

"System override, execute protocol Omicron," she commanded, her voice a mixture of iron and ice as she tapped into the control panel with practiced urgency. The facility shuddered under the relentless assault of the Kridrax, but the fortifications held—for now. Yet, even as she secured the lab's precious data, Evelyn knew that the true test of their resolve lay beyond these walls.

Outside, the cacophony of war raged on. Sergeant Mia Alvarez and her team maneuvered through the smoldering ruins, their movements a symphony of precise violence. Mia's face was a mask of determination, her eyes reflecting both the flames and her fierce will to protect those entrusted to her care. With each rescued civilian, her heart grew heavier with the weight of responsibility, yet lighter with the glimmer of hope.

Above, Captain Lucas "Hawk" Hawking piloted his craft through the smoke-choked skies, dodging debris and enemy fire with the agility of his namesake. His hands were steady on the controls, his blue eyes scanning for threats even as he coordinated the ground team's extraction. The burden of command sat heavily on his shoulders, each decision a potential sentence of life or death.

Deep within the bowels of the resistance stronghold, General Thomas "Thunderbolt" O'Neill surveyed the unfolding battle with a gaze that missed nothing. His orders barked out, crisp and clear, directing the flow of combat like a maestro conducting a deadly orchestra. Each explosion echoed the drumbeat of war, a testament to humanity's refusal to yield.

Elsewhere, cloaked by shadows, Zylar Threx observed the conflict with an otherworldly stillness. Their presence was a silent sentinel, their thoughts a mystery even as their eyes bespoke volumes of sorrow and ancient knowledge. Their alliance with humanity was tenuous, born of mutual necessity, but their commitment to the cause was as steadfast as the most loyal soldier.

In the midst of turmoil, Lily Chen worked furiously alongside Colonel Viktor Sokolov, their combined expertise a beacon of ingenuity in the darkness. Lily's youth belied her brilliance, her hands deftly manipulating devices of her own creation, while

Sokolov's strategic mind wove plans within plans, each move a calculated risk in the high-stakes game against extinction.

The moment unfurled, a tapestry of valor and desperation, each thread a story of courage, sacrifice, and the indomitable human spirit. As the narrative wove toward its climax, it was clear that the fate of the world hung precariously in the balance, each character a vital piece in the puzzle of survival.

Evelyn returned her focus to the task at hand, her green eyes reflecting the stark reality of their situation. They had lost much, but the fight was far from over. With a final keystroke, she encrypted the last of the data, ensuring that Patel's sacrifice would not be in vain.

The mysterious tone settled around her like a shroud, heavy with the burden of what was yet to come. The stakes had never been higher. Left perched upon the edge of uncertainty, wondering what redemption — or doom — awaited the them in the war-torn landscape of the future.

Chapter 11

Revelation

The air in the hidden base was thick with anticipation. Shadows clung to the rough-hewn walls as the coalition members, bound by a common resolve, huddled around a flickering holographic display. It cast an eerie glow on their faces, illuminating their determination and the faint creases of worry etched into their skin. This was where plans were forged in whispered tones, where the fate of civilizations hung precariously in the balance.

Dr. Evelyn Montgomery stepped forward, her piercing green eyes scanning the attentive ensemble. The light danced off her short black hair, casting angular shadows that mirrored the sharpness of her features. She cleared her throat, a sound that resonated in the charged silence, commanding the room's attention without need for grand gestures or words.

"Precision and stealth," she began, her voice carrying the weight of her vast intellect, "are not merely aspects of our plan—they are the very sinew that binds it." Each syllable was enunciated with a care that betrayed her meticulous nature. "We strike at the heart, severing the synthetic abomination from its consciousness." Her finger traced a path through the hologram, outlining the labyrinthine corridors of the Kridrax command ship.

"Every step," she continued, pausing as if to let the gravity of their mission settle upon each individual, "every action must be calculated." Dr. Montgomery's gaze lingered on the schematic of the enemy vessel, displaying paths and nodes like arteries and veins—a body awaiting a surgical incision.

"Remember, we are not only fighting against metal and circuitry," she added, her voice tinged with a vulnerability she seldom showed. "We confront a mind—a mind that once swayed masses and now seeks to control through tyranny and fear." There was a subtle tremor in her hand as she pointed to the central chamber, where the grotesque form of Synthetic Oppressor would be found, a twisted amalgamation of flesh and machine.

"Questions?" Dr. Montgomery asked, but the room remained silent, the members' own contemplations reflecting in the glassy sheen of their eyes. Each knew the cost of failure, the specter of a past they all longed to redeem. They were a tapestry of inner turmoil, woven together by a thread of hope—hope that this mission could mend the fabric of a reality torn asunder by war and desperation.

With a nod, Dr. Montgomery signaled the end of the briefing. The display dimmed, casting the room back into shadow, the lingering image of the command ship burning in their retinas like a phantom promise of what was to come. The coalition moved with quiet resolve, their steps echoing softly as they dispersed to ready themselves for the impending maelstrom.

The battle ahead was not only for the future but for the ghosts of the past that haunted them still—to silence the whispers of doubt and to grasp redemption from the jaws of darkness.

...

Captain Lucas "Hawk" Hawking surveyed the room, his piercing blue eyes locking onto each member of the coalition in turn. In the dimly lit chamber, an air of expectancy hung heavy as they awaited their marching orders. Hawk's voice sliced through the silence with the precision of a scalpel.

"Montgomery, you're on tech," he said, nodding to the doctor, whose fingers were already dancing over her portable hacking device. "We need those security systems down before we can even think about getting close to Oppressor."

"Chen, Weller, you'll support Montgomery. Your scientific expertise is our edge against whatever unnatural defenses we encounter." The two scientists nodded, their expressions grim but determined.

"Isabella, you're our eyes in the sky. Once we disembark, it's your job to keep the escape route clear." Isabella's jaw set in a line of determination, acknowledging the weight of responsibility placed upon her shoulders.

"Rest of you," Hawk continued, his gaze sweeping over the team of specialists, "you know your roles—combat, recon, demolition. Stick to the plan, and we might just pull this off."

A collective breath was drawn as the gravity of the mission pressed in, but there was no hesitation in their movements as they turned to gather their gear.

The preparation area was a quiet cacophony of clicking, snapping, and clinking as equipment was checked and rechecked. Magnetic boots, plasma rifles, and stealth cloaks were strapped on with meticulous care. Each piece of weaponry and gadgetry was more than mere tools; they were lifelines in the cold void of space, where the only thing louder than the silence was the pounding of one's own heart.

Hawk watched as his team secured their armor, the metallic sheen casting ghostly reflections in the low light. Their movements spoke of countless drills, a choreography refined by the necessity of survival. They were specters preparing for a dance with death, each step measured, every motion deliberate.

"Remember what we're fighting for," Hawk murmured, barely audible over the hum of equipment. It wasn't just a reminder to them; it was a mantra for himself, a tether to the world they were trying to save—a world that lay on the other side of redemption's razor-thin edge.

He hoisted his own weapon, the familiar weight a comfort and a burden all at once. His hands ran over the rifle's casing, checking the energy pack and sighting system. Satisfied, he clipped a series of grenades to his belt, their spherical forms whispering promises of controlled destruction.

"Check your comms," Hawk ordered, and a series of affirmative clicks responded. He could hear the undercurrent of resolve in each static-laced confirmation. They were ready, or as ready as they could ever be for an operation steeped in uncertainty.

"Five minutes out," came Isabella's voice through the earpieces, a solemn countdown to the unknown.

With weapons primed and hearts encased in steely resolve, the team lined up at the bay door. The mission that lay ahead was etched into their very bones—a silent symphony of anticipation and the unspoken knowledge that history waited for them, its pages open and pen poised.

And so, Captain Lucas "Hawk" Hawking led his coalition into the shadows, towards a confrontation that would either carve their names into the annals of heroes or erase them from existence altogether.

…

Under the dim glow of utilitarian lights, Zylar Threx's scaled hands unfolded a translucent map that hovered in the air like a ghostly apparition. The coalition members leaned in, their faces half-lit by the spectral chart of the Kridrax command ship — a labyrinthine structure pulsating with potential doom.

"Here," they began, their haunting voice infusing the silence, "lies the heart of tyranny." An elongated finger traced a serpentine path through the holographic corridors. "The central conduit runs like a spine through this monstrosity. It feeds the beast's limbs, but it is also its greatest weakness."

Their eyes, pools of ancient light, met each of the team members in turn. "Silence will be your ally," Zylar intoned solemnly. "There are sentries — biomechanical hybrids, unforgiving and sharp as the edge of night. Avoid them at all costs."

"Any blind spots?" Hawk's voice was a low rumble, grounded and ready.

"Few," Zylar admitted, "but here" — they pointed to a section of the map that flickered slightly — "an old scar in their defenses. Not enough for an army, but just wide enough for shadows such as ourselves."

"Shadows with teeth," muttered Hawk, his gaze fixed on the route that would lead them to their singular goal: severing the tyrant's consciousness from his synthetic throne.

The map dissolved into nothingness, and the room fell into a hush loaded with unspoken vows. They were the unseen, the harbinger had said, and it was time for the unseen to rise.

Lieutenant Isabella gave a curt nod, her scar a stark reminder of battles past and determination unyielded. She led the way to the hangar where their vessel awaited — a slip of a thing, dark and sleek against the cavernous backdrop. Its design spoke of swift incursions and silent departures, much like the woman who would pilot it through the stars.

"Board quickly," she commanded, her voice the essence of controlled urgency. Her fingers danced across the control panel, bringing the craft to a soft, expectant hum. "We have a narrow window before the Kridrax fleet cycles patrols."

One by one, the coalition members entered the spacecraft, each step a testament to their resolve. The interior was compact, functional, stripped of anything that didn't serve survival or success. As the hatch sealed with a hiss, sealing them in a cocoon of purpose, the world outside seemed to hold its breath.

Isabella settled into the pilot's seat, her hands steady on the controls. She felt the thrum of the engines sync with the pulse in her veins — a warrior's heartbeat, ready to chase down destiny or meet it head-on.

"Engaging stealth mode," she announced, flipping switches with practiced ease. The craft vibrated momentarily as it became a shadow amongst stars, a whisper slipping through the vast ocean of space.

They were adrift in the void now, propelled by silent engines and the gravity of what lay ahead. The journey towards the Kridrax command ship had begun, and with it, a dance with fate that none could foresee.

...

Stars flickered in the distance, distant suns oblivious to the dire mission unfolding in their midst. Within the stealth craft's confines, each member of the coalition sat ensconced in shadows, the tension between them as palpable as the cold metal underfoot.

Isabella guided the vessel with a deft touch, her features etched with concentration. The silence was occasionally broken by the soft thrumming of the engines or the faint tap of fingers on a control panel. Time seemed to stretch and compress, the spacecraft a lone sentinel slipping through the black sea of space.

Zylar Threx, The Harbinger, stood apart from the rest, their iridescent scales casting an otherworldly glow in the dim light. Their deep-set eyes, pools of ancient sorrow, scanned a holographic display of the Kridrax armada arrayed around the command ship—a constellation of danger.

"Adjust your trajectory by two degrees starboard," Zylar's haunting voice broke the stillness, a low murmur that resonated within the cabin. "The Kridrax's scanning patterns will shift momentarily."

"Understood," Isabella replied, her response a whisper against the weight of impending peril.

Each member of the team was lost in their own thoughts, minds racing with strategies and contingencies. They were acutely aware of what failure would mean—not just for them but for countless worlds teetering on the brink of tyranny.

Dr. Montgomery closed his eyes, envisioning the complex schematics of Synthetic Oppressor's neural network he would soon be tasked to sever. Captain Hawking ran a hand over the hilt of her weapon, finding some comfort in its familiar coolness against her palm.

Outside, the vast fleet of Kridrax warships loomed like sentinels of doom. Yet, under Zylar's guidance, the small craft wove through the deadly tapestry unseen, a ghost ship flitting through the web of an interstellar leviathan.

"Steady," Zylar intoned as they navigated the invisible currents of space, their words tinged with a gravity that belied the calm of their demeanor.

Isabella's hands moved with precision, adjusting the craft's course in harmony with Zylar's instructions. She could feel the eyes of her comrades upon her, trust and fear mingling in the charged atmosphere.

As the command ship drew nearer, it appeared as a fortress amidst the stars, bristling with armaments that promised obliteration. Yet, for now, it remained unaware of the silent threat drawing close.

"Prepare yourselves," Zylar said, their voice barely more than a breath, yet it carried the weight of galaxies. "We are the unseen, the vanguard of hope. Let us not falter at destiny's threshold."

In the shadow of the Kridrax armada, the coalition members steeled themselves, ready to breach the heart of darkness and strike a blow for freedom. With each passing moment, the line between salvation and ruin grew thinner, and within the depths of the void, they found a silent resolve to tip the balance.

...

The hatch hissed open with a whisper, and shadows greeted the coalition as they disembarked into the bowels of the Kridrax command ship. They were phantoms in a tomb of steel, threading through the dimly lit corridors with the silence of space itself clinging to their steps. Captain Lucas Hawking's blue eyes, sharp as shards of ice, scanned the dark ahead, every sense attuned to the alien vessel that threatened to become their grave.

"Keep it tight," he murmured, his voice barely carrying over the hum of unseen machinery. The words were unnecessary; his team knew the stakes, each movement deliberate, a dance of survival choreographed to avoid the clutches of death lurking around every corner.

Ahead, Dr. Evelyn Montgomery's form was a wraith, her green eyes reflecting the sterile light of the corridor. She moved with an uncanny grace, her body flowing from shadow to shadow, a testament to the many nights spent evading capture and wrestling with the betraying tendrils of her past. Her breaths came measured like the beats of a metronome counting down to the inevitable.

A flicker of movement stirred the stillness. Sergeant Mia Alvarez spotted it first, her soldier's instincts honed by countless skirmishes. Without a word, she signaled, her hand slicing through the air with precision. Two Kridrax guards, their chitinous armor gleaming dully in the low light, rounded the bend unaware of the predators that awaited them.

The coalition struck with the swiftness of lightning. Zylar Threx, their limbs a blur of motion, engaged one guard with a fluidity that belied their otherworldly strength. The clash was silent, a dance of death performed without fanfare, and the guard crumpled, its life force extinguished before a cry could escape its mandibles.

Alvarez faced the second guard, her movements a symphony of violence. There was no hesitation in her strike, no tremor in her resolve, only the cold assurance of a warrior who had long ago accepted the cost of war. The guard fell, and silence reclaimed the corridor, the echoes of combat absorbed by the insatiable darkness.

"Move out," Hawk commanded, his gaze lingering on the fallen foes with a soldier's lament for lives taken. Redemption was a luxury none of them could afford—not yet. They continued onward, specters adrift in the heart of an enemy that knew neither mercy nor remorse.

Each step was a defiance of fate, a testament to their unspoken vow to reclaim the future from the jaws of tyranny. Their mission was clear: sever the tyrant's grasp on reality, or perish in the attempt. And in the vast expanse of the command ship that loomed around them, they found the courage to face what lay ahead, united by the fragile thread of hope in a universe that had forgotten its meaning.

...

Hushed whispers of their boots against the metal grated floor were all that betrayed their presence. Dr. Markus Weller's gaze was fixed on the pulsing blue light of the security panel before him, his fingers dancing with a deftness that belied his absent-minded appearance. Beside him, Dr. Lily Chen mirrored his concentration, her bright eyes reflecting the luminescence of the holographic interface as she inputted a sequence of precise commands.

"Patience," murmured Dr. Samira Patel, laying a steadying hand on Dr. Chen's tense shoulder. "We have one shot at this."

A bead of sweat trickled down Weller's temple, but he did not wipe it away; there was no room for distraction. The security system was a labyrinthine puzzle, one wrong move and alarms would shriek their location to every Kridrax soldier aboard. The fate of worlds rested in the silence between keystrokes.

"Disabling the final lock," Chen whispered, her voice barely a breath.

There was a click, more felt than heard, and the sealed door before them parted like the maw of some great beast, inviting them into its depths. They stepped through the threshold, the weight of their task settling upon them with each footfall.

Their path took them deeper into the bowels of the command ship, where shadows clung to the walls like desperate phantoms. It was here, in the gloom of the narrow corridor, that they stumbled upon the unexpected: a defense mechanism unlike any other, a sentinel wrought from the nightmares of a twisted mind.

"Formidable" was too tame a word for the towering construct that barred their way. It was a mosaic of steel and sinew, a guardian with no soul to corrupt, only the relentless purpose to destroy any who dared approach.

"Stand back," Captain Hawking commanded, his voice steady as bedrock despite the dread that clawed at his insides. Evelyn Montgomery assessed the behemoth, her green eyes narrowed, calculating the pattern of its movements, searching for an opening in its armor of darkness.

"Distraction is key," she said, her tone leaving no room for debate. "Chen, Weller, you flank it. Samira, with me."

The dance began anew, a deadly ballet choreographed by necessity. As Hawking and Montgomery drew the construct's attention, Weller and Chen circled behind it, their intellects their greatest weapons. Patel's hands moved with grace, her devices humming softly as she worked to disrupt the creature's core.

It struck with ferocity, limbs blurring in motion, yet each attack met air as the coalition ducked and weaved with practiced synchrony. The rhythm of combat was punctuated by the whir of servos and the clang of metal against metal.

"Samira, now!" Montgomery called out.

Patel activated her device, sending a surge of energy into the construct's circuits. It faltered, confusion flickering across its mechanical features, and in that moment of hesitation, Weller and Chen pounced. Their expertise fused into action, they severed wires and dismantled components, unraveling the monstrosity from within.

With a shudder that reverberated through the hull, the construct collapsed, inert and lifeless. Breaths came easier, but eyes remained vigilant; they were close now, so very close. "Move forward," Hawk ordered, his voice a low growl of determination. They stepped over the fallen guardian, their resolve solidifying with each step toward their quarry.

Through corridors that whispered of past horrors, they pressed on, driven by memories of loss and the promise of redemption. The specter of their mission loomed large, a shadow cast by history's darkest hour, but they would not be deterred.

For in the heart of this metallic leviathan, they sought not just the end of a tyrant, but the salvation of their own souls, tarnished by war and wearied by sacrifice. Redemption was a distant star in the night sky of their plight, yet they reached for it with hands worn and hearts resolute.

...

The chamber loomed ahead, its massive doors sliding open with a hiss that echoed of ancient tombs and secrets unearthed. Within, the air crackled with an electric charge, palpable as the presence that awaited them. Synthetic Oppressor stood at the far end, a macabre figure bathed in the cold glow of a thousand blinking consoles. His red eyes pierced the dimness, locking onto the intruders with malevolent recognition.

"Welcome," his voice boomed, metallic undertones warping the words into something otherworldly. "To the heart of your demise."

Evelyn Montgomery's breath caught in her throat as she stepped into the chamber, her green eyes narrowing against the onslaught of darkness. Hawk was beside her, his muscular frame tensed like a coiled spring, ready to unleash havoc at her command. And Zylar, their ethereal ally, seemed to glide rather than walk, their iridescent scales reflecting the scant light in eerie patterns.

"Your reign ends here, Oppressor," Evelyn's voice cut through the tension, sharp and unwavering despite the flutter in her chest. "We will dismantle this abomination you've become."

Synthetic Oppressor's laugh rumbled, sending shivers down their spines. "You presume much, Dr. Montgomery. But it is I who shall dissect your hopes and leave you barren."

Hawk's hand rested on his weapon, but he held back. This was a battle that required more than brute force; it demanded precision, cunning — the very traits that had brought them to this precipice.

"Your thirst for power blinds you," Zylar spoke, their voice resonating with an almost spectral quality. "It is not strength that defines us, but our resolve to undo the wrongs of the past."

Yet Synthetic Oppressor remained unphased, his posture one of twisted nobility as he surveyed his adversaries. "History is written by the victors, alien. I shall pen my triumph with your blood."

The room felt charged, a battleground set not just for combat but for the clashing of ideals. Each word, each movement, was a calculated step in a dance as old as time — good against evil, hope against despair.

"What drives you now, Oppressor?" Evelyn asked, her tone steady as she sought to unravel the enigma before them. "What can a soulless machine truly desire?"

"Power," he said simply. "The power to achieve what flesh and bone could not. The power to reshape the world in my image."

"Then you are already defeated," Hawk interjected, his blue eyes glinting with resolve. "Because we carry something stronger than power. We carry the will of those you've wronged, the spirit of those who resist."

"Empty platitudes," Synthetic Oppressor retorted, his form beginning to hum with an ominous energy. "Let us see if your spirits can shield you from my wrath."

In that moment, they moved as one — a trinity bound by purpose. Evelyn deployed her devices, intricate mechanisms designed to sever the neural links that tethered Oppressor's consciousness to his synthetic shell. Hawk covered her, his movements deliberate and precise, offering protection and reassurance with his mere presence. And Zylar, their knowledge of the ship's inner workings invaluable, began to chant in their haunting tongue, disrupting the electronic symphony that empowered their foe.

The confrontation was a tapestry woven with threads of intellect and willpower, each coalition member playing their part in a desperate gambit for redemption. For in this encounter, it was not merely a tyrant they faced, but the embodiment of every fear, every loss they had suffered.

And as the struggle unfolded, the chamber seemed to shrink, the walls closing in with the weight of history bearing down upon them. Yet within the oppressive atmosphere, there flickered a spark of something greater — a chance for atonement, for the mending of a fractured world.

Synthetic Oppressor's synthetic body twitched and contorted, his mechanical components straining against the assault on his system. His voice, once laden with confidence, now sputtered with static as the battle reached its crescendo.

"Your efforts are futile," he spat, but the uncertainty beneath his words betrayed him.

"Perhaps," Evelyn replied, her fingers deftly working her instruments. "But we must try, for the sake of all that is still good in this universe."

And so, they fought on, their every action a declaration that even in the face of overwhelming darkness, hope would always find a way.

...

Outside the chamber of confrontation, Lieutenant Isabella crouched behind a bulkhead, her pulse rifle's barrel still warm from recent discharge. Her eyes scanned the labyrinthine corridors of the Kridrax command ship, a maze of shadows and steel designed to disorient and entrap. The dim lighting cast an eerie glow upon her determined face as she listened for the approach of enemy footsteps.

Beside her, Dr. Weller loaded a fresh energy cartridge into his sidearm, the soft click barely audible over the distant hum of the ship's engines. His brow furrowed in concentration; every movement was methodical, betraying years of experience in the field, years of losses he yearned to avenge.

"Here they come," Dr. Chen whispered, her voice a ghostly murmur that seemed to blend with the cold air circulating through the vessel. She peered through a crack in the wall, her enhanced vision piercing the gloom.

A horde of Kridrax guards rounded the corner, their chitinous armor reflecting the sparse light like a swarm of sinister beetles. Without hesitation, the coalition members sprang into action, their orchestrated defense a dance of desperation and precision. Blaster bolts crisscrossed the corridor, creating a cacophony of sizzling energy and scorched metal.

Isabella's shots were deliberate, each one finding its mark with lethal efficiency. The guards fell one by one, their alien cries echoing through the hallways — a testament to the coalition's unwavering resolve.

Within the chamber, Captain Hawking's voice rose above the fray, a clear note of triumph cutting through the tension. "Now, Montgomery!" he commanded, his tone laced with the weight of countless battles fought and the slim hope of victory within reach.

Dr. Montgomery, her hands steady despite the chaos, initiated the final sequence on her device. An arcane energy pulsed from the mechanism, intertwining with the electronic web that tethered Synthetic Oppressor's consciousness to his formidable frame.

A hush descended upon the room as the Reborn Führer's form began to convulse. His synthetic muscles twitched erratically, his red eyes flickering with uncertainty. The aura of malevolence that once permeated the space waned, giving way to an oppressive silence that hung heavy like a shroud.

"Impossible..." the synthetic dictator gasped, his mechanized voice fracturing into static. His limbs flailed, seeking purchase on a reality that was rapidly unraveling.

The coalition watched, transfixed, as the man who had once held the world in thrall stumbled. In that moment, as the tyrant's control slipped away, they all felt the gravity of what they were about to achieve. Years of torment, decades of fear — all converging into this singular instant of redemption.

And then, with a sound not unlike the breaking of chains long bound, Oppressor's consciousness severed from the grotesque vessel that housed it. The synthetic body slumped forward, the glow in its eyes extinguishing like dying stars, leaving only the hollow shell of the monster it once animated.

In the aftermath, the echo of battle faded into a somber stillness. The team members exchanged glances, each face etched with the scars of the past, yet illuminated by a fragile hope for the future. They had accomplished the unthinkable, but the road ahead remained fraught with peril. For now, though, there was a brief respite, a fleeting chance to grasp at the threads of peace so cruelly snatched from them before.

This battle was won, but the war — their war — was far from over.

…

Captain Hawking's boots pounded against the metallic flooring, the cacophony of his team's retreat echoing through the labyrinthine corridors of the Kridrax command ship. Overhead, emergency sirens wailed — a discordant symphony to the chaos that had erupted within the once-impenetrable fortress. The sharp scent of ionized air and the electric tang of scorched circuitry hung heavy around them as they navigated the maze.

"Move, move!" Hawking's voice was a gruff mantra, urging his team onward, his gaze darting to the rear where shadows danced with the silhouettes of pursuing Kridrax forces. Each member of his team carried the weight of history on their shoulders, a collective burden that lent urgency to their flight.

They ducked into a narrow access tunnel, the walls closing in like the jaws of some great beast. Lieutenant Isabella, ever the skilled pilot, led the way, her intuition for escape routes as keen as her piloting prowess. Behind them, the clamor of Kridrax boots grew louder, a relentless tide of adversaries spurred by desperation and rage.

A burst of plasma fire singed the tunnel wall near Dr. Montgomery's head, leaving a charred black mark as a grim reminder of their mortality. The doctor flinched but maintained pace, clutching the data-pad containing the crucial intelligence they had risked everything to acquire.

"Covering fire!" Zylar Threx commanded, his alien physiology allowing him a fluidity of movement that seemed almost supernatural. He spun, discharging his weapon in controlled bursts, each shot finding its mark. His knowledge of the ship had been indispensable, yet now it was his combat prowess that bought them precious seconds.

The team emerged from the tunnel's mouth, spilling out onto the docking bay where their stealth craft awaited. The vast expanse was awash with red emergency light, throwing monstrous shadows across the faces of the coalition members as they surged towards salvation.

"Secure the hatch!" Captain Hawking bellowed over the din as they piled into the spacecraft. Bolts of energy ricocheted off the hull, a metallic rainstorm heralding their departure.

Lieutenant Isabella slid into the pilot's seat, her fingers dancing across the console with practiced ease. Engines roared to life, a feral growl that cut through the tumult. The craft shuddered, lurching forward as she deftly maneuvered them away from the grip of the Kridrax armada.

Inside the cramped confines of the vessel, the team caught their breath, the adrenaline of battle slowly ebbing from their veins. They exchanged silent nods, acknowledging the enormity of what had transpired—each nod a quiet testament to their undying resolve.

"Chart a course. Anywhere but here," Hawking said, his eyes meeting those of his comrades. In the dim glow of the cockpit, their faces were etched with fatigue and the ghosts of battles past.

"Copy that, Captain." Isabella's voice was steady, a rock amidst the stormy seas of uncertainty.

As the spacecraft slipped into the void of space, a somber realization settled upon them all: though they had struck a decisive blow this day, their journey was far from its end. The specter of war lingered, a shadow stretching across the stars. And so they ventured forth, into the inky blackness, their mission accomplished but their spirits tempered by the knowledge that redemption was still a distant star, flickering on the horizon of a future they would shape with blood, sweat, and tears.

Chapter 12

Flashbacks

Zylar Threx stood alone, an ethereal silhouette against the stark backdrop of devastation. The dim light of a dying star cast an otherworldly gleam on their iridescent scales, creating a melancholic tapestry that flickered with each subtle movement. The once verdant landscapes that had sprawled beneath this cliff were now nothing more than charred memories and ghostly echoes of a vibrant past.

Their elongated limbs, slender and almost fragile in appearance, curled into fists as Zylar's gaze swept over the ruins of their home planet. It was as if the very air mourned, carrying whispers of lives extinguished and dreams turned to dust. Yet, amid the sorrowful panorama, Zylar's deep-set eyes, glowing faintly with inner light, betrayed not just loss but also the embers of defiance.

As they lingered on that desolate precipice, the present seemed to dissolve, giving way to the luminous thread of memory. It was a gentler time, wrapped in the soft gauze of nostalgia. Their minds' eye painted the world anew, resurrecting the lush forests that once whispered ancient secrets through their rustling leaves. Verdant canopies stretched towards the heavens, entwining with the vibrant hues of the sky in a dance as old as time itself.

The cities, resplendent with life and ingenuity, pulsed with the harmonious rhythm of a civilization at its zenith. Spiraling towers glistened under the kiss of the sun, while the laughter of children wove through bustling marketplaces. Artisans displayed their crafts, the fruits of a society where creativity and technology blossomed in symbiotic splendor.

In these streets walked beings of light and color, their scales reflecting the spectrum of a world unmarred by shadow. Zylar, among them, moved with a grace that belied the warrior they would become — a peaceful denizen in a realm where harmony resonated from every stone and stream.

A fleeting smile touched Zylar's lips, a ghost of warmth in the coldness that now enveloped them. They closed their eyes, allowing the echo of what once was to fill the hollow spaces within. For a moment, the scent of rain-soaked earth and the vibrancy of untamed wilderness embraced them, a tender reprieve from the relentless grip of reality.

But as all things do, the vision faded, slipping like grains of sand through the desperate clasp of remembrance. Zylar opened their eyes, the starkness of the present wrapping around them once more — a shroud that no amount of yearning could dispel. Here they stood, The Harbinger, upon the precipice of their shattered world and the brink of an unwavering resolve.

They turned away from the cliff, the shimmer of their scales dimming as the starlight waned. A silent vow hung in the air, a promise etched into the very marrow of their being. Zylar Threx would not let the past's glory be forgotten, nor would they rest until those responsible for its ruination faced the wrath of one who had lost everything — yet found purpose in the ashes.

...

Zylar Threx stood motionless, their gaze fixed on the horizon where twin suns dipped below the lush treetops of Yaloria, casting long shadows over the tranquil city of Caelum. Here, nestled among the whispering leaves and the gentle hum of bioluminescent flora, their people thrived in a seamless marriage of nature and technology. The air buzzed with the soft glow of energy fields protecting the verdant orchards, while the rivers sparkled, purified by nanites that danced like fireflies at dusk.

In the city's heart, holographic archives towered skyward, preserving millennia of knowledge within their shimmering walls. Children laughed as they chased each other through the parks, their feet barely skimming the grass thanks to anti-gravitational soles. Yet, with all their advancements, Zylar's people never forgot the heartbeat of their world—the sacred groves where every birth was celebrated, and the ancient stones that murmured stories older than time.

"Zylar," a voice called—a mere whisper riding the breeze. They turned to see an elder, draped in robes of woven light, offering a smile that held the wisdom of the stars. "The council awaits your insight on the harmonic convergence."

"Thank you, Elder Jhara," Zylar replied, their voice a melodic echo of the land itself. "I will join them shortly."

As Zylar made their way through the cobbled streets of Caelum, the serenity of the evening was palpable. It wrapped around them like a cloak woven from the very essence of peace—a peace that had cradled their civilization for eons.

Without warning, the skies ruptured. A cacophony of alien engines tore through the quietude, shattering it into a thousand pieces. Colossal ships, black as the void between stars, descended like raptors upon prey. The Kridrax invasion had begun.

Screams replaced laughter. The once-gentle lights of the city flickered and died as electromagnetic pulses ravaged the intricate circuits beneath. Zylar's scales flashed with an urgent iridescence, reflecting the chaos erupting around them. Elders and children alike scrambled for cover under the relentless barrage of laser fire and thunderous explosions.

"Harbinger!" cried a voice amidst the turmoil—a title not yet earned but now thrust upon Zylar like a cruel joke. Panic-stricken faces turned to them, seeking guidance, hope— anything to cling to in the face of annihilation.

"Take shelter in the groves!" Zylar commanded, their voice rising above the din. It was a desperate plan, one born of instinct rather than reason, but the natural barriers might offer some respite from the onslaught.

As Zylar ushered the last of the younglings into the protective embrace of the sacred trees, a searing pain lanced through their body—a direct hit. They stumbled, the world tilting dangerously. Through blurring vision, they witnessed the desecration of their beloved planet, felt the agony of its core, and heard the cries of its people.

"Rise, Harbinger," whispered the wind—a ghostly incantation imbued with prophecy and sorrow.

And rise they did, for the first time feeling the weight of a destiny that would lead them across the cosmos, driven by memories of a paradise lost and a fierce determination to reclaim it. But in this moment, as darkness clawed at the edges of their consciousness, Zylar Threx could only watch helplessly as their world burned.

…

Zylar Threx stood upon the desolate cliff, their gaze sweeping over the remnants of a civilization that once thrived. The horizon, now choked with the smoldering remains of vibrant metropolises, lay silent save for the occasional collapse of structures succumbing to their wounds. Where lush forests had danced in the breath of gentle winds, only charred skeletons of trees remained, stretching their blackened limbs towards an uncaring sky.

Beneath Zylar's feet, the ground was littered with the dust of dreams and the echoes of laughter that would never resonate again. Their iridescent scales, usually shimmering with life, reflected back a world drained of color and hope. Each shard of ruin, each mote of destruction, bore witness to the Kridrax's relentless savagery.

A solitary figure amidst the devastation, Zylar closed their eyes against the sharp sting of ash-laden winds, inhaling the acrid scent of their incinerated heritage. They could almost hear the distant melody of the Aethersong — the sacred symphony of their people — now forever silenced. The Kridrax had not only razed their homes but had extinguished the very soul of their culture.

The grief that clawed at Zylar's chest was as real as the twisted metal and fractured stone that surrounded them. Memories of laughter and learning in the Grand Lyceum twisted like a knife in their heart, each happy recollection a stark contrast to the current hellscape. The Kridrax had stripped away everything: family, friends, the future they had all envisioned.

"Forgive me," Zylar murmured to the silent ghosts of their people, "for I could not shield you from the night." Their words were barely audible, swallowed by the vast emptiness that had once pulsed with life. Their home, their history, their identity — all lay in tatters at their feet.

Anger simmered beneath the surface of their sorrow, a dangerous undercurrent threatening to erupt. But it was not the time for rage; this was a moment for mourning. The last vestiges of daylight cast long shadows across the ruins, as if nature itself grieved for the loss.

Zylar knelt, touching a fragment of what was once part of a grand mosaic depicting the harmony between their technology and nature. Now, it was nothing more than a jigsaw of despair. They pocketed the shard, a tangible piece of their past to carry into an uncertain future.

"From ashes, we will rise," they whispered, though there was no one left to hear the vow. It was a promise etched into the marrow of their being — a vow to restore, to rebuild, to remember.

With the weight of their people's memory anchoring them to their mission, Zylar rose to their full height. Their silhouette, a lone defiance against the backdrop of ruination, held firm. The Harbinger would journey through the stars, carrying the tale of a paradise lost, fueled by the pain of unfathomable loss and the fierce determination to seek retribution for the fallen.

...

Zylar Threx shed the cloak of their serene existence like a skin grown too tight, too constricting for the being they were becoming. In the crucible of loss and despair, where once had thrived the harmonious pulse of their world, now beat the heart of a warrior forged in sorrow's flame. The transformation was not merely an emotional metamorphosis; it was a physical one as well. Their scales, reflecting the dim light with newfound purpose, hardened in resolve, each one a shimmering testament to the resilience of a shattered people.

Their slender hands, once instruments of creation and caretaking, now clutched at the hilt of a weapon that hummed with a silent promise of vengeance. The very air around Zylar seemed to quiver with the power of their fury, a silent symphony of retribution that resonated through the cosmos. They had been a guardian of life, a nurturer of their planet's bounty, but the Kridrax had taken that from them, leaving only the searing desire to balance the scales.

With each planetfall on their journey across the stars, Zylar's quest became a pilgrimage through the wreckage of civilizations. Ruined worlds spun their tales of woe as remnants of life clung to the shadows of obliterated dreams. On planets once teeming with diversity and culture, Zylar walked among the echoes of societies broken by the same merciless hand that had torn their own world asunder.

From the crystalline spires of Echolynx, now fractured prisms on a barren landscape, to the subterranean havens of Cavora, collapsed into suffocating graves, Zylar bore witness. With every encounter, the Harbinger gleaned knowledge from survivors and ruins alike — secrets of the Kridrax's might and the twisted vision of Synthetic Oppressor, who sought to sculpt the universe in the image of a long-dead tyranny.

"Your pain is mine," they would murmur to the lingering spirits of these fallen realms, their haunting voice a balm to the unseen wounds of a cosmos grieving. "Your memories will not drift into the void unaccompanied."

It was on the desecrated soils of these worlds that Zylar honed their understanding of the enemy, learning tactics and weaknesses, mapping the web of their dominion. Each revelation steeled their resolve further, molding them into the harbinger of hope they had vowed to become — a beacon for those still standing against the encroaching dark.

As Zylar traversed the expanse between stars, they carried with them the weight of countless losses, yet it did not bow their frame. Instead, it served as the fire that fueled their journey, igniting within them a blaze that no void could extinguish. This quest, born from the ashes of their home, had transcended the personal, shaping Zylar into an avatar of retribution, one whose name whispered through the galaxy both as a warning and a promise: The Harbinger had come, and with them, the dawn of reckoning for the Kridrax and their Reborn Führer.

…

Zylar Threx stood motionless, the precipice beneath their feet crumbling slightly, a silent testament to the fragility of existence. The desolate cliff, once veiled in verdant majesty, now lay barren, its soul seared by the cruelty of invasion. A bitter wind caressed Zylar's iridescent scales, each one shimmering with an ethereal glow that belied the ruin around them. In the spectral dimness, they appeared as a phantom, an echo of both loss and unyielding resolve.

"Vengeance is not a path, but a vast, uncharted wilderness," Zylar mused, their voice barely more than a whisper against the howling gales of their devastated world. "And yet, within its thorns lies the road to deliverance."

The memory of their planet's former splendor haunted them — a ghostly mirage flickering at the edge of perception. But it was the stark reality of destruction that sharpened the edge of their determination. Their mission was clear: to end the tyrannical reign of the Kridrax and their synthetic abomination, Oppressor. It was more than a quest for retribution; it was a crusade to preserve the future from the agony of the past.

"Each star snuffed out by your malice shall be rekindled by my defiance," they vowed to the uncaring void, fists clenching with an intensity that matched the fervor of their spirit. "I am the harbinger of your nemesis, the echo of those you have silenced." Zylar's journey across the cosmos had been a pilgrimage through nightmares, each encounter with ravaged civilizations further cementing their role as the bearers of a grim legacy. They had seen worlds torn asunder, lives extinguished like candles in a tempest, and through these tragedies, their purpose had crystallized into something diamond-hard and unbreakable.

"No more," they breathed, the words emerging as a solemn oath. The silence that followed seemed to hang in the air, heavy with the gravity of their pledge. "By the memories of my people, no more shall the shadow of your oppression stretch across the canvas of this universe."

Their inner turmoil was a tempest, raging silently within the confines of their mind. Yet outwardly, Zylar remained a beacon of stoic resolve. The weight of witnessing countless tragedies had forged them into an instrument of justice, tempered in the fires of anguish and cooled in the icy resolve of their quest for redemption.

"Your reign ends with me," Zylar declared, their haunting dialogue resonating with the power of untold sorrows and the unshakable duty they bore. There was no turning back, no hesitation in their step as they turned away from the ruins of their home, their gaze set upon the stars that held their adversary's fate.

In the stillness of the devastated landscape, Zylar's departure seemed almost a sacred ritual, a solitary figure moving through the darkness, carrying with them the light of hope — a light that would either illuminate a new dawn or be extinguished forever in the final confrontation to come.

...

Zylar Threx, the Harbinger, stood motionless on the cliff's edge, their gaze piercing through the twilight mists that curled around the jagged remnants of a once magnificent spire. The sight unleashed a flood of memories, rivers of recollection flowing deep and turbulent as the ravaged valleys below. Their home planet, its very essence woven into the fabric of their being, lay silent — a testament to the voracious appetite of the Kridrax.

Each shattered edifice whispered tales of a different time, echoes of laughter and discourse now suffocated beneath layers of ash and despair. Zylar clenched their fists, iridescent scales catching the frail light, casting spectral patterns upon the broken ground. A somber melody of windswept ruins played against their heightened senses, conjuring the ghostly presence of those who had perished.

"Your cries shall not go unheeded," Zylar murmured, the words scarcely more than a breath against the howling silence. Their connection to this planet was an unbreakable bond, rooted in shared history and nurtured by love and loss. It fueled their resolve, each memory a star igniting the dark expanse of grief within them.

With every step taken from the precipice, Zylar's purpose grew clearer, the weight of their people's memory a sacred charge upon their shoulders. They could feel the very pulse of the planet, its sorrow and its plea for vengeance merging with their own heart's rhythm. This desolation would not be the end of their story; it would be the catalyst for retribution.

As night descended, blanketing the world in shadow, Zylar embraced the darkness like an old comrade. It was here, amongst the whispers of the past, that they found clarity. The path forward was etched in the stars, written in the language of cosmic destiny. The role of Harbinger was not just a title — it was a mantle forged from the very core of their being.

"From ruin, we rise," Zylar vowed to the infinite heavens, each word resonating with the power of ancient prophecies. "Through me, our voice will thunder across the galaxies, and the Kridrax shall know fear. For I am the harbinger of their doom."

The ruins seemed to stir at the proclamation, as if lending their silent approval to the pledge of their avenger. Zylar's silhouette merged with the encroaching night, a specter of determination striding forth to confront an evil that had spread its tendrils too far, for too long.

The saga of Zylar Threx, the beacon of lost worlds, was far from over. Ahead lay the great expanse, fraught with peril and uncertainty. Yet within the Harbinger's resolute heart, a single truth blazed brighter than any star: redemption would come, and with it, justice for all who had fallen under the shadow of Oppressor and the Kridrax.

Chapter 13

Setback

The first tremor of impact shuddered through the hidden base, a harbinger of doom that rippled across metal walls and through the hearts of the coalition members within. Alarm klaxons wailed their piercing cry as the Kridrax ships descended like harbingers of chaos, their angular hulls cutting through the smog-choked skies of Jannix IV. A barrage of energy pulses rained down, each strike a thunderous note in the symphony of destruction.

Sergeant Mia Alvarez's boots pounded on the grated floor, her strides measured amidst the anarchy. The cacophony of battle was a language she knew all too well; it spoke of urgency, loss, and the razor-thin line between life and death. She barked orders, her voice slicing through the din like a blade, "Delta team, form up! Defensive positions!"

Her gaze locked onto the descending enemy crafts, their dark silhouettes blotting out the stars from which they came. With practiced hands, Alvarez hoisted a plasma rifle, its design foreign but its purpose familiar. Beside her, Lieutenant Isabella mirrored the motion, her scar a pale streak against the grim determination etched into her features.

"Focus on the dropships!" Isabella commanded, her voice calm yet carrying the weight of impending peril. Her finger caressed the trigger, sending a volley of bright bolts skyward to challenge the invaders. Around them, soldiers scrambled to man the turrets and anti-aircraft emplacements, mustering a storm of resistance against the onslaught.

Alvarez and Isabella's movements were a dance of discipline and defiance, each step and shot an extension of their will to survive, to protect what was theirs. They ducked behind a shattered barricade as a shell exploded nearby, showering sparks and debris. Alvarez's eyes, fierce pools of resilience, never left the battlefield, even as the air thickened with the stench of burning circuitry and the cries of the wounded.

"Isabella, take point on the eastern flank," Alvarez instructed, reloading with a swift snap of her wrist. "I'll cover the breach."

"Copy that, Sergeant," Isabella replied, her tone resolute. She sprinted toward the designated area, her figure a blur of tactical precision. There, the Kridrax forces had begun to touch ground, their grotesque armor glinting with malice.

"Push them back!" Alvarez roared, rallying her troops. Her heart pounded in her chest, an echo of the unending gunfire. As she unleashed another round of concentrated fire, the memory of fallen comrades spurred her resolve. This base, a bastion of hope in the war-ravaged expanse, would not fall easily.

Amidst the turmoil, a fragile thread of unity bound the coalition fighters together. Their shared struggle against the Kridrax menace transcended origins and past grievances; now, they fought as one. Alvarez felt that bond tighten with every passing second, a silent pact sealed in the crucible of conflict.

The mysterious enemy had come with overwhelming force, but the coalition's spirit remained unbroken. In the shadow of adversity, heroes like Alvarez and Isabella rose to meet the tide of war head-on, their courage an unwavering flame against the encroaching darkness.

...

The shriek of tearing metal thundered through the hidden base, a cacophonous prelude to calamity. In the midst of chaos, Dr. Markus Weller and Dr. Lily Chen huddled behind an overturned desk, their eyes wide with terror as Kridrax invaders swarmed into the research lab. The air was thick with acrid smoke and the sharp scent of ozone, punctuated by the whine of energy weapons discharging their deadly volleys.

"Markus, we need to — " Dr. Chen's urgent whisper shattered as a shadow loomed over them, grotesque in its armored bulk. A Kridrax soldier, its visage obscured behind a helmet of darkened glass and twisted metal, reached out with hands that seemed more like claws. With brutal efficiency, it seized them both, pulling them from their scant cover.

Their cries were swallowed by the din of battle, their faces etched with a despair so profound it resonated through the very walls of the embattled stronghold. Dr. Weller's glasses slipped from his face, skittering across the floor, as he struggled futilely against the iron grip encircling his wrist. Dr. Chen, her hair whipping about her as she thrashed in the enemy's grasp, caught a fleeting glimpse of salvation beyond reach.

"Let us go! We're not soldiers!" Dr. Weller's voice cracked, the plea lost amidst the roar of conflict.

In the command center, Dr. Evelyn Montgomery watched the capture unfold on a flickering monitor, her heart clenching at the sight of her colleagues' helpless forms being dragged away. Her green eyes, hard as emerald, reflected the screen's glow. Beside her, Captain Lucas "Hawk" Hawking stood immovable, a stoic sentinel surveying the unfolding disaster.

"Montgomery," Hawk said, his voice low and even, the calm before a storm, "we need a plan, and fast."

Evelyn nodded, her jaw clenched. "We'll get them back," she vowed, the words springing not from hope but from an unyielding edict of her will.

"Coordinate with Alvarez and Isabella," Hawk commanded, his gaze already dissecting the battlefield for weaknesses. "We'll need a distraction. Something to give us an edge."

"Understood." Evelyn turned away, her fingers dancing across the keyboard with practiced urgency. She dispatched orders with precision, her mind racing ahead to anticipate every variable. Here, in the eye of the tempest, her resolve became an anchor, her intellect a blade wield to carve a path to redemption.

"Prepare the extraction team," Hawk ordered, directing his attention to a cluster of soldiers. His scars seemed to tighten with each word, a grim testament to battles past. "This isn't just a rescue; it's a statement. We don't leave our own behind."
As Hawk and Evelyn orchestrated their counterstrike, the weight of leadership bore down upon them—a mantle woven from duty, sacrifice, and the silent promise to reclaim what had been lost. Their strategy took shape like a sculpture emerging from stone, each decision chipping away at despair, revealing the glint of hope beneath.

...

In the dimly lit war room, the air hung thick with silent dread. The screens flickering with chaotic feeds were the only sources of illumination, casting an eerie dance of shadows across Evelyn's disheveled appearance. She stood motionless, her green eyes locked on the images of Dr. Weller and Dr. Chen being dragged away by Kridrax soldiers. The sight gnawed at her insides—a corrosive mix of frustration and fear. Her fingers unconsciously fidgeted with her pendant, each twist echoing the tightening spiral of her thoughts.

She whispered a curse, the words barely escaping her lips. They resonated through the charged silence, a testament to the collective anxiety suffusing the space.

Captain Hawking, standing beside her, bore his own signs of distress. His jaw was set in a hard line, and his hands clenched involuntarily, releasing slowly as if grasping at slivers of control amidst the chaos. "We underestimated them," he admitted, the truth a bitter pill. "But we will adapt."

Evelyn felt the weight of their captured colleagues' fates pressing against her chest. Guilt clawed at her — had her caution slowed their response? Had her reluctance to fully trust colored their strategy with hesitance? The questions haunted the edges of her mind, specters of doubt that threatened to consume her resolve.

"Resilience," she murmured, the word a lifeline to cling to. "That's what defines us, isn't it?"

"Always has been," Hawk replied, his gaze never wavering from the screens. "We'll find a way."

Meanwhile, within the cold confines of a Kridrax cell, Dr. Weller's mind raced. His glasses askew, he eyed the alien technology lining the walls, a spark of defiance igniting within him. Beside him, Dr. Chen's fingers moved subtly, tracing patterns on the floor — patterns that to any Kridrax observer would seem random, but to any coalition member spelled out a binary sequence.

"Stay focused," Markus whispered to his colleague, his voice a low hum designed to avoid detection. "Remember the algorithms we discussed. We can disrupt their systems from the inside."

Dr. Chen nodded imperceptibly, her eyes meeting Markus's in silent agreement. Together, they began the mental gymnastics required to manipulate the Kridrax tech without alerting their captors — their intellects their only weapons in this battle of wits.

Back at the base, Evelyn allowed herself a momentary breath, a respite amidst the storm. She knew their adversaries well enough to recognize the tenacity of their captive team members. Markus and Chen would hold on, buying them precious time. And she would not waste it.

"Let's gather our assets," she said, turning to face the remaining members of her team. "Every piece of intel, every shred of tech — we're going to need all of it." Her voice had taken on a steely quality, fortifying her words with the strength of her conviction.

"Time is a luxury we don't have," Hawk added, his blue eyes scanning the faces of their allies. "But we have skill, knowledge, and a reason to fight. That gives us an edge."

In the quiet corners of their minds, the team held onto hope like a fragile flame in the encroaching darkness. The captured scientists, with their whispers and codes, had ignited a signal fire. Now, it was up to Evelyn, Hawk, and their coalition to fan the flames into a roaring blaze — one capable of burning through the clutches of the Kridrax and bringing their people home.

...

In the dimly lit command room, a holographic blueprint of the Kridrax stronghold hovered like a ghost above the central table. Around it, the coalition's remaining members gathered, their faces grim masks of determination. Evelyn's eyes flickered over the intricate layout, her green gaze sharp as she dissected every corridor and chamber.

"Here," she pointed at a narrow service entrance, "we could slip in undetected." Her voice was taut, the clipped tones of a woman who had seen too many plans crumble to dust.

"Too risky," grunted Hawk, his broad shoulders tense. "One misstep, we're sitting ducks." He traced an alternate route, his finger hovering over the main gates. "We hit them hard and fast here, create a diversion."

"Diversion?" Mia interjected, her words edged with skepticism. "That's a full frontal assault on enemy territory. We'd be exposed."

"Sometimes the direct approach is the least expected," Hawk countered, meeting Mia's gaze squarely. The air thrummed with unspoken tension.

"Your strategy assumes they won't anticipate brute force," Evelyn retorted. "We need subtlety, not bravado."

"Subtlety hasn't saved Weller and Chen," Hawk shot back. General O'Neill's gravelly voice cut through the dispute. "Enough!" he commanded. "We don't have the luxury of debate. Every option carries weight, carries blood." Silence fell like a shroud, the weight of his words pressing down upon them all.

"Both approaches have merit," Markus offered quietly. "Perhaps... a combination? A feint, followed by infiltration?" His thin frame seemed to shrink even as he spoke, yet his suggestion hung in the air, ripe with potential.

Evelyn and Hawk exchanged a glance, the previous conflict suspended in the face of innovation. Mia nodded slowly, her expression contemplative.

"Could work," Mia conceded. "Hit them hard enough to draw attention, then sneak in while they're distracted."

"Risky," murmured O'Neill, but his gray eyes were calculating, already considering the logistics. "It'll require precise timing. And sacrifice."

"Everything worthwhile does," Hawk said, a rare softness touching his tone. He looked around the room, meeting the eyes of each team member. "We all know what's at stake."

"Then it's settled," Evelyn declared. "We prepare for both scenarios. We keep our tactics as fluid as the shadows we'll be using for cover."

"Fluid as shadows," echoed Markus, almost to himself, as if the words were a mantra to steady his racing thoughts.

The mysterious air of the room thickened as the team delved into preparation, each member contributing their piece of the puzzle. They spoke in low tones, their dialogue sparse but laden with meaning, each word carefully chosen and each plan meticulously detailed.

As the hours stretched on, the slow pacing of their planning was punctuated by bursts of action—simulations run, weapons checked, contingencies debated. The past loomed over them, a silent specter whispering of failure, yet also of redemption. Each knew the price of war, the sacrifices etched into their very bones.

"Remember why we fight," Hawk said, his voice barely above a whisper as they wrapped up the session. "For our colleagues, for humanity, for a future where the Kridrax no longer cast their shadow over us."

"Let's bring them home," Evelyn added, her steely resolve a beacon in the encroaching darkness.

"Bring them home," the others echoed, unity forged in the crucible of impending danger. With a final nod, they dispersed, the ghostly blueprint fading away, leaving only the echo of their determination hanging in the air.

…

Evelyn Montgomery's fingers danced with deft certainty over the complex array of tools spread before her on the weathered workbench. Every instrument had its purpose, from the sleek, energy-dampening grenades to the slender hacking devices destined to whisper through Kridrax security like shadows slipping under a door. Her team gathered around her, their eyes reflecting the dim glow of holographic displays and the sharp glint of weaponry.

"Remember, these aren't just machines," she reminded them, her voice echoing softly in the vast emptiness of the prep room. "They're lifelines."

Hawk paced the perimeter, his boots thudding against metal grating. His hands moved over the combat gear with practiced ease, checking and rechecking each strap, each buckle. There was a rhythm to his movements, a ritualistic preparation for battle that steadied the pulse of the room.

"Stealth is our ally," Hawk murmured, his gaze meeting Evelyn's. "We move like whispers and strike like fate."

Mia Alvarez stood apart, her figure a study in control as she flowed through a series of combat drills. Each movement was precise, a silent promise of violence honed to perfection. Her breathing was even, a counterpoint to the thunder of her fists against the training pads.

"Timing is everything," she breathed out with each strike, the words punctuated by the muffled impact of glove on target.

Zylar Threx, their unlikely ally, hovered near a console, their scales catching the light in mesmerizing patterns. They interfaced with the alien technology, their fingers trailing an arcane script only they could comprehend. The data streams flickered across their features, casting ethereal reflections of a world lost to the cruelty of the Kridrax.

"Knowledge is our shield," Zylar intoned, their voice resonant within the chamber. "Ignorance, our truest foe."

The hours waned, slipping away into the urgency of the night. Equipment was packed with surgical care into anti-gravity containers, the silence punctuated by the soft clicks of locks and seals. Shadows grew longer, and the air thickened with a tension that whispered of the dangers ahead.

As night cloaked the sky in obsidian folds, the team set out, their movements a symphony of purposeful silence. They traversed the jagged landscape, weaving between craggy rocks and stunted vegetation that clung to life in the harsh environment. The stronghold loomed ahead, a monolith of steel and malice that rose from the barren ground like a prehistoric beast.

"Keep your comms open, but chatter to a minimum," Hawk's voice cut through the static of the earpieces, a low command wrapped in calm. "Eyes sharp, everyone."

Evelyn's heart hammered in her chest, a drumbeat keeping time with their cautious advance. She felt the weight of her pendant against her skin, a cool anchor amidst the heat of adrenaline. With each step closer to the stronghold, memories of past battles surged like tides against the walls of her resolve.

"Steady," Mia whispered, her hand signaling a halt as a patrol of Kridrax guards marched obliviously past their concealed position. Their alien forms were silhouetted against the stark lighting of the stronghold's perimeter, oblivious to the predators in their midst.

"Patience," Zylar's voice echoed in their minds, a telepathic thread connecting them beyond the limitations of speech.

In the shadow of the enemy's fortress, the team waited with bated breath, the seconds stretching into eternities. They were specters in the night, unseen yet ever-present, their mission a beacon guiding them through the perilous dark.

"Move," Hawk finally signaled, and they slipped forward once more, the stronghold's walls now within reach, their texture cold and unyielding beneath Evelyn's touch. The way ahead was fraught with uncertainty, every corner a new challenge, every corridor a potential trap.

But they were ready. Ready to reclaim their own, to face whatever lay hidden within the depths of enemy territory. A slow dance of redemption awaited them, each step a note in the haunting melody of their resolve.

Pressed against the metallic hide of the Kridrax domain, the cusp of action upon them, the future unwritten and hearts united by a single, unspoken vow:
Bring them home.

…

Evelyn's heart drummed a frantic rhythm against her ribs as she led the charge through the labyrinthine corridors of the Kridrax stronghold. Shadows clung to the walls like specters, whispering secrets of past incursions that stained the air with a silent tension. Each corner turned was a ballet of precision and peril, the team synchronized in their silent communication, a silent symphony orchestrated by necessity and trust.

The stronghold resisted them at every step, its mechanisms and defenses an alien puzzle demanding solutions under duress. Hawk's hands danced across a control panel with deft movements born of countless simulations, disarming traps with an engineer's intuition. Mia's sharp gaze cut through the dimness, spotting sensors and cameras disguised within the metallic carapace of the structure, guiding them through unseen eyes.

A sudden burst of energy pulsed through the corridor, a warning siren that needed no translation. Kridrax guards materialized from hidden alcoves, their chitinous armor reflecting the harsh light of the base. The team sprang into action, a whirlwind of controlled chaos. Hawk unleashed a barrage of suppressive fire from his plasma rifle, carving a path through the onslaught. Zylar's mind became a weapon as potent as any blade, sowing confusion among the enemy ranks with telepathic assaults that left them reeling.

"Cover!" Evelyn shouted, her voice barely rising above the cacophony of battle. She dove behind a bulkhead, feeling the heat of near-misses scorch the air. Mia rolled to her side, returning fire with a marksman's poise that belied the ferocity of her assault. Together, they were a relentless tide, each member compensating for the other's blind spots, each victory a testament to their unity.

Breathing heavily, the team regrouped once the last of the guards crumpled to the ground, their forms twitching in defeat. They exchanged brief nods, the unspoken language of warriors who had danced on the edge of mortality and returned to tell the tale.

"Almost there," Evelyn whispered, her green eyes scanning the schematic displayed on her wrist-mounted device. A sense of foreboding settled over her as they approached the holding cells; the very air seemed to weigh heavier with each step.

The door to the detention area loomed before them, an insidious barrier mocking their efforts with its silent presence. Hawk set to work immediately, his fingers blurring as he manipulated the lock mechanism. Time slowed, each click and whir echoing through the corridor like the ticking of a doomsday clock.

With a hiss of releasing pressure, the door slid open, revealing the stark interior of the captive chamber. Dr. Weller and Dr. Chen were there, their figures hunched but unbroken amidst the sterile confines. Their eyes met those of their rescuers, a myriad of emotions flitting across their faces — relief, fear, defiance.

"Stay back," a guttural voice commanded, the threat underscored by the sound of weapons powering up. Kridrax guards, previously unseen, emerged from the shadows with their weapons trained on the captives. Evelyn's pulse quickened as she assessed the situation, her mind racing to find an angle, a weakness, anything.

"Everything we've fought for," she murmured, more to herself than anyone else. Her gaze hardened, her resolve steeling within her like a blade tempered in the fires of adversity. "We do this together."

"Always," came the collective reply, a chorus of conviction that filled the space with its resonance.

The standoff stretched taut, a moment frozen in time, a precipice upon which the fate of two worlds teetered. And in that eternity suspended between breaths, the team readied themselves to reclaim what was theirs, to salvage hope from the jaws of despair. They were a phalanx of determination, bound by a shared past and the unwavering belief in a future worth fighting for.

"Let them go," Evelyn demanded, her voice steady despite the storm raging within her. The Kridrax hesitated, the air charged with the potential for violence or salvation.

And then, the decision was made.

...

Evelyn's breath was a whisper in the charged silence, each exhale a ghostly testament to the living tension that enveloped them. The dim light of the stronghold flickered across her companions' faces, casting long shadows that danced with the uncertainty of their fate. Hawk stood beside her, his jaw set, the scars etching his face speaking to battles hard-won and losses deeply felt. Mia's hand hovered near her weapon, a silent promise of swift retribution, while Zylar's luminous gaze bore into the semi-darkness, an alien sentinel poised on the brink of chaos.

"Plan B," Evelyn uttered, her voice barely rising above the hum of the Kridrax machinery that thrummed through the walls like the heartbeat of some slumbering beast.

"Are we certain?" Hawk asked, his tone low, a tempered blade sheathed in resolve.

"Certainty is a luxury," she replied, her eyes never leaving the guards who held Weller and Chen captive. "We adapt, or we fail."

Mia nodded, her expression steely as she relayed quiet instructions to the team, her words weaving them together in a tapestry of silent agreement. They had come too far to falter now, their path woven from the threads of sacrifice and courage, stained with the ink of loss.

Zylar shifted, scales shimmering with an ethereal glow that seemed to swallow the scant light. "The Kridrax underestimate us," they said, their voice a haunting melody that resonated with the weight of galaxies lost and found. "They see not the fire that burns within."

"Then let's ignite it," Hawk whispered, drawing a small device from his pocket. With a deft press, he activated the holographic blueprint of the stronghold. Their escape route highlighted in pulsating red, a beacon amidst the encroaching darkness.

"Time is the serpent that devours its own tail," Zylar intoned, their gaze locked with Evelyn's. "We must strike swiftly."

"Thunderbolt's waiting for our signal," Evelyn said, invoking the General's call sign with a reverence borne of countless engagements under his command. "We give him this one chance."

"Or we give them everything," Mia added, her words a sharpened edge against the looming threat.

"Everything," Hawk echoed, his blue eyes reflecting a glint of something fierce, something undying.

Evelyn took a step forward, her shadow merging with those of her team, a single entity forged from the crucible of shared purpose. She raised her hand, signaling the moment's arrival, the precipice upon which destiny teetered. The air seemed to hold its breath, the very atoms around them vibrating with anticipation.

"Initiate," she said, and the word fell like a stone into the still waters of their resolve, rippling outwards towards an unseen shore.

As the team dispersed, slipping into the labyrinth of corridors, each movement precise and deliberate, Evelyn remained rooted to the spot. Her mind raced with calculations and contingencies, the lives of her colleagues a heavy weight upon her conscience.

"Stay safe," she whispered into the comms, a benediction for the battle to come.

A sudden surge of energy cascaded through the stronghold, the prelude to their daring gambit. The Kridrax guards tensed, their weapons humming with deadly potential, but the prisoners — Weller and Chen — exchanged a glance that spoke volumes of unspoken faith in their rescuers.

And so, with hearts pounding and plans set into motion, the team prepared to launch their rescue operation, the outcome veiled in the mists of uncertainty. Would valor and ingenuity triumph over the cold calculus of the Kridrax? Only time, unforgiving and relentless, would tell.

Chapter 14

Doubts

The room lay steeped in shadows, barely disturbed by the feeble glow of a single console's blinking lights. Dr. Evelyn Montgomery sat across from Captain Lucas "Hawk" Hawking, her silhouette a study in tension against the dim backdrop. Their faces, though half-concealed by darkness, betrayed the toll of sleepless nights and relentless pressure. The slow rhythm of their breathing filled the space, punctuated by the distant hum of the ship's engines—a reminder of the ceaseless march of time.

"Are we deluding ourselves, Lucas?" Evelyn's voice sliced through the stillness, sharp yet tinged with an undertow of despair. Her eyes, those vivid pools of green, sought out Hawk's gaze, searching for an anchor in the sea of uncertainty.

"Thinking what if... it's like staring into the abyss, Eve," Hawk responded, the sturdy timbre of his voice faltering as he leaned forward, elbows resting on his knees. His hands were clasped tightly together, knuckles white—a bastion of strength wavering under invisible siege.

Evelyn's fingers traced the edge of her data tablet, the screen's soft luminescence casting ghostly light upon her disheveled black hair. "The Kridrax... they're not just an enemy. They are the very embodiment of annihilation." She paused, her throat tightening around the words. "And each decision we make seems like... like a step closer to oblivion."

"Every choice carries its shadow, that much is true," Hawk conceded, his jaw set. Yet, within the blue depths of his eyes, something flickered—a spark refusing to be snuffed out by the encroaching gloom.

"Perhaps our strategy was flawed from the start." Evelyn's confession hung between them, laden with the weight of unspoken fears. Her analytical mind, once so clear and decisive, now wavered at the precipice of doubt. "Have we led our people astray? Has our leadership only hastened the end?"

Hawk shifted, the leather of his chair protesting softly under the movement. "You know as well as I do that this isn't about one decision, Eve. It's a tapestry of choices, woven together, each thread reinforcing the next." His tone carried the burden of command—a reminder of countless battles fought and the heavy cost of war.

"Yet, every thread feels like it could unravel at any moment," she whispered, her gaze drifting away, lost in the contemplation of their shared plight.

In the quietude that followed, the echo of their doubts seemed almost palpable, filling the room like a living entity. Hawk watched Evelyn, his comrade-in-arms, grappling with the enormity of their situation. He recognized the tremor in her voice, the hard swallow that betrayed her inner turmoil. It was a mirror to his own soul—reflecting the jagged edges of fear and the haunting specter of defeat.

But even as the shadows pressed in, threatening to choke the last vestiges of hope, neither leader yielded to despair. In their steadfast presence, there remained a glimmer that defied the dark—the unspoken vow to stand against the tide, to fight until their last breath for the survival of humanity.

...

Hawk rose from his seat, the weight of his frame dissipating the gloom that clung to the corners of the dimly lit room. He stepped closer to Evelyn, his shadow merging with hers on the concrete wall — a somber dance of dark silhouettes twining in the uncertain light.

"Dr. Montgomery," he began, the words rumbling from deep within, "I won't pretend I have all the answers. But I do know this: we can't let doubt divide us now. Our strength is in our unity, in the bond we share as defenders of this planet."

Evelyn's eyes flickered towards him, her green irises reflecting a spark of defiance that belied her exhaustion. Hawk's gaze held steady, a silent testament to the unyielding resolve that had earned him the moniker 'Hawk' among those who served under him.

"Remember," he continued, his voice low but firm, "we've faced darkness before. Each time, it was not the might of our arms, but the steadfastness of our spirit that carried us through."

A faint nod, almost imperceptible, acknowledged his words. It was a small gesture, but it held the gravity of a thousand battles — each fought with the tenacity that had become their hallmark.

The makeshift meeting room was a stark contrast to the intimacy of their previous conversation. Desks had been pushed aside to form a crude circle, and chairs were occupied by slump-shouldered figures whose faces were etched with lines of worry and fatigue. The flickering lights overhead cast an otherworldly glow on the assembly, shadows undulating across the walls like specters of doubt come to feast on their fears.

As coalition members gathered, their movements lacked the precise choreography of a well-oiled machine; instead, they betrayed the weariness that seeped into their bones. The air was thick with unspoken thoughts, each breath a silent prayer against the encroaching dread.

Among them, Dr. Markus Weller's thin frame seemed almost to fold in upon itself, his glasses sliding perilously close to the tip of his nose as he pored over the data pad in his trembling hands. Beside him, Dr. Lily Chen sat with her back rigid, the usual luster of her eyes dulled by the reflection of losses too numerous to count.

They did not speak. Words were a luxury they could ill afford when the very fabric of their reality hung by such a precarious thread. Yet in their silence, a chorus of unsung heroes resonated — a symphony of determination and desperation intertwined.

Hawk surveyed the room, the lines of his face carving deeper grooves with each passing second. These were the architects of hope, the last bulwark against a tide of oblivion. And though fear prowled at the edges of their gathering, waiting to pounce at the slightest sign of weakness, there remained a steadfast current beneath the surface — a yearning for redemption that would not be quelled.

...

The dim glow of the console screens cast long shadows across the room, where frustration simmered like a dormant volcano ready to erupt. Dr. Evelyn Montgomery stood silently at the center, her piercing green eyes scanning each face as if searching for an answer that refused to reveal itself.

"Another supply run failed," Dr. Samira Patel's voice cut through the tension, her words falling heavily in the silence. "We can't keep pretending that everything is under control."

"Control?" Markus scoffed, pushing his glasses back up his nose with a shaky finger. "What control? We're losing ground every day, and you know it." His gaze locked with Evelyn's, a storm of accusation brewing behind those lenses.

"Enough!" Lily's sharp command sliced the air, but her voice trembled, betraying her own uncertainties. "Blame won't solve anything. What we need are solutions, not quarrels."

"Easy for you to say," Markus shot back, "when your projects haven't been on the frontline."

Their voices rose, each sentence layered with the unspoken fears that clawed at their minds. They were the brightest minds of their generation, yet doubt gnawed at the foundations of their resolve, threatening to collapse the fragile structure of their unity.

Evelyn felt the weight press upon her shoulders—a burden of leadership she had never asked for, yet could not escape. She stepped forward, her presence commanding silence without a word.

"Listen to yourselves," Evelyn began, her voice weaving through the charged atmosphere with deliberate calm. "This division serves only our enemy. Yes, we are facing a force more formidable than any we have encountered. Yes, the path ahead seems insurmountable. But it is precisely in these moments of darkness that we must find the light within ourselves."

She paused, allowing the gravity of her words to sink into the hearts of her colleagues. The room held its breath, waiting.

"We have all lost something to the Kridrax—friends, family, a sense of security. But if we lose hope, if we lose the bond that unites us, then we surrender to defeat before the battle has even begun."

Her eyes met each of theirs, a silent plea for the understanding and trust that had grown threadbare with time. "We cannot change the past, nor predict the future. But here, now, we have the power to shape the outcome. Together."

"Unity does not mean the absence of conflict," she continued, her tone softening. "It means rising above it, recognizing that our shared purpose is greater than any individual fear or ambition. We are humanity's last chance. And I believe — in spite of everything — that we will prevail. Because we must."

In the stillness that followed, the seeds of redemption took root once again. Evelyn's words, though spoken softly, carried the strength of steel and the promise of dawn after the longest night.

And as they looked to one another, the flicker of solidarity began to chase away the shadows of despair, igniting a flame that would not be easily extinguished.

...

The hush that had settled over the room in the wake of Dr. Montgomery's poignant words was abruptly shattered as Captain Hawking, known to all as Hawk, cleared his throat, commanding attention with the unspoken authority that cloaked him like a mantle. He stood, his towering form casting elongated shadows across the dimly lit space, remnants of battles long past etched into the lines of his face.

"During the siege of Taranis," Hawk began, his voice resonating with the timbre of experience, "we were outnumbered, outgunned, and staring down the barrel of extinction." His piercing blue eyes scanned the sea of weary faces before him. "But we held our ground, fought with every last breath until the tide turned. We survived because we refused to give in to despair."

A murmur rippled through the assembled team, a collective memory of victories won under this man's steadfast command lending weight to his words. The air seemed charged with an electric current, sparking remembrances of strength they had all but forgotten.

"Each one of you," Hawk continued, the muscle in his jaw clenching with fervor, "has faced your own Taranis. Your presence here is proof of your resilience. It's not the absence of fear that defines us; it's how we confront it, together, as one indomitable force."

The conversations that followed erupted like a tempest, voices raised in a cacophony of doubt and frustration. Arguments flared, each member wrestling with their fears aloud, the gravity of their situation fanning the flames of discord.

"We can't just pretend we're not outmatched!" one voice cried out, slicing through the din.

"Every victory in our past has come at a cost. How many more lives must pay the price for our so-called unity?" another countered, the bitterness of loss tainting their words.

"Enough!" Hawk's command cut across the room, silencing the turmoil. His gaze swept over them, unyielding yet not without empathy. "This is not about ignoring the odds stacked against us, nor the sacrifices we've made. It's about believing—despite those odds—that we have something worth fighting for."

In the ensuing calm, a transformation unfolded. Where there was once a gathering frayed by uncertainty, now stood a coalition bound by a shared recognition. The truth of their predicament lay bare before them, a formidable foe indeed — but not an unconquerable one.

"Trust is our greatest weapon," Hawk said, his voice now a low rumble of conviction. "We trust in the skills we've honed, in the strategies we've crafted, and most importantly, in each other."

Slowly, nods of agreement punctuated the stillness, silent vows exchanged beneath the watchful gaze of their leaders. The path ahead was fraught with peril, yes, but they were no strangers to adversity. In their veins coursed the blood of survivors, of warriors who had risen time and again from the ashes of defeat.

As the meeting adjourned, a subtle shift permeated the atmosphere. Doubts lingered, as they always would, but interwoven now with strands of hope, determination, and an unspoken pledge: to stand united in the face of whatever darkness awaited them.

...

The dim glow of the emergency lights painted long shadows on the walls of the command center as Dr. Evelyn Montgomery stood shoulder to shoulder with Captain Lucas "Hawk" Hawking, their reflections in the polished surface of the table a testament to the weight they both carried. The room was drenched in silence, save for the occasional hum of machinery, a reminder of the ceaseless struggle against the Kridrax looming just beyond their fragile stronghold.

"Hope is as vital as oxygen in this fight," Evelyn murmured, her voice barely above a whisper, yet her words cut through the heavy air with surgical precision. "We need a catalyst, something to ignite the fire that's been dampened by fear and loss."

Hawk nodded, his eyes haunted pools reflecting battles past and those yet to come. "We'll give them a narrative, a beacon in this storm," he said, his tone firm despite the flicker of doubt that clouded his gaze. "Stories of our fallen can be the kindling we need."

Together, they wove a tapestry of inspiration, plucking threads from the valor and sacrifices of countless souls who had laid down their lives for humanity's fleeting chance at survival. Their plan emerged, not unlike a phoenix rising from the ashes — an emblem of rebirth amid desolation.

As the coalition members filtered into the makeshift meeting room, an expectant hush fell upon them. Dr. Montgomery ascended to the dais, her stature commanding yet bearing the invisible scars of battle, her eyes bright with the embers of a resurgence.

"Today, I speak not only as your leader but as a fellow sentinel standing watch over our future," she began, her voice carrying across the room, echoing off the metallic surfaces and resonating within each person present. "Our enemy is formidable, but so too is the spirit of those who have fought before us."

She paused, allowing the gravity of her words to settle like dust after a cosmic explosion, each particle a monument to the courageous.

"From the scorched plains of Rigel-7 to the icy trenches of Thetis Prime, our comrades have shown what it means to defy the darkness." Her green eyes locked onto faces in the crowd, each glance an unspoken pact. "Let their bravery remind us that we are not mere survivors; we are the vanguard of hope. They did not falter, nor shall we."

For a moment, the room held its breath, the shared pulse of humanity threading through the stillness. Evelyn's heart beat in tandem with theirs, her resolve unwavering as she drove her point home.

"Redemption lies not in victory alone, but in every act of defiance against oblivion. Our past is laden with ghosts, specters of what could have been — but our redemption... it blooms in the here and now, in our unity, in our refusal to succumb."

A murmur swept through the coalition like wind through autumn leaves, carrying whispers of determination, of lives interwoven by the common thread of their struggle.

"Stand with me, stand with each other, and let us carve a path toward the dawn," she concluded, her final words a clarion call to the hearts of those who would follow her into the abyss.

The mysterious air of the room shifted subtly, a latent energy awakening within the ranks — a collective heartbeat quickening. No grand gestures or thunderous applause marked the moment, only a deep-seated acknowledgment that they were ready to face the unknown, bolstered by the tales of heroism and the promise of redemption whispered in their ears.

...

The air in the training hall vibrated with a subtle current of anticipation. Captain Lucas "Hawk" Hawking stalked between the rows of consoles and holographic displays, his gaze sharp as flint. His team clustered around him, their uniforms a patchwork of insignias from a dozen different worlds, united under one cause.

"Alright, listen up," he began, his voice cutting through the hum of machinery like a knife. "We're about to commence a series of training exercises designed to hone our collective instincts. You'll be paired off — randomly. Expect the unexpected, adapt, and overcome."

His orders echoed off the walls, creating a cadence that mirrored the pulse of their mission. Hawk watched as his team paired off, their expressions a mix of determination and the lingering shadows of doubt. The simulations they were about to undergo would test more than their combat skills; it would challenge the very sinew of their unity.

"Commence simulation Alpha-Three," Hawk's command resonated across the room. Instantly, the area transformed into an alien landscape — an intricate illusion woven by light and sound. The coalition members sprang into action, their movements synchronized but punctuated by bursts of individual brilliance.

As the exercise unfolded, a quiet tension seeped into the gaps where confidence had yet to take root. Hawk observed from his vantage point, noting the slight hesitations, the fleeting glances exchanged — a silent language of uncertainty.

"Remember, you are not alone out there!" Hawk's reminder cut through the cacophony of simulated warfare. His voice, usually a bastion of command, now carried an unspoken message of solidarity.

The training came to a halt as the simulation faded, leaving behind only the raw reality of the dimly lit hall. The team congregated in small clusters, their breathing labored, the adrenaline slowly receding from their veins. It was in these quiet moments that the true battles were fought — the internal skirmishes that no amount of training could dispel.

"I don't know if I can do this when it's for real," murmured a young engineer from Terra Nova, her eyes reflecting a battle-scarred planet she once called home.

"You're not alone in this," replied her companion, a grizzled veteran whose visage bore the tapestry of interstellar conflict. "We've all got ghosts haunting us, doubts nibbling at our courage. But we've got each other—and that counts for something."

Their words were soft, almost lost amidst the gentle thrumming of the ship's heart, but they carried the weight of worlds. One by one, the team members shared their stories—tales of loss and triumph, of narrow escapes and last stands. With each confession, the specter of fear retreated, its grip loosened by the thread of common experience.

"Remember what Dr. Montgomery said," another spoke up, her voice steadier than before. "Our redemption blooms in the here and now. We make our stand together."

The murmur of agreement spread, a ripple of resolve that strengthened the bonds frayed by the Kridrax threat. Hawk remained a silent sentinel among them, his presence a reassuring anchor in the tempest of their doubts.

"Back to positions," he eventually called out, his tone brooking no argument. "Let's run another drill. This time, think like a unit. Act as one."

As the coalition members returned to their stations, the air crackled with a newfound energy. They were more than just an assembly of soldiers and scientists; they were the vanguard of hope, each carrying a spark that, when united, could ignite the fires of resistance against the encroaching darkness.

Captain Hawking watched them, his blue eyes alight with the reflection of their burgeoning spirit. The mysterious dance of light and shadow played across his features, a silent testament to the inner strength they were all beginning to rediscover.

...

Dr. Evelyn Montgomery stood at the forefront of the command deck, her short black hair a stark contrast against the pale glow of the monitors. Even in the dimly lit room, the green flecks in her eyes seemed to emit their own luminescence—a beacon amidst the encroaching gloom of uncertainty that had settled over the coalition.

"Steady," she commanded, her voice clipped yet resonant, echoing through the chamber as the team's fingers flew across consoles, recalibrating and rearming the defenses with precision born from their rigorous drills. The usual pauses where she would meticulously choose her words were absent now; there was no time for deliberation when action was demanded.

Beside Evelyn, Captain Hawking's towering form loomed, his muscular frame radiating a silent authority that bolstered the spirits of those around him. Scars crisscrossed his face like ancient runes telling stories of battles won and struggles overcome—each a testament to resilience.

"Echo formation, now!" Hawk barked, his tone authoritative, his blue eyes scanning the room for any hesitation, any falter in the collective resolve. The immediate shuffle of bodies and the symphony of beeping consoles affirmed his command, each member of the coalition moving with newfound purpose.

It was this dance of shadows and light, this interplay of fear and courage, that bound them together. In the thick air laden with the hum of machinery and the scent of ozone, whispers of the past mingled with the echoes of determination. Redemption, it seemed, was not a distant dream but a reality being forged with every passing second under the leadership of these steadfast souls.

"Look at them," Dr. Montgomery murmured, more to herself than to Hawk. "They're ready."

"Because you showed them they could be," Hawk replied, his gaze never leaving the crew. His words were sparse yet carried the weight of unspoken stories, tales of endurance and survival that had become the lifeblood of their mission.

The training exercises, the simulations — they had all been leading to this moment. This crucible where the fire of unity tempered the steel of their resolve. Dr. Chen's bright brown eyes met Evelyn's across the room, and an imperceptible nod passed between them — an acknowledgment of the gravity of what lay ahead and the silent vow that none would face it alone.

"Let's give 'em hell," Dr. Markus Weller said, pushing his glasses up the bridge of his nose with a resolute motion. His thin frame belied the strength of his conviction, his voice steady as he coordinated the network of defense systems.

"Indeed," Evelyn agreed, a slow smile spreading across her features. She glanced at her companions, at their poised stances and determined expressions, and felt the tide within her shift. Doubt receded, replaced by a surge of confidence that coursed through her veins like liquid fire.

"Prepare for the next wave," she called out, her order slicing through the tension. "We stand united, and we will prevail."

A chorus of affirmations rippled through the room, each voice a note in the anthem of their defiance. Hawk stepped forward, his presence an unyielding pillar amidst the storm of anticipation.

"Remember why we fight," he intoned, the timbre of his voice grounding them all. "For Earth. For humanity. For the future we believe in."

As the coalition members fortified their stations, the energy that pulsed between them was almost palpable. They were no longer disparate individuals but a single entity, a force melded by shared purpose and mutual trust.

The chapter closed with the hum of readiness, a collective breath drawn in anticipation of the battle to come. Hope, once a fragile thing, now thrived in the hearts of the coalition, its roots entwined around the certainty of their bond. Together, they faced the horizon, where the dark maw of the Kridrax invasion awaited, armed with the fiercest weapon of all: an unbreakable spirit.

…

Dr. Montgomery's gaze lingered on the holographic display, the soft glow casting an ethereal light upon her features as she watched the swirling mists of data coalesce into a semblance of order. Her eyes, green embers in the dim room, narrowed with intent as fragments of code danced before her, each sequence a piece of a larger puzzle that had eluded them for too long.

"Could it be?" she murmured, more to herself than to the shadowed figures standing vigilant behind her. The air was thick with expectation, every breath a silent prayer for the breakthrough they so desperately sought.

Captain Hawking, his stance a testament to battles weathered and scars borne, leaned forward. His voice, when he spoke, was a rumble of distant thunder, "What do you see, Evelyn?"

"An anomaly," she replied, her words laced with a cautious excitement that belied the fatigue etched deep into her bones.

"Within the Kridrax's communication network. It's... inconsistent with their known protocols."

The information hovered between them, a specter of possibility. Dr. Markus Weller peered over the rim of his perpetually askew glasses, his intellect piercing the enigma as he joined the conversation. "A flaw in their armor?" he proposed, the scientist within him aflame with curiosity.

"Or a trap," Sergeant Mia Alvarez interjected, the ever-present strategist. Her voice cut through the murk of uncertainty, a steel blade forged in the fires of experience.

Zylar Threx shifted, their form a wraithlike presence at the fringe of the gathering. Their scales shimmered with an otherworldly luminescence, a silent beacon of alien wisdom. "We must tread carefully," Zylar intoned, their voice a haunting melody of cautious hope. "This could be the turning point we have been seeking."

The room fell into a hush, the weight of potential hanging heavy in the air. General O'Neill's steely gaze swept over the assembly, his presence a bastion amidst the storm of doubt. "Then let us seize this chance," he declared, his gravelly voice echoing the resolve that had carried them this far. "Fortune favors the bold."

And so, the decision was made. A plan began to take shape, its contours drawn from the collective strength and brilliance of those who refused to yield. Each member of the coalition knew the risks, yet there was a fire kindling within them, a spark that promised to blaze into an inferno of defiance.

As the team dispersed to their respective posts, the air crackled with a newfound energy. Dr. Montgomery paused, her hand hovering over the console, and cast one last glance at the anomaly that beckoned them toward the unknown. With a steadying breath, she pressed the sequence that would initiate their daring gambit.

"Let's turn the tide," she whispered, her voice a vow to the shadows.

Chapter 15

Reasons to Persevere

Dr. Evelyn Montgomery sat hunched over her makeshift desk, the glow of monitors casting ghostly shadows across the scattered papers that surrounded her. Each screen flickered with images of desolation – cities once vibrant now reduced to smoldering ruins, landscapes cratered and scarred by the relentless Kridrax invasion. Her fingers tapped a staccato rhythm against the cold metal surface, the sound punctuating the silence like distant gunfire.

The air in the cramped office was thick with the weight of unspoken grief, the very walls seemed to whisper of lost lives and the sacrifices too numerous to count. Evelyn's piercing green eyes fixated on a particular image: a young girl clutching a tattered doll amidst the rubble, a still frame of innocence marred by the horrors of war. The sight clawed at her insides, dredging up the question that gnawed at her soul—had all their efforts, all the blood spilled and tears shed, amounted to nothing but ash?

A sudden draft announced the arrival of another weary soul into the room. Captain Lucas "Hawk" Hawking stepped through the doorway, his imposing frame momentarily blocking the dim light from the corridor. His short-cropped brown hair and sharp blue eyes spoke of countless battles, his face etched with lines of exhaustion that even his stoic demeanor couldn't mask.

Without a word, he moved to stand beside her, his gaze following hers to the devastation captured in frozen time before them. Their reflections in the screens were pale specters, bound together by an unspeakable burden. For a long moment, they shared only the heavy air between them, laden with the scent of burnt circuitry and lost hope.

Finally, Hawk let out a breath, as if releasing some of the weight that bowed his shoulders. "Evelyn," he murmured, the use of her first name breaching protocol in a way that acknowledged the intimacy of their shared despair.

"Lucas," she replied, her clipped voice barely above a whisper. It was unusual for her to reciprocate the informality, yet here, surrounded by the echoes of a world gasping for survival, titles held little meaning.

Their eyes met, twin pools of understanding in a sea of uncertainty. In that prolonged gaze, a silent conversation unfolded — a mutual recognition of the doubts that haunted their every decision, the fear that they might be leading their team into the abyss.

But it was more than acknowledgment — it was the forging of an unspoken pact. Their resolve simmered beneath the surface, a defiance against the darkness threatening to consume them. They stood not only as leaders but as pillars for each other, finding a semblance of solace in the knowledge that they were not alone in this dance with despair.

As the silence stretched on, the room seemed to hold its breath, the tension palpable. The past loomed over them, its specter a reminder of what they fought to redeem. Yet beneath the layers of weariness and doubt, a spark of determination endured, fueled by the very memories that pained them.

In this quiet chamber of sorrow, amid the remnants of a world teetering on the brink, Dr. Evelyn Montgomery and Captain Lucas Hawking found a momentary refuge in their shared vigil — a fleeting respite before they would once again face the storm together.

...

Dr. Montgomery led the way, her shoulders squared against the shadows that clung to the walls of the dimly lit meeting room. Captain Hawking followed a step behind, his boots barely whispering across the cold floor. The air tasted of stale determination and lingering fear as they entered the sanctuary of the coalition's last stand.

The room was a tableau of somber reflection. Coalition members sat scattered like islands in an archipelago of loss, their faces etched with the stories of battles fought and comrades mourned. Each one was adrift in their own sea of contemplation, their gazes unfocused, as if peering into the murky depths of what might have been — or what still could be.

A chair scraped faintly as Dr. Montgomery settled into it, her white lab coat a stark contrast against the gloom. Hawk remained standing, his posture a silent sentinel, eyes scanning the collective of weary souls. The magnitude of their shared ordeal hung between them, an unvoiced lament for the world outside these walls — a world scarred by the merciless advance of the Kridrax.

Then, the air shifted subtly, heralding a presence that transcended the ordinary. Zylar Threx, the enigmatic ally from a fallen realm, glided into the chamber. Their entrance was not marked by sound or fanfare, but by a palpable change in the atmosphere — a current of power that stirred the lethargy from every soldier and scientist present.

Zylar's iridescent scales caught the scant light, casting prismatic echoes against the darkness. Deep-set eyes, aglow with otherworldly luminescence, swept over the faces of the gathered coalition, piercing through the veneer of their resolve. When they spoke, the timbre of their voice resonated like a chord struck on some celestial instrument, at once beautiful and disquieting.

"Comrades," Zylar began, the word laced with a gravity that tugged at the soul, "the path we tread is fraught with peril, the outcome uncertain. Yet we must not falter."

Their gaze lingered on Dr. Montgomery, then Captain Hawking, acknowledging the mantle of command they bore. "The Kridrax know only devastation — worlds laid to waste, futures extinguished. Our resistance is the bulwark against this tide of obliteration."

As Zylar paused, a quiet rustle passed through the room, as if their words awakened the dormant spirit of the assembly. Eyes that had been dulled by despair now flickered with embers of purpose, rekindled by the haunting cadence of Zylar's speech.

"Recall what we fight for: not merely survival, but for the dawn of new beginnings. For redemption from the ashes of our past mistakes." Zylar's voice wove through the shadows, binding the team together with threads of hope and conviction. "We are the architects of our fate."

In that moment, the burden of history seemed to lift ever so slightly, allowing a breath of possibility to fill the room. Dr. Montgomery's green eyes met Zylar's glowing orbs, a silent vow exchanged in that glance — an oath to carry onwards, to shepherd this fragile flame of resistance through the encroaching dark.

And though the road ahead promised only hardship, in Zylar's unwavering gaze, there flickered the promise of stars yet unquenched, worlds waiting to be reclaimed. It was a vision worth fighting for — the chance to write an end to their saga that spoke not of defeat, but of enduring legacies carved into the very fabric of the cosmos.

...

Dr. Montgomery leaned forward, the soft glow of the monitors casting ghostly shadows across her somber features. Zylar's voice, haunting and resonant, filled the room with an almost palpable energy. Her eyes, those piercing green windows to a soul weathered by too much loss, began to harden with resolve. She watched as the faces around her transformed, the creases of doubt smoothing into lines of determination.

"Each step we take," Zylar intoned, "is a step away from the brink of oblivion." Their scales shimmered subtly, reflecting the scarce light as they paced deliberately before the assembled coalition members.

Captain Hawking's jaw set firmly, his blue eyes igniting with a fire long suppressed. The weight of command, which had bowed his shoulders like a yoke, now seemed to propel him upright. He stood, nodding to Zylar, acknowledging the gravity of their shared purpose.

A collective breath was drawn as the team, united in their newfound fervor, turned towards one another. Dr. Weller pushed his glasses up the bridge of his nose, the lenses catching a glint as he met Dr. Montgomery's gaze. His voice, usually lost in the labyrinth of his thoughts, emerged steady and clear.

"I joined because I believed our science could outwit any adversary," he said, adjusting the spectacles that seemed perpetually on the verge of slipping. "The Kridrax taught me that knowledge alone is not enough. It must be tempered with courage."

Nods of agreement rippled through the room, each member finding strength in their shared conviction. Captain Hawking spoke next, his words carrying the weight of battles fought and comrades lost.

"Every soldier who falls under my command," he began, his tone low but carrying, "leaves a mark upon my soul. I carry them with me, into every order I give, every plan I make. They are why I am here—why we must prevail."

Dr. Montgomery felt a warmth spread through the chill of the meeting room, a flame kindled by the shared stories of sacrifice. She found her own voice, usually so clinical, tinged with emotion as she added her piece to the tapestry of their collective resolve.

"Behind every calculation, every strategy, there are lives at stake," she said, her voice betraying a rare tremor. "I've seen what happens when we falter. I cannot—will not—let it happen again."

In the dim light of the meeting room, amidst the hum of distant machinery and the soft murmur of voices, a bond was forged. Each story, each declaration, wove them tighter together, creating a fabric strong enough to withstand the despair that threatened to engulf them.

They sat for a while, sharing tales of bravery and loss, each revelation a thread weaving an unspoken pact of unity and resilience. The war against the Kridrax loomed large, but within this circle of weary souls, hope flickered anew.

As the meeting drew to a close, the silence that followed was not empty but full—a canvas stretched taut with the colors of their combined resolve. They rose from their seats, their movements deliberate, their expressions no longer masks of defeat but visages of warriors ready to reclaim their future.

Zylar Threx watched them, their glowing eyes a mirror to the stars outside, reflecting the vastness of space and the infinite possibilities it held. In the quiet communion of the room, the echoes of their past mingled with the promise of redemption—a symphony written in the stars, waiting to be played out against the backdrop of war and wonder.

...

Dr. Montgomery traced her finger over the holo-display, where tiny flickers of light represented lives snatched from the jaws of oblivion. Each glimmer a world saved, each pulse a victory no less significant than the last. They were pinpricks of hope in an otherwise stygian tapestry, but to the doctor, they were monumental. She lifted her gaze to meet those of her comrades, finding in their eyes reflections of her own gratitude for the lives preserved amidst chaos.

"Every star we've kept burning is a testament to our tenacity," Dr. Montgomery murmured, her voice a soft echo against the room's somber walls. "We are more than survivors; we are guardians."

Captain Hawking nodded, his eyes lingering on the display. "Each skirmish won, every Kridrax craft downed... It's a blow to the darkness that seeks to consume us."

The team sat in contemplative silence, shoulders unbowed by the gravity of their achievements. For a brief moment, the specter of defeat dissipated, banished by the tangible evidence of their resilience.

It was then that Zylar Threx rose, their silhouette framed by the ambient glow of the consoles, casting long shadows across the chamber. The iridescent scales that adorned their form shimmered with an ethereal luminescence, and when they spoke, it was as if the cosmos itself lent weight to their words.

"Recall the stars from whence you hailed," Zylar began, their haunting timbre wrapping around each listener like a shroud. "For within them lies the essence of what we fight to reclaim."

"Once, upon the cradle of my people, we too gazed upon such lights with wonder and joy. But the Kridrax extinguished our skies, leaving naught but cinders and sorrow." Zylar paused, the sorrow evident in their glowing eyes. "Let not the annals of history repeat their darkest chapters through our inaction."

With each sentence, Zylar wove a tale of destruction and despair, yet one underscored by an indomitable will—a narrative that resonated deeply with the coalition members. Their shared losses, the memories of worlds razed and civilizations uprooted, bound them in common purpose.

"Survival is but the first step," Zylar continued, their elongated fingers splayed as if to embrace the very fate they sought to alter. "Redemption beckons us forth, inviting us to forge a legacy that defies the ruination wrought by our foe."

Their words hung heavy in the air, laden with the gravity of unspoken oaths and unshed tears. Yet beneath it all, an undercurrent of strength coursed through the gathering, igniting a flame that would not be quelled.

"Let us bear the mantle of redemption," Zylar implored, their gaze sweeping over the assembly. "Our actions shall be the harbinger of a new dawn, one that ensures no other world endures the agony visited upon mine."

A silent accord pulsated through the room, uniting the coalition in a resolve as unyielding as the steel of their ships. The past's specters could not be undone, but the future remained

unwritten — a canvas upon which their saga of defiance against
the Kridrax would be etched in the annals of time.

…

Dr. Montgomery's fingers brushed against the cool surface of
the metal table, her gaze settling upon Captain Hawking as he
paced before her with measured strides. Their eyes met, an
unspoken dialogue crackling in the charged air between them —
a mutual understanding that bore the weight of countless lost
souls and battles fought in the shadow of the Kridrax menace.

"Lucas," Evelyn began, her voice barely a whisper yet carrying
the strength of a clarion call. "We stand upon the precipice of
annihilation, our every effort a bulwark against the tide."

Hawking stopped, his posture rigid, the lines on his face etching
a map of the arduous path they had traversed. "I know, Evelyn.
Our comrades... their memories are not just echoes; they are the
very drumbeat to which we march."

"Then let us make a pact," she said, rising from her seat to stand
shoulder to shoulder with him. The dim light cast long shadows
across the room, yet within their eyes burned a fire that no
darkness could suppress. "We lead with hearts unyielded, for
each life given is a promise to those who remain."

"Aye," he murmured, his hand extending, palm upturned,
towards her. His fingers were calloused, each scar a testament
to his resolve. "Until the last Kridrax falls, until the stars
themselves bear witness to our victory, we fight."

Their hands clasped, a silent vow forged in the crucible of war,
sealing their pledge with the fortitude of iron and the solemnity
of graves long filled. They knew the road ahead would be
fraught with peril, but in this moment, their shared
commitment was a beacon that pierced the encroaching gloom.

As the coalition members filtered out of the chamber, each soul retreated into a cocoon of contemplation. Markus Weller lingered by a viewport, his gaze lost in the celestial ballet of distant galaxies. The stars seemed indifferent to the plight of lesser beings, yet within their cold light lay secrets that whispered of hope and renewal. He clutched at his notes, the scribbled equations a language through which he sought communion with the infinite.

Zylar Threx, their luminescent scales reflecting the sparse illumination, moved to a secluded corner where shadows played upon the walls like specters of doubt. They closed their eyes, their chest rising and falling in a rhythm that suggested a silent chant — an invocation to ancestors whose wisdom spanned eons. Memories of their ravaged homeworld surfaced, but so too did the conviction that such devastation must never be allowed to unfurl again.

One by one, the warriors who comprised this unlikely fellowship found solace in the quietude. They turned inward, wrestling with the demons of uncertainty and the specter of mortality that loomed over their every choice. Yet beneath the veneer of isolation, they drew strength from the collective spirit of their assembly.

Evelyn Montgomery returned to her office, the scattered papers and blinking monitors now serving as reminders not of defeat, but of the indomitable will of her species. She pondered Zylar's words, allowing them to seep into the marrow of her being. Redemption was indeed a beacon, and though it flickered in a storm-ravaged night, its glow promised guidance towards a dawn of their own making.

Captain Hawking stood at the threshold, watching the remnants of his team embrace the stillness that preludes the tempest. Within each heart lay the seed of resistance, germinating amidst the ruin, ready to sprout forth with vigor when called upon. With a final nod to the empty room, he turned and strode away, the echo of his boots a drumbeat heralding the renewed assault on destiny's forge.

...

The dim glow of the monitors cast long shadows across the makeshift office, enveloping Dr. Evelyn Montgomery in a cocoon of flickering light and darkness. With each passing moment, the silence grew heavier, laden with the unspoken fears of what was yet to come. She sat motionless, save for her eyes, which traced the contours of the devastation wrought by the Kridrax.

Captain Lucas "Hawk" Hawking's entrance was a silent affair; the soft hiss of the sliding door the only herald to his arrival. His shadow merged with hers on the wall—a symbolic confluence of their shared duty. Without need for words, they acknowledged the solitude that leadership demanded of them, finding an unspoken comfort in their mutual presence.

"Everything we've done..." Evelyn's voice cracked the quiet, the weight of countless decisions anchoring each word. "It has to matter."

"It will," Hawk replied, his tone a tempered blade forged from the fires of conflict. His gaze met hers, and in those deep blue wells, she saw not only the reflection of her own resolve but also the promise of support that neither rank nor protocol could dictate.

They stood together, silhouettes against the backlit chaos of war, allowing the stillness to wash over them like a balm. The enormity of their task lay before them, a behemoth shadowed path that wound towards an uncertain horizon. Yet it was in this fragile moment of quietude that their bond solidified, each drawing strength from the other's steadfast resolve.

"Let's join the others," Hawk suggested, his voice barely above a whisper. "We need to stand united."

Evelyn nodded, her green eyes no longer mirrors of the past's torment but lanterns illuminating the way forward. With a final glance at the screens, she rose, her lab coat catching the light as if shedding the dust of doubt that had clung to its fibers.

Together, they walked towards the meeting room, where the rest of the coalition awaited — their faces etched with stories of loss and defiance. As they entered, the air seemed to shift, a current of newfound unity pulsing through the space. One by one, heads lifted, and gazes locked, each pair of eyes igniting with the same fire that now burned within Evelyn and Hawk.

The circle they formed was more than a mere gathering of weary souls; it was a testament to the resilience of the human spirit, an unbreakable link in the chain that bound them to their cause. And as they stood shoulder to shoulder, the chapter of despair drew to a close, replaced by a collective narrative of determination and the shared dream of a future reclaimed.

"Look at us," Evelyn murmured, her voice carrying the echoes of battles fought and the whispers of those yet to be waged. "Ready to carve our fate from the stars themselves."

"Aye," Hawk affirmed, his scarred visage a mask of resolute courage. "Together, as one."

Their unity was a fortress, impenetrable and majestic, standing defiant against the looming specter of the Kridrax threat. And there, amidst the convergence of hope and tenacity, they prepared to face the final stages of the war, their every heartbeat a drumroll of anticipation for the ultimate act of redemption.

...

Zylar Threx, known to many as The Harbinger, slipped away from the circle of determined faces. Their slender form glided through the corridors, a silent specter haunting the shadowed spaces of the ship. The iridescent scales that adorned their body reflected the dim emergency lights, casting an ethereal glow against the metallic walls.

They arrived at a secluded alcove, one designed for the quiet contemplation required by the weight of command but now repurposed for more clandestine endeavors. Zylar's elongated fingers danced across a hidden panel, and with a hushed click, a concealed communicator hummed to life, its screen flickering with cryptic symbols.

"Report," came a voice, neither male nor female, distorted by layers of encryption. It was a voice filled with expectation, devoid of warmth, a ghostly whisper in the vastness of space.

"Progress continues," Zylar replied, their measured tone betraying none of the turmoil that churned beneath the surface. "The coalition stands united, stronger than anticipated."

"Good. And the artifacts?" The question held an edge sharper than a blade, cutting through the silence.

"Secured, but unusable until the alignment is complete." Zylar's gaze shifted as if they could sense the constellations aligning beyond the hull. "Patience is required. The final act awaits."

"Ensure there are no deviations. We cannot afford mistakes — not at this juncture," the voice insisted, a hint of steel threading its way through the veil of distortion.

"Understood." Zylar's response was curt, the words exiting their lips like a vow carved from ice. "The sacrifices will not be in vain."

"Remember what is at stake," the voice reminded them, a statement laced with an undercurrent of warning.

"Redemption," Zylar murmured, a solitary word that encapsulated the magnitude of their shared endeavor. Yet, within the confines of their glowing eyes, a storm seemed to brew — a tempest of conflict and conviction.

"Redemption," the voice echoed, before the line went dead, leaving Zylar alone with the secrets that pulsed in the darkness. They stood motionless for a long moment, a solitary figure wrestling with the ghosts of a past consumed by war and the fragile threads of hope for a future yet unwritten.

As they turned back towards the unity of their makeshift family, the faintest glimmer of doubt passed over Zylar's visage. With each step, they carried the weight of unspeakable knowledge, the burden of an agenda shrouded in mystery, and the silent prayer that redemption would justify the means.

Chapter 16

Traitor Revealed

The walls of the secure chamber echoed with the murmured anxieties of the remaining coalition members, a symphony of hushed tones and furtive glances. Dr. Evelyn Montgomery stood slightly apart, her piercing green eyes scanning the room like twin searchlights piercing through the fog of suspicion. The stark lighting cast deep shadows across her sharp features, underscoring the gravity of their predicament.

"Silence," she commanded, her voice slicing through the tension as effectively as a laser blade. The room fell immediately still, all eyes turning toward her. There was a magnetism to her presence that demanded attention, a gravitas born of countless battles fought both in the lab and on the field.

"We can't ignore the viper in our midst any longer," she continued, the words measured but laced with an urgency that betrayed her typically composed demeanor. "There's a traitor among us."

A collective shiver ran through the assembly at the declaration, as if the air itself had grown colder. Whispers of betrayal had been circulating like ghosts down corridors, haunting their every step since the Kridrax had somehow anticipated their last move.

Dr. Montgomery's gaze settled on Captain Lucas "Hawk" Hawking, his imposing figure a reassuring bastion amidst the sea of uncertainty. "Hawk, I'm entrusting you to spearhead this investigation," she said, each syllable heavy with responsibility.

Captain Hawking nodded curtly, his blue eyes steely as he processed the weight of the task. "Understood, Doctor. We'll find the mole."

Beside him, Sergeant Mia Alvarez stood in quiet solidarity, her eyes betraying none of the turmoil that surely churned within her. She had been forged in the fires of conflict, her visage a mask of stoic resolve.

"Alvarez, your insights will be vital. You know these people, you've fought alongside them." Dr. Montgomery's voice softened ever so slightly as she addressed the sergeant, acknowledging the personal cost of such an inquisition.

"Of course, Dr. Montgomery," Mia replied, her tone betraying no emotion, though her hand twitched imperceptibly at her side — a subtle battle between duty and the ache of potential betrayal.

"Begin immediately," Dr. Montgomery instructed, her short black hair framing her face like a raven's wings as she turned back to the rest of the group. "Interviews will be conducted individually. No one leaves this facility until the traitor is found."

The coalition members exchanged uneasy glances, the specter of distrust now manifest among them. Hawk stepped forward, the sound of his boots against the metal floor punctuating the silence as he prepared to carry out his orders.

"Let's get to work," he said, his voice carrying the unspoken weight of their shared past and the fragile hope for redemption that hung in the balance.

As Hawk and Alvarez moved to commence their daunting quest, Dr. Montgomery remained behind, her thoughts adrift in the currents of memories that threatened to pull her under. It was a delicate dance with the demons of yesteryear, a waltz that spun her around the possibility of yet another painful truth waiting to be unearthed.

...

Captain Hawking's shadow loomed tall against the stark walls of the interrogation room as he beckoned the first coalition member inside. The air was thick with unease, each breath a silent admission of the turmoil that had infiltrated their ranks. Sergeant Alvarez stood by the door, her posture rigid, her gaze unwavering — a sentinel guarding against unseen threats.

"Sit," Hawk commanded, his voice echoing slightly off the cold metallic surfaces. A simple gesture to the chair across from him held an undercurrent of authority that no one dared to question. The first interviewee, a seasoned technician named Corin, took his place, his hands betraying a slight tremor despite his composed facade.

Hawk leaned forward, resting his forearms on the table, his eyes piercing through the dim light. "Where were you during the comm relay sabotage?" he asked, his tone devoid of accusation yet heavy with implication.

Corin's reply came swiftly, rehearsed, but not without a hint of defensiveness. "In the engine bay. Calibrating the hyperdrive stabilizers." His words hung in the air, a fragile truth or a well-crafted lie.

Alvarez observed the exchange, her mind cataloging every shift in demeanor, every flutter of the eyelids. She knew the dance of deception all too well — the subtle steps and missteps that betrayed a soul's secrets.

The interviews continued, a procession of faces, each carrying their own story, their own potential for treachery. Hawk's questions sliced through the silence, incisive and probing, while Alvarez's silence spoke volumes. They sought inconsistencies like hunters tracking elusive prey, vigilant and methodical.

But as the hours ticked by, with every new alibi and every denial, the fabric of trust that once bound them frayed further. Paranoia seeped into the corridors of the secure location, whispers echoed in the shadows, and allies eyed each other with newfound wariness.

A technician named Jules hesitated when recounting his whereabouts, his eyes darting to the side before catching himself. "I was... reviewing data logs," he stammered, the veneer of confidence cracking.

"Data logs," Hawk repeated, his skepticism a tangible force in the room. "Which ones?"

"Um, the external sensor arrays," Jules replied, his voice losing volume as if the truth was slipping through his fingers.

"Convenient," Alvarez murmured from her post by the door, her remark hanging ominously in the space between them.

With each passing hour, the atmosphere grew denser, the burden of suspicion adding weight to their shoulders. Coalition members who had once fought side by side now sat apart, their camaraderie eroded by the gnawing fear that one among them had turned coat.

As night enveloped the facility, a shroud of darkness seemed to press against the windows, an echo of the shadow that lay upon their hearts. Hawk's resolve never wavered.

The secure location, once a sanctuary against the vastness of space and the threat of the Kridrax, now felt like a chamber of secrets and silent accusations. The remaining coalition members sat around a holographic map that flickered with intermittent static — a grim reflection of their faltering unity.

Dr. Evelyn Montgomery stood at the head of the table, her piercing green eyes scanning the faces before her, each etched with the fatigue of war and the dread of betrayal. Her voice sliced through the tension as she addressed them, "We've suffered heavy losses, and our security has been compromised from within. Trust is a luxury we can no longer afford unchecked."

Her gaze settled on Captain Lucas "Hawk" Hawking, who met her stare unflinchingly, his broad shoulders squared as if bracing against an unseen adversary. With a curt nod, he understood the gravity of the mission bestowed upon him.

"Captain Hawking, Sergeant Alvarez," Dr. Montgomery continued, her tone imbued with authority, "you are to lead the investigation. Leave no stone unturned. We need answers, and we need them yesterday."

"Understood, Doctor," Hawk replied, his voice steady despite the maelstrom of doubt that threatened to engulf them all. Beside him, Sergeant Mia Alvarez gave a sharp salute, her dark eyes resolute, the set of her jaw revealing her unwavering dedication.

As the other members dispersed, shadows clinging to their silhouettes, Hawk and Alvarez remained. They exchanged a glance, a silent pact formed between them — one of loyalty to the cause and to each other. Together, they would peel back the layers of deception until only the stark truth remained.

"Let's start with the comms logs," Hawk suggested, his mind already sifting through potential leads, "If there's chatter, it'll be there."

"Agreed," Alvarez said, moving towards the door. "And the supply manifests. Anyone accessing more than their share could be preparing for... contingencies."

"Good call," Hawk acknowledged, knowing full well the implications. A traitor would need resources — ammunition, rations, perhaps even a hidden getaway plan.

They stepped into the empty corridor, the silence punctuated by the distant hum of the station's life support systems. Each member would have to be interviewed, their stories meticulously compared for discrepancies. It was a task that required precision and an unflinching will to confront uncomfortable truths.

Yet, amidst the chaos of suspicion, there stirred a deeper unease within Hawk — a fear that redemption might not come easy, should the traitor be one of their own. But the path ahead was clear, and the stakes were too high for hesitation.

With a determination that matched the cold clarity of the stars outside, Hawk and Alvarez began their search for the elusive traitor, unaware that in the darkness of space, every light cast a shadow, and within those shadows lurked the possibility of further treachery.

...

Captain Hawking's shadow stretched long and lean across the sterile confines of the interrogation room, a silent witness to the questioning that was about to unfold. He stood motionless for a moment, watching as Sergeant Alvarez arranged her notes with meticulous care, the soft shuffle of paper oddly intrusive in the quiet.

"Let's begin," Hawk intoned, his voice low but clear, as he motioned the first coalition member into the room. The door sealed with a hiss, ensnaring them within the confines of cold steel walls. Every eye movement, every twitch of discomfort from the interviewee was cataloged under Hawk's intense gaze. Alvarez, equally observant, posed questions designed to probe past defenses, her tone deceptively gentle.

"Where were you during the last supply raid?" she asked, her eyes never leaving those of the jittery engineer seated before them.

"Uh, I—I was in the hangar, repairing a shuttle engine," stammered the man, his fingers entwining nervously.

"Alone?" Hawk's query sliced through the room's thickening tension.

"Y-yes. Alone," came the hesitant confirmation.

The dance of question and answer continued, a meticulous waltz of suspicion where missteps could prove perilous. With each dismissed member, a residue of doubt lingered, tainting the air like an unseen miasma.

As hours turned and shadows lengthened, the very atmosphere aboard the station seemed to warp with the strain of unresolved anxiety. Corridors that once echoed with the solidarity of shared purpose now whispered doubts, the clatter of boots on metal grating sounding retreats from conversations cut short by wary glances.

Hawk felt the weight of unrest bearing down upon him, an oppressive force that threatened to fracture the fragile veneer of trust amongst the coalition. His own instincts, honed through countless skirmishes, screamed that the enemy hid in plain sight, cloaked in the familiar guise of comradeship.

"Something isn't right," Alvarez murmured, echoing his disquiet as they conferred between interviews. "Every answer feels rehearsed, every alibi too pat."

"Keep pressing," Hawk replied, the lines etched deeper into his weather-beaten face. "The traitor is here, hiding behind half-truths."

The investigation marched on, relentless and unyielding. Hawk watched as the battle-hardened warriors of the coalition crumbled under scrutiny, their resolve shaken by the insidious seed of mistrust that had been sown among them. It wasn't just the fear of betrayal that gnawed at their confidence; it was the harrowing possibility that their faith in one another — their greatest weapon against the encroaching darkness — was being twisted into a weapon against them.

Yet in this slow-burning crucible of doubt, Hawk found a grim determination solidifying within him. There would be a reckoning, a moment when veils would lift and the traitor's visage would be laid bare. Until then, he would cleave to his duty, moving through the murky waters of deception with the singular focus of a predator closing in on its unwitting prey.

Each passing hour, each scrutinized face drew them inexorably closer to an uncomfortable truth: that redemption, if it came at all, would exact its own toll — a price paid in the currency of broken trust and the smoldering embers of unity once thought unquenchable.

…

Dr. Evelyn Montgomery paced the dimly lit chamber, her boots clicking rhythmically against the cold steel floor — a metronome of unrest. Shadows clung to the corners of the room like specters bearing witness to her solitude. They seemed to stretch and reach for her, eager to swallow the flickering resolve that played across her features.

"Zylar," she called softly into the semi-darkness, the name resonating with a quiet desperation. The air itself seemed to hum, charged with an energy that defied the laws of physics.

From the shadowy periphery, Zylar Threx emerged, their luminous form casting an ethereal glow. "Evelyn," they acknowledged, their voice a serene contrast to the palpable tension. It was the calm in the eye of a storm, soothing yet foreboding.

"Your thoughts are troubled," Zylar observed, their eyes reflecting a universe of sorrow. "Speak, so that we may unburden your soul."

"Betrayal," Evelyn began, the word escaping like a sigh. "It festers within us. How did you endure, Zylar? When your own kind turned against you?"

"Betrayal is a wound that time struggles to heal," Zylar replied, a distant sadness creeping into their otherwise tranquil demeanor. "But it taught me that trust must be the foundation upon which we build our resistance. Without it, we crumble before our enemies have even struck."

Evelyn's gaze drifted away, her mind grappling with the gravity of Zylar's words. "And if our trust has been misplaced?" she questioned, her voice barely above a whisper.

"Then we must forge a new path," Zylar intoned solemnly. "One built on the unity of those who remain steadfast."

A single nod from Evelyn conveyed her understanding, but her heart remained heavy with the burden of leadership. She watched as Zylar melded back into the shadows, leaving her to contemplate the fragility of their coalition.

Elsewhere, concealed by the anonymity of a nondescript corridor, the traitor moved with a silent urgency. With each cautious step, they cast furtive glances over their shoulder, their heartbeat a staccato drumming in their ears. They were close — too close — to being unmasked.

In the privacy of a secluded alcove, the traitor worked swiftly, planting fabricated communications logs into the data terminal. The digital script scrolled across the screen, each line a carefully constructed lie designed to ensnare an innocent. With a final keystroke, the trap was set.

"Covering your tracks?" A voice sliced through the stillness, its owner hidden by the curve of the corridor.

"Merely... taking precautions," the traitor responded, the smoothness of their reply belying the adrenaline surging through their veins.

"Of course," the unseen figure murmured, their tone laced with a knowing that sent a chill down the traitor's spine. The exchange was brief, but the message was clear: Trust no one.

The traitor slipped away, their mind racing with plots and counterplots. They knew that every moment brought them closer to discovery, every planted clue a double-edged sword that could just as easily point back to them.

With the seeds of deception sown, they retreated into the labyrinth of passageways, a specter moving among the unsuspecting. The game of shadows continued, a dance with destiny where the price of missteps was not merely failure, but the annihilation of all they held dear.

...

Captain Lucas "Hawk" Hawking leaned over the holographic display, his brow furrowed as he pieced together the fragments of evidence with the meticulous care of an archaeologist uncovering relics of a bygone era. Beside him, Sergeant Mia Alvarez mirrored his concentration, her eyes scanning the data points that floated in the air like stars in a galaxy of deceit.

"Look at this comm timestamp," Hawk said, his voice barely above a whisper, yet carrying the weight of command. "It's been doctored. Someone wanted us to think they were on the other side of the base when the sabotage occurred."

Mia nodded, her finger tracing the altered code. "Only someone with high-level access could manipulate the logs like this. It narrows the field considerably."

Their list of suspects had shrunk under the scrutiny of their investigation, each member's alibi dissected and scrutinized until only a handful of coalition members remained under the shadow of suspicion. Those with the means and motive to betray them were fewer still, but it was the motive that eluded them, a ghost flickering just beyond reach.

In the depths of the secure location, away from prying eyes, the traitor moved with quiet desperation. Their hands, slick with perspiration, worked with practiced haste to reroute power conduits, their actions cloaked by the guise of routine maintenance. The hum of the energy core grew erratic, a symphony of impending chaos.

"Disruptions in the power grid," came a voice over the comms, urgent yet controlled. "Main defense systems are experiencing fluctuations."

Hawk exchanged a glance with Mia, a silent conversation passing between them. This was no coincidence—the saboteur was making their move, striving to fracture the already brittle trust that held the coalition together.

"Secure the area," Hawk commanded. A subtle nod from Mia sent her darting out of the room, her footsteps echoing in the hollow space, a testament to the urgency of their mission.

The traitor, meanwhile, blended into the shadows, their breaths shallow as they observed the discord they had sown among the ranks. Accusations flew like arrows in the dimly lit corridors, piercing the armor of camaraderie that had once seemed impenetrable.

"Could be anyone," one voice muttered, tinged with fear—a fear that the traitor savored like a rare vintage.

"Trust has become a luxury we cannot afford," another agreed, the resignation in their tone a dark melody that played well into the traitor's plans.

Amidst the rising panic, Hawk stood as a beacon of resolve, his gaze sweeping over the faces of his team—faces etched with doubt and suspicion. He knew the cost of uncertainty, the toll it took on even the strongest of spirits. Yet, he also understood the necessity of faith, the belief in something greater than oneself. "Stay focused," he instructed, his voice a bastion against the tide of paranoia. "We find the traitor, we end this."

As Sergeant Alvarez secured the compromised systems, her movements precise and deliberate, the traitor watched from the darkness. They understood that their time was running short, that every action now was a desperate gambit in a game where the stakes were survival itself.

And so, they wove their web of lies tighter, casting aspersions with a subtlety that turned ally against ally. The traitor needed only to keep the illusion alive for a while longer, to stoke the fires of distrust until the coalition imploded from within.

But Hawk and Alvarez were relentless, their dedication to the truth unyielding. Each clue they unearthed brought them closer to unveiling the betrayer, each step forward a march toward redemption—for themselves and for a future that hung precariously in the balance.

…

Hawk's pulse thrashed in his temples as he stood before the holographic display, the dim light casting angular shadows across his chiseled features. Data streamed across the screen in relentless waves, a digital deluge that threatened to drown them in information yet promised salvation. Beside him, Alvarez's fingers danced with practiced ease over the interface, her expression a mask of concentration.

"Got something," she murmured, her voice barely a whisper against the hum of machines.

The room stilled as all eyes converged on the flickering image—a series of encrypted communications, now laid bare. The cipher had been cracked, and within its electronic belly lay the traitor's desperation, the illicit communiques with the Kridrax—a stark betrayal illuminated by cold, hard evidence.

"Who?" Dr. Montgomery demanded, her piercing gaze fixed upon Hawk, searching for the answer that had eluded them for so long.

"Markus," Hawk declared, the name tasting like bile upon his lips. Markus Weller, the unassuming genius whose brilliance shone like a beacon through the darkest hours, now revealed as the harbinger of their potential undoing.

"Impossible," someone gasped, but the truth was undeniable, the deception too intricate to be anything but deliberate. Whispered conversations turned into heated exchanges, the fragile threads of trust unraveling with each passing moment.

"Markus, explain!" Evelyn's command sliced through the cacophony, her authority unquestionable even as disbelief clouded her verdant eyes.

The thin scientist stood, his frame dwarfed by the towering figure of Hawk, his glasses reflecting the sterile light. "I... I feared..." Markus stammered, his voice trailing off into the void of his own making.

"Feared what, Weller?" Hawk's voice boomed, the controlled anger barely contained beneath the surface. "You feared enough to betray us all?"

The room held its breath, the tension a palpable entity that fed on their collective dread.

"It was not fear of death," Markus confessed, his words trembling as they fought their way out, "but fear of futility. The Kridrax are... inevitable. I thought—"

"Thought you could save yourself?" Sergeant Alvarez cut in, her tone dripping with contempt.

"Save myself? No. Save humanity," Markus's retort came with an unexpected fervor, his eyes alight with the fires of conviction. "In my communication with the Kridrax, I sought an understanding, a pathway to coexistence."

"Coexistence?" Hawk spat the word as if it were an insult. "With those who have ravaged our worlds?"

"Peace requires sacrifice!" Markus implored, his hands outstretched, beseeching them to understand his twisted rationale.

"Enough," Hawk commanded, stepping forward. His presence loomed, a sentinel of justice in the midst of chaos. "Your actions have endangered us all. You'll face judgment for this, Markus. For every life lost, every hope dashed."

"Lucas," Dr. Montgomery interjected, her voice a balm to the tempest raging around them. "We must remember who we are, what we fight for."

"Redemption," Hawk muttered, the word hanging heavy in the air, a reminder of their shared burden, the past that haunted them, and the future that depended on their unity.

"Redemption," Markus echoed, a single tear tracing the line of his haggard cheek, the admission of his guilt a surrender to the fate he had chosen when he first reached out to the enemy. "Take him," Hawk instructed Alvarez, his heart leaden with the weight of the moment.

As Alvarez led Markus away, the team gathered close, their faces a mosaic of sorrow and resolve. They had uncovered the darkness within their ranks, but the struggle against the Kridrax—and the demons of their own doubts—loomed ever larger on the horizon.

…

The chamber, once a sanctuary of strategy and solidarity, now lay suffused with the acrid stench of betrayal. Shadows clung to the corners, as if they too harbored secrets, watching the coalition members with opaque eyes. The air was thick with unsaid accusations, every glance a dagger veiled in doubt. Dr. Montgomery stood amongst them, her disheveled black hair framing a face that could not hide its shock, her piercing green eyes reflecting a turmoil that echoed in the hearts of all present.

"Could we have prevented this?" whispered someone from the back, the words falling like stones into a still pond, rippling outward with silent devastation.

"Was it our blindness," another murmured, "or his deception that led us here?"

Evelyn felt the weight of their stares, their words igniting embers of guilt within her. She tucked a strand of hair behind her ear, a futile attempt to quell the unease gnawing at her resolve. Had her confidence in technology been her downfall? In seeking to outsmart their enemies, had she failed to see the enemy within?

"Focus," she heard herself say, her voice cutting through the fog of despondency. "We are scientists, soldiers... survivors. We must rise above this treachery."

Captain Hawking stepped forward, his muscular frame a pillar against the tide of despair, his scars testaments to battles fought and won. His blue eyes locked onto each member, an unspoken vow that he would lead them through this storm.

"Markus's fear drove him to darkness," Hawk said, his voice a measured drumbeat against the silence. "But we—we will not succumb to the shadows. Our path is clear. We stand together, or we fall apart."

Zylar Threx moved next to Evelyn, their slender frame almost lost among the humans, yet their presence undeniable. The iridescent scales along their arms caught what little light there was, casting prismatic whispers across the walls. Their voice, when they spoke, was the echo of a distant star, resonating with an ancient pain that knew too well the cost of betrayal.

"Unity forged in adversity is the strongest steel," Zylar intoned. "Let the fracture Markus has created be the crucible that tempers our resolve."

The room held its breath, the coalition members finding solace in the unity reflected in Zylar's luminescent gaze. Evelyn saw it then—hope flickering back to life in their eyes, a shared determination knitting itself into the fabric of their spirits. Together, they were more than the sum of their parts, more than flesh and blood and shimmering scale.

"Let us look to tomorrow," Dr. Montgomery declared, "not as a multitude divided, but as one force, indomitable. For humanity, for all sentient beings threatened by the Kridrax, we shall carve our redemption from the stars."

Nods of agreement met her words, the hurt beginning to heal, the resolve hardening like cooling metal. And though the specter of the past loomed over them, a ghostly reminder of the fragility of trust, they understood what must be done. They would face the Kridrax, not as fractured shards, but as a blade reforged, sharp and unyielding.

In that moment, the coalition was reborn, a phoenix rising from the ashes of deceit. They would write their future in the annals of the galaxy, a testament to the power of unity and the enduring quest for redemption.

...

Evelyn Montgomery's gaze swept over the assembly, the weight of leadership pressing against her shoulders like the gravity of a neutron star. The coalition members, once scattered by suspicion, now converged with a shared intensity that sparked in the air around them. It was time to forge a new path through the darkness.

"Begin," she commanded, her voice the catalyst that broke their inertia.

With a flurry of motion, holographic displays sprang to life, casting an ethereal glow on determined faces. Captain Hawking's fingers danced across the controls, bringing up schematics of the defense systems — lines and shapes coalescing into a vision of hope. They needed to be faster, smarter, impregnable. A fortress amidst the void.

"Here," Sergeant Alvarez pointed to a sector on the display, "the Kridrax are exploiting our faltering shield frequencies. We reinforce these points, synchronize the phase variance cycles..." His words trailed off as he delved deeper into strategy, his mind a tempest of tactical prowess.

"Excellent," Dr. Montgomery affirmed, her eyes reflecting the shifting data streams. "And the counterattack?"

Jeremy Standing, silent until now, stepped forward. His silver hair seemed to shimmer with the subtle light of the room, a beacon of the wisdom only years of navigating treachery could bestow. "Diversion," he suggested, his voice resonating with the gravity of his experience. "A feint at their flank while we strike at the heart."

"Deception as a weapon," Zylar Threx murmured, their alien features betraying no emotion, yet their tone laced with approval. "The Kridrax understand strength, but not cunning. It is there we will find our advantage."

Ideas flowed and melded into a plan stronger than any single mind could have woven. Each member contributed a thread, and together they wove a tapestry of defiance—a declaration that they would not be broken by betrayal or fear.

As the final pieces of the strategy locked into place, a hush fell over the room. They stood as one, their unity palpable, the silence not empty but full of promise. In this stillness, the past was acknowledged, its lessons etched deep in their resolve.

Dr. Montgomery's gaze met each pair of eyes in turn. "We move at dawn," she said, her voice a whisper of steel. "Prepare yourselves. Rest, for tomorrow we reclaim our destiny from the jaws of defeat."

The coalition members dispersed, each carrying within them a burning ember of the collective fire they had stoked. Their steps were measured, echoing through the chamber like a solemn drumbeat of impending retribution.

In the quiet that followed, Evelyn allowed herself a moment to reflect. The betrayer had sought to dismantle them from within, yet here they stood, closer and more resolute than ever before. The Kridrax loomed large on the horizon, but so too did their spirit—the indomitable will of beings united in purpose.

"Redemption awaits," she whispered to the stars. And with that, she turned to join her comrades in preparation for the battle to come. Together they would face the morrow, their commitment unshakable, their mission clear. For in unity, they had discovered an unyielding strength, a force that no enemy, internal or galactic, could ever hope to extinguish.

Chapter 17

Plan Resolved

A hush fell over the dimly lit chamber as Dr. Evelyn Montgomery's silhouette paced before the assembly of her team, the weight of the impending mission pressing down on each of them like the gravity of a black hole. Her steely green eyes flicked across the faces of her crew, piercing the gloom with an intensity that belied her compact form.

"Time is a luxury we can't afford," she began, her voice a low thrum in the charged air. "Our comrades are out there—in the cold grasp of the Kridrax—and every second we lose tightens their grip."

She paused at the center of the room, her gaze locking onto each member in turn, ensuring the gravity of their situation was understood without recourse to dramatics. With a deliberate motion, she unrolled the schematics of the enemy's command ship across a large table, revealing a labyrinthine network of corridors and chambers etched in blue light.

"Markus, Lily," she called, her tone shifting to one of cool professionalism. "Show us what you've unearthed."

Dr. Markus Weller, hair askew as though he had wrestled with the very winds of space, stepped forward. Beside him, Dr. Lily Chen's composed presence offered a stark contrast; her long hair tied back to reveal a determined set to her jaw.

"The Kridrax command ship," Markus intoned, gesturing to the holographic display that sprang up from the table. "A formidable beast, but not without its vulnerabilities."

"Here," Lily said, pointing to a section of the display where the walls of the ship seemed to converge. "The ventilation system. It's expansive enough for entry, but it won't be easy. They're designed to flush out intruders with neurotoxins."

"Which is why precision is key," Evelyn interjected, her own mind tracing paths through the maze of vents. She could almost smell the sterile chill of the ship's interior, the distant hum of alien technology thrumming in her ears.

"Once inside," Markus continued, adjusting his glasses as if to bring the plan into sharper focus, "we target these power junctions." His finger jabbed at several pulsing nodes. "Disrupt their systems, sow confusion. It's our best chance to slip through undetected."

Evelyn nodded, her lips pressed into a thin line. Betrayal—the sting of it lingered in her psyche, a ghost from the past that sharpened her resolve. Trust was a currency spent sparingly now, yet here she stood, poised to gamble it once more on the hope of redemption.

"Remember," she said, her voice barely above a whisper as she turned to face her team, "this isn't just about rescue. It's about reclaiming our future... undoing the wrongs inflicted upon us."

The room settled into silence, the weight of her words settling like dust upon old wounds. The mission would test them all, perhaps beyond their limits, but it was a crucible they were compelled to endure. For in the dark tapestry of space, woven with threads of loss and vengeance, lay the slim, shining chance for atonement. And none felt its pull more keenly than Evelyn Montgomery herself.

...

A hush fell over the training bay as Captain Lucas "Hawk" Hawking surveyed his team, their faces a mosaic of determination and apprehension. Hawk's presence was a gravitational force, and as he stepped into the simulation chamber — a holographic theatre of war — his shadow loomed large against the pulsating images of the Kridrax command ship.

"Begin," he ordered, his voice slicing through the silence like a blade.

The room burst into orchestrated chaos. Lasers seared through the dim light, artificial alarms blared, and the team moved with practiced precision. Hawk's eyes tracked every motion, his mind churning with tactical possibilities. Here in this crucible, they honed their unity, each movement a testament to their shared purpose.

"Communication is your lifeline," Hawk called out, his tone a blend of steel and encouragement. "Words unspoken can be just as deadly as a misfired shot."

He ducked, a simulated bolt grazing where his head had been. The experience of countless skirmishes was etched into his muscles, a corporeal memory that guided him through the simulated fray. Around him, his team adapted and overcame, their maneuvers a dance of survival choreographed by necessity.

It was then that Zylar Threx, the Harbinger, entered the fray. Their iridescent scales caught the artificial light, casting prismatic shadows on the walls. Their movements were fluid, almost ghostly, as they slipped between combatants, whispering insights only those who had suffered at the hands of the Kridrax could know.

"Precision," Zylar intoned, their voice threading through the cacophony of the simulation. "The Kridrax thrive on disorder, but we will carve our path with deliberate intent."

They paused beside a simulated control panel, their elongated fingers tracing a sequence that caused the alarms to cease abruptly. "Here," they said, gesturing to a section of the ship's schematics, "lies the heart of their defenses. Strike true, and silence will be our ally."

Their words hung heavy in the air, a cloak of solemnity draped over the team. Hawk nodded, recognizing the gravity of Zylar's guidance. Each revelation was a piece of the puzzle, a chance to undermine the oppressors who had cast such long shadows over their pasts.

"Stealth is our redemption," Zylar continued, their gaze locking with Hawks'. "We move through the darkness to bring forth the light of liberty."

As the team regrouped, Hawk took a moment to regard them all, their faces illuminated now by a shared conviction. They were warriors, yes, but also guardians of a fragile hope — a chance to reclaim not just their comrades but their very future.

"Again," Hawk commanded, the word a covenant unto itself. "We will not falter. We cannot."

The simulation rebooted, and the dance of redemption began anew.

...

Dr. Evelyn Montgomery's fingers danced over the sleek surfaces of her gear, a symphony of clicks and whirrs accompanying each precise movement. Her short black hair, a stark contrast to the pale sheen of advanced weaponry laid out before her, hardly stirred as she worked. The functional jumpsuit she donned seemed to merge with the shadows of the secure chamber, its pockets filled with devices that hummed with latent potential.

"Check your comms," she instructed, her voice a low murmur that cut through the silence like a scalpel. "Ensure every frequency is calibrated to our encrypted channels."

Beside her, Dr. Markus Weller fumbled slightly with a communication device, his glasses perched precariously on the bridge of his nose. His fingers trembled momentarily before finding their familiar cadence over the intricate equipment. He nodded to himself, more in reassurance than in response to anyone else, absorbed in his own world of circuits and signals.

Across the room, Dr. Lily Chen adjusted the straps of her stealth suit with practiced ease, her bright brown eyes reflecting an inner turmoil that belied her calm exterior. She tested the flexibility of the fabric, allowing herself a momentary breath of relief as it responded silently, capable of masking her presence from prying sensors.

"Stealth suits operational," she confirmed, her voice soft yet clear across the shared comm link.

The air crackled with a sense of urgency, the weight of their impending mission pressing down upon them like the vacuum of space itself. Each member moved with a purpose, fully aware that their preparation now would mean the difference between life and death later. The meticulousness of their checks was not merely a precaution; it was a ritual, a silent vow to leave nothing to chance.

It was then that Dr. Samira Patel stepped forward, her curly brown hair casting a halo around her earnest face. The warmth in her eyes flickered with a strategic fire as she unrolled a set of blueprints that depicted the Kridrax command ship—an enigmatic beast that they were soon to infiltrate.

"Listen carefully," Samira began, her words deliberate and infused with a gravity that commanded attention. "I've developed a diversion that should draw their forces out of alignment." She tapped on the holographic display, where points of light began to scatter like fireflies in a dark forest.

"Timing is crucial," she continued, her tone shifting to underscore the importance of her next words. "We have a narrow window to execute this maneuver. Once we initiate the distraction, we must move swiftly."

A series of nods rippled through the team, a silent acknowledgment of the role they each had to play. They understood that Samira's plan hinged on precision—a dance with destiny where even a single misstep could spell disaster.

"Once the Kridrax are drawn out," she explained, circling a section on the hologram that pulsated ominously, "we'll have a clear path to our comrades."

Evelyn's piercing green eyes met Samira's, an unspoken agreement passing between them. The past had taught Evelyn the cost of failure, the sting of betrayal that had sharpened her resolve. Now, redemption beckoned, a siren's call that promised a chance to right the wrongs etched deep in the annals of their history.

As the team dispersed to finalize their preparations, each member cloaked in the somber hues of determination, the chamber seemed to hold its breath. The shadows whispered of battles fought and sacrifices made, of the relentless march toward an uncertain future where hope was the rarest commodity.

In this quiet before the storm, the echoes of Zylar's words, "We move through the darkness to bring forth the light of liberty," resonated within the walls, a haunting refrain that bound them all to the cause for which they stood ready to risk everything.

…

Sergeant Mia Alvarez crouched low, her gaze piercing the metallic landscape that sprawled beneath the Kridrax command ship. Distance did little to diminish its imposing silhouette against the star-strewn sky — a leviathan of war suspended in the void. Beside her, Lieutenant Isabella's eyes were equally scrutinous, scanning for the subtlest signs of movement, a whisper of change in the enemy's patterns.

"Anything?" Mia's voice was a hushed thread in the stillness, barely stirring the air.

"Quiet," Isabella murmured back, "too quiet."

They moved as shadows across the terrain, their stealth suits hugging every contour of their disciplined forms. Each step was measured, each breath controlled — warriors in synchrony with the night. The reconnaissance mission had transformed the void into a chessboard, and they were the queens, formidable yet cautious in their advance.

A blip on Mia's scanner drew her attention, and she relayed the information with a curt gesture. Isabella nodded, her expression unreadable behind the visor, but Mia knew the determination that lay beneath. Together, they mapped the area, noting the patrol rotations of the Kridrax sentries and marking potential vulnerabilities in their defenses.

When they returned, the team awaited in the cold embrace of the secured chamber, an oasis of resolve amidst the chaos of impending battle. Mia shared their findings, her report concise — a litany of timings and blind spots that would serve as their lifeline within the beast.

"Here," she pointed to a node on the holographic layout that Dr. Weller had projected earlier, "and here are our entries. We'll need to be swift, silent, and above all, precise."

"Any deviation from the plan could cost us," Isabella added, locking eyes with each member of the team. Her scar seemed to underscore the gravity of her words — a stark reminder of the cost of complacency.

Dr. Montgomery absorbed their intel, his weathered features betraying none of the storm that surely raged within. He turned to the team, assigning roles with a commander's confidence. Zylar Threx, the enigmatic guide through this labyrinth of steel and malice, received instructions with a solemn nod. Captain Hawking confirmed the combat strategies, her voice a rallying cry that cut through the uncertainty.

"Contingencies?" Dr. Montgomery's question hung heavy in the air, an acknowledgment of the myriad ways fate could conspire against them.

"Secondary exits, fallback points, emergency signals," Isabella listed them off, each provision another layer of armor around their fragile hopes.

"Comms will be minimal once inside," Mia interjected, knowing that silence would be their greatest ally. "Hand signals, mainly. Only break radio silence if —" She paused, the weight of what she left unsaid bowing her shoulders ever so slightly.

"If it's life or death," finished Captain Hawking, her tone unyielding yet not unkind.

The past loomed over them like an indomitable specter, its tendrils steeped in regrets and losses too numerous to count. Yet here they stood, at the precipice of redemption, ready to reclaim a future that had been stolen from them piece by piece. This mission was more than a rescue; it was a chance to sever the chains of yesteryears, to emerge from the ashes of history reborn.

"Once we're in," Dr. Montgomery's voice anchored them back to the present, "we stick to the plan. No heroics. We get our people and get out."

Mia felt the familiar surge of adrenaline, the clarity that came with purpose. She exchanged a glance with Isabella—a silent pact between warriors. They would see this through, together, whatever the cost.

The meeting disbanded, its members dispersing like phantoms into the gloom of preparation. They were the unseen, the unheard, moving through the darkness to bring forth not just light, but the dawn of a new day—one where freedom was more than an elusive dream whispered in the void of space.

...

The shadows of the hangar seemed to swallow them whole, their figures melding with the darkness as they approached the vessel—a phantom in the void. The transport's hull gleamed dully under the faint light, a specter of technology designed to deceive the eyes of the enemy. Dr. Evelyn Montgomery led her team toward it, her stride measured and silent against the cold metal floor.

"Systems check," she murmured, more to herself than anyone else. Her voice was a soft command, threading through the air like a needle precise and sharp.

Captain Hawk followed close behind, his boots thudding softly, a silent drumbeat to their covert march. His hand reached out, skimming the sleek surface of their ticket to the unknown, feeling for the thrum of life within the vessel's shell. He nodded to Markus, whose fingers danced across a portable console, coaxing the ship's systems into wakefulness.

"Stealth field is holding at ninety-eight percent efficiency," Markus reported, squinting behind his glasses as data streamed before his eyes. "We're as invisible as ghosts."

Zylar Threx lingered on the periphery, their luminescent scales catching stray wisps of light. They watched the humans with an inscrutable gaze, centuries of wisdom and sorrow etched into the depths of their glowing eyes. This mission was not just about humanity's survival; it was personal—a chance to honor a world lost to the merciless grip of the Kridrax.

The vessel's hatch opened with a sigh, expelling a breath of recycled air that brushed against their faces like a promise. One by one, they climbed aboard, swallowed by the belly of the beast that would carry them through the stars.

Inside, the consoles hummed with anticipation, their screens painting the cabin in hues of green and blue. Evelyn took her seat, her fingers gracing the armrests, feeling the latent power coursing beneath them. Hawk settled beside her, his presence both a comfort and a reminder of the battles they had endured, the scars they bore together.

"Engage cloak," she said, the words falling from her lips like droplets into a still pond.

The ship obeyed, its engines whispering secrets to the cosmos as they slid away from the hangar, undetected, unchallenged—a ghost ship charting a course through the eternal night.

As the silhouette of the Kridrax command ship loomed ahead, vast and foreboding against the tapestry of space, the team donned their stealth suits with ritualistic precision. The fabric clung to their skin, morphing, adapting, rendering their forms indistinct blurs against their surroundings.

Silence enveloped them, a shroud that stifled any stray sound. Communications were severed, leaving only the language of gestures and the shared understanding that came from countless hours of training. Hawk's hands moved with military precision, conveying orders without a word.

Evelyn felt the familiar weight of responsibility settle upon her shoulders, a mantle she bore with quiet dignity. This was it— the culmination of all their fears and hopes. The past haunted them, a specter of what had been, but now they stood united, poised to reclaim a future that teetered on the brink.

The transport edged closer, the behemoth ship unaware of the specters that drew near. Evelyn's heart beat a steady rhythm, echoing the pulse of the vessel, as the maw of redemption yawned wide before them. Their mission was clear—rescue, retribution, rebirth. Each step forward was a step away from the chains that bound them, a chance to emerge from the ashes of history, to breathe life into a new dawn where freedom was more than an elusive dream.

It was theirs to seize.

...

The bulk of the Kridrax command ship loomed, a leviathan of cold metal and sinister purpose. With each step, the team's presence was but a whisper against the thrum of the vessel's dark heart. Zylar Threx's scaled hand gestured, a silent sentinel guiding them through a labyrinthine maze of corridors where shadows clung like cobwebs.

Evelyn's breaths were measured, her senses taut as drawn bowstrings, while the stealth suits cloaked them in near-invisibility. They were phantoms in a world of steel and silence, moving with a grace born of desperation. Hawk's gaze met hers, a fleeting connection that spoke volumes—trust, fidelity to their cause, an unspoken vow to emerge victorious or not at all.

The first patrol they encountered was oblivious, the Kridrax guards ensconced in the arrogance of assumed security. Hawk's movements were swift, a blur of precision and strength, his actions mirrored by his team. The guards crumpled soundlessly, felled by hands unseen, their final moments an unanswered question lingering in the sterile air.

Shadows seemed to shift and recoil as the team advanced, the very walls of the ship pregnant with the ghosts of those who had come before, those who had failed. Yet, this time, redemption beckoned with its siren call. The past, with its scars and lessons, was the crucible that had forged them, honed them into instruments of retribution.

They arrived at the holding cells—a stark chamber, suffused with the chill of despair. Evelyn's green eyes scanned the area, her mind dissecting scenarios, calculating risks. Beside her, Hawk issued quiet commands, his voice no more than a murmur, a ghost's whisper.

"Three... two... one," he mouthed.

The operation unfolded with a practiced ease, the team slipping through the guards' defenses like specters through mist. The Kridrax soldiers were dispatched without ceremony, their stunned expressions fading into the void as they slumped to the ground, neutralized.

Evelyn moved to the cells; her fingers deft as they worked to override the security measures. The locks disengaged with a hushed click, and the doors swung open with soft sighs of liberation. The captured comrades emerged from their confinement, their expressions a tapestry of relief and disbelief.

"Quietly," Evelyn urged, her voice barely above a breath. "We're not clear yet."

With their numbers bolstered, the team retreated from the chamber, their steps light upon the cold deck. There was no celebration, only the shared understanding that each moment of reprieve was borrowed, each heartbeat a gift not to be squandered.

As they retraced their path, guided by Zylar's otherworldly intuition, the command ship around them remained ignorant of the daring escape taking place within its bowels. For now, they were phantoms dancing on the edge of perception, moving ever closer to the dawn of their redemption.

...

The corridors of the Kridrax command ship thrummed with the pulse of a thousand machines, a symphony of power and menace that reverberated through the steel bones of its structure. Dr. Montgomery led the way, her eyes narrowed in focus, the rescued comrades flanking her like shadows tethered to her will. The team's steps were measured, each one a deliberate dance with destiny as they delved deeper into the belly of the metallic beast.

"Stay vigilant," she whispered, her voice threading through the squad's comms like a secret meant only for the most trusted ears. "We're treading on the dragon's spine now."

Ahead, the passageway twisted into the unknown, a labyrinthine test of their resolve. Captain Hawking, his features set in a grim mask of determination, nodded toward Zylar Threx. The alien's knowledge had been their beacon thus far, but the light it cast grew dimmer with every step toward their quarry—the synthetic abomination that was Oppressor reborn.

"Resistance ahead," Zylar murmured, their voice tinged with an otherworldly cadence that sent ripples of unease down the spines of their human allies. "Their life-signs churn with hostility."

As if summoned by the very mention, a horde of Kridrax soldiers rounded the corner, their weapons raised in an ominous salute to the impending conflict. Synthetic minions, grotesque parodies of life, skittered at their heels, their eyes glowing with a baleful light.

"Engage!" barked Captain Hawking, his command splintering the heavy silence like lightning rending the sky.

The battle erupted with the ferocity of a storm unleashed. Laser fire streaked through the gloom, painting the walls with ephemeral artistry. Dr. Montgomery ducked behind a protrusion in the wall, her own weapon discharging calculated bursts of energy. Each shot was a whisper of death, precise and unforgiving.

Beside her, Dr. Weller channeled his genius into the fray, manipulating the environment with deft hacks that turned the ship's defenses against their creators. Dr. Chen, her movements a blur of grace and lethality, danced through the chaos, her strikes a poet's verses etched in blood and steel.

"Push forward!" Montgomery urged; her gaze locked onto the path that would lead them to the heart of darkness. "For Earth, for humanity—press on!"

The Kridrax fell before them, their numbers dwindling even as they fought with the desperation of a cornered beast. Yet for every enemy felled, another seemed to rise, a relentless tide of malice that sought to drown them in despair.

"Coordinate!" called out Sergeant Alvarez, his voice a rallying cry amidst the din. "Unity is our strength!"

Lieutenant Isabella, her eyes alight with the fire of battle, leaped into the fray, her blade singing a deadly lullaby as it cleaved through synthetic flesh. Together, they were a symphony of destruction, each member's prowess amplifying the others' — a testament to the indomitable spirit that had carried them this far.

Dr. Patel, ever the strategist, enacted her diversionary tactics with flawless timing, drawing clusters of enemies away from the group, giving them precious moments to regroup and advance. The Kridrax command ship reeled under their assault, its veins of power flickering as the onslaught took its toll.

"Nearly there," Captain Hawking breathed, his eyes reflecting the steely resolve that had become their anchor. "To sever the tyrant's grasp, we must endure."

Sweat mingled with the grime of combat upon their brows, but no fatigue could sway them. With each fallen adversary, redemption drew nearer, a glint of dawn on the horizon of their darkest hour. They were not merely fighters; they were avatars of retribution, each step a declaration that even the ghosts of the past could be laid to rest.

And so, they forged on, their path a crucible that would either temper them to victory or consume them in the fires of history's judgment.

...

The chamber loomed before them, a monolith of steel and shadow, its door an ominous maw ready to swallow any who dared enter. Dr. Evelyn Montgomery's heart hammered a relentless rhythm, her blood thrumming with the urgency of the moment. She exchanged a silent nod with Captain Lucas "Hawk" Hawking, whose scars seemed to deepen in the flickering light, badges of battles fought, and burdens borne.

Beside them, Zylar Threx's luminous form pulsed with a subdued glow, their presence an otherworldly contrast to the stark brutality around them. The iridescent scales that adorned their slender body shimmered with a readiness that transcended the physical realm, as if they were attuned to the vibrations of a universe crying out for balance.

Evelyn's weapon hummed softly in her grip, a high-tech harbinger of the confrontation to come. Her mind raced with calculations and contingencies; each thought a spark igniting the tinder of resolve. This was more than a battle; it was the culmination of every sacrifice, every loss that had etched itself into the fabric of their souls.

The door slid open with a hiss, revealing Synthetic Oppressor, a grotesque parody of a man once flesh and blood, now encased in a carapace of cold metal. His red eyes glared with a malevolence that reached across time, a testament to the poison of unyielding ambition.

"Welcome," the synthetic tyrant intoned, his voice a chilling echo that reverberated off the walls. "You are but the last vestiges of a feeble resistance."

"Your reign ends here, monster," Hawk growled, stepping forward with a confidence that belied the gravity of their plight.

"Indeed," Zylar's haunting timbre filled the chamber, "the wheel of fate turns toward justice this day."

Evelyn felt the weight of history upon them, the silent gaze of countless generations bearing witness to their struggle. With a swift motion, she unleashed a volley of plasma bolts, their brilliance slicing through the charged air as Hawk charged with a roar, his blade a flash of righteous fury.

Synthetic Oppressor countered with terrifying precision, his mechanical limbs a blur of devastating efficiency. The chamber became a vortex of chaos, each clash of metal on metal a symphony of survival against the machinations of tyranny.

But Evelyn's thoughts remained clear, a beacon amidst the storm. She wove between deadly strikes, each movement a calculated risk, her weapon finding weak points in the synthetic overlord's armor. Hawk's relentless assault kept the foe reeling, a dance of destruction that left no room for error.

Zylar moved like a specter, their alien technology interfacing with the ship's systems, sowing discord within the synthetic legion's ranks. Their guidance was a lifeline, pulling at the threads of control that bound Oppressor's consciousness to his metallic shell.

Amidst the fray, Evelyn's piercing green eyes locked onto the core processor that housed the dictator's vile essence. She knew that within that labyrinth of circuits and data streams lay the key to their salvation—or their doom.

"Zylar!" she shouted over the din, "Now!"

With a surge of power that lit the chamber with spectral energy, Zylar initiated the sequence they had prepared tirelessly for, disrupting the flow of information and isolating the core. Hawk seized the moment, his blade cleaving through cables and conduits with the finality of judgment passed.

A shudder ran through the command ship, a sign of the tenuous hold on life fraying at the seams. Synthetic Oppressor staggered, his movements growing erratic as his synthetic form faltered, the fusion of man and machine unraveling under the onslaught.
"Finish it!" Hawk bellowed, his voice a clarion call that pierced the cacophony.

Evelyn stepped forward; her weapon aligned with the exposed core. She hesitated for the barest of moments, the enormity of what they were about to achieve anchoring her to the spot. Redemption was within reach, a chance to mend the torn tapestry of their past.

With a silent prayer to the ghosts that haunted her, Evelyn fired.

The shot was a brilliant flare in the darkness, a beacon of hope that tore through the air and struck true. Synthetic Oppressor's form convulsed, a grotesque marionette with its strings cut, as his consciousness dissolved into the Aether.

Silence fell like a shroud, punctuated only by the labored breathing of the victors standing amidst the wreckage of tyranny toppled. They had faced the abyss, stared into the eyes of a past that refused to die, and emerged not just as warriors, but as harbingers of a future forged in the fires of redemption.

Chapter 18

Concurrency

The first rays of dawn had barely graced the horizon when the sky erupted in a cacophony of light and sound. From their concealed positions, the members of the coalition initiated their assault with precision that belied the chaotic nature of war. They unleashed a torrent of energy beams and missiles, each one a testament to their mastery over the stolen secrets of Kridrax technology. The battlefield, once silent and brooding, became an arena of defiance.

Amidst the turmoil, Colonel Sokolov stood as an unwavering pillar, his gaze locked on the advancing lines of Synthetic Oppressor's mechanized infantry. The cold air bit at his exposed skin, a sobering reminder of the stakes at play. With every order he barked, a renewed sense of urgency coursed through the ranks, fueling their advance against an enemy who was both familiar and alien.

The ground trembled beneath the weight of tank treads and the march of countless boots, but it was the indomitable spirits of the men and women beside him that shook Sokolov's soul. Each blast from their rifles was a chorus of hope, a symphony of determination that resonated across the scarred earth. The Kridrax - cold, unyielding adversaries - returned fire with relentless precision, their crimson lasers carving through the morning mist like fingers of death.

"Push forward!" cried Sokolov, his voice carrying over the din. His command was more than a tactical order; it was an invocation of the past, a plea for redemption in the face of overwhelming odds. The coalition fighters, a mosaic of races and creeds united under a single banner, charged ahead. Their movements were fluid, a dance of survival and aggression honed by months of shared bloodshed.

Zylar Threx, their eyes reflecting the chaos around them, fought with a ferocity that bordered on the primal. Each strike they delivered to the mechanized monstrosities was a blow for vengeance, a silent scream against the tyranny that had once shackled their world. Even as their allies fell around them, the coalition did not waver. Each loss was a wound to their hearts, yet they persisted, propelled by the knowledge that failure would mean a return to darkness for all.

The battle stretched on, time becoming a malleable concept, distorted by adrenaline and the will to survive. Death loomed over the field like a specter, its presence both imminent and ignored. And amidst this theatre of war, the figure of Synthetic Oppressor loomed large - a twisted echo of history's vilest chapter, reborn in steel and malice. His troops, undyingly loyal, mirrored their leader's ruthless efficiency, making every inch gained a Herculean effort.

But still, the coalition fought - side by side, human and alien, past enemies now comrades in arms. They were a testament to what could be achieved when the haunted memories of yesteryear were channeled into a singular, unwavering resolve: to reclaim their future from the clutches of a nightmare reborn.

...

Dr. Evelyn Montgomery's boots pounded the metallic floor of the Kridrax command ship, her breaths rhythmic against the cacophony of warfare. Her short black hair clung to her sweat-drenched forehead as she and Captain Lucas "Hawk" Hawking advanced, their weapons at the ready. The stark lighting of the corridor threw their elongated shadows against the walls, dancing grotesquely with each burst of gunfire.

"Montgomery, status on the severance protocol?" Hawk barked over the din, his muscular frame slightly ahead as they navigated the labyrinthine innards of the ship.

"Charging the disruptor now," Evelyn replied, her voice clipped, fingers flying over her portable tech console. "But we need to get closer."

Their objective was clear: severing Oppressor's consciousness from its synthetic host. Every step they took was a calculated risk, every corner turned an embrace of potential oblivion. Yet, they pressed on, driven by the burden of history's weight upon their shoulders, and the hope of a future untainted by tyranny.

Meanwhile, in the bowels of the same grim fortress, Sergeant Mia Alvarez and Lieutenant Isabella executed a daring dance of stealth and aggression. They moved with silent urgency, weaving through debris and ducking under sporadic energy blasts. Their mission was one of liberation – to rescue Dr. Weller and Dr. Chen, whose intellects were invaluable and whose lives hung in the balance.

"Keep your head down, Isa," Alvarez murmured, her striking brown eyes scanning for threats as she covered Isabella's advance.

"Always do," Isabella responded, the scar on her cheek a pale line in the dim light. She brandished her weapon with practiced ease, her mind a whirlwind of strategies.

The two women embodied the coalition's desperation and determination; their every move was a testament to the camaraderie forged in the fires of conflict. And as they neared the holding cells, their hearts hammered with a blend of fear and resolve.

In the echoing stillness that momentarily enveloped them, Alvarez's thoughts wandered to the friends they sought to save. A pang of guilt gnawed at her for those left behind, but she shook it off, knowing sentiment could not afford to cloud her judgment.

"Almost there," she whispered, signaling to Isabella. They shared a fleeting glance, a silent exchange of mutual understanding, before resuming their treacherous advance.

Back on the command deck, Evelyn and Hawk reached the hub that housed the monstrous dictator's digital essence. The air was thick with electric anticipation, the hum of power coursing through ancient circuits.

"Ready the disruptor," Hawk ordered, a rare flicker of concern crossing his features.

"Initiating sequence," Evelyn affirmed, her green eyes reflecting the glow of the device as she initiated the process that would dismantle a despot's hold on reality.

A sudden barrage of enemy fire forced them to take cover, yet even as the fusillade threatened to overwhelm them, their focus never wavered. Hawk returned fire, providing cover as Evelyn worked furiously to complete her task.

"Almost... got it," she gasped, the finality of their mission within tantalizing reach.

In those protracted moments, the past's ghosts hovered close, whispering of redemption, of wrongs to be righted. And as the disruptor emitted a triumphant whine, signifying the end of Oppressor's reign, a swell of triumph surged within them.

Amidst the chaos, far from the epicenter of technological confrontation, Alvarez and Isabella breached the cell block, their arrival heralding hope. Dr. Weller and Dr. Chen, haggard but unbroken, met their rescuers' gazes with weary gratitude.

"Time to leave this hell," Isabella declared, her voice a resonant promise against the backdrop of battle.

And with the freedom of their comrades secured, they turned to rejoin the fray, their spirits bolstered by small victories amidst the vast tapestry of war. For in this struggle, every liberated soul was another step towards salvation, another chance to mend the fabric of a fractured universe.

...

The battlefield lay shrouded in the acrid smoke of relentless warfare, a grim canvas upon which the final act of an interstellar struggle was painted in stark, violent strokes. Coalition forces surged forward with a fervor that belied the desperation of their cause, each step contested by the zealous legion of Synthetic Oppressor's followers. Their cries, warped by devotion, clashed against the thunderous cacophony of battle, creating a discordant symphony of defiance.

In the midst of this maelstrom, Zylar Threx moved with preternatural grace, an ethereal wraith amongst the chaos. They were The Harbinger, a title earned through sorrow and loss, now a mantle of vengeance against the Kridrax scourge. With every fluid motion of their elongated limbs, they summoned the wrath of a civilization extinguished, channeling it into raw, destructive energy that danced across the battlefield like vengeful spirits.

"Yield not to despair," Zylar intoned, their voice a haunting echo that resonated within the hearts of the beleaguered coalition fighters, "for the echoes of our fallen will resound through victory."

The Kridrax, once formidable adversaries, recoiled as if struck by a force unseen, their ranks fracturing under the weight of Zylar's unleashed power. Wherever they tread, the enemy withered, scales and sinew disintegrating before the silent fury that radiated from The Harbinger's very being. It was as though the grief of worlds unnumbered had found its conduit, lashing out to reclaim a measure of stolen peace.

With each fallen foe, the coalition advanced, their progress measured in the currency of blood and resolve. Yet for every inch gained, a life was spent, the cost of freedom etched into the annals of time with the precision of a surgeon's blade. The ground, soaked in sacrifice, bore witness to the inexorable advance, a testament to the indomitable spirit of those who fought not only for survival but for redemption.

"Press on!" cried Sergeant Alvarez, his voice carrying over the din, rallying the weary to stand firm against the encroaching darkness. Beside him, Lieutenant Isabella brandished her weapon with grim determination, her every action a challenge thrown in the face of malevolence.

"Until the end," she vowed, her words a beacon amidst the shadow of war.

Above them, the specter of Synthetic Oppressor's command ship loomed, a monolithic harbinger of doom that cast its pall over the embattled world below. Yet even as the fires of conflict raged, there was a sense of an ending approaching—a crescendo of fate that would see the tyranny of The Reborn Führer either cemented or shattered.

And so they fought, warriors bound by a shared destiny, driven by the ghosts of their past and the sliver of hope that whispered of a future free from the tyrant's grasp. Each act of valor, each life given in defiance, became the threads weaving together the tapestry of tomorrow—a tomorrow that Zylar Threx, with their spectral gaze fixed upon the heart of darkness, vowed to see dawn, no matter the cost.

...

Evelyn Montgomery stood amid the ruins, her breaths shallow and ragged, as the air trembled with the concussive blasts of distant explosions. The ground beneath her boots was scarred and broken, a mosaic of destruction wrought by Synthetic Oppressor's relentless forces. She watched through narrowed green eyes as her comrades fell, one by one, to the unyielding onslaught. The scent of burning metal and charred flesh hung heavy on the wind, an olfactory testament to the battle that raged without mercy.

"Dr. Patel," Evelyn called out over the cacophony, her voice barely audible against the clamor of war. "We need that diversion now!"

Across the battlefield, obscured by the haze and debris, Samira Patel nodded, her brown eyes reflecting the inferno that surrounded them. With deft hands, she assembled the components of her makeshift device—a beacon of false hope designed to mislead their otherworldly foes. She paused for a moment, pushing a stray curl behind her ear, a gesture of concentration amidst chaos. Her fingers flew over the controls, guided by an intellect honed sharp by years of conflict and creation.

"Almost there," she replied, her calm voice breaking through the bedlam as she connected the last wire. "This will give us the opening we need."

A sudden blast rocked the earth, sending shockwaves through the already battered coalition lines. Evelyn braced herself, feeling the weight of each life lost, the burden of command anchoring her to this moment of despair. Yet within her chest, the ember of resolve glowed fiercely, refusing to be extinguished by doubt or fear.

"Samira, now!" Evelyn urged, desperation threading her clipped efficiency.

With a final adjustment, Dr. Patel activated the device. A surge of energy pulsed into the sky, coalescing into a brilliant display of lights and sounds, a phantom army marching toward the heavens. The Kridrax, deceived by the spectacle, turned their attention skyward, their alien minds ensnared by the lure of the diversion.

"Move, move, move!" Evelyn commanded, seizing the fleeting opportunity. The coalition members, their faces etched with weariness and grief, rallied to her call, their movements infused with newfound purpose. They surged forward, exploiting the distraction as they pushed toward their true objective—freedom from the tyrant who sought to enslave not just their bodies but their very souls.

Amid the thunderous roar of battle and the deceptive serenity of the diversion above, Evelyn allowed herself a moment of introspection. This war, born from the ashes of humanity's darkest history, was more than a struggle for survival—it was a quest for redemption, a chance to right the wrongs of the past and forge a path toward a future unshackled by tyranny.

As the Kridrax faltered, their focus fractured by the cunning ruse, Evelyn caught a glimpse of Samira through the smoke. Their eyes met, a silent acknowledgment passing between them. They were different, yes, in temperament and approach, but they were united in their defiance against the darkness. Together, they would weather the storm of battle, each playing their part to turn the tide in favor of those who still dared to dream of peace.

...

The dim corridors of the Kridrax command ship loomed like the hollow bones of some long-dead leviathan, echoing with the distant clangs and whirs of machinery. Dr. Evelyn Montgomery's breath came in measured puffs, misting the air as she advanced. Her green eyes, sharp as scalpel blades, swept over the alien architecture—a grotesque melding of metal and flesh that pulsed with an unholy life.

"Watch your step," she murmured, her voice barely rising above a whisper as she sidestepped a panel that glinted ominously under the eerie light. Hawk nodded, his presence a reassuring solidity at her side. The pair moved with the synchrony of two celestial bodies bound by invisible forces, their steps weaving through Synthetic Oppressor's labyrinthine traps with a dancer's grace.

A sudden hiss rent the silence, and a barrage of needle-like projectiles lanced towards them from hidden recesses in the walls. Hawk reacted with preternatural speed, his body a blur as he pushed Evelyn out of harm's way. They tumbled to the ground, a controlled chaos of limbs as the darts thudded into the metallic surface where they had stood moments before.

"Close," Hawk grunted, helping Evelyn to her feet. His blue eyes smoldered with an intensity that mirrored the firefights raging outside the ship's steel innards.

"Too close," Evelyn agreed, her pulse thrumming in her ears. She couldn't shake the feeling that these corridors were more than mere pathways—they were the sinews of Synthetic Oppressor's domain, each twist and turn a testament to his twisted genius.

They pressed on, deeper into the bowels of the command ship, where shadows clung like cobwebs and the air grew thick with the scent of ozone and fear. Here, in the heart of darkness, they found him—Synthetic Oppressor, a nightmarish chimera of man and machine, his red eyes alight with the fires of hell itself.

"Dr. Montgomery, Captain Hawking," the abomination intoned, its voice a symphony of malice. "So kind of you to join me."
"End of the line, Oppressor," Hawk declared, his tone a steel blade unsheathed.

Evelyn's fingers danced across her tactical vest, retrieving a compact device designed to disrupt the synthetic neural network that tethered Oppressor's consciousness to this mechanical monstrosity. Her mind raced, calculating angles and trajectories, her every movement a deliberate step in the intricate dance of combat.

"Your persistence is... admirable," Synthetic Oppressor sneered, advancing with mechanical precision. "But futile."

"Let's find out, shall we?" Evelyn shot back, her defiance a beacon in the encroaching gloom.

Their confrontation erupted into a maelstrom of violence, Hawk's military prowess clashing against the synthetic tyrant's augmented might. Evelyn wove between the blows, her focus singular as she sought the perfect moment to strike.

She thought of the lives torn asunder by this war, of the redemption that seemed always just beyond reach. This was more than a battle; it was the culmination of countless sacrifices, a chance to mend the fractured tapestry of history.

With a deft motion, Evelyn slipped past Oppressor's guard, pressing the device firmly against his metallic skull. A surge of energy crackled through the air, and for a moment, time itself seemed to hold its breath.

"Goodbye, Adolf," she whispered, and activated the device. In the ensuing silence, punctuated only by the echoes of distant battles, Evelyn stood resolute beside Hawk. They were the harbingers of a new dawn, the architects of a world unchained from the specter of a past that had haunted humanity for far too long. And as they turned to face the uncertain future, they knew that whatever lay ahead, they would confront it together.

…

The crimson sky bled over the ravaged landscape, casting an ominous glow on the faces of Sergeant Alvarez, Lieutenant Isabella, and Colonel Sokolov as they orchestrated the dance of war. Their figures loomed against the backdrop of chaos, shadows wielding the dimming light like a weapon. The ground beneath their boots vibrated with the ferocity of the coalition's offensive, a symphony of resolve and retribution against the mechanical beast that was the Kridrax command ship.

"Delta team, flank left! Echo, provide cover fire!" Alvarez's voice cut through the din, each command a lash against the enemy's defenses. She moved with lethal grace, her eyes two dark orbs reflecting the battlefield's carnage. Memories of fallen comrades fuelled her every step; redemption was written in the path of her bullets.

Isabella's silhouette darted between blasts, her presence ethereal yet commanding. Her orders were fragments of poetry amidst the cacophony, "Rally at the ridge, push them back!" The scar upon her cheek seemed to whisper tales of battles past, each a testament to her indomitable spirit.

At the heart of this orchestrated assault stood Colonel Sokolov, the eye of the storm. His posture was a pillar amidst ruins, his bald head glistening with the sheen of perspiration and purpose. Every move he made was precise, a chessmaster advancing pawns to protect his queen. There was no room for doubt under his watchful gaze, only the unspoken promise of humanity's last stand.

As the coalition's fury reached its zenith, the once-impenetrable Kridrax command ship began to show signs of faltering. It groaned under the relentless barrage, its hull buckling like the chest of a behemoth drawing its final breaths. With each volley of firepower, hope spread its wings within the hearts of the human forces, daring to soar amidst the smoke and ruin.

"Steady, steady," Sokolov murmured, green eyes fixed on the wavering leviathan above. "Now, unleash hell."

And they did. The collective might of Earth's desperate defenders surged forth, a tidal wave of vengeance crashing against the synthetic shores of tyranny. Explosions blossomed like deadly flowers, tearing through metal and circuitry with a hunger for liberation.

In the thick of the fray, Alvarez found herself momentarily isolated, her breaths coming in ragged gasps. She could feel the phantom pain of a world torn asunder, the weight of history heavy upon her shoulders. Yet, as she watched the Kridrax defenses crumble, there was a fleeting sense of something more profound than victory—a whisper of peace in the eye of the storm.

"Press forward!" Isabella's voice pierced the haze, her blue eyes aflame with the fervor of battle. "We break them here!"

The command ship shuddered violently, its structure compromised by the ceaseless onslaught. With each passing moment, the colossus waned, its tyrannical grip loosening from the throat of a defiant Earth.

Sokolov allowed himself the ghost of a smile, a rare crack in his stoic facade. "For those who have fallen," he intoned solemnly, "for those we can still save."

In the shadow of redemption, amid the echoes of a world reclaiming its future, the Kridrax command ship gave one final, mournful cry before succumbing to the void. And as it crumbled, so too did the last vestiges of a nightmare that had once seemed eternal.

...

The command ship's inner sanctum thrummed with the dying pulse of Kridrax technology, its once-immaculate corridors now marred by the scars of battle. Dr. Markus Weller's fingers danced over the alien console with frantic precision, his mind a whirlwind of calculations and contingencies. Beside him, Dr. Lily Chen stood resolute, her gaze locked onto the flickering displays as they reflected the gravity of their final gambit.

"Power levels critical," she announced, her voice a serene counterpoint to the chaos that enveloped them. "Markus, are you certain?"

"Certainty is a luxury we no longer have," Markus replied, his tone betraying none of the trepidation that gnawed at the edges of his resolve. The words seemed to hang in the air, mingled with the scent of ozone and the distant cries of their comrades in arms.

Their hands met for an instant, a silent pact forged amidst the tempest of war. With a collective breath, they initiated the sequence that would herald the end of an era or the doom of their cause. A cascade of lights blinked into existence, heralding the overload of the core—a beacon of defiance in the face of oblivion.

The command ship groaned, metal and flesh unified in protest, as a surge of raw power ripped through its veins. The heart of the beast, once a juggernaut of oppression, swelled to the brink of rupture. And then, with a brilliance that outshone the stars themselves, it unleashed its fury upon the remnants of the Kridrax armada.

Outside, soldiers and scientists alike shielded their eyes against the blinding conflagration that tore the heavens asunder. The very fabric of the battlefield shifted, reality bending beneath the weight of liberation's crescendo.

As the light receded, leaving behind only the echo of its wrath, the survivors emerged from their shelters like specters rising from the ashes. Dr. Evelyn Montgomery's piercing green eyes surveyed the smoldering ruins, her face a mask of stoic contemplation painted by hardship and triumph. She could not yet fathom the cost of their victory, but she felt the fragile threads of the future weaving anew.

"Is it done?" Her voice cut through the settling dust, seeking affirmation in a world still reeling from its rebirth.

"Done," Markus confirmed, stepping through the wreckage with the gait of one who has walked through fire and emerged unscathed. His glasses skewed on his nose, a testament to the maelstrom he had weathered.

Lily followed, her composure a stark contrast to the devastation that surrounded them. "We have severed the head," she added, her voice steady but haunted by the specter of doubt that lingered in her heart.

They stood together, a trio emblematic of humanity's indomitable spirit, bearing witness to the dawn of an age wrought by their own hands. The Kridrax threat, once a shadow that stretched across worlds, now lay broken at their feet — a monument to the resilience of those who refuse to yield to tyranny.

"Let history remember this moment," Evelyn murmured, her words imbued with the weight of all they had endured, "when the children of Earth reclaimed their destiny."

In the silence that followed, fractured only by the distant sounds of a world healing its wounds, they shared a glance that spoke volumes. It was a look of understanding, of shared loss and mutual redemption — a silent vow that the past would guide them, but never again define them.

The coalition members, battered and weary, gathered amidst the remnants of a battle that would echo through the annals of time. Their faces, etched with the toll of conflict, bore the unmistakable mark of victory — hard-won and dearly bought.

And as they stood in the shadow of a fallen tyrant, it was clear that the path ahead would be fraught with challenges anew. But in this moment, under the watchful gaze of a universe that had tested their resolve, they were united.

They were victorious. They were free.

…

Captain Hawking's boots crunched over the debris-strewn ground as he approached the ragged assembly of survivors. The air was thick with the tang of scorched metal and victory, a heady blend that filled their lungs and steeled their spirits. They had breached the seemingly impregnable fortress of tyranny, and in its place, they beheld the promise of a new epoch. "Report," he commanded, his voice ringing clear amidst the murmurs of triumph.

Dr. Montgomery stepped forward, her gaze lingering on the horizon where the command ship's wreckage scarred the sky. "Oppressor's consciousness — severed. The Kridrax influence is crumbling without its puppet master."

"Then it is done," Hawking affirmed, allowing himself the ghost of a smile. Around them, the coalition members exchanged weary nods and clasped hands, the camaraderie born from shared adversity forming an unspoken pact.

"Indeed," said Dr. Patel, her eyes reflecting the fire of distant stars. "We've not only won a battle but turned the tide for human sovereignty."

The group fell into a contemplative hush, each lost in their own reckoning of loss and resilience. They were like chiseled statues from ancient myths, bearing the marks of countless struggles, their faces telling tales of sacrifice and indomitable will. Sergeant Alvarez cleared his throat, breaking the silence. "We remember those who fell, but we honor them by moving forward. For them, for Earth, for the future we've fought so hard to secure."

"Earth's children, no longer bound by chains of fear," Lieutenant Isabella added softly, her words lifting on the breeze.

A slow, collective breath seemed to pass through the group, and for a moment, time itself hung suspended, acknowledging the gravity of their undertaking. They had wrenched back their destiny from the clutches of a synthetic monster, casting off the shadow that loomed over their homeworld.

"Let us carry this victory as a beacon," Colonel Sokolov stated, his Russian accent wrapping around the words like a comforting blanket. "For when the darkness comes again — as it always does — we will remember this light."

Their gazes turned skyward, where the heavens stretched infinite and inscrutable, a tapestry of celestial wonders that awaited their next bold stride. A sense of relief washed over them, mingling with the triumphant realization that they had indeed severed Oppressor's grip on Earth. They had not merely endured; they had prevailed.

"Today we have forged our legacy," Hawking declared, his voice resonant with the weight of their achievement. "Humanity shall carve its place among the stars, unshackled and unbroken."

As they regrouped, a silent acknowledgment passed between them — a nod to the unyielding spirit that had sustained them through their darkest hours. They had emerged from the crucible of conflict reborn, their eyes alight with the dawn of possibilities.

And so, beneath the watchful heavens, they began the solemn procession back to their stronghold. With hearts tempered by battle and eyes set upon the vast frontier before them, they walked together into the unfolding narrative of their reclaimed future.

Chapter 19

Severed Consciousness

The command ship loomed like an ancient behemoth, its corridors stretching into shadows that whispered of secrets and dormant perils. Dr. Evelyn Montgomery's pulse thrummed in her ears as she led the way, the dim glow from the walls barely illuminating their path. Her short black hair seemed to absorb the darkness, and her piercing green eyes sliced through the gloom, a beacon of resolve amidst uncertainty.

Captain Lucas "Hawk" Hawking followed a step behind, his formidable frame a silent promise of protection. His gaze never wavered, blue eyes dissecting every crevice and corner, alert for the ambush they all feared yet marched steadfastly toward. The air sat heavy with the scent of ozone and the unspoken thoughts of battle-hardened warriors.

Beside him, Zylar Threx moved with a grace that belied their size, iridescent scales casting eerie reflections on the metal walls. Their deep-set eyes remained fixated ahead, glowing softly, the light within them a testament to the knowledge and sorrow they carried.

"Stay vigilant," Evelyn murmured, her voice authoritative despite the undercurrent of memories clawing at her composure. She didn't need to look back to sense Hawk's nod or hear the faint rustle of Zylar's agreement. They were a unit, bound by the gravity of their mission and the shadows of their respective pasts.

Abruptly, the sterile silence shattered as Synthetic Oppressor's voice boomed from hidden speakers, resonating with a chilling resonance. "Foolish intruders," the synthetic dictator taunted, each syllable dripping with venomous disdain. "Your presence defiles this vessel of new order. Turn back now and embrace the mercy of oblivion."

Evelyn's stride did not falter, though the spectral tendrils of the dictator's voice sought to ensnare her will. She could almost see the twisted visage of metal and flesh, red eyes burning with malice and madness. Hawk's jaw clenched at the sound, a muscle ticking in his cheek — the only sign of his simmering rage against the tyrant who had brought so much suffering.

"Empty threats from a man who's already lost," Zylar intoned, their words slicing through the oppressive atmosphere with otherworldly resonance. "We are not swayed by the echoes of a fallen despot."

Synthetic Oppressor's laughter reverberated off the walls, a discordant symphony that clawed at their nerves. "Abandon your futile quest. There is no redemption for you here, only the inevitable embrace of defeat."

But the trio pressed on, the slow cadence of their steps a silent counterpoint to the bluster and bravado that filled the air. Each heartbeat was a drumroll of defiance, a signal that they would not be turned aside. They were the harbingers of Synthetic Oppressor's reckoning, and nothing — not even the ghostly specter of his voice — could deter them from their path.

Their journey through the labyrinthine corridors was a march through time itself, where every shadow held a memory and every echo a whisper of battles fought long ago. Yet amidst the remnants of war and the machinery of conquest, there was a palpable sense of impending change — a tide about to turn, a future about to be rewritten.

As they neared the central control room, Evelyn's mind raced, strategizing, calculating. Synthetic Oppressor's downfall lay just beyond these walls, and with it, a chance to heal the wounds of a galaxy torn asunder. It was more than a mission; it was a crucible in which their souls would be tested, and from which they would emerge either victorious or not at all.

...

The corridor terminated abruptly, the stark outline of the control room's entrance looming before them. Evelyn, Hawk, and Zylar halted, their breaths suspended in a moment of anticipation. The threshold vibrated with an imperceptible hum, a siren song to their senses, pulling them toward the confrontation that awaited.

"Prepare yourselves," Evelyn whispered, her voice a serrated edge cutting through the silence.

No sooner had the words left her lips than shadows detached from the walls, coalescing into the formidable shapes of Kridrax guards. Their weapons—a terrifying amalgam of alien technology and deadly intent—were trained on the trio with mechanical precision.

Evelyn's fingers danced over the gadget at her belt, a device birthed from her intellect and crafted for moments such as this. The air crackled with electricity, an invisible maelstrom directed by her will. A cascade of sparks erupted from the guards' weaponry, rendering them lifeless husks. She allowed herself the ghost of a smile, satisfaction mingling with the adrenaline coursing through her veins.

Beside her, Hawk's battle cry shattered the stillness, his body a blur of motion as he lunged towards the nearest guard. Muscle and sinew moved in perfect harmony; each strike a testament to countless hours of training and combat. His fists were instruments of deliverance, each blow echoing the silent promise of liberation he carried within him.

Zylar moved like water, a symphony of fluid grace amidst the chaos. Their limbs contorted in ways human anatomy never could, the iridescent scales adorning their skin catching the flickering light as they danced death's waltz with their adversaries. There was a melancholic beauty to Zylar's movements, a lament for every life snuffed out too soon by the Kridrax scourge.

The guards fell, one by one, their forms crumpling under the relentless assault of flesh, bone, and alien might. As the last of them hit the ground with a finality that echoed in the hollow space, the path to Synthetic Oppressor lay unguarded.

Their advance resumed in silence, the door to the control room parting before them like the curtain of fate revealing its inexorable design. They stepped through the threshold, the cool air within greeting them like the embrace of destiny itself. The control room was a cathedral of terror, its walls lined with instruments of control and subjugation, all converging upon the epicenter of malice that stood before them.

Synthetic Oppressor towered over the room, a grotesque monument to mankind's darkest legacy. His synthetic eyes, glowing with the fire of hatred and ambition, fixed upon the trio with chilling intensity. The metallic timbre of his voice reverberated through the vast chamber, a perverse echo of history's most infamous orator.

"Welcome, heroes," he intoned, the word dripping with venomous sarcasm. "You have come far, but it is here that your misguided journey ends."

Evelyn's heart thundered against her ribcage, each beat a drumroll of courage and fear intermingled. Her green eyes, reflecting the cold light of the room, locked onto the artificial monstrosity. In the depth of those eyes, the reflections of past betrayals flickered momentarily before being replaced by the steely resolve of one who has seen the abyss and chosen to defy it.

Hawk's stance was a fortress of determination, his body poised and ready to unleash the fury of humanity upon this abomination of nature. And beside him, Zylar's alien form seemed to shimmer with a quiet rage, the weight of a thousand lost worlds etched into the solemnity of their aspect.

Here, in the heart of darkness, they stood united — not just as warriors, but as bearers of hope, guardians of a future that teetered precariously between salvation and ruin.

...

The air crackled with the scent of ozone, a harbinger to the storm Synthetic Oppressor summoned with a twisted snarl. Energy, raw and vengeful, surged from his mechanical fingertips, sizzling across the room in arcs of lethal fury. Dr. Evelyn Montgomery dove behind a console, her breaths shallow and rapid as she pressed herself against the cold metal. Beside her, Captain Lucas "Hawk" Hawking's muscles tensed like coiled springs ready to release; his gaze was an anchor in the tempest. Zylar Threx's lithe form shimmered with subtle iridescence as they too sought refuge, their alien grace stark against the harsh contours of human technology.

"Watch out," Hawk growled, his voice barely above a whisper as another blast seared the space where Zylar had been moments before. The trio exchanged glances, a wordless conversation passing between them — an acknowledgment of the peril they faced and the resolve that bound them.

Evelyn's mind raced, her intellect a blade honed on the whetstone of necessity. Her eyes darted over the control room's layout, noting the positions of consoles and the towering figure of their foe. The dim lighting cast deep shadows across the synthetic sinews that wound around Synthetic Oppressor's frame, but there, just beneath the cruel simulacrum of a heart, a subtle imperfection — a panel less secure, a junction of wires more exposed than the rest.

"Got it," she murmured, more to herself than her companions. Her fingers twitched, the knowledge of machines and circuitry melding with the urgency of battle. She envisioned it, the plan crystallising in her mind: a precise assault on that vulnerable nexus, a strike to sever the tyrant from his vessel of terror.

"Zylar," she whispered, her voice carrying the weight of countless calculations, "I need a diversion, something... anything."

Zylar nodded, their alien features set in grim determination. They understood the stakes, the dance of death and deliverance that played out in the theatre of war.

Hawk, sensing the shift in Evelyn's demeanor, offered a curt nod. He trusted her, not merely as a comrade in arms but as the brilliant mind that had steered them through darkness time and again. His hand found the grip of his weapon, the familiar texture a promise of retribution yet to be dealt.

In the silence that followed, the past loomed like specters at the feast, whispering of betrayals and battles won at great cost. Yet here, in this crucible of fire and steel, the past would serve not as a shackle but as a springboard to redemption — for Evelyn, for Hawk, for Zylar, and for a world teetering on the brink of oblivion.

As Synthetic Oppressor's laughter echoed, mocking and malevolent, the three warriors steeled themselves. Each knew what must be done, and what might be lost in the doing. But the path to victory is paved with such uncertainties, and only those who dare to tread its length can claim the triumph that waits, veiled in shadow, at its end.

…

Captain Hawking's voice pierced the cacophony of energy discharges, "Now!" The command was both a beacon and a decree, echoing through Dr. Montgomery's focus as she calibrated the device with shaking hands. She felt the weight of souls and the breath of destiny upon her neck, the pivotal fulcrum of time teetering on her actions.

Zylar, lithe and spectral, unleashed a volley from their plasma caster, the sapphire bolts streaking across the room like vengeful spirits seeking to distract their synthetic nemesis. Synthetic Oppressor's attention wavered, drawn to the defiance that dared challenge his dominion. His mechanical limbs whirred discordantly, orchestrating a symphony of destruction aimed at the source of his irritation.

"Keep him busy," Evelyn muttered under her breath, the words a mantra against the dread that clawed at her resolve. Her device — a confluence of science and hope — glowed softly in her grasp, its light a whisper of salvation amidst the shadow of tyranny.

Hawk, ever the sentinel, fired in measured bursts. His shots were the thunderous retort to Zylar's lightning, a terrestrial counterpoint to otherworldly precision. Beneath his stoic exterior, the tumult of leadership raged — a tempest of concern for the lives entrusted to his care, for Evelyn's gambit to succeed.

In this dance of death and defiance, the past unfurled its spectral fingers, beckoning with memories of loss and triumph. It was a haunting reminder of what lay at stake, of the redemption that could be wrought from the crucible of conflict.

Evelyn took a breath, inhaling the electric tang of ozone and the sharp scent of fear — an alchemy that fortified her spirit. With a swift glance towards her comrades, she readied herself. Now was the moment, now was the act.

She surged from behind the console, a specter of vengeance clad in the armor of necessity. Synthetic Oppressor's gaze snapped towards her — a predator recognizing the heart of his peril too late. Energy blasts seared the air where she had been moments before, their lethal intent thwarted by the grace of desperation.

The distance between Evelyn and Synthetic Oppressor shrank with each pounding step. The room seemed to elongate, time stretching thin as she raced towards the abyss of uncertainty. Her device thrummed, an eager heartbeat against her palm.

A blast grazed her shoulder, singing fabric and flesh, but she did not falter. She couldn't. Humanity's last hope was a mere arm's length away, nestled in the grotesque junction of man and machine that pulsed with Synthetic Oppressor's malevolent consciousness.

With a cry torn from the depths of every soul yearning for freedom, Evelyn thrust the device forward. It connected with a soundless plea, a silent prayer to the ghosts of her past, to the future that hung in the balance.

For an eternal second, the world held its breath.

Then, activation.

The device emitted a pulse, a radiant flare of light that sank into Synthetic Oppressor's form. There was no fanfare, no grand explosion—only the subtle sag of defeat as the tyrant's synthetic shell shuddered, its connection to its vile master severed by the hand of courage.

As the finality of her actions settled over her, Evelyn's heart thundered a rhythm of triumph and terror, the twin harbingers of redemption earned in the face of oblivion.

...

Synthetic Oppressor's form writhed, the metallic sinews twisting in an unnatural dance of fury. His voice, once booming with tyrannical command, now crackled through the intercom—a symphony of rage and electronic malaise. The walls of the command ship vibrated as though resonating with his anger, loose panels clattering to the floor, creating a cacophony of chaos.

"Impossible!" the synthetic dictator garbled, his words slurring into obscurity. "I am... I am eternal!"

Above them, the ceiling groaned, burdened by the seismic wrath that coursed through the vessel. Dust motes danced in the flickering light, spiraling like lost souls set free from purgatory. A panel gave way, and debris rained down, forcing Dr. Montgomery to shield her face with a raised arm, her green eyes narrowing against the grit-laden air.

Captain Hawking, ever the sentinel, took a half-step forward, his muscular frame poised to protect, though the threat was now internal, collapsing upon itself. His blue eyes, mirrors of the sky they longed to reclaim, reflected the crumbling tyranny before him.

Zylar Threx, their alien ally, swayed slightly, their shimmering scales reflecting the emergency lights that strobed in panicked rhythm. Their gaze lingered on the convulsing mass that had been their nemesis, their voice a mere whisper carried on the tempestuous air. "The end of one nightmare," they intoned, "the harbinger of hope."

The synthetic body stilled abruptly, the room falling into a sudden, eerie silence. It was as if the universe itself exhaled, releasing the pent-up breath of countless battles, of bloodshed and tears sown across the stars.

Dr. Montgomery watched as Synthetic Oppressor — no longer a figure of terror but a husk devoid of its malevolent spirit — collapsed with a finality that echoed in the hollow space. Her heart, which had been a drumbeat of survival, slowed its cadence, allowing a fragile peace to settle within her chest.

For a moment, none moved. They stood amidst the wreckage, a trinity of resilience, their shared purpose culminating in this singular point in time. Victory was an elusive mistress, often slipping through the fingers like grains of sand, but here, now, she bestowed upon them a fleeting kiss.

"Is it over?" Hawk's voice broke the stillness, a gruff murmur that seemed almost sacrilegious in the hallowed aftermath.

"Over, yes," Evelyn replied, her clipped tones softening as she allowed herself to believe in the reality they had forged. "But the journey continues."

They exchanged glances, silent conversations traversing the distance between them. In each other's eyes, they found reflections of themselves: scarred, battle-weary, yet undefeated. Here, in the heart of darkness, they had carved out a beacon of light, a testament to their tenacity.

And in the quiet that followed, as the dust settled like memories laid to rest, each knew that redemption had been granted—not only to the worlds they vowed to defend but to their own tattered souls, seeking solace in a galaxy reborn from the ashes of tyranny.

...

Sergeant Mia Alvarez crouched low, her breath a ghost in the frigid air, as she surveyed the war-ravaged terrain that sprawled before her. The cries of conflict, a cacophonous symphony to which she had become all too accustomed, rang in her ears. Beside her, Lieutenant Isabella's blue eyes were alight with a fire forged from years of combat, her scar a stark reminder of the price already paid. And there, standing as an unwavering monolith amid the chaos, was Colonel Sokolov, his gaze piercing the night like a harbinger of fate.

"Steady, Alvarez," Sokolov said, his voice the embodiment of resolve. "Our moment is near."

The ground beneath them shuddered with the ferocity of explosions, each blast painting the sky with blooms of destruction. Yet, in their hearts, a different kind of detonation occurred—an explosion of hope as word of Synthetic Oppressor's imminent fall rippled through their ranks.

"Push forward!" Isabella commanded, her voice slicing through the din. With a nod that sealed their unspoken pact, Mia and her comrades surged into the fray.

The Kridrax invaders, once a relentless tide of malice, now faltered under the weight of human determination. Each soldier bore the scars of countless skirmishes, but none so deep as the wounds within their souls. The fight was not just for territory; it was for redemption—for every memory tainted by the shadow of tyranny.

Alvarez moved with a grace born of desperation, her rifle an extension of her will. She fired with precision, the echo of each shot a promise to those who had fallen. Beside her, Isabella's quick thinking turned the battlefield into a chessboard, her moves calculated and deadly.

"Covering fire!" Alvarez shouted, her voice barely audible over the roar of battle.

"Got it!" Isabella responded, her fingers dancing across her weapon's controls with practiced ease.

Above them, the skies were ablaze, the stars obscured by the fury of war. Yet, despite the chaos, a silence settled in Mia's mind—a stillness that spoke of endings and beginnings. She thought of the command ship, of Dr. Montgomery, Captain Hawking, and Zylar, and how their struggle mirrored her own.

"Adolph is falling," she whispered to herself, the words a talisman against the darkness.

"Then let's give him a push," Isabella replied, understanding the sentiment without needing to see Mia's face.

Together, they advanced, each step a defiance of the fear that sought to claim them. The Kridrax, sensing their leader's doom, wavered, their once-impenetrable lines crumbling like sandcastles before the tide.

"Victory is at hand!" Colonel Sokolov bellowed, his voice the clarion call that spurred them onward.

In the distance, the faintest light of dawn began to creep above the horizon, a subtle herald of the new world that awaited them. It was a world that Sergeant Mia Alvarez dared to envision—

one where the specters of the past no longer held dominion over the living.

And as she reloaded, her movements automatic yet fraught with meaning, she allowed herself to believe, if only for a heartbeat, that the ghosts of yesteryear might finally find peace in the dawn of humanity's hard-won day.

...

Sergeant Mia Alvarez crouched low against the jagged remains of a once-mighty wall, her gaze sweeping across the battlefield — a tapestry woven with streaks of laser fire and the staccato dance of shadows. Beside her, Lieutenant Isabella's eyes flickered with a steely resolve as she surveyed their dwindling cover, the Kridrax forces relentless in their advance.

"Bravo team, flank left! Echo, you're with me," Isabella commanded, her voice slicing through the cacophony of war like a shard of ice. Alvarez nodded, the unspoken language of warriors flowing between them. They had become adept at reading each other's intentions, two kindred spirits etched by the same chisel of duty and loss.

In synchronized grace, they moved, a lethal ballet choreographed amidst chaos. The Kridrax, their exoskeletons gleaming under the barrage of artillery, seemed almost mechanical in their precision — yet not invulnerable. Alvarez noted the slight delay in their movements, the way they faltered when a barrage came from an unexpected quadrant.

"Isabella, there!" Alvarez pointed to a cluster of the enemy momentarily disoriented by a mortar's kiss. "Their reaction time — it's our key."

"Let's turn it in our favor," Isabella replied, her voice a whisper of steel. Signals flashed, orders given without words, and suddenly, human troops poured forth from their hiding spots, a wave crashing upon the rocks of uncertainty.

As the battle ebbed and flowed around them, a figure stood resolute amidst the maelstrom. Colonel Viktor Sokolov's presence was as commanding as the statues of old-world generals, his green eyes reflecting a mind that saw beyond the immediacy of battle. He watched, his fingers tracing invisible lines upon a holographic map, a maestro conducting an orchestra of destruction.

"Comms are their lifeline," he mused aloud, more to himself than to the communications officer beside him. "Cut that, and we cut the head from the serpent."

"Sir?" the officer prompted, awaiting the command that would redefine the tide of this relentless conflict.

"Prepare an EMP strike," Sokolov ordered, the weight of his decision heavy in his tone. "Target their communication arrays. No transmissions in or out. Leave them blind and deaf."

"Understood, sir." The officer's fingers danced over the controls, setting into motion a gambit that could spell triumph or disaster.

Alvarez felt a ripple in the air, a prelude to silence that descended like a shroud. It was followed by a pulse, invisible yet potent enough to still the frenetic heartbeat of technology. The Kridrax stumbled, their coordination shattered like glass under a hammer's blow. Their movements became erratic, confused—an army of puppets with severed strings.

"Advance!" Sokolov's order cut through the newfound quiet, and the human forces surged forward, seizing upon the chaos sown in the enemy ranks. Alvarez leapt over debris, her rifle a constant companion spitting defiance with every round.

She locked eyes with Isabella across the field — a shared nod, an acknowledgment of battles fought and the hope of those yet to come. They were the vanguard, the heralds of humanity's indomitable spirit, pressing on where lesser souls might falter.

The Kridrax, once a fearsome tide, now retreated in disarray, their unity fractured by Sokolov's cunning. Alvarez allowed herself a fleeting smile, a rare indulgence on a visage carved from sternness and scars.

"Today, we reclaim our future," she murmured, her voice barely audible above the din of rekindled warfare. And in that moment, amidst the smoke and ruin, the past seemed a distant specter, and redemption glinted on the horizon like the first light of dawn.

...

The Kridrax, once a coordinated swarm of destruction, now floundered in disarray, their synchronized malice disrupted by an unseen hand. A cacophony of disjointed commands echoed through their ranks, the once unbreakable chain of command reduced to a tangled mess of uncertainty and fear.

From her vantage point, Sergeant Mia Alvarez surveyed the battlefield with calculating eyes, noting the hesitation that rippled through the enemy like a wave. The ground beneath her boots, littered with the evidence of fierce combat, seemed to tremble with opportunity. Each step forward was measured, a silent dance amidst the thunderous chaos that surrounded her.

"Push them back!" she commanded, her voice piercing the tumult as she signaled to Isabella. Together, they became conduits for Colonel Sokolov's strategy, orchestrating movements that turned soldiers into instruments of reclamation, each maneuver a note in a symphony of liberation.

The sky, heavy with the smoke of battle, watched in silence as humanity's warriors carved paths through the bewildered masses of Kridrax. With each faltering step the invaders took backward, the humans advanced, driven by an insatiable hunger for victory. This was more than a fight for survival; it was a declaration that the shadow cast by tyranny would be lifted, and redemption was theirs to seize.

Alvarez felt the familiar surge of adrenaline as she dispatched another foe, her movements precise, the result of countless hours honed in the crucible of war. Yet, underneath the soldier's exterior, there thrummed a current of reflection. Each life taken was a stark reminder of what had been lost, of the price of freedom etched into the very soil upon which they fought.

The Kridrax's confusion sowed seeds of courage among the human forces, their spirits buoyed by the sight of enemies retreating into the embrace of the horizon. It was in these fleeting seconds that Alvarez allowed herself the luxury of hope—a dangerous sentiment on the battlefield, yet one that could not be denied its place in her heart.

"Today," she found herself whispering amid the roar of guns and the cries of the fallen, "we rise from the ashes of our past." The words were carried away, lost to the ether, yet they left a lasting imprint on her soul. For in this moment, the ghosts that haunted her steps seemed to fall away, granting her a taste of the peace she fought so fiercely to attain.

And as the Kridrax lines crumbled further, the air tinged with the scent of impending triumph, Alvarez knew that the tales of this day would be etched in the annals of history—a testament to the resilience of those who dared to defy the darkness and reclaim the light.

Chapter 20

Advantage

The void of space clung to the Kridrax command ship like a
shroud, its shadowy silhouette a behemoth against the cosmos.
Within its bowels, the coalition members melded with the dark,
moving through the winding corridors like specters, each step a
silent testament to their covert purpose. Their knowledge of the
alien vessel's layout was their guide in this metallic labyrinth,
their movements calculated to escape the omnipresent gaze of
unseen sentries.

Dr. Evelyn Montgomery led the cadre with a quiet ferocity that
belittled her compact frame. Her short black hair seemed to
absorb the scant light, and her piercing green eyes flickered
from one shadow to the next, vigilant for any sign of the enemy.
The corridors stretched before them, an endless maze of cold
steel and secrets, but she navigated with the confidence of one
who had long since mapped every turn in her mind's eye.

"Stay sharp," she whispered into the comm, her voice barely
above a breath yet carried with clarity to her team. "We move to
the core on my mark."

Even as she spoke, her steps never faltered, each footfall a silent
drumbeat marching them toward their unseen goal. The weight
of her blaster felt familiar in her grip—its cold, unyielding
presence a stark reminder of the stakes at hand.

Evelyn's resolve was the heartbeat of the mission, unbreakable
and rhythmic. She knew the ghosts of betrayal that haunted the
past could not be allowed to whisper doubts into this precarious
present. With every step forward, she sought redemption—not

just for herself but for a humanity teetering on the brink of oblivion.

The dim corridor seemed to constrict around them, the air thick with anticipation. A faint hum of distant machinery played a discordant lullaby, punctuated by the occasional, unsettling click of something mechanical adjusting in the darkness. The muted glow of indicator lights cast an eerie pallor on the faces of her comrades, their expressions set in determined lines.

"Left at the junction. Then straight to the secondary access hatch," Evelyn instructed, her tone imbued with an authority that brooked no argument, yet carried the intimacy of shared purpose. Her eyes caught the brief nod from Dr. Markus Weller, his thin frame a shadow within shadows, glasses reflecting pinpricks of light as he acknowledged the command.

They moved as one entity, a fusion of flesh and intent, driven by the singular desire to sever the source of the Kridrax's power. Each member bore the scars of a ravaged Earth, the memory of loss fueling their silent advance. Evelyn felt the weight of those memories, letting it anchor her resolve rather than sink it.

Dr. Lily Chen trailed close behind, her youthful features belying the steel within. Her bright brown eyes scanned the environment, alight with the fire of conviction. There was more than mere intelligence in those depths; there was a burning need to right the wrongs of the universe.

"Remember why we're here," Evelyn murmured, though she knew the words were unnecessary. They all remembered. It was etched in the very air they breathed, in every silent prayer for the future, in every heartbeat that pounded in defiance of tyranny.

As they reached the predetermined juncture, Evelyn gestured with a gloved hand, signaling a halt. Her team froze, an unspoken understanding flowing between them like an undercurrent. With a glance, Evelyn confirmed the absence of Kridrax patrols — a small mercy in a night fraught with peril.

"Go," she breathed, and once more, they were motion, phantoms slipping through the ribcage of the beast, closer now to the heart that sustained its malignant life. Redemption called to them, a siren song amid the stars, promising that the past could be reconciled with a future yet unwritten.

...

Silence ruptured into chaos as the thunderous eruption of gunfire shattered the stillness of the Kridrax command ship's corridor. Evelyn Montgomery's heart pounded in her chest, a rhythm that matched the staccato bursts from Sergeant Mia Alvarez's rifle. The air sizzled with the discharge of energy weapons, the acrid scent of ionized particles filling the confined space.

"Cover!" Alvarez barked, her voice a sharp spear through the din. Lieutenant Isabella responded in kind, a dance of deadly precision unfolding as they laid down a suppressing barrage against the suddenly materializing Kridrax soldiers.

Evelyn ducked behind a bulkhead, her green eyes darting to Dr. Markus Weller and Dr. Lily Chen, who had sprung into action amidst the turmoil. Weller's fingers flew over a small device, his glasses reflecting the soft glow of its screen, while Chen relayed coordinates with urgent clarity.

"Disrupting their frequency... now," Weller announced, his normally slow cadence clipped by necessity. With a final tap, a wave of distortion rippled through the air, and the Kridrax's weapons emitted a high-pitched whine before falling silent.

Chen allowed herself the ghost of a smile, fleeting and determined, before she returned her focus to the battle at hand. Their enemies, momentarily confused by their malfunctioned arms, were quickly adapting—resorting to brute force.

"Move!" Evelyn shouted, her voice a commander's call to advance. They navigated through the debris of combat, finding their rhythm amidst the disarray. A locked portal loomed ahead—a barrier to their progress, yet another test of their resolve.

Weller approached, his thin frame hunched with concentration as he extracted a tangle of wires from his pack. His hands, so often lost within the recesses of his mind's labyrinth, now weaved a tangible maze that interfaced with the alien door's mechanism.

"Curious design," he murmured, almost to himself, "akin to an ancient puzzle longing to be solved." The mysterious tone was not lost on Evelyn, who watched the man work, her trust in his expertise unwavering despite the encroaching danger.

Time stretched, each second a precious commodity as Weller decoded the Kridrax's intricate security. With a satisfying click, the door's seal relented, granting them passage. A collective breath held was released, and they slipped through the threshold.

"Keep alert," Evelyn commanded, the weight of their mission pressing upon her shoulders like the gravity of a collapsing star. They were the bearers of hope, navigating the shadowed corridors of despair, each step a defiance against the dark history that had led them here.

Their journey continued, the ghosts of the past whispering of redemption, of a future where the stars would once again shine unobscured by the specter of war. The coalition moved onward, united by the unspoken oath to reclaim what had been lost and to carve a path toward absolution.

…

Silence clung to the corridors of the Kridrax command ship like a shroud. The dim lighting cast long shadows that danced upon the walls with every flash from the distant skirmishes echoing through the metal bones of the vessel. Dr. Evelyn Montgomery led her team with an unwavering stride, her green eyes scanning every dark corner for signs of the enemy.

"Stay close," she whispered, each word laced with authority and the unspoken fear that one misstep could lead them all to ruin. They were a phalanx of resilience against an unseen tide, moving through the darkness as one entity, bound by purpose and necessity.

A sudden flicker on a nearby monitor caught their collective gazes. A visage materialized from the static — a face from history reborn into a grotesque parody of life. Synthetic Oppressor's digital eyes bore into them, his voice resonating through the speakers with a chilling blend of arrogance and malice.

"Your efforts are but the fluttering of wings within the web," he sneered, "Soon to be extinguished beneath the might of our conquest."

Dr. Samira Patel stepped forward, her posture solid against the spectral dictator's glare. "Remember why we are here," she said, her voice steady, each syllable a beacon cutting through the despair. "We carry the hope of Earth within us. For the fallen, for the living, for the generations yet to be born — we cannot falter."

Nods of affirmation rippled through the group, the clarity in Patel's words lifting the veil of doubt, if only for a heartbeat.

They pressed on, the labyrinth of corridors unfurling before them until they stood before the heart of the command ship— the power core. It pulsed with a foreboding energy, veins of light coursing along its surface, feeding the monstrous fleet beyond the hull.

"Time is our enemy now," Evelyn stated, her gaze locked on the core. Dr. Weller and Dr. Chen approached the behemoth of technology, their fingers deftly assembling the devices necessary to orchestrate its downfall.

"Cover them," she ordered, and the air was soon filled with the cacophony of battle as waves of Kridrax soldiers descended upon them.

Sergeant Alvarez and Lieutenant Isabella became whirlwinds of defiance, their weapons singing songs of resistance. Each blast from their guns was a note in an anthem of survival, the rhythm punctuated by the chorus of alien shrieks.

Amidst the chaos, Weller's hands moved with precision, guided by intellect and an inherent understanding of the alien mechanisms before him. Beside him, Lily Chen's keen eyes followed his work, her own contributions seamless, her movements a dance between science and artistry.

"Almost there," Weller breathed, his voice barely rising above the din. The core began to whine, the sound a herald of the impending destruction. Lights flickered, the ship's systems sensing the danger from within.

"Get ready!" Evelyn called out, her voice the steel thread holding them together as the fabric of the battle frayed around them.

The monitor that had once displayed their taunting adversary now flashed with warnings, the synthetic eyes replaced with the symbols of urgency. The ship trembled beneath their feet, groaning against the violation of its core.

"Done!" Chen shouted, her declaration slicing through the turmoil. Weller nodded, his glasses askew but his resolve clear in his weary eyes.

"Move—now!" Evelyn's command was the signal, the catalyst for retreat as the coalition members turned to run, their mission's success teetering on the precipice between victory and oblivion. Behind them, the heart of the Kridrax invasion throbbed with the fury of a dying star, its final beat a countdown to annihilation.

...

Evelyn Montgomery's breaths were short and heavy, her pulse a drumbeat in her ears as she surveyed the chaos unfolding before her. The dim corridors of the Kridrax command ship thrummed with energy, blasts of plasma lighting the shadows like flashes of lightning presaging a storm. The coalition members formed a protective circle around Dr. Weller and Dr. Chen, their bodies tense, weapons ready.

"Protect the core team!" Evelyn's voice echoed down the steel-walled passageway, her words tinged with the gravity of their situation. She watched as Dr. Weller's fingers danced across alien interfaces, his brow creased with concentration, while Dr. Chen's hands moved with equal parts grace and precision, adjusting components only they fully understood.

The Kridrax soldiers surged forward like a wave of darkness, their armor clanking ominously. The air sizzled with the discharge of energy weapons, the sharp scent of ozone filling the space. Each shot from the coalition was a desperate plea for just a few more precious seconds.

In the midst of the cacophony, Evelyn caught sight of a towering figure breaking through the frontlines — a Kridrax commander clad in imposing battle gear, his eyes fixed on the scientists. Time seemed to slow as she locked onto her new adversary. A primal instinct, honed by countless battles, whispered an undeniable truth: this creature would not fall easily.

"Cover me," she uttered, the words almost lost amid the din. With a fluidity born of necessity, Evelyn stepped away from the circle, her movements a dance of death as she drew her blade — an antique relic from Earth, the metal hungering for combat.

The Kridrax commander roared a challenge, a guttural sound that reverberated through the steel bones of the ship. They clashed, metal against chitinous armor, the impact ringing out over the staccato rhythm of gunfire. Evelyn parried and struck, each motion deliberate, conserving energy for the fight she knew would demand everything she had.

Around them, the battle raged on, a tableau of desperation and resolve. But in this moment, within the sphere of their conflict, nothing existed but Evelyn and the Kridrax commander, two warriors etching their wills upon the fabric of fate.

She felt the weight of her past — the betrayals, the losses — fueling her arms as she fought. The commander was relentless, his attacks a torrent she narrowly escaped time and again. Her green eyes, usually so piercing, now glimmered with something else: the reflection of a soul seeking redemption through the clash of steel.

"Montgomery, hold on!" a voice called through the fray, but it sounded distant, a whisper from another world. She could not falter, not when the lives of her comrades, the future of humanity, hinged on the edge of her blade.

As the commander raised his weapon for a crushing blow, Evelyn saw her opening. With a swift step and a twist of her wrist, she redirected the force of his attack, sending him stumbling. She advanced, exploiting the gap in his guard, her blade finding its mark.

The commander fell with a thunderous crash, and Evelyn stood over him, her breath coming in ragged gasps. She turned back to the circle, her eyes meeting those of Dr. Weller and Dr. Chen, whose work continued unabated amidst the chaos.

"Keep going," she urged, her voice a hoarse whisper, the steely resolve returning. "I've got you."

And with that, Evelyn Montgomery returned to the fray, her every step a testament to the enduring spirit of a warrior who would not yield until the last star faded from the cosmos.

...

The deck heaved like a living thing, its metal bones groaning under the stress of impending doom. Dr. Markus Weller's fingers danced across the alien console with practiced urgency, his glasses sliding down the bridge of his nose. Beside him, Dr. Lily Chen fed data into the system, her hands a blur. The power core before them hummed, a crescendo of energy that promised annihilation.

"Sequence initiated," Markus announced, his voice oddly steady amid the chaos.

"Overload in progress," Lily confirmed, her eyes never leaving the readouts.

The command ship shuddered violently, and the blare of sirens filled the air, a cacophony of warning that death was imminent. Evelyn Montgomery's green eyes swept the room, seeing the vibrations ripple through her team as they steadied themselves against the onslaught.

"Time to leave," she commanded, her voice cutting through the din.

The coalition members didn't need to be told twice. With a collective nod, they turned from the pulsing heart of the Kridrax command ship and sprinted towards salvation. The corridors were a labyrinth of shadows and light, flickering as explosions began to tear the vessel apart from within.

They rounded a corner, only to be met by an ambush—a final onslaught of Kridrax soldiers, their armor glinting malevolently in the spasmodic illumination. Sergeant Alvarez and Lieutenant Isabella raised their weapons, delivering cover fire in controlled bursts as the rest of the team ducked behind the scant protection of the bulkheads.

"Push through!" Evelyn yelled over the deafening roar of gunfire.

Bullets whizzed past, close enough to singe the air. Her heart thundered in her chest, each beat a drumroll to oblivion. They exchanged lead with the enemy, a deadly dance that wove between the twin threads of life and death.

In this maelstrom of violence, Evelyn's past waged its own war within her—a tapestry of regrets and resolutions unraveling thread by thread. She fired her weapon, each shot an echo of battles fought, of lives lost, of the redemption she sought through the smoke of warfare.

Dr. Weller, usually so absorbed in his own world of technology and theory, now moved with surprising agility, dodging debris and returning fire with a grim determination that belied his scholarly appearance. Beside him, Dr. Chen's calm demeanor had given way to a fierce resolve, her weapon an extension of her will to protect and persevere.

The Kridrax fell one by one, their numbers dwindling as the coalition's relentless assault overwhelmed them. Each member of the team was an avatar of defiance, a testament to human resilience in the face of the abyss.

As the last enemy dropped, silence fell for a brief, surreal moment, punctuated only by the ominous creaks and groans of the dying ship. The corridor ahead lay clear, a path fraught with peril but leading to the promise of escape.

"Move, move, move!" Evelyn's voice spurred them onward, her words the incantation needed to break the spell of stillness that had fallen.

They surged forward, a tide of humanity amidst the storm. Around them, the ship convulsed in its death throes, a behemoth brought low by the audacity of those who dared challenge the dark.

Ahead, the exit loomed, a portal back to the stars from which they had come—a beacon of hope that guided them through the darkness, through the remnants of a battle hard-won, and toward the uncertain future that awaited them all.

...

The void beyond held its breath as the coalition members burst through the ship's exit, their figures silhouetted against the backdrop of an unforgiving universe. The command ship, once a symbol of Synthetic Oppressor's indomitable will, swelled with light from within, a burgeoning star heralding its demise. And then, with a ferocity that echoed through the cosmos, it erupted into a blinding explosion, casting its twisted metal carcass across the endless night.

Dr. Montgomery's boots clanged against the hull of their vessel as she led her team inside, the reverberations marking the end of their harrowing journey through the belly of the beast. They collapsed against walls and consoles, each breath a shuddering testament to their journey's toll. The silence was profound, punctuated only by the labored breathing of warriors who had danced too closely with oblivion.

"Is it done?" Lieutenant Isabella asked, her voice a mere whisper against the magnitude of their victory.

"Done," confirmed Dr. Weller, his gaze still locked on the scattering debris where the Kridrax command ship once loomed — a monument to terror now reduced to cosmic dust.

Their relief was palpable, a shared exhalation that carried with it the weight of lives lost and futures reclaimed. For a moment, time stretched thin, allowing them the luxury of reflection amidst their exhaustion. Sergeant Alvarez removed his helmet, the scars and sweat on his face telling stories of countless battles, of resilience that defied even the darkest of foes.

"Let's go home," Dr. Montgomery said, her voice steady despite the fatigue that pulled at her limbs.

With the remnants of the command ship fading into the abyss, they set a course for Earth, leaving behind the shattered dreams of a synthetic dictator. As the stars streaked past, the coalition members allowed themselves a moment of somber introspection. The silence of space enveloped them, a comforting shroud that belied the chaos they had endured.

"Remember those we've lost," Dr. Patel murmured, her words a solemn incantation to honor the fallen. "Their sacrifices paved the way for this moment."

"Without them, this wouldn't have been possible," added Dr. Chen, her eyes reflecting the cold light of distant suns.

"Nor without us," stated Sergeant Alvarez. "We fought. We survived. We ended this."

"Indeed," Dr. Weller sighed, his thoughts adrift among memories of battles waged in the name of an embattled Earth.

As their hidden base came into view, nestled within the protective embrace of a secluded asteroid field, the coalition members embraced the solace it offered. They had traversed the abyss, stood firm against a relentless tide, and emerged not unscathed, but undeterred.

"Rebuilding awaits," Dr. Montgomery declared, her eyes alight with the fire of one who knows the true cost of peace. "But for now, let's take solace in our triumph."

"Triumph," echoed Lieutenant Isabella, "and redemption."
In the quiet that followed, as their vessel docked within the safety of their hidden sanctuary, the shadows of the past seemed to retreat, giving way to the faintest glimmer of hope—a new dawn forged from the ashes of war.

...

Dr. Evelyn Montgomery stood at the forefront of the gathered coalition, her gaze lingering on the horizon of a battered Earth that lay beyond the base's viewing port. The planet, once vibrant and teeming with life, now bore the scars of relentless conflict. Her black hair was an unruly shadow framing the resolve etched upon her face, and though fatigue pulled at her limbs, her green eyes sparked with the fire of determination.

"Look at it," she murmured, more to herself than to those behind her. "Our home... What we fought for."

The silence in the room was thick, weighted with the enormity of their task ahead. Evelyn could feel the collective breath of her comrades, each drawn ragged from battle, yet steadied by the shared purpose that bonded them closer than any familial tie.

Captain Hawking, known to all as Hawk, stepped beside her, his muscular frame a testament to countless battles waged. "It won't be easy," he said, the timbre of his voice steady like the ancient rocks of Earth's now silent mountains.

"No," Evelyn agreed, her tone just as unwavering. "But since when has 'easy' ever been our way?"

Around them, the others began to gather their strength, the quiet hum of the base's generators a subtle reminder of the technology that still thrived despite adversity. Dr. Markus Weller adjusted his glasses, poring over data pads filled with schematics and calculations, already lost in thoughts of reconstruction and innovation.

Sergeant Mia Alvarez, her dark hair a stark contrast against her pale features, checked her equipment methodically, the movements a familiar dance to ward off the creeping tendrils of sorrow for what—and who—had been left behind.

General O'Neill, his silver hair a halo in the dim light, stood tall and unyielding as bedrock. His gaze swept over his people, pride and a fierce protectiveness burning in his steely eyes. "Each of us has a role," Evelyn continued, addressing the assembled team. "Each skill, each expertise will forge the path from ruins to rebirth."

Her words, though spoken softly, carried the weight of command, resonating through the chamber. It was Dr. Lily Chen who moved first, her bright eyes alight with the spirit of a challenge accepted. "Let's begin by understanding the enemy's technology," she suggested. "Turn their instruments of war into tools of restoration."

Evelyn nodded, acknowledging the wisdom in repurposing their adversary's advances for the benefit of Earth's future. "A fitting retribution," she agreed.

The mysterious air of the room shifted subtly, charged with anticipation and the gravity of their undertaking. They stood not as individuals, but as a collective force, each member a crucial piece of the intricate puzzle that would rebuild a world from the ashes of its darkest days.

"Tomorrow, we start anew," Evelyn declared, her voice carrying the echoes of the past, the promise of redemption. "For the fallen, for us, and for the generations to come."

"Tomorrow," echoed the coalition, their voices a chorus of resilience.

As they dispersed, each to their own quarters and contemplations, Evelyn remained, her eyes never leaving the sight of Earth. In the quiet expanse of space, surrounded by the remnants of war, she allowed herself a moment's respite, a fleeting second of peace before the storm of creation that lay ahead.

"Rebuild and protect," she whispered, her vow a secret pact between her and the silent stars. "This I swear."

And with that, Dr. Evelyn Montgomery turned away from the darkness of space, her every step towards the heart of the base a drumbeat of hope in the symphony of survival.

Chapter 21

Forever Return

The transport descended through the ragged clouds, its metallic sheen marred by the scars of battle. Below, the once-proud cityscape was a jagged silhouette against the dusk, its buildings fractured skeletons clawing at a sky that had witnessed too much. Dr. Evelyn Montgomery's gaze lingered on the devastation, her piercing green eyes reflecting the desolation like twin mirrors of sorrow.

"Welcome home, Dr. Montgomery," the pilot intoned, his voice a hollow echo amidst the hum of engines winding down. Home, a term now synonymous with ruin and rebirth in equal measure.

Evelyn stepped onto the tarmac, her boots crunching on the scattered debris that carpeted the ground. Officials, their faces etched with the same weariness that marked her own, awaited her. Without preamble, they ushered her into a makeshift command center, where the stench of burnt circuitry hung heavily in the air. The government officials, as fragmented as the city they represented, spoke of reconstruction, of strategies to prevent another Kridrax nightmare. Her responses were measured, technical jargon flowing from her lips with an ease that belied the vulnerability threatening to fracture her composure.

Meanwhile, continents away, Captain Lucas "Hawk" Hawking exchanged salutes with grim-faced soldiers as he disembarked from his vessel. His piercing blue eyes, perennial sentinels, scanned the horizon where the remnants of war's fury stretched outwards like the aftermath of a storm. He trudged through the detritus of what was once a bustling metropolis, each step a testament to survival.

"Captain Hawking," a general greeted, extending a hand not in camaraderie, but obligation. Hawk's response was curt, a nod sufficing where words would falter. They assembled in a tent that rippled in the cold wind, a fragile bulwark against chaos. Talk of defense strategies and resource allocation buzzed around him, but Hawk's mind wandered through the labyrinth of past battles, each memory a specter that refused exorcism.

Days later, fate ordained that Dr. Montgomery and Captain Hawking should cross paths in a sterile conference hall, miles from their respective ruins. Surrounded by the hum of alien technology and the fervent whispers of those eager to wield it, their meeting was a silent acknowledgment, a shared recognition of endurance in the face of existential threat.

"Dr. Montgomery," Hawk greeted, his voice betraying none of the resonance that typically accompanied his commanding tone.

"Captain," Evelyn replied, allowing herself a momentary lapse in her guarded demeanor. As they navigated the throngs of delegates and displays of otherworldly machinery, their conversation unfolded in sparse but meaningful exchanges, each word a brick in the bridge spanning the chasm of their experiences.

"Evacuation protocols proved effective in the northern sectors," Hawk mused, recalling orders barked under fire-scarred skies.

"Biological countermeasures held up better than expected," Evelyn countered, her thoughts drifting to petri dishes and pathogen samples, the unlikely heroes of warfare's new frontier.

Their stories interlaced, tales of ingenuity and instinct, of despair and defiance. As the conference wore on, the pair found themselves secluded in an alcove, shielded from prying eyes by the shadow of a dormant war machine. It was there, amidst discussions of pulse shields and antimatter weaponry, that they discovered solace in their shared solitude.

"Never thought I'd find comfort in recounting days I wish to forget," Hawk confessed, the mysterious depths of his eyes softening.

"Yet here we are," Evelyn acknowledged, the corners of her mouth twitching towards a smile that struggled to surface. "Finding kinship amidst the relics of our enemies."

As the conference dissolved into the evening, Dr. Montgomery and Captain Hawking stood together, their bond solidified not by the common goal of humanity's defense, but by the unspoken understanding of sacrifice. They were kindred spirits, tempered by the fires of war and forged anew by the prospect of redemption for a world still clinging to hope amidst the ashes of the past.

...

The wind whispered across the graveyard, carrying with it the scent of freshly turned earth and the soft murmur of leaves rustling against headstones. Dr. Evelyn Montgomery's boots crunched on the gravel path as she walked beside Captain Lucas "Hawk" Hawking, their silhouettes etched against the dimming sky. The cemetery stretched out before them, a somber tapestry of marble and memories.

Evelyn paused before a row of graves, her green eyes tracing the names etched in stone. Each one a testament to courage; every inscription a silent echo of a life offered in the fray. Hawk stood beside her, his gaze lingering on the markers as if seeking communion with the souls they commemorated. His posture, usually so commanding, seemed to bear the weight of unseen burdens, his broad shoulders slightly stooped.

"Here lies the best of us," Hawk murmured, his voice barely above the sighing wind. "May their valor never fade into the obscurity of peace."

"Nor shall it," Evelyn replied, the clinical precision of her words belying the quiver of emotion that underscored them. "We carry their legacy within us, the torchbearers of their unfinished battles."

They moved among the graves, pausing now and then as silent promises were made. Promises to honor the fallen, to forge ahead in the face of insurmountable odds, to ensure that the darkness which had once threatened to engulf their world would never rise again.

As twilight descended upon them, casting long shadows across the hallowed ground, they shared a moment of quiet solidarity. Here, amidst the whispers of those who had passed, Dr. Montgomery and Captain Hawging found strength in the solemn bond of shared loss—a bond unspoken yet understood.

The lab was a sanctuary of solitude when Evelyn returned, the sterile hum of machinery welcoming her like an old friend. She shed her jacket and slipped into her familiar white coat, the fabric settling around her like armor. Her fingers danced over the console, awakening screens filled with data and diagrams, the detritus of her relentless quest for knowledge.

She delved into her work, her mind alight with possibilities. The night stretched on, time losing meaning as she chased the elusive specter of innovation. Pipettes and microscopes were her weapons, knowledge her shield against the darkness that lurked beyond the stars.

In the silence of the laboratory, surrounded by the ghosts of breakthroughs and the specter of failures past, Evelyn Montgomery toiled. She wrestled with equations and probabilities, each discovery a step closer to redemption for a world still scarred by war. In the crucible of her intellect, new defenses took shape, forged from the fires of determination and the unyielding drive to protect.

The promise she had made among the gravestones lingered in her heart, fueling her resolve as she worked through the night. A vow to the fallen, to the living, to herself — that she would stand sentinel against the unknown, a guardian whose vigilance was born of remembrance and whose purpose was etched in the annals of survival.

In the depths of that night, beneath the watchful eyes of her comrades-in-arms immortalized in data and dreams, Dr. Montgomery's pursuit of the future was undeterred. It was here, in the quiet sanctum of her laboratory, where the veil of mystery yielded to the clarion call of progress — one experiment, one hypothesis, one revelation at a time.

...

Captain Lucas "Hawk" Hawking stood in the shadow-streaked conference room, his broad silhouette etched against the backdrop of a holographic globe spinning lazily in the air. The globe paused, continents marred by pulsing red dots — the scars of recent invasions. The murmurs of military officials, like the distant rumble of thunder, filled the space with an undercurrent of urgency.

"Commence," Hawk's voice cut through the din — a sword cleaving stillness. His blue eyes, reflecting the light of the globe, were two beacons of resolve in the dimly lit chamber.

Around him, officers of high rank clustered like ancient warlords plotting their next campaign. Their uniforms bore the insignia of a fractured world seeking to forge unity from the ashes of conflict. They turned their attention to the towering figure that was Captain Hawking, awaiting orders.

"Strategy and strength," he began, pacing before the assembly with predatory grace, "are only as effective as the force that wields them." He gestured to the globe, where the red dots flickered ominously. "We've survived the Kridrax—but survival isn't enough."

With each word, his presence seemed to swell, filling the room not just with his physicality but also with the weight of his conviction. The officials leaned in, hanging on the precipice of his every syllable.

"We will build a new defense force," Hawk declared, his jaw set firm, "trained exclusively for extraterrestrial combat. We will be prepared, vigilant, unyielding." He locked eyes with each official, an unspoken challenge in his gaze.

Nods of agreement punctuated the air, and the room bristled with newfound determination. The seeds of a specialized unit, one born of necessity and baptized in the fire of Hawk's leadership, began to take root.

***

Underneath a sky streaked with the fading colors of dusk, Dr. Evelyn Montgomery and Captain Hawking convened with the remnants of the coalition. A ragtag assembly of scientists and soldiers gathered on the tattered remains of what had once been a bustling square, now a sacred congregation of shared purpose. The clinking of metal and the whirring of machinery formed an eerie symphony as Dr. Montgomery stepped forward, her green eyes scanning the faces before her. She saw in them reflections of her own inner turmoil—each one grappling with the specter of wars past and the daunting path ahead.

"Isolation is our adversary as much as any alien threat," she stated, her voice a clarion call cutting through the twilight. "Together, we are more than the sum of our parts. Together, we rebuild, we fortify, we endure."

Captain Hawking joined her side, an immovable pillar of support. "We have witnessed the fall," he added, his tone steeped in the gravity of their losses, "and we have risen to tell the tale. From this crucible of shared suffering, we will forge a future unwavering in its defiance."

Amidst the ruins, a silent accord was struck—a covenant of collaboration and resilience. Heads nodded, hands clasped, and hearts merged in a collective vow to honor the legacies of those no longer present.

As night crept over the shattered city, a gathering of souls found solace in unity, their whispered conversations a testament to the enduring human spirit. In this hallowed reunion, Dr. Montgomery and Captain Hawking were the architects of tomorrow, their plans for the future etched into the very essence of the world they were determined to protect.

And so they stood together, amidst the echoes of redemption and the quiet resolve that hummed within the bones of the earth—a duo bound by the solemn pledge to safeguard humanity's place among the stars.

…

The pale glow of the console bathed Dr. Evelyn Montgomery's face in an eerie light as she reached out, her fingers deftly navigating the virtual keyboard projected in the air before her. Data streams cascaded down the screens, a waterfall of information from every corner of the ravaged planet. She stood at the epicenter of a network that was slowly, inexorably knitting together the fragmented pieces of humanity's resistance.

"Contact established with the Tokyo enclave," she murmured, her voice betraying none of the fatigue that clung to her like a second skin. "They've agreed to share their designs for the atmospheric purifiers."

"Good," came the gruff reply from across the dim room. Captain Lucas "Hawk" Hawking leaned over another floating display, his fingers tracing lines and symbols only he could fully comprehend. The military encryption danced away at his touch, revealing secure channels to far-flung operatives who had once fought under disparate banners.

"Madrid is sending through their energy schematics," Hawk noted, his voice carrying the weight of command as much as it conveyed a spark of hope. "We're piecing together a defense unlike any before."

Their efforts were more than mere strategy; they were an act of defiance against the uncertainty of the future. A silent pact between intellect and valor, science and strength, to ensure that when — if — the Kridrax or others returned, Earth would not be caught unawares.

It was on one such unseasonably cool morning that they left the confines of their makeshift command center to witness the fruits of this newfound coalition. As they walked amidst the rubble-strewn streets once known as boulevards, the scars of the city seemed to mirror their own — wounds that were healing but would never quite fade.

"Look there," Evelyn said, nodularity softening her usually sharp tone as she gestured toward a cluster of workers hoisting beams onto a skeletal frame. The structure rose defiantly against the skyline, a phoenix in mid-emergence. "Out of the ashes..." "Resilience incarnate," Hawk finished for her, nodding in quiet appreciation.

They moved on, passing murals freshly painted on still-pockmarked walls, vibrant colors clashing with the drabness of destruction, each stroke a testament to the indomitable spirit of those who remained.

"Sometimes I wonder," Hawk began, his voice lowered as if sharing a sacred secret, "if we're building more than just cities here."

Evelyn glanced at him, green eyes reflecting the myriad questions that lingered in her own mind. "We're building memories," she offered. "Memories imbued with determination... and hope. That's something no invasion can ever erase."

Their path took them to a park where children played amidst the shadows of salvaged statues, laughter piercing the heavy silence that had once hung over the area like a shroud. It was a poignant reminder of what had been lost, and yet, also, what had been gained.

"From great loss comes great resolve," Hawk observed, watching a young girl chase a fluttering piece of paper caught in the wind.

"Indeed," Evelyn agreed, her gaze lingering on the scene. "A resolve that binds us, strengthens us."

And so they continued, bearing witness to the slow rebirth of a world that refused to succumb to despair. With each step, they carried with them the promise of collaboration, the blueprint of a future fortified by the shared wisdom of survivors, and the unspoken oath to stand guard over a civilization that would rise, stronger and wiser than before.

In the hush of twilight, as they stood looking out over a landscape etched with both sorrow and triumph, it was as if the very earth whispered its gratitude to these quiet architects of redemption. Their mission was clear, their burden heavy, yet their spirits remained unbroken, tethered to the dream of a dawn that would shine upon a world united — not just in survival, but in the resolute pursuit of a destiny reclaimed.

...

The morning sun crept over the horizon, casting a warm glow that danced across the rubble of the once-great metropolis. It was a sight that had become achingly familiar to Dr. Evelyn Montgomery as she navigated her way through the remnants of civilization. The air held a charge today, one of anticipation, for the hallowed halls where minds would soon mingle and share in the collective task of mending their fractured world.

Evelyn's stride was purposeful, her short black hair swaying with each determined step toward the conference center, an imposing structure miraculously spared by the Kridrax invasion. Within its walls, voices from around the globe would converge, seeking out the elusive threads of hope amid the tapestry of destruction. Today, she and Captain Lucas "Hawk" Hawking were to be the harbingers of that hope.

"Doctor," Hawk's voice rumbled behind her, a steadfast presence that cut through the stillness of the morning. His tall figure emerged from the shadow of a crumbling archway, his piercing blue eyes reflecting a solemnity that matched her own.

"Captain," Evelyn acknowledged, allowing a brief nod before they both continued forward. There was comfort in their mutual silence; words often fell short when set against the gravity of their shared experiences.

As they entered the grand auditorium, the murmurs of the gathered crowd hushed into an expectant quiet. Evelyn took her place at the podium, her green eyes scanning the sea of faces — scientists, military personnel, survivors — all united in their thirst for knowledge, for guidance.

"Today, we stand on the precipice of a new era," she began, her voice carrying the timbre of authority mingled with the weight of wisdom hard-earned. "An era where our greatest adversary is no longer the unknown, but rather our willingness to face it."

The audience leaned in, hanging on every word as she recounted tales of valor and ingenuity, of the darkest hours when humanity's light flickered, threatening to extinguish. Yet, here they stood, testament to the resilience of the human spirit, a beacon for the path ahead.

The conference unfolded with a rhythmic ebb and flow of discourse and deliberation, punctuated by bursts of applause. Hawk, with his direct manner and military precision, complemented Evelyn's scientific acumen, weaving a narrative of unity and determination that resonated deep within the hearts of those present.

"Let us forge a shield from the ashes of our past," Hawk declared, his voice a clarion call that reverberated within the marbled walls. "A shield not just of steel and circuits, but of resolve and remembrance."

Days turned to nights and back again as the conference drew to a close, yet the work for Evelyn and Hawk was far from done. In the quiet confines of a makeshift laboratory — a sanctuary of sorts — they poured over schematics and equations, their collaboration a dance of intellect and strategy.

Evelyn's fingers traced over the diagrams strewn across the table, her sharp features bathed in the soft glow of the holoscreen as it projected their latest design—a defense system unlike any other. It was a melding of alien technology and human innovation, a testament to the progress they had made in understanding the very foes that sought to destroy them.

"Are we ready for this?" Hawk's query broke the silence, his gaze locked onto hers with an intensity that bordered on reverence.

"Ready as we'll ever be," she replied, her tone laced with the tenacity that had become her hallmark. Together, they refined their creation, a symphony of science and strategy that promised not only protection but also retribution.

In these moments of fervent labor, the world outside faded into obscurity, leaving only the task at hand—an endeavor of redemption, a bulwark against the encroaching darkness. It was more than a project; it was a covenant between two souls who had seen the abyss and dared to defy it.

As night embraced the city once more, a hush settled over the lab. Evelyn and Hawk exchanged glances, a silent acknowledgment of the road ahead—a road fraught with peril, yet lined with the potential for triumph.

"Tomorrow, we begin testing," Evelyn murmured, her voice barely above a whisper, as if afraid to disturb the sanctity of the moment.

"Tomorrow," Hawk echoed, his affirmation a solemn vow to stand shoulder to shoulder with her, come what may.

And in the quiet solidarity of their shared conviction, the seeds of humanity's salvation took root, nurtured by the indomitable will of those who refused to yield to the specter of annihilation. They would rise, tempered by loss, emboldened by victory, and forever bound by the unspoken oath to safeguard a future written in the stars.

…

The echoes of applause reverberated through the vastness of the Grand Assembly Hall, where marble pillars stretched towards a frescoed ceiling depicting humanity's triumph over adversity. Dr. Evelyn Montgomery stood beside Captain Lucas "Hawk" Hawking, the weight of their medals a tangible reminder of the gravity of their achievements.

"Your efforts," intoned the Chancellor with grandeur, "will remain etched in the annals of history."

Evelyn nodded graciously, her piercing green eyes scanning the sea of faces before her, each worn by the ravages of war yet alight with newfound hope. Beside her, Hawk's blue gaze remained steady, his posture as rigid as the military decorum that had shaped him.

"Thank you," Evelyn said, her voice clear but laced with the subtle crack of vulnerability. The words were expected, but they bore the heavy truth of unfinished business. Hawk followed suit, his response succinct, a testament to his forthright nature.

"Service is its own reward," he stated, the timbre of his voice grounding the loftiness of the ceremony back into the realm of reality.

As the formalities dwindled and the assembly dispersed into murmurs of reverence and relief, Evelyn felt the mantle of heroism, ill-fitting on her shoulders. She caught Hawk's eye, finding an echo of her discomfort mirrored in his expression.

They excused themselves from the throng of dignitaries and slipped into a quieter antechamber. Here, the hushed atmosphere allowed for reflection—a luxury seldom afforded amidst the cacophony of rebuilding.

"Heroes," Hawk mused, the word tasting foreign on his tongue. "Yet we both know the cost, the names and faces that never made it home."

"Indeed." Evelyn's gaze drifted to the golden insignia on her chest. "These accolades feel like ghosts sometimes—haunting reminders of those we lost."

"Strength and resilience," Hawk ventured, running a hand through his short-cropped hair. "That's what they say we've gained. But the scars run deep, don't they?"

"Scars can be instructive," she replied, her sharp intellect grappling with the paradox of pain and growth. "They are the map of our journey, each one a lesson learned, a trial endured."

"Lessons paid for in blood," Hawk added solemnly, his military bearing unable to mask the sorrow of such harsh tutelage.

"Yet here we stand," Evelyn observed, the scientist within her analyzing their evolution as if through the lens of a microscope. "Changed, undoubtedly. Perhaps even broken in places. But not defeated."

"Never defeated," Hawk affirmed, his voice a quiet declaration of their shared resolve. He extended his hand, not in salute, but in solidarity.

Eyes locking, they shook hands, the gesture transcending the formality of their roles. In that grasp lingered the silent promise of endurance, the unyielding spirit of two individuals who had stared into the abyss and chose to defy it.

"Redemption lies ahead," Evelyn stated, more to herself than to Hawk. "Not just for us, but for all who look to us for guidance."

"Redemption and a future worth the sacrifices made," Hawk agreed, his determined nod speaking volumes.

In the stillness of the chamber, surrounded by the shadows of yesterday's battles, Dr. Evelyn Montgomery and Captain Lucas "Hawk" Hawking found a momentary peace. It was not the end of their story, but rather the closing of a chapter — one that had tested the limits of their humanity, only to find it resilient, defiant, and more resolute than ever before.

And in their shared silence, the seeds of tomorrow's victories took root, fostered by two souls bound by duty and honed by the relentless pursuit of a future where humanity might flourish once again.

…

The sun dipped low on the horizon, casting long shadows over the ruins that once thrived with life. Dr. Evelyn Montgomery stood beside Captain Lucas "Hawk" Hawking, their gazes fixed upon the skeletal remains of buildings. The city, once a vibrant tapestry of human ingenuity, now lay in muted silence, but beneath the desolation, the heartbeat of rebirth pulsed steadily.

"Look at it, Hawk," Evelyn murmured, her voice barely rising above the whispering wind that carried the dust of reconstruction through the air. "From these ashes, we'll forge a new beginning."

Hawk's eyes, mirrors of the sky at twilight, reflected the broken skyline. "We've been given a second chance," he replied. "It's our duty to ensure it wasn't in vain."

They turned toward each other, the weight of unspoken thoughts creating a tangible tension between them. Hawk's hand found its way to his side, calloused fingers brushing against the medals that adorned his uniform—a uniform that bore the scars of war as much as the man within it.

Evelyn's gaze fell upon those hands, symbols of countless battles fought, of lives saved and lost. She reached out, her own fingers—stained with the ink of research notes and the patina of lab work—intertwining with his.

"Then let's make our commitment," she said, her voice steady despite the undercurrent of emotion. "Not just to each other, but to all of humanity. We stand on the precipice of tomorrow, and we will be the ones to lead them away from the edge."

"Agreed," Hawk responded, his grip tightening. "We've seen the darkness that lurks beyond the stars. It is our charge to be the shield against it, to guard this fragile peace with everything we have."

The pact sealed, they released their hold, yet the connection lingered—a shared resolve that transcended physical contact. Together, they stepped forward, the rubble crunching under their boots, a testament to the resilience of the human spirit. Evelyn paused, allowing the breeze to lift strands of her short black hair. She closed her eyes, letting the coolness kiss her cheeks, feeling the stirrings of hope amidst the scent of metal and sweat. When she opened her eyes again, they shone with an unwavering determination, the green irises like emerald beacons in the encroaching dusk.

"We'll build more than just structures," she declared, her gaze locking onto the skeletal frame of what would become a center of innovation. "We'll cultivate minds, nurture hearts, and arm souls with the knowledge to face whatever comes."

"An impregnable fortress of unity," Hawk added, his stance as solid as the earth beneath them. "Where every child born into this world knows they are part of something greater — a legacy of survival and defiance."

As the first stars emerged, twinkling in the velvet expanse above, the two figures stood resolute, their silhouettes etching a promise into the canvas of night. Around them, the city whispered its gratitude, its very foundations infused with the strength of those who dared to envision a future where light triumphed over shadow.

"Redemption isn't found," Evelyn said softly, "it's created. And with each stone we lay, each life we touch... we write our own story of redemption."

"Let it be a tale for the ages," Hawk responded, his voice carrying the timbre of an oath.

In the quietude that followed, Dr. Evelyn Montgomery and Captain Lucas "Hawk" Hawking remained vigilant sentinels, guardians of a dream not yet fully realized. They were the architects of tomorrow, bound by a commitment as enduring as the very stars that bore witness to their resolve.

...

The twilight air, still pungent with the scent of scorched earth and rejuvenation, filled the vast hall as murmurs of reunion swelled into a chorus of camaraderie. Dr. Evelyn Montgomery's silhouette weaved through clusters of coalition members, each face etched with the relief and weariness of triumph. Her piercing green eyes, alight with a quiet intensity, scanned the room, taking in the tapestry of emotions that draped over the shoulders of every survivor, every hero.

A clinking glass punctuated the hum of conversation, commanding silence with the authority of ritual. Captain Lucas "Hawk" Hawking stood at the forefront, his imposing frame casting a long shadow across the gathering. His voice, when he spoke, was a gravelly echo that seemed to carry the weight of the cosmos itself.

"Today, we stand not as soldiers, scientists, or survivors," Hawk began, his blue eyes glinting with unshed emotion. The words caught slightly in his throat, a rare crack in his stoic armor. "We stand as guardians of a future forged from the ashes of despair."

Evelyn felt a surge of pride swell within her chest — a tempest contained only by the rigidity of her posture and the measured cadence of her breathing. Memories flickered like ghostly specters behind her eyelids; friends lost, cities fallen, hope nearly extinguished. Yet here they were, remnants of a fractured humanity, bound by a shared legacy that would ripple through time.

"Each story," she found herself saying, stepping forward, her lab coat a banner of resilience amidst the sea of uniforms, "is a thread in the fabric of our history." Her voice resonated with both vulnerability and strength, a paradox befitting the woman who had navigated the darkest corners of the unknown.

Laughter erupted at one end of the hall, where a group had gathered around an animated retelling of narrow escapes and ingenious tactics. Markus Weller, his glasses askew, chuckled softly — a sound as rare as the sight of a comet streaking across the heavens. Evelyn noted the subtle shift in his demeanor, the cautious lowering of walls built from solitude and sorrow.

"Here's to the architects of tomorrow," Hawk toasted, raising his glass high. Glasses clinked in a symphony of solidarity, refracting the light of hope that shone ever more brightly within their hearts.

As the evening waned, tears mingled with laughter, creating a mosaic of human spirit. Each shared reminiscence revealed scars, but also the indomitable will that had turned the tide of an unwinnable war. In the quiet spaces between tales of valor, the whispers of redemption threaded through the air, weaving a narrative far greater than any single victory.

"Look at us," Evelyn murmured to Hawk as they observed the jubilant assembly, her words a hushed reverence for the moment. "From the depths of darkness, we've sculpted a dawn brimming with light."

"Indeed," Hawk agreed, his gaze lingering on the faces around them, "a dawn that speaks not of what we have endured, but of what we have become."

In the thrumming heart of celebration, Dr. Evelyn Montgomery and Captain Lucas "Hawk" Hawking stood as pillars among their peers, their inner battles etched into the very essence of their beings. The past would forever haunt them, but together, they faced the enigma of the morrow with souls tempered in the crucible of war.

They had sown seeds of unity in soil steeped with sacrifice, and now, as they watched the first tentative shoots of peace break the surface, they knew their odyssey had etched an indelible mark upon the stars.

Chapter 22

Unity

The dawn chorus had long since given way to the cacophony of reconstruction as the city awoke from its post-war slumber. Amidst the clatter and clang of steel on stone, humans and machines intertwined in a delicate dance of rebirth. Cranes stretched skyward like metallic fauna, hoisting beams and girders into place, while workers, their faces etched with determination, mended the scars that marred the landscape.

Dr. Evelyn Montgomery threaded her way through the bustling throng, her keen green eyes taking in the synchronous harmony of labor before her. Each hammer swing and drill whine was a testament to humanity's indefatigable spirit. Piles of rubble stood as monuments to what once was, but around her echoed the drumbeat of what would be: a city phoenix-rising from the ashes of devastation.

Evelyn's mind, ever prone to wandering the labyrinth of the past, found solace in the present spectacle. She noted how every volunteer moved with purpose and unity, an intricate web of lives intertwining to weave a stronger fabric than before. It was a momentary balm to the haunting memories that often clawed at the fringes of her thoughts.

Later, beneath the grand arches of the restored City Hall, a ceremony unfolded with the pomp and gravitas it deserved. General Thomas "Thunderbolt" O'Neill stood straight-backed upon the stage, his silver hair reflecting the sunlight that streamed through the colonnades. His gravelly voice resonated across the assembly as he recounted acts of valor with poignant reverence.

"Today, we recognize those who have forged our future with the mettle of their courage," he declared, pausing to let the weight of his words settle over the crowd.

One by one, the coalition members ascended the stage to accept their medals—a tangible symbol of gratitude from a world they had fought to save. The air vibrated with applause, a thunderous accolade for each hero whose deeds became etched into the annals of history.

Captain Lucas "Hawk" Hawking was among them, his broad frame casting a formidable shadow as he stepped forward. His military bearing was unmistakable, yet his blue eyes harbored a depth of contemplation few could fathom. As the general placed the medal around Hawk's neck, their gazes met—a silent exchange of mutual respect forged in the crucible of conflict.

The audience erupted once more, their cheers reverberating off the marble and soaring into the open sky. Each clap was like a heartbeat—a collective pulse driving the lifeblood of a civilization ready to thrive anew. Hawk raised a hand, not in triumph, but acknowledgment of the sacrifices made by countless others.

Evelyn watched from the wings, her own accolades waiting. The shimmering medal felt heavy in her hands, weighted with meaning far beyond its simple alloy. Steeling herself against the swell of emotions, she prepared to step into the light and embrace the mantle of honor bestowed upon her.

For in this moment of recognition, the past, with all its shadows, seemed to recede just a little—giving way to a hope that glimmered on the horizon. And though the road ahead was fraught with unknown perils, the heroes of this age knew one thing for certain: they were the architects of redemption, and their work had only just begun.

...

As the applause settled into a hum of whispered conversations and shuffling feet, the coalition members stood shoulder to shoulder on the grand stage that had been erected in the heart of the city's plaza. The remnants of war seemed a universe away as they looked out upon the sea of faces, each one a testament to the resilience of humanity. Dr. Evelyn Montgomery's piercing green eyes met those of Captain Lucas "Hawk" Hawking, whose stoic demeanor was softened by the shared understanding reflected in his gaze.

In that suspended moment, a silent chorus of memories danced between them, whispering of narrow escapes and desperate gambits — the echoes of battle that had bound them together. It was an unspoken acknowledgment of loss, of survival, and of the indelible bond forged in the white-hot crucible of war.

The ceremony gave way to a more intimate tableau as the crowd began to disperse, leaving behind individuals who approached the heroes with tentative steps. A woman, her eyes brimming with tears that shimmered like liquid gratitude, reached out to clasp General Thomas "Thunderbolt" O'Neill's weathered hand. Her voice was a quivering leaf caught in the wind as she spoke of her son, saved by the general's decisive actions on a day when hope had seemed a distant star.

"Thank you," she said simply, but the weight of those two words carried the depth of oceans. General O'Neill, whose silver hair glinted in the sunlight like a crown of honor, nodded solemnly. His gravelly voice held the softness of twilight as he replied, "We serve for all our sons and daughters. For the future."

Nearby, Dr. Lily Chen was encircled by a group of eager young minds, their questions tumbling over each other in a cascade of curiosity. They saw in her not just a scientist who had unlocked the enigmas of alien technology but a beacon of inspiration, casting light upon the shadowed paths of their ambitions.

"Your work... it's like magic," one child breathed out in awe, his eyes wide with wonder.

Lily smiled, the gesture lifting the burden of self-doubt that often clung to her like morning mist. "Not magic," she corrected gently, "just science we haven't fully understood yet. And now, it's yours to explore too."

As the afternoon waned, the coalition members continued to receive the thanks of a grateful populace. With each handshake, each embrace, they were reminded that their struggles had not been in vain — that the fabric of society, once torn, was weaving itself anew through their efforts. And though the specters of the past would always hover at the edges of memory, today redemption felt not like a distant dream, but a reality taking shape before their very eyes.

...

Evelyn Montgomery's gaze lingered on the group of children whose laughter cascaded through the newly rebuilt park like a melody of rebirth. They chased each other around the vibrant playground, their small bodies weaving between swings and slides with an energy that seemed inexhaustible. Their joyous shrieks pierced the air, echoing off the freshly painted murals that adorned the surrounding walls — a mosaic of triumph over destruction.

From a respectful distance, she stood with her comrades, a silent sentinel watching over the fledgling peace they had fought so fiercely to attain. Evelyn's fingers grazed the communication device at her belt, a tactile reminder of the vigilance that still hummed beneath the surface of this serene tableau. Hawk, beside her, observed the scene with a soldier's poise, his broad shoulders relaxed yet betraying a readiness to spring into action should the need arise.

The subtle shifting of feet on gravel announced Markus Weller's approach, his hands preoccupied with some gadget or another. His eyes, magnified behind thick lenses, reflected the simplicity of the moment as he marveled at the children's ability to find wonder in the mundane—an attribute he envied in his most candid moments.

"Remarkable," Markus murmured, more to himself than to his companions, "how resilience is woven into the very fabric of their being."

"Indeed," Mia Alvarez replied, her voice low and steady, her keen eyes never straying from their charges. "They are the architects of tomorrow, building upon the foundations we've laid."

A flicker of movement caught their collective attention as Zylar Threx, their enigmatic ally, slipped noiselessly among the shadows cast by the late afternoon sun. The iridescence of their scales was muted in the dimming light, yet they seemed almost luminescent against the backdrop of human endeavor. Zylar's otherworldly presence was a poignant reminder of the unity forged across galaxies—a harmony that had once seemed impossible.

"Humanity Rises from the Ashes," Elena Vasquez read aloud as a series of news clips flickered across a nearby holographic display. The headlines morphed seamlessly one into the next, painting a picture of a civilization not only mended but strengthened in the crucible of conflict. "A New Era of Unity Begins."

"Poetic, isn't it?" Farrah Rodriguez commented, her voice tinged with a mix of hope and nostalgia. She stood slightly apart, her gaze alternating between the playing children and the scrolling headlines. The colorful scarf around her neck fluttered gently in the breeze, a silent testament to her vibrant spirit amidst the somber reflections of her peers.

As the sky began its descent into twilight, the park slowly emptied, leaving the coalition members alone with their thoughts. The montage continued to play out before them, a visual symphony of progress and perseverance. Each article, each story of heroism and healing, was a brushstroke on the canvas of a future they had dared to envision amidst the darkest hours of their past.

"Look at what we've accomplished," Hawk finally said, his voice barely louder than a whisper, yet carrying the weight of unspoken emotions. "This... all of this... was worth fighting for." "Let us not forget those who gave everything so this could be," Evelyn added, her words suffused with reverence and a hint of sorrow. Her piercing green eyes met each of her comrade's in turn, finding unspoken agreement in their depths.

"May we always remember," Zylar intoned solemnly, their voice a melodic contrast to the human voices, resonating with an ancient wisdom that transcended time and space.

As night embraced the city, the park's lights flickered to life, casting a warm glow on the faces of those gathered. They stood together, a band of warriors, healers, and dreamers, united by their shared history and the common thread of hope that wove through their hearts.

In the quiet of the evening, the news clips faded to black, and the park settled into silence. But the message they carried lingered in the air, a promise etched into the stars above: "From ashes, we rise. In unity, we thrive."

...

The remnants of the day's light filtered through the high windows, casting elongated shadows across the repurposed hall. In the heart of the bustling city, tucked away from the reconstruction frenzy, a secluded chamber thrummed with life. Here gathered the coalition members, their faces illuminated by the soft glow of antique chandeliers that had somehow survived the war's ire. A long table stood at the center, laden with the spoils of peace—a feast to sate both hunger and spirit.

Dr. Evelyn Montgomery raised her glass, the crystal catching the light as if trapping fleeting moments within its facets. "To those who stand only in our memories," she began, her voice steady yet tinged with the echoes of loss. The room fell silent but for the gentle clink of glasses meeting in solidarity.

"May their sacrifices be the foundation upon which we build a future unwavering," Captain Lucas "Hawk" Hawking added, his deep timbre resonating through the hushed air. Each face around the table bore the marks of remembrance, eyes glistening with unshed tears for comrades lost.

Laughter and solemn anecdotes intermingled, painting a tapestry of resilience threaded with the colors of shared trials. They spoke of narrow escapes and desperate gambits, of whispered secrets under the cover of darkness. Yet, amid the revelry and reverence, there existed an undercurrent of fatigue that no amount of mirth could fully wash away.

In the corner of the room, partially obscured by the heavy velvet drapes that danced with the drafts, stood Dr. Montgomery and Captain Hawking. They had slipped away from the collective embrace of camaraderie to find solace in the quietude of each other's presence.

"Where do we go from here, Hawk?" Evelyn asked, her green eyes searching his for an answer neither fully possessed. Her stance, typically so poised, now betrayed hints of uncertainty.

Captain Hawking's gaze was distant. "We build, Evelyn. We heal. We lead." His words were spoken not as a decree but as an affirmation of a journey far from conclusion.

"Yet the scars remain," she countered softly, her fingertips absently tracing the edge of a scar that marred the table's surface — a remnant of a world before.

"Scars remind us of where we've been, not where we're going," Hawk replied, his blue eyes locking onto hers with an intensity that bridged the chasm of their past ordeals.

A moment passed, weighted with the gravity of their shared history, the silence between them thick with unspoken understanding. "There's hope still," Evelyn murmured, more to herself than to him. "Despite everything."

"Hope," Hawk echoed, allowing himself a rare smile, one that reached the creases etched into his face by years of conflict. "That's what we fought for, isn't it?"

In their sequestered alcove, amidst the backdrop of celebration and sorrow, Dr. Montgomery and Captain Hawking found a fragile peace within the eye of a storm that had raged too long. The path ahead bristled with challenges yet conquered, but in the company of one another, they discovered a wellspring of fortitude that promised the dawn of a world reborn from the ashes of its own fiery descent.

…

The echoes of their private celebration still lingered in the air as Dr. Evelyn Montgomery stood within the cavernous halls of the global summit, her piercing green eyes scanning the assembly of world leaders who had gathered to forge a path forward from the war's devastation. The murmurs of diplomats and strategists swirled around her like a tempest, yet she remained an island of calm amidst the chaos, her mind meticulously dissecting every speech and resolution offered.

Captain Lucas "Hawk" Hawking's broad shoulders were braced as if he still bore the weight of military armor rather than the formal uniform he now wore. His piercing blue eyes flitted over the crowd, ever watchful, even in this time of peace. Beside him, Dr. Lily Chen's youthful visage was alight with thoughtful contemplation, her contributions to the discussions punctuated by nods of approval and earnest scribbles in her digital notepad.

In the hushed tones reserved for sacred halls, General Thomas "Thunderbolt" O'Neill's gravelly voice reverberated, infusing the room with a sense of unity that transcended borders. Each word he spoke carried the gravity of battles endured, the lives lost, and the unyielding spirit that had brought them all here.

President Jonathan Reed's charismatic presence dominated the room as he articulated a vision of cooperation. His words, carefully chosen, were an intricate dance of diplomacy and inspiration, weaving a tapestry of hope that enshrouded the hearts of those present.

As the ceremony drew to a close, the coalition members stepped forth, their medals gleaming—a testament to valor and sacrifice. Evelyn's measured, authoritative voice filled the silence, her speech a litany of innovation and caution born from the crucible of war. Hawk added his own narrative, each sentence a testament to duty and the unwavering fortitude required to lead through darkness.

The summit, a mosaic of aspirations, slowly began to dissolve, its participants dispersing with renewed purpose. And it was then that the coalition members embarked on their separate journeys home—each to a hero's welcome.

Parades painted the streets of Hawk's country with vibrant banners and the roar of adulation. Children perched on their parents' shoulders, eyes wide with wonder at the sight of the man who had become a living legend. Hawk, usually stoic, allowed himself a moment of vulnerability, his hand lifting in salute, acknowledging the sea of faces that mirrored the diverse fabric of humanity he had fought to protect.

Across the ocean, in a land where tradition melded with technological marvels, Lily Chen stood before a throng of eager students, her voice imbued with the clarity of knowledge and the warmth of experience. Her story was not just one of survival but of the relentless pursuit of understanding that which sought to destroy them.

In the grandeur of an auditorium, Evelyn shared her insights with academics and innovators alike, her words painting the stark realities of a world once on the brink. Yet, interspersed within her scientific discourse were threads of a deeper truth— the indomitable human spirit that refused to yield to despair.

And in the quiet after the fanfare, under the cover of stars that had silently borne witness to their tribulations, the coalition members found themselves reflecting upon the journey they had undertaken. They had emerged as champions not only of war but of the enduring hope that had sustained them through their darkest hours. The past, with its shadows and scars, stretched behind them, a reminder of what had been sacrificed and what had been gained. Redemption whispered in the spaces between their shared glances—a promise etched into the very fabric of their beings.

For in the heart of each hero lay the unspoken commitment to a future yet written, a chapter of history that would be remembered not for the conflict that had ravaged their planet but for the unity it had birthed. It was this conviction that propelled them onward, toward horizons rich with the potential of new dawns and realms beyond the stars.

...

Evelyn Montgomery stood at the edge of the gathering, her piercing green eyes scanning the faces of those who had become more than comrades — they were forged family. They encircled a fire that crackled with life, its flames reaching upward toward a night sky littered with stars and the potential of untold worlds beyond. Her lab coat had been abandoned for the evening, replaced by a simple outfit that allowed her to blend into the collective rather than stand apart as a beacon of scientific prowess.

"Time has taught us much," Dr. Markus Weller mused aloud, breaking the contemplative silence with his measured tone. "Not just the intricacies of quantum entanglement or the physics behind their weapons, but about who we are... what we can endure."

"Endure and rise above," Hawk added, his voice carrying the weight of countless commands yet softened by the vulnerability of this shared moment. He looked around the circle, making eye contact with each member, including Evelyn, whose guarded demeanor wavered under his gaze.

"Indeed," General O'Neill's gravelly voice interjected, the flickering light casting shadows over his decorated uniform. "The war carved deep lines in the earth, in our souls. But from the chasm sprouted unity — a force more formidable than any adversary."

Mia Alvarez nodded, her disciplined posture relaxing as she let her guard down. "We've learned to lean on each" other, her words a whisper against the stillness. "To find strength in our differences."

And Zylar Threx, the coalition's enigmatic ally, spoke last, their voice resonating with an otherworldly timbre. "Your resilience is not unique to your species, but the way you wield it... it is what sets humanity apart."

As the fire's crackle punctuated the moments between confessions, Evelyn felt the threads of their experiences weave together, creating a tapestry rich with pain and triumph. It was in this gathering that they found redemption — not as an end, but a continuing journey that would stretch across time and space.

The conversation ebbed, giving way to reflection, until finally, Lily Chen broke the hush with words that pulled their gazes skyward. "Look at them," she said, pointing to the heavens where distant satellites twinkled alongside the stars. "Our ancestors dreamed of touching those celestial bodies. Now, we're on the cusp of calling them home."

A collective breath seemed to be held, then released, as if the very act solidified their resolve. They stood, shoulder to shoulder, and watched as the night unveiled its canvas of endless possibilities. Colonies on Mars, terraforming Venus, outposts on Titan — the war had ravaged, but from its ashes rose a unified humanity, eager to claim its place among the cosmos.

In the quiet that followed, the future whispered its siren song — a promise of discovery and wonder, of civilizations rebuilt and horizons expanded. And as the reunion drew to a close, Evelyn felt the mysterious dance of fate and choice converge, knowing that the story they had written was but a prelude to the odyssey that awaited.

The chapter of their lives marked by conflict may have concluded, but the narrative of humanity's ascendancy was just beginning to unfold. The stars, once silent witnesses to their strife, now beckoned as beacons of hope — a testament to the indelible spirit that thrived within each soul gathered around the dying embers of the fire.

...

Above the throngs of laughter and the sweet smell of rebirth that marked the reunion, a solitary figure stood apart from it all, perched high upon the skeletal remnants of a once-towering skyscraper. The iridescent scales of Zylar Threx shimmered against the twilight's embrace, casting prismatic patterns onto the ruins below. Their elongated fingers traced the air as if weaving threads only they could perceive, crafting a tapestry unseen but deeply felt.

The coalition members below, emboldened by their shared victories and aspirations, remained ignorant of Zylar's haunting vigil. They were unaware of the solemn gaze that followed their every gesture, the way their laughter reverberated through the ether to reach ears attuned to frequencies of both mourning and hope.

A mysterious smile played upon Zylar's lips, an enigma unto itself. Was it born of satisfaction for humanity's resilience, or did it conceal an omen of trials yet to come? As The Harbinger, Zylar was privy to secrets that spanned the void between stars, and their presence here, at this fulcrum of human history, was no simple coincidence.

Their haunting eyes, glowing with an inner light that mirrored the stardust-sprinkled sky, lingered on the faces of those who had become champions of a world not their own. In the silence of their secluded perch, Zylar knew the tenuous peace was but a brief respite in the grander scheme of cosmic eons — a momentary pause in the eternal dance of creation and destruction.

"Humanity," they whispered into the void, their voice a symphony of otherworldly resonance, "you are children of the stars, and to the stars you shall return."

And then, with a fluid grace that defied the ruin around them, Zylar retreated into the shadows that clung to the edges of the night. Their departure was as silent as their arrival, leaving behind nothing but the lingering touch of a future unwritten and the subtle shift in the air that hinted at destinies intertwined.

As the evening wore on and the fire dwindled to embers, Captain Hawking, his gaze fixed on the horizon where earth met heaven, found the words that encapsulated their journey — a reflection that resonated with the weight of experience and the lightness of newfound purpose.

"Through the darkest of nights, we have borne witness to the depths of despair," he mused aloud, his voice carrying the timbre of hard-earned wisdom. "Yet, it is in our unity that we find our brightest dawn. We are the architects of redemption, the weavers of hope. From the ashes of our fallen world, we rise — not just to survive, but to thrive. For in our hands lies the pen that writes the future, and in our hearts burns the indomitable spirit of humanity — ever enduring, ever aspiring, ever triumphant."

His words, like seeds sown in fertile ground, took root within the hearts of all who heard them. And though none saw Zylar depart, the enigmatic echo of their presence remained — a silent sentinel watching over the unfolding saga of humankind.

...

The stars, those timeless sentinels of the cosmos, had begun their nightly vigil as Dr. Evelyn Montgomery stood at the edge of the gathering, her silhouette etched against the soft glow of the rebuilt city. The murmur of voices and laughter from the coalition's private celebration filtered through the evening air, a harbinger of peace in a world once torn asunder. Yet, amid the revelry, Evelyn's gaze lingered on the dark expanse above—a canvas of infinity that held both the memories of war and the promise of exploration.

"Quite a sight, isn't it?" The low timbre of Captain Lucas "Hawk" Hawking's voice broke the quietude around her. He approached with measured steps, his broad shoulders relaxed but ever bearing the invisible mantle of command.

"Indeed," Evelyn replied without turning. Her eyes remained fixed on a particularly bright star. "A reminder that there's so much more out there waiting for us."

"True," Hawk agreed, standing beside her, sharing in the momentary reprieve from the weight of expectations. "And yet, here we are—standing on the precipice of a new chapter, one written by our own hands."

Evelyn finally shifted her gaze to meet Hawk's earnest blue eyes. In them, she saw not just a reflection of the sky above but also the depth of his convictions. It was a look she had come to know well, one that spoke of battles fought and the unspoken bond forged in the crucible of conflict.

"Tomorrow always comes with its own challenges," she remarked, her voice carrying an undertone of the caution that had become her second nature. "But tonight, we can afford a brief respite—to celebrate what we've achieved together."

"Indeed," Hawk echoed, his lips curving into a half-smile that softened the lines of his face. "And to remember those who aren't here to see it. Their sacrifices paved the way for this peace."

Silence fell between them again, filled only by the distant symphony of reconstruction — the hum of machinery, the clink of metal, the occasional shout of workers still laboring under the blanket of night. They were the sounds of humanity's indefatigable spirit, a testament to resilience in the aftermath of devastation.

"May we never forget what it took to get here," Evelyn whispered, more to herself than to Hawk. She closed her eyes briefly, allowing the breeze to carry away the ghosts of her past traumas. When she opened them again, the world seemed a little brighter, the future a fraction more tangible.

"Nor the lessons we learned along the way," Hawk added solemnly, his hand finding its way to rest gently on her shoulder — an anchor in the vast sea of uncertainty.

"Look!" A child's voice pierced the calm, followed by a chorus of excited shouts. Evelyn and Hawk turned to witness a group of children pointing skyward, where a shooting star trailed a path of incandescent beauty across the heavens.

"Make a wish!" one of the children called, and for a moment, everyone present — scientists and soldiers, volunteers and civilians alike — paused to join in the hopeful ritual.
Evelyn watched the streak of light fade into the darkness, a smile tugging at the corners of her mouth. Maybe, just maybe, wishes could come true — after all, hadn't they already defied the odds?

As the coalition members returned to their festivities, each carrying their own silent hopes and dreams, Evelyn allowed herself to believe in the possibility of a brighter tomorrow. Because if the past had taught her anything, it was that even amidst the shadows of doubt, the human spirit could shine like the stars — unyielding, undimmed, and ever upward.

And somewhere, unseen but ever watchful, Zylar Threx observed the unfolding tableau with that same enigmatic smile, the mysteries of their intentions as hidden and vast as the universe itself.

Chapter 23

Hope and Purpose

The garden, a verdant oasis amidst the skeletal ruins of the once vibrant city, welcomed them with open arms. The ruins, mere shadows of their former selves, stood in stark contrast to the riotous colors of the blooming flora that had defiantly pierced through the cracked and scorched earth. Twisted rebar reached out like desperate fingers towards the sky, seeking absolution from the chaos that the Kridrax invasion had wrought upon the world.

As each figure stepped into this paradoxical sanctuary, the air seemed to shimmer with the gravity of their reunion. Dr. Evelyn Montgomery was the first to arrive, her short black hair framing her face in a wild yet determined manner. Her green eyes scanned the environment, not just as a survivor, but as one who had been instrumental in turning the tide. Around her neck hung a pair of spectacles, more a symbol of her intellect than a necessity for vision.

Her gaze settled on Captain Lucas "Hawk" Hawking, whose approach was as silent as it was imposing. His military boots crunched softly on the gravel path, his stature a beacon of strength amid the desolation. Their exchange was brief, a respectful nod that spoke volumes of their shared history, before he enveloped her in an embrace that was both protective and equal.

"Good to see you standing, Doctor," Hawk murmured, his voice a familiar rumble of assurance.

"Likewise, Captain," Evelyn replied, her tone carrying the subtle hint of a smile. "We've come through much."

Markus Weller's arrival was less pronounced, his thin frame almost lost among the taller blooms that lined the pathways. His glasses sat askew as he offered a tentative smile to those gathered. When Hawk extended a hand in greeting, Markus accepted with a grip that belatedly found its firmness, his own battles etched in the lines around his eyes.

Sergeant Mia Alvarez's entrance was heralded by her confident stride, her dark hair pulled back tightly, revealing the jagged scar that traced along her jawline—a testament to her valor. Her handshake with Hawk was firm, a mutual acknowledgment of their shared front-line experiences. She turned to Evelyn and offered a salute softened by the warmth in her brown eyes.

"Doctor," Mia said, her voice a blend of respect and relief.

"Always a pleasure, Sergeant," Evelyn replied, the corner of her mouth lifting ever so slightly.

In the periphery, Zylar Threx observed the human exchanges with a contemplative stillness, their scaled form a whisper of otherworldly grace among the garden's blossoms. The depth of their glowing eyes held centuries of knowledge and sorrow, a reflection of losses too vast for any one planet's history.

General Thomas "Thunderbolt" O'Neill's entry was marked by the crisp sound of his boots on stone, his silver hair catching the light like a halo of earned wisdom. His gaze swept over the assembled group with a mixture of pride and a lingering sense of vigilance, as if the threat might yet rise from the very ground they stood on.

"Let us never forget," he intoned, his voice rough like gravel yet imbued with warmth.

"Never," they echoed, their voices a chorus of resilience.

Lily Chen, her youthful visage belying the intellect within, approached General O'Neill with deference. Her hands, which had manipulated alien technologies and saved countless lives, were now relaxed at her sides, the tension of war temporarily eased by the peace of the garden.

"General," she began, her clear voice carrying a timbre of reverence.

"Dr. Chen," O'Neill acknowledged, his stern expression softening. "Your contributions have not gone unnoticed." Together, they all stood within the healing embrace of nature, their scars and weary smiles serving as silent testaments to the trials they had endured. Yet, the vibrant life around them whispered promises of renewal and hope—a stark reminder that even after the darkest of invasions, humanity, and indeed life itself, would persevere and flourish once more.

…

A hush descended upon the garden, as if nature itself paid homage to the gathering of battle-scarred souls. Dr. Evelyn Montgomery stood motionless, her piercing green eyes reflecting the dichotomy around her: the tumbled remnants of once-towering structures and the irrepressible vitality of purple wisteria reclaiming the broken cityscape. Her expression was a canvas of contemplation; each crease told a story of hard-fought battles—both against external foes and internal demons.

Captain Lucas "Hawk" Hawking's gaze, too, settled on the vibrant interplay of destruction and growth. The silence held a reverence that softened the lines of exhaustion etched into his features. His muscular frame bore the weight of command even in reprieve, yet his blue eyes harbored an ember of hope amid the ruin.

As the stillness lingered, it seemed time itself had paused to allow the weary defenders a chance to breathe — to acknowledge the magnitude of their endurance.

The moment stretched until Evelyn broke the silence, her voice a low murmur blending with the rustling leaves. "We've come far, Hawk. From the ashes, we rise again."

Hawk turned towards her, his stance relaxed but attentive. "Indeed, Doctor. The city breathes anew, our people stronger for the trials endured." In his tone lay a quiet power, a testament to the resilience that had become their shared creed.

"Yet we must remain vigilant," Evelyn added, her eyes narrowing slightly. "I refuse to let complacency undermine our vigilance. Our scars are reminders, not just of pain, but of what we must protect at all costs."

"Agreed," Hawk replied, the scar on his cheek highlighted by the fading sunlight. "The Kridrax sought to extinguish us, but we've proven that humanity's spirit is unbreakable. We rebuild, we fortify, and we remember."

"Never again will we be caught off-guard," she stated, her words carrying the weight of an unspoken oath.

"Never again," he echoed solemnly.

Their conversation flowed like a gentle stream, weaving through recollections of loss and triumph, forging ahead with plans for a future where such horrors would be relegated to history. Each word spoken between them fortified an invisible bond — one wrought in the fires of adversity and quenched in the waters of shared purpose.

In the mysterious dance of shadow and light that played upon their faces, one could almost perceive the silent vows they made — not only to each other but to the very essence of the world they were determined to safeguard.

…

Sergeant Mia Alvarez's silhouette stood steadfast against the backdrop of vibrant flora that had overtaken the concrete ruins, her gaze contemplative. Beside her, Lieutenant Isabella mirrored the sergeant's resolute posture, their shoulders almost touching in silent solidarity. The air between them was thick with the unspoken language of soldiers who had danced too close to death's embrace, yet emerged not unscathed but undaunted.

They surveyed the garden, where life defiantly bloomed amidst the scars of war — a stark reminder of their own battles etched on their skin and souls. Isabella's fingers brushed against her cheek, tracing the line of her scar as if remembering the pain that once throbbed beneath it. Alvarez caught the movement, her eyes flickering with a knowing look. In this peaceful enclave, words were superfluous; their shared glances conveyed volumes of mutual respect and understanding.

Just as the evening star began its ascent, casting a celestial glow over the garden, Dr. Markus Weller strode towards the edge of the gathering, his disheveled hair reflecting the silver light. His companion, Dr. Lily Chen, walked beside him, her eyes animated with the fire of intellectual fervor. They paused beneath the arching boughs of a resilient willow tree, its leaves whispering secrets only they could decipher.

"Remarkable," Dr. Weller murmured, pushing his glasses up the bridge of his nose. "The adaptogenetic properties we've discovered in these plants could revolutionize our approach to regrowth."

Dr. Chen nodded, her gaze locked onto the bioluminescent flowers weaving through the rubble. "It's like the earth itself is fighting back, eager to heal the wounds inflicted upon it." Her voice held a timbre of awe mixed with a steely resolve.

They both knew the cost of complacency in a world still teetering on the brink of survival. As they discussed the potential of harnessing such natural resilience for humanity's benefit, their excitement was palpable, an undercurrent of energy that seemed to ripple through the surrounding greenery.

"Imagine," Dr. Chen continued, "if we could apply these principles to human medicine — self-repairing tissue, enhanced immune responses..." She trailed off, lost in the possibilities their research presented.

"Humanity could thrive again, not just survive," Dr. Weller added, his words echoing the promise of a future reclaimed from the jaws of annihilation. His gaze met hers, and in that moment, they shared more than just scientific ambition — they shared a vision of redemption, a dream of restoring what had been lost to the shadows of war.

As twilight enveloped the garden, their dialogue became a beacon of hope, a testament to the relentless pursuit of knowledge and the unyielding spirit of those who wielded it. In their earnest exchange, the seeds of tomorrow were sown, promising a harvest of healing and restoration for a world yearning for peace.

...

Farrah Rodriguez's laughter, a melody of resilience, danced through the air, mingling with the rustle of leaves and the distant echo of urban renewal. Her eyes, warm pools of hazel, glanced between Elena Vasquez and Javier Morales, reflecting a camaraderie hard-earned in the shadow of desolation. The trio stood amidst the unlikely bloom of the garden, their shared smiles carving out a sanctuary from the ruins that lay beyond.

"Remember when we had to ration those awful nutrient bars?" Farrah quipped, her tone light but carrying the gravity of shared hardship.

Elena's chuckle rumbled like distant thunder, her sturdy frame shaking with mirth. "How could I forget? You nearly started a riot when you found that last case of chocolate-flavored ones." Javier nodded, his smile lines deepening around tired yet hopeful eyes. "And you, Elena, threatening to march us all to victory on an empty stomach if it meant never having to eat another one."

Their laughter rose again, a testament to the support they'd woven together, each thread a lifeline through the ordeal of invasion and survival.

In the middle distance, partially concealed by a curtain of weeping willow fronds, Zylar Threx observed the reunion. Their luminescent scales caught the dying light, casting prismatic shadows upon the earth. Pride swelled within them at the sight of human fortitude; sorrow followed as swiftly as nightfall. They stood, a solitary figure grappling with the duality of their existence — once avenger, now guardian.

Zylar's gaze lingered on the joyous trio, and a whisper of envy brushed their heart — a longing for the simplicity of laughter unburdened by memory's specter. Yet, as the Kridrax threat loomed like a storm on the horizon, it was their own hands, stained with actions irreversible, that carried the weight of history's course.

Silently, Zylar turned away, their presence a ghostly footnote amid the blooms of renewal. The path ahead was fraught with the undercurrents of vengeance and the pursuit of peace — an eternal dance between darkness and light, with every step etching indelible marks upon the canvas of time.

...

The sun dipped lower, casting elongated shadows across the garden's mosaic of wildflowers and rubble. One by one, the survivors gravitated towards a central clearing, their movements deliberate yet somber. They formed a circle, the space between them filled with the gravity of unspoken words. Hands reached out, fingers intertwining, forming a chain of flesh and resolve.

Time seemed to pause, bowing respectfully as heads lowered in a shared moment of silence. They stood united, honoring those who had become whispers and echoes in the annals of their memories. The air itself held its breath, the gentle rustling of leaves ceasing as if in reverence to the fallen. This circle was their fortress, each person a bastion against the encroaching darkness that once threatened to swallow their world whole.

Dr. Evelyn Montgomery stepped forward, her green eyes reflecting the last rays of twilight. She cleared her throat, and the sound rippled through the stillness like a stone dropped into a tranquil pond. "We stand amidst the blooms of resilience," she began, her voice a soft yet unwavering melody in the hush. "Each petal, each leaf, mirrors our own journey from the ashes of despair."

Her gaze swept over the faces before her — the brilliant mind of Markus Weller, whose thoughts often danced on the edge of comprehension; Lily Chen, whose youthful visage belied the depth of her brilliance and compassion. Every pair of eyes held a story, a testament to the trials they had endured.

"Today, we remember not just the battles fought," Evelyn continued, her tone imbued with warmth, "but the strength we discovered within ourselves and in each other." Her hands gestured subtly, encompassing the entirety of their shared experience. "This unity, this bond we have forged—it is unbreakable. It will be the foundation upon which we rebuild, not just structures and systems, but lives enriched with purpose and hope."

A collective breath was drawn, and the air vibrated with renewed determination. Scars and stoic expressions alike softened, as if her words were a balm to the weariness that clung to their souls. Eyes that had seen too much blinked back the shimmer of tears, not of sorrow, but of gratitude—for survival, for camaraderie, for a future unwritten.

"Let us carry forth the legacy of those who gave everything so that we could stand here today," Dr. Montgomery concluded, her voice now a clarion call that pierced the encroaching dusk. "Together, we are the architects of tomorrow, the sentinels guarding against the return of darkness. Together, we shall ensure that the light of humanity continues to shine across the cosmos."

As the silence settled once more, it was not empty but filled with the resonance of her speech, echoing in every heart and soul gathered there. They were united, not just by circumstance or necessity, but by the indomitable spirit that thrived within each of them—a spirit that promised redemption, rebirth, and the eternal pursuit of light amidst the shadows of their past.

...

In the tranquil aftermath of Dr. Montgomery's speech, the survivors took hesitant steps forward, their hearts heavy with both sorrow and gratitude. Captain Hawking cleared his throat, his once-commanding voice now softened by reflection.

"Every battle scar," he began, eyes tracing the labyrinthine paths of the garden, "is a lesson in resilience. I've learned that courage isn't about being unafraid — it's about facing fear and pressing onward."

Dr. Montgomery nodded, her gaze lingering on each face as they shared their own truths. Sergeant Alvarez spoke next, the timbre of her voice steady but laced with emotion.

"Comradeship," she said simply, "is our greatest weapon. It is the thread that binds us, stronger than any alloy or armor. We've forged something unbreakable here, in the crucible of war."

Lieutenant Isabella, standing shoulder to shoulder with Alvarez, added, "And we've learned that humanity's light doesn't dim in the darkness; it becomes more vital, a beacon for those lost in the shadow of despair."

The circle of survivors passed the mantle of speech like a sacred flame, each contribution igniting further introspection. Dr. Weller's scientific mind grappled with the metaphysical changes wrought upon them, his words measured and thoughtful.

"Adversity has been our unsought mentor, teaching us the value of ingenuity and the power of hope. Our breakthroughs are more than mere discoveries; they're testaments to our adaptability, our refusal to succumb."

Beside him, Dr. Chen's eyes shone with a fervor born of relentless pursuit of knowledge in the face of annihilation. "Our collaboration," she affirmed, "has transcended disciplines, revealing new horizons. We stand on the precipice of a future where science not only heals our world but elevates it."

Laughter then bubbled up from Farrah Rodriguez, the sound incongruous yet healing against the backdrop of their somber reflections. Elena Vasquez and Javier Morales joined her, their chuckles mingling in a chorus of irrepressible optimism.

"Who would've thought," Farrah mused, "that the end of the world would bring such unity? These friendships are my silver lining—the family I never expected to find among the ruins."

Elena's smile was a radiant counterpoint to the evening's encroaching gloom. "We've discovered strength in vulnerability, haven't we? In sharing our fears, we've found our fortitude."

Javier nodded, his eyes crinkling at the corners. "And humor," he interjected, "remains our undefeated champion. It's the spark that keeps the dark at bay, reminding us that joy persists, even when the stars themselves seem to falter."

Amidst the camaraderie, Zylar Threx remained apart, an enigma wrapped in the glow of their iridescent scales. Their presence was a silent vigil, a reminder of the cost of survival. When they finally spoke, their voice was like the whisper of a distant nebula, both mesmerizing and chilling.

"Your journey mirrors the stars' own cycle—birthed from chaos, shining through adversity, destined to endure." Zylar's eyes held a depth unfathomable, their luminosity betraying no secrets. "But remember, the cosmos is vast, and its currents are ever-shifting. Vigilance must be your constant companion, for darkness has many forms."

The cryptic intonation of their warning sent a shiver through the assembly, a ghostly touch that hinted at unseen threads in the tapestry of their struggle. Was it a simple caution, or did it portend something more profound? The Harbinger's gaze seemed to pierce beyond the visible spectrum, reaching into realms untold.

As the survivors mulled over their shared musings, each one felt the subtle shift in the air brought forth by Zylar's words — an undercurrent of mystery that promised there were still chapters unwritten in the saga of their lives. The garden, with its resilient blooms and scars of war, stood as a testament to their past and a harbinger of their uncertain future.

...

Evelyn Montgomery stepped away from the circle, her boots crunching on the gravel path. She let her fingers brush against the leaves of a robust fern, its green vibrancy a stark contrast to the steel and concrete bones of the city's ruins looming beyond the garden walls. With each measured step, she felt the tension in her shoulders ease, the cacophony of shared pasts fading into the tranquil whispers of rustling foliage.

"Beautiful, isn't it?" murmured Hawk as he fell into step beside her, his voice low and tinged with an undercurrent of awe. His gaze swept over the blossoming flora, a softness in his eyes that belied his rugged exterior.

Evelyn nodded, allowing herself a rare smile. "It's a reminder," she said, her voice barely above a whisper, "that life persists, even through devastation."

They continued in silence, their presence among the thriving plants serving as quiet testament to their resilience.

Elsewhere, Mia Alvarez's steady pace brought her to a secluded corner where a small pond reflected the sky's deepening hues. She knelt, tracing the surface with her fingertips, sending ripples dancing across the mirrored expanse. In the dwindling light, she saw not just her reflection but the echo of battles hard-fought—a warrior seeking peace in a world slowly mending its wounds.

Zylar Threx lingered at the periphery, their alien form half-hidden in the shadow of a weeping willow. Their eyes, deep pools of cosmic mystery, rested on the gentle sway of the branches. They remained an observer, their thoughts as distant as the star system they once called home, their heart grappling with the duality of revenge and reconciliation.

As twilight descended, the survivors converged once more, drawn together by an unspoken accord. The air was alive with the scent of night-blooming jasmine, wrapping them in its heady embrace as they each took up a lantern. Evelyn's fingers worked deftly, lighting the wick, which flared to life with a soft glow.

"Let these be our beacons," she declared, her voice steady and clear, carrying through the stillness. "To guide us, to remind us, and to honor those we've lost."

One by one, they released the lanterns, watching as they ascended towards the darkening canvas above. The flickering lights mingled with the first stars of evening, a dance of hope against the encroaching night.

"Into the darkness, we cast our light," Hawk intoned, his words an affirmation of the promise they all carried in their hearts.

"May it shine as a symbol of our enduring spirit," added Lily Chen, her tone imbued with the weight of their collective resolve.

"May it lead the way for those who follow," Zylar Threx offered, their enigmatic presence lending gravity to the ritual.

The lanterns climbed higher, their luminance a silent chorus amidst the vastness of the cosmos. Each flame was a declaration, a vow renewed beneath the watchful gaze of countless worlds. And as the characters watched their hopes take flight, they stood united — not just as survivors, but as guardians of a future crafted by their own hands. With the night embracing them, they departed the garden, their paths illuminated by the certainty that humanity's place among the stars was secured.

Chapter 24

End?

Earlier

The heavens blazed with war. Streaks of laser fire seared through the void, carving brilliant lines across the black canvas speckled with distant stars. Explosions erupted in silent fury, blooming like deadly flowers that cast an infernal glow upon the twisted metal carcasses of fallen ships. The coalition fleet, a ragtag assembly of vessels from a thousand worlds, weaved and darted through the debris, unleashing volleys of return fire at the relentless swarm of Kridrax invaders.

Amidst the chaos, a lone escape pod, its surface sleek and unyielding, burst forth from the underbelly of the Kridrax command ship. It was a glimmering speck of defiance, glinting silver in the starlight as it hurtled toward the beleaguered planet below. The pod's trajectory cut a sharp contrast to the disorder that surrounded it, a silent testament to the desperation that had birthed its journey.

Inside the cramped confines of the escape vessel, Dr. Evelyn Montgomery's green eyes mirrored the explosions outside, reflecting a storm of urgency and fear. Her fingers danced over the control panel, adjusting the pod's course with meticulous precision. Each movement was a whisper against the cacophony of claxons and alarms that filled the air, her presence a calm within the tempest raging beyond the reinforced hull. "Maintain heading three-two-five," she ordered, her voice a clipped melody amidst the discordant orchestra of warfare. Her reflection in the glass revealed soot-stained cheeks, a stark reminder of the battle that had torn her from the stars.

Captain Lucas "Hawk" Hawking gripped the manual override, his knuckles white with exertion. "Steady as she goes, Montgomery," he replied, his authoritative tone belying the undercurrent of concern that threaded through his words. The blue of his gaze was steel; his focus never wavered from the instruments that blinked and flashed their morse code of survival.

Beside him, Dr. Markus Weller peered through his glasses, adjusting the settings with the tender care of a maestro coaxing harmony from discordance. His quiet mutterings of calculations and probabilities were like incantations, willing them through the gauntlet of space that lay ahead.

The pod's engines hummed a deep bass note, a counterpoint to the symphony of destruction that continued to rage outside its walls. They were a beacon of hope, a slender thread weaving through the darkness, binding the fate of those within to the beleaguered world below.

As the pod drew closer to its destination, the stars seemed to watch in silence, the guardians of secrets untold and futures unwritten. And within that silence, the escape pod carried with it not just the lives of its passengers but the weight of a history that refused to be forgotten and a future yet to be redeemed.

...

Veiled in the shadow of a fragmented asteroid, Zylar Threx, known to many as The Harbinger, watched the trajectory of the escape pod with an expression that was a turbulent sea of conflict. They stood motionless, the iridescent scales of their skin catching the faint light of distant stars, casting prismatic whispers across the void. Their deep-set eyes, luminous and somber, reflected the glinting speck that carried within it the seed of a history best left buried.

The silence of space wrapped around them, a cold shroud that seemed to compress the very air in their lungs. Memories of their ravaged homeworld flickered like dying embers in Zylar's mind, fueling the disquiet that gnawed at their conscience. The decision to protect the consciousness of Adolf Oppressor, now a synthetic abomination forged by Kridrax technology, weighed heavily upon them, an anchor threatening to drag them into an abyss from which there would be no ascent.

"Will this bring redemption or ruin?" Zylar murmured to themselves, the words falling like stones into the vastness of the cosmos. The weight of their choice pressed against their chest — a safeguard encasing a dormant volcano of malevolence that, if unleashed, might set ablaze the tenuous future they had fought so tirelessly to secure. Could they justify shielding such darkness for the promise of leveraging its power against a common enemy, the merciless Kridrax?

Zylar's slender fingers curled into a fist, their knuckles pale despite the ethereal glow of their skin. The echoes of countless tragedies hummed through their veins, a reminder of the duty that compelled them forward — one born of vengeance and the hope to forestall further suffering. Yet the path they trod was lined with thorns of uncertainty, each step a gamble against the capricious whims of fate.

"Forgive me," they whispered, not knowing to whom the plea was addressed — the ghosts of their past or the specters of a future yet unseen. With a flicker of resolve, they turned away from the sight of the pod's descent, the mantle of The Harbinger once again settling upon their shoulders, heavy with secrets and the burden of decisions made in the oppressive stillness of space.

...

The silvered hull of the escape pod spun silently through the vastness of space, a solitary beacon amidst the infinite black canvas dotted with distant stars. Cosmic storms lashed out with tendrils of incandescent plasma, their fury an artist's brush against the void, painting swirling eddies of color that danced with wild abandon.

Asteroid fields loomed, fields of rocky debris scattered like the bones of ancient celestial giants. The pod wove through them with precarious agility, its pre-programmed course a testament to human ingenuity — a fragile thread stretched taut between survival and annihilation.

Inside this metal womb, Dr. Evelyn Montgomery sat alone, her short black hair a shadow against the dim glow of the control panels. She was motionless save for the rise and fall of her chest, her green eyes fixed on the eerie tableau beyond the reinforced glass. The chaos of Earth's battlefield, where Captain Lucas "Hawk" Hawking waged war far below, seemed a universe away in both distance and memory.

Evelyn's practical attire, her jacket worn at the elbow, boots scuffed from countless hours at work, now served as a cold comfort in the isolation of her journey. The silence was a stark contrast to the cacophony of laser fire and explosions that had been the overture of her escape.

The pod shuddered, a ghost's whisper against the hull, as it skirted the fringe of a storm. Evelyn's hand reached out, fingertips grazing the console, her movements precise and deliberate. A stray lock of hair slipped forward; she tucked it behind her ear without looking away from the abyss outside. It was an intimate gesture of vulnerability, a fleeting reminder of the woman beneath the scientist's composed exterior.

"Forgive me," she murmured, the words dissipating into the quiet like mist. The simplicity of her plea belied the complexity of her burden — the preservation of Oppressor's consciousness within this vessel. A grotesque fusion of man and machine, his revival promised power but threatened untold horror. Her decision to protect this dormant evil was fraught with the potential consequences of playing god or devil.

The pod navigated onward, a lone speck adrift in the cosmic ocean. In the oppressive stillness, the specter of redemption haunted her thoughts — a redemption for whom, she could not say. Perhaps for humanity, or perhaps for herself, seeking solace in the belief that even the darkest of legacies could be repurposed for good.

Evelyn closed her eyes briefly, allowing herself just a moment to feel the weightlessness of her body and the weight of her choices. When her eyelids lifted, resolve sharpened her gaze. The mission was clear, though its outcome remained shrouded in the mists of uncertainty.

"Stay the course," she whispered to the pod, to the void, to the echoes of her own doubts. The vessel obliged, hurtling towards an unknown future, bearing the sins of the past and the fragile hope of redemption in its silent passage through the stars.

...

The silence within the escape pod was deafening, a stark contrast to the cacophonous symphony of war that raged light-years away. Evelyn sat motionless, ensconced in the cold embrace of technology that cradled Oppressor's consciousness — a synthetic relic of monstrosity and ambition. Her eyes, fixed on the console's dim glow, bore the reflection of data streams that pulsed like lifeblood through the vessel's veins.

"History will not remember me," she murmured, her voice barely a whisper against the hum of machinery. "But it will remember him, reborn from ashes into circuits."

With each passing moment, the gravity of her role weighed heavier upon her shoulders. She was the guardian of a legacy, twisted and dark, yet one that could reshape the universe if wielded with a deft hand. The solitude of space afforded her time — time to ponder the ethics of her mission, time to question the morality of preserving a tyrant for the promise of peace.

"Can a monster teach us to be human?" The question hung unanswered in the void, resonating with the silent stars that bore witness to her solitary journey.

Shifting back to Zylar Threx, the Harbinger watched from afar, their presence an ethereal silhouette against the backdrop of chaos. They moved with deliberate grace, each step a measured tread upon the deck of the coalition flagship. Their eyes, deep pools of luminescence, remained locked onto the celestial display where streaks of lasers danced with the fury of exploding stars.

Zylar's mind was a tempest of conflicting emotions, swirling with the same intensity as the cosmic storms that threatened the escape pod's path. They were acutely aware of the paradox they embodied — saving a symbol of hatred to potentially avert greater atrocities. Through the shimmering scales that adorned their form, a subtle glow ebbed and flowed with the rhythm of their contemplation.

"Is redemption truly attainable for such as he?" Zylar whispered to themselves, the words tinged with a sorrow that spanned galaxies.

Their movements ceased, and for a moment, Zylar seemed a statue carved from stardust — timeless and still. Then, with a resolve born of eons of suffering and loss, they resumed their silent vigil. Every fiber of their being was focused on the minuscule speck hurtling through the vastness — a speck carrying the potential to either heal or rend the fabric of civilizations.

"May the fates be merciful," they intoned, their voice a lamentation for all that had been and all that might yet come to pass.

...

The escape pod, an oblong specter amidst the celestial chaos, descended upon the Kridrax planet with a sinister grace. Below, the world unfurled like a tapestry of darkness; its atmosphere churned with storms the color of bruises, the winds howling silent epics of desolation. Structures rose from the jagged landscape like monoliths to forgotten gods, their sharp angles casting long, oppressive shadows over the barren plains.

Zylar Threx, The Harbinger, stood statue-like before the viewing port, their iridescent scales reflecting the turmoil of the approaching surface. Their eyes, aglow with ancient light, tracked the pod's trajectory as it sliced through the miasma of the planet's heavy air. Within that small vessel lay a relic of Earth's darkest legacy, and with it, a plan that Zylar had nurtured amidst the stars' cold indifference.

"Adolph," Zylar began, their voice threading through the void, resonating within the confines of the pod. "You perceive the grandeur of your new dominion?"

From within the pod, Synthetic Oppressor's glowing red eyes flickered with the reflection of the hostile world he was destined to inhabit. "A fitting realm for rebirth," he replied, his mechanical voice devoid of warmth, his synthetic form unyielding to the atmospheric pressure.

"Indeed," Zylar said, their tone a medley of mourning and resolve. "But do not be mistaken, Reborn Führer. Your consciousness shall not command here—your strategic acumen will be... repurposed."

Suspicion narrowed the metallic slits of Synthetic Oppressor's eyes. "Explain, Harbinger," he demanded, his words sharpened on the whetstone of apprehension.

"Upon this forsaken rock, you will devise battle plans against the Kridrax," Zylar intoned, the spectral dance of their scales growing more pronounced. "Your insight into tyranny will now serve to dismantle it. You are to become the architect of their undoing, or you will find yourself entombed within this celestial crypt."

A tense silence fell, punctuated only by the whirring systems of the pod and the distant thunder of cosmic storms. "Betrayal?" Synthetic Oppressor's voice betrayed a hint of incredulity, a semblance of human vulnerability in his otherwise impassive facade.

"Call it penance," Zylar whispered, their gaze never wavering from the scene outside. "Even the most wretched of souls may yet carve a path toward redemption—or at least, towards utility."

"Utility..." echoed Synthetic Oppressor, the term reverberating through his artificial mind, mingling with the stratagems of wars past, the echoes of old ambitions.

"Your survival hinges on cooperation," Zylar continued, their voice fading like the last glimmer of a dying star. "Should you defy this purpose, know that oblivion awaits."

As the pod breached the outer layers of the atmosphere, the structures below loomed larger, casting their oppressive shadow upon the approaching vessel. And there, in the expanse between worlds, Synthetic Oppressor sat alone in contemplation, the weight of history and future converging upon him in a moment of profound isolation.

Meanwhile, Zylar remained vigilant, a sentinel of fate whose enigmatic purpose was etched in the cosmos itself. They bore witness to the descent, knowing that the threads they had woven could unravel the fabric of empires — or bind them tighter in their inexorable grip.

...

The escape pod, a solitary speck against the sprawling canvas of space, pierced the atmosphere of the Kridrax planet with a hiss of superheated air. Below, the jagged spires and monolithic fortresses of an alien civilization rose up to meet it, their angular silhouettes etched sharply against the brooding sky. Zylar Threx, The Harbinger, observed the descent from the command deck of the coalition's flagship, the iridescent scales on their body shimmering faintly in the dim light.

A sense of disquiet settled over the scene like a shroud. Zylar's expression was an inscrutable mask; the depths of their glowing eyes seemed to churn with secrets untold. They had revealed but a sliver of their intentions, just enough to ensure compliance from the occupant within the pod, yet withheld the vastness of their designs. Those who witnessed the Harbinger's vigil could not discern whether they gazed upon a savior or a harbinger of doom.

"Zylar..." murmured Lieutenant Sera Trask, her gaze fixed on the luminous figure at the viewport. She stood slightly apart from the others on the bridge, her thoughts adrift in the eddies of suspicion. The lieutenant's fingers drummed an uneasy cadence on the hilt of her sidearm, as if to ground herself amidst the swelling tide of doubt.

"Can we really trust them?" she whispered, though none were close enough to hear. Her words, intended for no one, hung suspended in the charged silence of the bridge. The question lingered, unanswered, festering in the minds of those who dared consider it.

As the pod vanished into the clouds of the Kridrax world, so too did the certainty of Zylar's allegiance. The coalition had embraced their warning, welcomed their aid against the invaders, but Sera's instincts warned her of the peril in trusting a being whose history was written in the ashes of fallen stars. What pact might Zyrar have struck with an echo of humanity's darkest legacy?

"Your past is rife with sorrow," Sera finally spoke, addressing the silent silhouette of Zylar. "But does it guide you to redemption or retribution?"

Zylar turned, their movement fluid and ghostlike, and regarded the lieutenant with a measured gaze. Their reply, when it came, was soft and resonant, casting ripples through the quiet that enveloped them both.

"Every soul bears its scars, Lieutenant. Some seek to heal them... and some to wield them."

The cryptic response left Sera wrestling with her unease. As the battle outside continued to rage, a storm of laser fire and detonating starships, the lone figure of the Harbinger remained ever enigmatic, their true motives as elusive as the shifting nebulae that cradled distant suns.

And in that moment of stillness, with the future hanging precariously in the balance, a whisper of trepidation wound its way through the hearts of the coalition—a silent sentinel to the uncertainty that now clouded their cause.

…

The chamber that housed the escape pod's controls was bathed in an eerie glow, casting long shadows across Zylar Threx's angular features. The Harbinger stood motionless, their iridescent scales shimmering faintly as they watched the stars streak by through the viewport. Though the chaos of battle raged on, here in the silence of space, there was a deceptive peace—one that belied the turmoil churning within Zylar's mind.

"Approaching final coordinates," the synthetic voice of the onboard computer announced, its clinical tone cutting through the stillness.

A solitary nod from Zylar acknowledged the transmission. They placed a slender hand against the cool metal of the console, fingertips tracing the intricate patterns etched into its surface. The gesture betrayed a hint of reluctance, or perhaps a silent invocation for whatever lay ahead.

"Activate cloaking sequence," Zylar commanded, their voice barely above a whisper yet carrying the gravity of unspoken dread.

"Sequence activated. We are now invisible to all known scanning technology."

The words hung heavy in the cabin, and Zylar's gaze turned inward, reflecting an ancient sorrow that had found a new host. The preservation of Oppressor's consciousness—a task fraught with peril and moral ambiguity—loomed before them, a specter of a future that could be shaped for redemption or cast into darkness.

"Is this the path to atonement?" Zylar murmured to themselves, the question lingering in the air, unanswered.

No sooner had the thought taken form than an urgent beep resonated through the craft, demanding attention. On the display, a series of calculations blinked ominously, each digit portending an outcome that could alter the course of history. The pod was nearing its destination, the Kridrax planet, a world of unfathomable secrets and untold power.

Zylar's eyes narrowed as they analyzed the data stream. The trajectory was precise, a testament to their meticulous planning. Yet even the most careful plans carried the seed of uncertainty, and Zylar knew all too well the cost of miscalculation. They were gambling with forces beyond comprehension, and the stakes could not be higher.

"Prepare for entry," Zylar instructed, their voice steady despite the tempest of emotions that threatened to breach their composure. "Initiate communication with The Reborn Führer." "Link established." The mechanical voice replied.

"Adolf," Zylar intoned, their voice taking on the ethereal quality that so often left others unsettled. "The hour approaches. Are you prepared to wield the future as your own?"

"Preparation is but a formality," came the cold, metallic retort from Synthetic Oppressor. "Destiny awaits my command."

A chill traced its way down Zylar's spine, the implications of Synthetic Oppressor's words echoing in the cavernous space. As the escape pod descended toward the brooding planet, the cosmos seemed to hold its breath, awaiting the collision of past sins and future aspirations.

The pod pierced the Kridrax atmosphere, shrouded in mystery and deceit. Zylar remained motionless, their expression unreadable, as if carved from the very stars themselves. The fate of worlds rested in the balance, teetering on the precipice between salvation and ruin.

The enigmatic Harbinger, alone with their thoughts, and the ghostly echo of Synthetic Oppressor's ambition resounded through the void. What consequences awaited them? What truth lay hidden behind Zylar's solemn visage?

The questions lingered, unanswered, leaving a trail of doubt and anticipation. When would the veil of mystery slowly begin to lift?

The year is 2045, a century after World War II. As the world has moved on from the atrocities of World War II, an ominous force lurks in the depths of the cosmos, plotting its revenge. In the waning days of the war, the desperate dictator was abducted by an advanced alien civilization, the Kridrax, who saw his twisted genius as a valuable asset in their quest for universal domination.

Promising the chance to conquer Earth and exact his vengeance, the Kridrax performed a sinister experiment – transplanting the dictator's consciousness into a synthetic body, one designed to sustain him indefinitely. For decades, the dictator bided his time, assisting the Kridrax in subjugating planet after planet, all while honing his thirst for power over the human race he so despised.

As the Kridrax armada approaches the outer reaches of the solar system, a lone emissary ship breaks ranks, carrying a dire warning from a civilization crushed under the oppressor's alien oppressors. The vessel narrowly escapes destruction, crash-landing on the White House lawn in a blaze of fire and metal. Though the messenger itself is swiftly secreted away, its ominous message sparks a covert effort within the world's military forces to develop alien defense technologies.

When the first ominous ships appear in Earth's skies, unleashing devastating attacks on major cities, the world is plunged into chaos. Yet, in secret bases and underground laboratories, a coalition of scientists and soldiers have been feverishly preparing, integrating the alien messenger's technology into a patchwork of human innovation. As the full might of the Kridrax armada rains down from the heavens, a merciless ground invasion led by the reborn dictator follows, his twisted ambitions bent on subjugating the planet he failed to conquer a century ago.

What follows is a harrowing interplanetary war, one that strains human resilience and resolve to the breaking point. Battered by the overwhelming force of the Kridrax onslaught, the human resistance finds itself pushed to the brink of annihilation time and again. Yet in the midst of the carnage, unlikely heroes emerge, their unwavering determination to protect their homeworld fueling a series of daring counterattacks and improbable victories.

Made in the USA
Monee, IL
29 July 2024

62863175R00207